The men who reigned over Eleanor of Aquitaine

Louis VII. Raised to be a priest, he ruled France but was no match for his strong and beautiful bride, Queen Eleanor.

Henry II. Bold and brilliant founder of the Plantagenet line in England, the great love of Eleanor's life. He became her husband and her jailer.

Thomas à Becket. Henry's Archbishop of Canterbury, whose murder nearly wrecked England.

Richard the Lion-Hearted. Eleanor's handsome and chivalrous favourite son. He brought her joy and grief in equal measure.

King John. Eleanor's youngest son, whose career of misrule started with intrigues against his own family.

THE COURTS OF LOVE

The Courts of Love

Jean Plaidy

FAWCETT CREST • NEW YORK

A Fawcett Crest Book
Published by Ballantine Books
Copyright © 1987 by Jean Plaidy

Library of Congress Catalog Card Number: 87-13814

ISBN 0-449-21657-8

This edition published by arrangement with G. P. Putnam's Sons, a Division of The Putnam Publishing Group, Inc.

Manufactured in the United States of America

First Ballantine Books Edition: February 1990

Contents

In the Courts of Love

When I look back over my long and tempestuous life, I can see that much of what happened to me—my triumphs and most of my misfortunes—was due to my passionate relationships with men. I was a woman who considered herself their equal—and in many ways their superior—but it seemed that I depended on them, while seeking to be the dominant partner—an attitude which could hardly be expected to bring about a harmonious existence.

I inherited my good looks and fiery passionate nature from my forebears—and my surroundings no doubt played a big part in forming my character, for until I was five years old I lived at the Court of my grandfather, the notorious William IX of Aquitaine, poet, king of the troubadours, adventurer, lecher, founder of the 'Courts of Love', and the most fascinating man of his day.

It was true that I knew him when he was past his adventuring and had reached that stage when a man who has lived as he had is casting uneasy eyes towards the life hereafter and forcing himself into reluctant penitence; but, all the same, even to my youthful eyes, he was an impressive figure. Engraved on my memory forever are those evenings in the great hall when I sat entranced watching the tumblers and listening to the *jongleurs*— and most of all hearing my grandfather himself singing songs of his exploits in those days when he was a lusty young man, roaming abroad in search of love. I thought him godlike. He was as handsome as Apollo, as strong as Hercules and as ingenious a lover as Jupiter. I was sure he could assume any shape in his love adventures. All the songs were of beautiful women, mostly unattainable, which seemed to make them more desirable than they would otherwise have been. Women were glorified in his Court, and when I left Aquitaine and discovered how differently they were treated in other countries I was amazed.

Seated beside him would be the exciting Dangerosa. I had heard her called Dangereuse, which was appropriate. She was tall, statuesque and flamboyantly handsome. He was my father's father and she was my mother's mother; but they were lovers. Nothing in my grandfather's Court followed conventional lines.

My grandfather often sang of how he had ridden into the castle where he found her; and he had fallen in love with her the moment he set eyes on her. She was married to the Viscount of Châtellerault to whom she had borne three children; but that was no obstacle to my grandfather's passion. He abducted her and brought her to his castle—a willing captive—and he set her up in that part of the castle known as the Maubergeonne Tower. Not that her presence was kept a secret. All knew what had happened; and when my grandfather's wife, Philippa—who had been away at the time—returned to the castle to find a rival actually in residence, understandably she left my grandfather for ever.

I never knew my grandmother Philippa. She died before I was born, but of course I knew the story of that stormy marriage. My grandfather's affairs were openly discussed and he himself sang of them.

However, I was enchanted by my dashing troubadour grandfather and my merry, wicked grandmother, Dangerosa, living in riotous sin together.

I think my mother was a little shocked and would have liked the household to have been run on more orthodox lines. She was Aénor, daughter of Dangerosa and the Viscount of Châtellerault; as Dangerosa could not be the Duchess of Aquitaine, she decided that her daughter should marry my grandfather's eldest son so that her grandchild could inherit Aquitaine in due course. This was adding to the unconventionality, and I believe even my grandfather hesitated, but he was so besotted with Dangerosa that he gave in.

Very soon after the wedding, to the delight of all, I appeared.

No doubt they would have preferred a boy, but because of the status of women in Aquitaine I was warmly welcomed.

I heard afterwards that before I was born one of the holy pilgrims came to the castle. They were always turning up like birds of ill omen. The man was understandably shocked by the situation at the castle: the abduction, the blatant living together of the unmarried pair, and the flight of the true Duchess to Fontevrault Abbey, and to follow that the marriage of the son and daughter of the guilty pair.

He stood before my poor pregnant mother and declared: 'Nothing good will come of this.'

What I am wondering now is: Was the pilgrim right?

Aquitaine is one of the richest provinces in France. It had been a law unto itself since the time of the Romans when the Emperor Augustus divided Gaul into four provinces and added to Aquitaine the land between the Garonne and the Loire. It included Poitou and Gascony and contained some of the most beautiful scenery in France. Fruit and flowers grew in abundance; the grape flourished and the wine was the best to be found anywhere. My grandfather ruled over a prosperous land.

Living was easy in Aquitaine and that made its people pleasure-loving. Nature was indulgent towards us and we were a contented community, my grandfather a popular ruler. People liked his merry ways; they did not care that he was often in conflict with the Church; they did not criticize his way of life; his amorous adventures were a cause for laughter, and his exploits were recounted throughout the Duchy.

I learned a little about him during those five years when I knew him and I discovered a great deal later. He really had an influence on my life, for he it was who set the tone of the Court which my father was later to inherit and which was to continue to be my home during my childhood.

My grandfather had come to the throne when he was fifteen or sixteen years old, and even at that time the pursuit of women seemed to be the great aim of his life. At the Court of Poitou this was considered a lovable failing. Perhaps his ministers thought that such a youth would be easy to handle; they soon found their mistake. He might first and foremost wish to play the part of lover, but he was determined to rule as well and he intended that one pursuit should not deter him from following the other.

It was thought a good idea to get him married quickly. On our northern borders was the province of Anjou, and the daughter of Fulk of Anjou was chosen for William. She was Ermengarde and reckoned to be a great beauty—as most royal brides are made out to be—and they were married.

He appeared to be delighted for a while but he was not a man to give up old habits, and there was friction between them. Moreover she failed to produce an heir—a terrible fault in women of noble families—and there was agreement between them that divorce would be desirable.

This was obtained without too much difficulty but of course a man in my grandfather's position was in duty bound to produce an heir so he must again think of marriage.

An interesting situation had arisen in the neighbourhood. Count William of Toulouse had gone to fight in the Holy Land and had been killed. He had a daughter but no son, and his brother, Raymond, immediately seized Toulouse and the title that went with it. Philippa, Count William's daughter, had married Sancho Ramirez, the ruler of Aragon, and, fortuitously, just at this time he was killed in battle, leaving her a widow. William, having heard accounts of her outstanding good looks, decided she was the wife for him and set out to woo her, and with his handsome looks and gift of words he was soon a successful suitor.

At first the marriage was successful. Moreover, inspired by religious fervour, Raymond of Toulouse joined the First Crusade and on the way to the Holy Land met his death; so all my grandfather had to do was ride with Philippa into Toulouse and take it.

While this was happening, Philippa gave birth to a son—my father.

There was a great deal of religious enthusiasm at that time. A certain monk who had once been a soldier and was the father of several children had what he called a revelation from God and became a recluse. He was known as Peter the Hermit and created a great stir when, having been on a pilgrimage to Jerusalem, he returned with such stories of the manner in which Christians were being treated that he attracted the attention of Pope Urban II. Together they preached about the wickedness of the villainous Turks who were desecrating the Holy Shrine, and such was the mystic power of Peter the Hermit that all over Europe men rallied to his call, eager to join the crusade which was to free Jerusalem from the Infidel.

My grandfather was caught up in the excitement, no doubt seeing that by such a venture he could wipe out his sins with one stroke and save himself years of wearying virtue. As an important ruler, he must set out in great style, and for that he needed money. He then did what in Philippa's eyes must have been unforgivable. He sold Toulouse to Raymond—son of that other Raymond—without asking Philippa's permission; and she, who was in Toulouse at the time, knew nothing about the transaction until Raymond came to take possession.

William found the Turk a formidable enemy and had the mortification of seeing his army cut to pieces in battle. He himself managed to escape, but all he came back with was some poems glorifying the crusade and telling of the cruelty of the wicked Infidel.

Philippa must have forgiven him, for she bore him two more children—there were five girls and another boy—but their relationship had been seriously impaired. She turned to religion and came under the influence of Robert d'Abrissel. I later took notice of this man for he founded Fontevrault, which consisted of four convents—two for women and two for men. He was the first of his kind to show a respect for women, and for that I applauded him. I came to love Fontevrault and could well imagine what a haven it would be to a woman who could embrace the cloistered life. I could not imagine myself doing so, but that did not stop my loving Fontevrault.

William had no interest in the place and did his best to discourage Philippa from the religious life she was leading. He deplored d'Abrissel's view of women for he wanted to keep them in that niche which men of his kind arranged for them. Had I been older, I would have made known my disagreement with him. I should have enjoyed doing battle with him on the subject.

He ridiculed d'Abrissel and talked of building a convent for courtesans. He was the sort of man who enjoyed shocking all those about him. Philippa was determined to pursue her own way of life; and the final break between them came with the appearance of Dangerosa, which was more than any woman could be expected to endure.

So Philippa left him for ever and retired to Fontevrault.

I was called Eleanor, named after my mother, for Eleanor meant 'That other Aénor'.

They made much of me. Like many sinners my grandfather and grandmother were indulgent. I doubt the virtuous Philippa or the Viscount of Châtellerault would have given me so much loving attention. My mother was there in the background, gentle, rather timid, an alien in this flamboyant Court. She was devoted to me and I know did her best to counteract the effect of the spoiling. I am afraid she was not very successful in this; but I did love her dearly and she represented a steadying influence in my young life which was certainly necessary.

When my sister Petronilla arrived, I was not quite sure of the effect she would have on my position; but very soon I was in charge of her. The elders watched me with amusement as I exerted my influence over her and by the time she could walk she was my abject slave. She was pretty and charming, but just as my father lacked the charisma of my grandfather, so Petronilla, for all her prettiness and charm could only take second place to me.

So all was well. I was the little Queen of the Court. I would sit on my grandfather's knee and make my quaint remarks which set his beard wagging, implying that he was amused. I was the one who received most of the sugarplums fed to us by Dangerosa.

At this time I heard someone say that the Lady Eleanor could well be the heiress of Aquitaine. That was a great revelation. Aquitaine, that beautiful country with its rivers, mountains, flowers and vineyards, its many castles . . . all would one day be mine! I was a very contented little girl.

And then it happened. My mother had been sick for a long time. Her shape changed; she rested a good deal. There was a great fuss about what they called 'her condition'. I was told: 'There is going to be another little one in the nursery.'

I naturally thought of another Petronilla—someone for me to mould and direct and who would become my ardent admirer.

The great day arrived. One of the nurses came to me in great excitement.

'What do you think, my lady!' she said. 'You have a little brother.'

What rejoicing there was throughout the castle. 'Now we have a male heir,' they said.

My grandfather was full of glee; so were Dangerosa and my father.

It was treachery. *I* was the heir of Aquitaine. But it seemed that, in spite of all the songs dedicated to the glory of women, they were forgotten when a boy was born.

This was the first setback.

I sat on my grandfather's knee and voiced my protests.

'But you see, little one, men want a leader.'

'I could lead them.'

'Sometimes we go into battle.'

'*You* don't.'

'I did . . . when I was a younger man.'

Dangerosa said: 'Never mind. Women have their way of ruling.'

My father tried to console me. 'You will make a great marriage when the time comes.'

My mother said: 'Happiness does not come with great titles, my child, but with the good life. If you marry and are a good wife, that will bring you more happiness than great estates.'

I did not believe her. I wanted to be the heiress of Aquitaine.

But no one could help loving little William Aigret. He was such a docile child; and I still ruled the nursery.

Soon after that my grandfather died and my father became the Duke of Aquitaine.

My grandfather was genuinely mourned. I spent a great deal of time with Dangerosa; she used to tell me stories about him; and it was from her I pieced together the events of his turbulent life. She loved to tell the story of her abduction and how he had come to the castle to talk business with his vassal the Viscount of Châtellerault and as soon as he set eyes on her all thought of business was driven from his mind. I felt I was there during those periods in the castle when they had planned their flight. I seemed to have ridden with them through the forest, she riding pillion, clinging to him as they sped away to happiness. It was very romantic. I did not spare a thought for the poor deserted

Viscount and my wronged grandmother Philippa. My sympathies were with the lovers.

Philippa was dead now but in the Courts of Love, which my grandfather had created, their story would be sung for years to come.

The Court changed of course. My father was a very different man. He was not the great lover; he was more of a fighter. At least he was constantly embroiled in some dispute with his vassals. He was quick-tempered and ready to go to war on the slightest pretext; and he was absent a good deal during the years which followed my grandfather's death.

There were plenty of young people at the castle, for girls were sent to my mother to be brought up as the Court ladies they would eventually become. There were boys too, who must be taught the art of chivalry and horsemanship. We girls had to learn how to embroider and do delicate needlework, which was so much a part of a lady's education; we had to sing and dance and make gracious conversation; but I was taught other things besides, such as reading and writing. I had shown such an aptitude for learning when it was thought I might be Duchess of Aquitaine that they decided I should continue. I was, therefore, apart from the other children, and I intended that none should forget it.

There was still a great deal of music in the evenings but my father, although he loved it, was no composer. He sang well, and this he liked to do; and he enjoyed the ballads and stories about his father. But he was so often away and the character of the Court had changed from what it had been in his father's day.

When my father came home he would want to know how we had progressed. He was very interested in William Aigret's performance, but I fancied he had a special fondness for me.

Then one day fever struck Poitou. Several people died and there were restrictions as to who should be allowed to come into the castle.

My mother became ill and she died within a few days. That was not all. William Aigret caught the fever from her and very soon afterwards he was dead.

It was a time of great mourning. It was then that I realized how much I had cared for my mother and that William Aigret had been such a loving little boy.

It was a great loss. There were only two children now—

Petronilla and myself; but I had become the heiress of Aquitaine.

My father called me to him. He held me close and said that I was his precious child. He was very sad. He told me how much he had loved my mother and their son, and to be deprived of them both was almost more than he could endure. He thanked God he had his daughters; and I knew that he was especially thankful for me.

I was eight years old now but more like a girl of ten, and ten was nearing maturity. Girls were married at thirteen—twelve even. So I did not seem like the child my years might suggest.

We wept together over our loss. My mother had not been a great beauty but perhaps there were qualities which some men found even more attractive. She had been gentle, tender and uncomplaining; and he had loved her as my grandfather had never loved the beautiful Ermengarde and Philippa. Of course Dangerosa had reigned supreme for several years but she had been a perfect match for my grandfather.

'This has made a difference to your position, daughter,' he said. I nodded. 'You will inherit this duchy when I am gone.'

'That will be years and years away.'

'I pray God so. For we are both unready as yet . . . I to go, you to rule. You will have to learn a great deal.'

I nodded again, but I felt I already knew a great deal.

'These are troublesome times. There is always some vassal ready to make mischief. That is why I am so often from Court.'

'I know, Father.'

'We have to remember that we ourselves are vassals of the King of France. You and I must talk together. There will be times when I shall take you with me on my journeys. You will have to know the domain which one day . . . unless I remarry and get a male heir . . . will be yours.'

'Will you marry?' I asked with trepidation.

He shook his head and there were tears in his eyes. 'No, no,' he said. 'How could I think of replacing your mother?'

I rejoiced. I could not bear the thought of a boy replacing me.

Life had certainly changed with the death of my brother. Everyone was subtly different towards me. I had become important.

They were writing songs about me now. I loved to hear them sing of my beauty and my cleverness. I noticed that several of the young men—even those of quite mature years—glanced at me in a special way. It was exciting.

My father took me on a journey with him. It was wonderful to ride beside him over the hills and through the forests with the courtiers about us, and then to receive the lavish hospitality at the castles where we stayed.

I had thought of Poitiers as home because that was where I had spent most of my childhood, but we had other castles and palaces of which I could grow fond.

Best of all these was the Ombrière Palace at Bordeaux, where we stayed for a time. My father had to deal with disgruntled vassals, many of whom had made trouble. He wanted me to be with him so that I could see how justice was meted out. It was illuminating.

I loved Bordeaux. There was evidence of Roman occupation there and I liked to dream of those old days and wonder what life had been like then. The palace was built on the old Roman wall, and from its windows I could look down on the Garonne winding its way to the sea.

I think that in the year following the death of my mother and brother I grew up. I was like a plant in a greenhouse where the atmosphere tends to force growth. My father was beginning to treat me like an adult. I do not think I am being unduly conceited when I say that I did have a rather special aptitude for ruling. That was to develop and bring me trouble later, but at the time my father rejoiced in it.

He talked often of the King of France. I would see his eyes on me and there would be an uneasy expression in them. I asked him if anything worried him.

He said frankly: 'In a duchy of this size there will always be trouble. It is too big for a ruler to be everywhere at once. It is necessary for that ruler to be loved by his people . . . loved and respected. It is the only way.'

'They do love you and respect you.'

He smiled ruefully. 'We do have trouble, you know. There are some who think they can do as they will and because of the distance between us will never be found out. There could be uprisings.'

'You will stop that.'

'If I can.'

'Is it worse now than it used to be?'

'Your grandfather was respected. It is strange. He was a man who defied the Church and who even died excommunicated; but he was loved throughout the Duchy . . . partly for what the Church deplored. That is the strangeness of human nature.'

'Perhaps you should be like him?'

'My child, we can only be like ourselves.'

I knew that he was quick to anger and perhaps acted recklessly. I was learning that it was no easy matter to keep order over a vast territory. And there was more trouble than there had been in my grandfather's day.

'One needs friends,' he said.

'And you have them?'

He lifted his shoulders. 'The King of France is very powerful,' he said.

'We are his vassals.'

'Yes. I think he casts envious eyes on Aquitaine.'

'Do you mean he will try to take it from you?'

He shook his head. 'He has sons and I have daughters.'

'You mean . . . marriage?'

'My child, I should like to see you married to the son of the King of France.'

'Marriage! Me!'

'One forgets how young you are. But the years pass quickly, daughter, and one day a husband will be found for you.'

'Perhaps I shall find my own.'

'That would not be easy for you. The Duchess of Aquitaine could not choose from those around her. It would have to be someone worthy. I should like to see you Queen of France.'

'But I am to be Duchess of Aquitaine.'

'Queen of France *and* Duchess of Aquitaine.'

'Queen of France!'

'Why not? The King of France has a son who will be King when his father dies.

I was excited. It was impossible in the Courts of Love not to be aware of the relationships between men and women. Looks came my way even now. I had noticed the men's eyes watching me, assessing me. It excited me to attempt to probe their thoughts.

I knew instinctively that marriage was not something I should shrink from. But Queen of France! I had not thought of that. Duchess of Aquitaine had seemed a glorious enough title. We were all vassals of France, and although we in Aquitaine might be richer, France was the master of us all.

'Tell me about the King of France and his son,' I said.

'Louis VI. Let me see. He must be in his late forties. He is the son of Philip I. Philip's story is not unlike that of your own grandfather. He married Bertha of Holland and there was a son, Louis, the King's heir. Philip fell in love with Bertrade de Montfort who was the wife of Fulk of Anjou, who as you know has connections with our own family. As your grandfather did with your grandmother, Dangerosa, he abducted Bertrade.'

'It is indeed the same story,' I cried.

'Love stories often resemble each other, and when you have two powerful men who act according to their whims and desires, similar results often come about. The Holy See rose in protest and Philip was obliged to promise to give up Bertrade, which he failed to do and consequently was excommunicated.'

'Just like my grandfather.'

He nodded. 'The trouble is that when a leader is excommunicated, the edict can fall on the entire community. This is what happened. Churches were closed and people were in revolt against that, so Philip eventually had to make a show of giving up Bertrade, and when he died he was reconciled to the Church. Bertrade was an ambitious mother and wanted her son by the King to be heir to the throne. When Philip was alive she made an attempt to poison his son Louis—her stepson—but that attempt fortunately failed and on his father's death Louis came to the throne.'

'And he is the father of the man I shall marry?'

'The man I should like you to marry. This is between ourselves at the moment. There will be many to seek alliance with France, my dear, but we have much to offer. We have the rich duchy of Aquitaine and with it one who must be the most beautiful girl in the whole of France.'

I smiled complacently. I had no doubt of my ability to capture the son of the King of France.

'Louis VI has two sons—Philip and Louis.'

'It will be Philip for me,' I said.

'The elder, no less.'

'Does he . . . know?'

My father shook his head. 'Though Louis will be looking out for his son's best interests.'

'Tell me about the Court of France. Is it like ours?'

'Oh, no, no. I doubt there is another Court in the world like ours. Your grandfather founded it, and although he is no longer with us, it does not change greatly. There will be differences. They call the King of France Louis the Fat . . . for obvious reasons. He is a great eater . . . a great drinker . . . and it is difficult for him to move about, so large is he. He is a very religious man which is why France is called ''the Elder Daughter of the Church''.'

'It would not be very merry at his Court.'

'If you were Queen of France, you would see that your Court was how you wanted it to be.'

'That is true,' I said. 'But the King of France has said nothing as yet regarding his son's marriage.'

'Not as yet, but I am his most powerful vassal, and Aquitaine covers about a quarter of France. He would be hard put to it to find a more worthy bride for his son.'

'So you think it will come to pass.'

'I am as sure as a man can be of anything.'

After that I thought a good deal about France and tried to learn all I could from the travellers who came to our Court.

It was at Ombrière that I first saw Raymond.

I was in the gardens with a group of girls who were being brought up at Court with us, and Petronilla was beside me. Some of them were embroidering altar cloths, while others took it in turn to recite verses and sing to us.

It was a pleasant summer's day—not too hot for the shade under the trees was pleasant.

I saw him walking through the gardens with my father, and I thought he was the most handsome man I had ever seen. He was very tall and upright, with blond hair, blue eyes and a merry expression. Since my talk with my father about marriage, I was paying more attention to young men. I had always been aware of them and liked to see what effect I had on them, and I was accustomed to receiving ardent looks which delighted me. I liked to think of myself as one of those sought-after maidens who kept themselves aloof because they were far too precious to fall into the hands of lesser men and must wait for the perfect knight.

I left the group of girls, Petronilla at my heels; she followed me everywhere.

My father saw us and smiled. 'Oh, Raymond,' he said, 'here are my daughters Eleanor and Petronilla. Daughters, your uncle Raymond.'

We curtsied. Uncle! I was thinking. There must be some mistake. He gazed at me and murmured my name.

'And Petronilla,' said my father.

Petronilla gave him a dazzling smile but I was delighted to notice that it was I who held his attention.

'I did not know that I had such enchanting nieces,' he said.

'You should have come before,' my father told him. 'It is not good for there to be rifts in families.'

We went into the palace with him. I think he was rather surprised by the easy manners between us. We were doubtless expected to be in awe of our father instead of making light conversation with him . . . at least I did. Petronilla said little, but I could see that she was as enchanted by this new uncle as I was.

He proved to be about eight years older than I, and he was Philippa's youngest son, born just after she had left the castle on the arrival of Dangerosa.

Alas, his visit was brief, but I was with him a great deal during the ten days he stayed in the palace for he was as attracted by me as I was by him. Each morning I awoke with the joyous thought: Raymond is here. We would ride together. I would sing for him. Petronilla was often with us and so was my father but I liked best the times when we were alone.

He told me that I was the most enchanting little girl he had ever met. There was a certain regret in his eyes and in his voice, and being precocious I knew what he meant by that. This was love, of which the troubadours sang, but he was a man, and for all my sophistication I was but a child, and he was my uncle, so there was too strong a blood tie between us for us to be lovers. But all our looks and gestures spoke of love; and I shall always remember Raymond as my first love.

He talked to me of serious things. I had an idea that he believed that by pretending I was not a child I should miraculously become a woman and then we could both give expression to what we felt.

He reminded me of my grandfather although I had only known him as an old man and this was a radiant young one. He was after all my grandfather's youngest son but he had never known him because he had been born after Philippa had left.

He told me that he was without fortune which was why he was setting out to make it. He was starting first in England, for he had met Henry, the King, who had promised him a welcome. I was sure he would make a name for himself, for he was meant for greatness . . . even though at this stage it was difficult to see how he would do this.

He was a great talker and I loved to listen.

He told me much of what was happening around me and of which I had been ignorant before. I had thought that my father was all-powerful; it was a revelation to learn that this was not the case and that he had dangerous enemies.

The greatest of these was the Church.

I began to see my father through new eyes. Not that Raymond ever spoke against him. But when he told me of affairs in Europe I realized that my father had only a very small part in them.

Raymond was interested in Bernard of Clairvaux, who was at this time in conflict with my father.

'He is a very powerful man,' Raymond told me, 'and it is unwise to cross swords with him.'

'And that is what my father is doing . . . crossing swords?'

'I should not be talking to you thus, dear child. Let us sing a beautiful song together. That is more suitable to the occasion, I am sure.'

'Let us sing certainly . . . but first I would hear of this Bernard of Clairvaux.'

'If you have not heard of him, assuredly you soon will. He is a monk and he is renowned for his power with words. He draws the most hardened sinners to the monastic life. It is said that mothers hide their sons, wives their husbands and friends their companions for fear that he will lure them away from them. As a young man he went to the monastery of Cîteaux because it was noted for its austerity, and that was the life he chose.'

I grimaced. 'How tiring such people are!' I cried. 'They want to be miserable themselves and to make everyone else so at the same time. If they want to starve and mourn, I say, let them, if they will allow those who want to enjoy life to do so.'

He laughed at my vehemence. 'I see you are a little hedonist. I am of your opinion. But we cannot ignore this Bernard. He is becoming too powerful a figure in the world.'

'It seems to me that one must either be very wicked or very good to win the approval of the people.'

He laughed again. 'And an observer of human nature too, I perceive. What a wise niece I have.'

'Tell me more of this Bernard.'

'He and his followers became so well known that many wanted to join their Order and there was not room at Cîteaux to hold them so they decided to build a new monastery. They went in search of a place where they could build it and they came upon the wooded valley of Langres which was very dark and gloomy and would have to be cleared.'

'They make me impatient,' I said. 'Why choose a place which demanded a lot of hard work before they began to build? They might have chosen a sunny plain somewhere.'

'But that would not suit Bernard. He believes that only by suffering can a man come to God. So they worked hard; they cut down trees; they settled there and built the famous abbey of Clairvaux. They endured great hardship and as a matter of fact, Bernard became so ill because of the austere life he led that they feared he would die.'

'He had none but himself to blame.'

'You are a realist, my dear little niece. Of course you are right. But there was great consternation. He was regarded as a saint. You have heard of the great doctor William of Champeaux. He went to Bernard. He cured him, taught him that it was possible to live frugally and be healthy. So now we have Bernard travelling the country, urging people to forsake their evil ways and whipping them up to a frenzy of piety. But the point of his discourse now is the acceptance of Innocent II as the true Pope.'

'I know of the rivalry between the two Popes.'

'It is splitting not only France but the whole of Europe. There are the supporters of Anacletus and those of Innocent.'

'But why are there these two Popes?'

'Because there was a split among the Cardinals and each candidate for the Papacy declares himself the winner. It is dividing the whole of Christendom. Italy stands for Anacletus and France for Innocent. At least that was how it was until Bernard took a hand in the dispute. You see, Louis sent for Bernard. Louis, indulgent as he is to his own appetites—and his immense body bears witness to that—is a very religious man. How the ascetic Bernard and gross Louis became so reconciled to each other it is hard to say, but the fact is that Louis has persuaded Bernard to stand for Innocent; and that means that he will win the whole of Europe to his side with his honeyed words.'

'So this matter will be settled then?'

'What I am telling you is that there are some who still stand for Anacletus and your father is one of them.'

'Is that why he is so troubled lately?'

'It may well be.'

'Why should we in Aquitaine be bothered by what is happening in Rome?'

'What happens in the world affects us all. Does your father talk to you of these matters?'

'Of some. He did not talk of this.'

'I would guess that it is because it weighs heavily on his mind.'

'What is Anacletus to him?'

'It is hard sometimes for people to change a course when they have set out on it.'

I knew what he meant. My father was a stubborn man and he would often cling to a decision because he had made it even when he discovered it could do him harm. He had an innate pride which would not let him do otherwise.

Raymond was smiling at me. 'Why do I talk to you so?' he said. 'Eleanor, there are times when I forget you are so young.'

'Then go on forgetting,' I begged him.

He took my face in his hands and kissed me gently. I flung my arms about his neck and cried: 'Do not go away. Stay here at our Court.'

He sighed. 'I would that I could!' he said.

'Why not?' I demanded. 'You are seeking your fortune. Why not do it here?'

He laughed. 'What a glorious prospect! Every day to be with Eleanor. Ah, the temptation is great. Tell me this, little wise one, why are the best things in life so often out of reach?'

'The clever ones stretch out far enough to reach them,' I replied.

Then he took me in his arms and held me tightly against him. I was deeply stirred, and if I could have shut out of my mind the knowledge that he would soon be going away, that could have been the happiest moment I had ever known.

But he released me and said he must leave me. He had much to do and he must prepare for his departure and not delay too long or King Henry would have forgotten his invitation, and that would be another lost chance.

When he went away, I was sad for a long time.

The conflict between the Popes dominated the country. From what I could gather, we stood apart, for now that the King of France had persuaded Bernard to give his approval to Innocent, it seemed the whole world followed him. Bernard only had to appear with his spare, emaciated figure and his loud condemnation of sin, for people to know that they were in the presence of a saint. They immediately followed him—all except my father.

'I will not be told what to do by this man just because he tortures his body and talks like a fanatic,' declared my father. 'I will go my own way.'

I was a little alarmed for him. To my way of thinking it was of little importance to us which Pope ruled. They were all the same, all in search of the same thing: self-aggrandisement, power.

But my father was stubborn. When an invitation came for him to meet Bernard at the Abbey Montierneuf, he refused to go at first. It was only when he was advised that this was a dangerous attitude to take, for the King of France was firmly behind Bernard as was most of Europe, that he finally decided to go.

I wanted to accompany him. I should have loved to see the celebrated Bernard.

Of course I was not allowed to, and when he did come back I was amazed to see how chastened he was.

'There is something about the man,' he admitted. 'Something spiritual.'

'Have you promised to withdraw your support from Anacletus?' I asked him.

'I was bemused by him,' he admitted. 'One really did feel that one was in the presence of a saint.'

Now, I thought, all will be well. This silly business will be settled. We shall be at peace with our neighbours. Raymond would have said this was the wise thing to do.

My father was a strange man. He had certainly been impressed by Bernard. He had come back subdued, and remained so for a whole week.

One evening, when we were in the great hall, my father sat listening to the singing with a brooding look in his eyes. I was beside him as I often was at this time. The lute-player was singing a love song about a lady who bore a strong resemblance to myself. Petronilla was at my side listening intently.

Then my father spoke. He said quite softly so that only I heard him: 'A plague on these reformers. I'll have my own way. I'll not be led by them.'

I said: 'Do you speak of Bernard?'

He said in a loud voice: 'I speak of all who would seek to rule me. This is my land and I am the master of it.'

The next day he rode with a party to Montierneuf and smashed the altar on which Bernard had said Mass, and he declared that all those who supported Innocent should be driven from his kingdom.

I was beginning to learn that my father was not the great ruler I had thought him to be; nor, I supposed, had my grandfather been. Neither of them had had any great success in battle; both were men who followed their own desires to such an extent that they could not see any other point of view. My grandfather had died excommunicated from the Church—and the Church was a force to reckon with. Because of his colourful personality, he had won the affection of his people; my father did not have that.

It is all very well for a ruler to be strong; that he must be. But when the forces against him are so great that they are superior in every way, he should reconsider his position and avoid unnecessary danger. My father was a stubborn man. If he found himself on the wrong path, his pride would not allow him to retrace his steps. He must go on. Only a miracle could change him. Who would have thought that a miracle was possible?

Bernard must have had some spiritual power. I would not have believed it could happen any more than my father did; but

both of us were forced in the end to believe what was an actual
fact.

It was hardly likely that my father's intransigence would be
allowed to pass.

Bernard of Clairvaux was not accustomed to being flouted.
He had preached to my father; he had persuaded him; he had,
he believed, led him out of his evil ways—and as soon as Bernard had gone my father reverted to them!

Bernard came once more to Poitou to see him.

Although my father refused to see him, that did not deter
Bernard. He remained in Poitou, visiting the town, preaching
to the people. Wherever he went there were crowds. He was a
later Jesus Christ—and I believe that was how he saw himself.
People fell down and worshipped him; they declared themselves
enemies of sin and the Devil for ever more.

And my father still refused to admit him to the palace.

When Bernard arrived in Poitiers and preached in the square,
people came from miles around to beg for his blessing.

My father could not allow him to use his city, his church. He
rode into the town to see what was happening. I do not know
what he intended to do. I was afraid that in his stubborn recklessness he would seek open conflict with Bernard; and I could
guess what the outcome of that might be.

When he arrived in the centre of the town, Bernard was already in the church celebrating Mass. The crowd outside was
great, for the church was not big enough to hold all the people.
My father pushed his way through the press of people and stood
at the door of the church. I can imagine the silence. Bernard
was holding the Host and when he saw my father, still carrying
the Host, he walked slowly down the aisle towards him. I could
imagine my father, choking with anger, because this man who
had come into his territory was acting as though he owned it.
So great would his anger have been that he drew his sword.
Nearer and nearer to each other came the two men. My father,
sword in hand, and Bernard holding the Host. It must have been
the most dramatic confrontation the watchers had ever seen.

Then Bernard began to castigate my father; he said he had
spurned God, that he had desecrated the Church and had rejected God's servant.

Closer and closer they came to each other and the people

waited breathlessly for what would happen next. Would my father slay the saint?

Bernard had no fear. Such men never have. They embrace martyrdom as the worldly do their lovers. It would not surprise me if, at the moment, Bernard *hoped* my father would kill him, for if he did that would no doubt be the end of my father—and such men as Bernard are vengeful—and for Bernard the crown of glory.

Then the miracle happened. My father lifted his sword, for having come so far a man such as he was could not retreat. Bernard came nearer, waiting for the blow, but as my father raised his arm, he fell suddenly at Bernard's feet.

This was seen as the power of God against the forces of evil. The sword had no power to strike the Host.

My father lay on the floor, and Bernard made him rise and make his peace with God.

The strange thing was that my father was able to get to his feet, and Bernard embraced and kissed him.

'Go in peace, my son,' he said.

The miracle had brought about the effect which Bernard had desired. My father had been vanquished. There would be no more objections to Innocent, no more support for the man whom his enemies called the anti-Pope.

My father came back to us, a changed man.

He was never the same again. He was given to moods of melancholy. Immediately after his return he shut himself in the palace. It was a shattering experience to have been shown so clearly that God was displeased with him.

Bernard was a saint. He was sure of that. The man had proved it. And he himself was a miserable sinner.

Everyone was afraid to go near him—with the exception of myself, and even I went tentatively at first. But I soon found that he wanted me with him. He wanted to talk to someone, and he could do that with me more easily than with anyone else.

He explained to me how he had lifted his sword. 'I was going to strike a holy man. What if I had? I should have been damned forever.'

'But you did not,' I soothed. 'You were saved in time.'

'Bernard saved me. He looked into my eyes . . . such glittering eyes *he* has. I seemed to lose myself in them; and there he was . . . holding the Host, and my knees buckled under me. I found myself swaying like an aspen in the wind. It was as though something flowed over me . . . like a gigantic wave . . . and there was I, helpless at his feet.'

'Try to forget it,' I said. 'It is over.'

'It will live with me forever. I see that I have failed and not done what I should for my country . . . and for God. What shall I do, Eleanor my child? What shall I do?'

'Forget what has happened. Have no more trouble with these Popes. Let them fight their own battles. Rule Aquitaine. This is your country. What else matters?'

'I fear I have not done well. There is unrest in the country more than there was during my father's time.'

'Your father did not worry with such matters as you do.'

'No, he was content in his Courts of Love.'

'As you must be.'

'I am different from my father. I see how neglectful I have been of my duties. My dear wife died . . . and our son with her. I am left with two daughters.'

'We are as good as any sons, Father.'

He smiled at me. 'There is none like you, my dear child, nor ever could be, but you are a woman. There will be trouble when I am gone if there is not a strong hand on the reins.'

I held out my hands to him. 'They are strong, Father.'

'They are beautiful . . . soft as a woman's should be. You do not understand, dear child. There should be a male heir.'

'You have me now.'

I was shaken with horror at his next words. 'It is not too late.'

'What do you mean?'

'I must do my duty. It is expected of me. I am going to change my ways. I have been brought face to face with the truth. Because I did not wish to marry again I thrust the matter out of my mind. But I see that I must.'

'No!' I cried.

'My dear daughter,' he said, 'you want to be the ruler of Aquitaine. That is because you do not know what it entails. It would bring you little joy. It is a task for a man.'

'But you have said *you* have not done well, and you are a man.'

'This is not the time to twist words, dear daughter. I have

been thinking over the past days that I must marry. I must give Aquitaine a son. If only your brother had lived . . .'

I stood up and, without asking permission, left him.

How weak he was, how clinging. He could not bear that I should withhold myself from him. When I look back, I am amazed at the power I had in that Court. I was thirteen years old but more like eighteen. I was both physically and mentally developed beyond most girls of my age. I had been in the forcing-ground of maturity ever since I was born. I had seen romantic love and lust in my grandfather's Court; I had gradually become aware of my father's weakness; I had seen him disintegrate before my eyes. Oddly enough, this made me feel strong. It made me more certain than ever that when the time came I should be capable of ruling Aquitaine. I should not have made the mistakes I had seen my father make. I should not have considered the Popes' quarrel mine. I should never have given way to the influence of Bernard.

And now my father, in his weakened state, was reaching out to me. I felt strong, important. Aquitaine was going to be mine.

My father sent for me. He told me with some humility that he had not meant to hurt me. He thought I was wonderful. Many of the young men at Court admired me, looked up to me as an ideal. That pleased him. He, too, venerated me. He knew that I was no ordinary girl. He was proud of me.

'And yet you would replace me by some sickly boy!'

'I merely feel that a son would be more acceptable to the people. I have not thought enough of my people, Eleanor. There is no reason why the boy should be sickly.'

'You are becoming old now. I believe the age of its parents has an effect on a child. Here am I strong and healthy, the daughter of your youth. I can read and write with ease; I can reason. Rest assured I shall be fit to govern when the time comes.'

'I doubt it not. But the people want to look to a man.'

'Where will you find this bride?'

'I must look for her.'

'Then I suppose you will go on a pilgrimage to some shrine or other to pray for a fertile wife.'

'A pilgrimage,' he said slowly. 'Perhaps I should go on a pilgrimage.'

I thought: If it is going to stop these thoughts of marriage, yes, certainly you should go.

I said: 'You have been deeply disturbed by what has happened to you in the church. You need to make your peace with God before you think of marriage.'

He stared at me incredulously. 'By all the saints, I believe you are right.'

He had made up his mind. He would go on a pilgrimage; he would earn complete forgiveness for his past sins; he would find favour in the eyes of God. He would go not as a great ruler but as the humblest pilgrim without splendour of any sort; his garment should be a sackcloth robe; he would endure all the hardships of a long journey; and the more discomfort he endured the more quickly his sins would be wiped away. He would return to Aquitaine in triumph, and God would give him a fruitful bride.

Being headstrong, as he always had been, when he came to a hasty decision he found it hard to wait to put it into action; and when what he thought of as a great opportunity came, he was ready to seize it.

Emma, daughter of the Viscount of Limoges, had been married to Barden of Cognac who had recently died. The heiress of Limoges seemed to my father an excellent bride. He became convinced that God had removed Barden of Cognac to show him, William, the way.

He did not stop to assess the situation. He talked of the honour he was about to bestow on Limoges, for the Limousin was a vassal state to Aquitaine. He forgot that there had been a great deal of friction between the two states in the past; he believed that now he was a changed man, everyone's attitudes must change towards him.

The last thing the people of Limousin wanted was to come under the direct rule of Aquitaine; and there were others who did not wish to see Aquitaine become more powerful and who would do a great deal to prevent William's marrying Emma.

They managed very skilfully and prevailed on the Count of Angoulême to abduct Emma. He came in strength and took her from her home as Philip of France had taken Bertrade and my grandfather Dangerosa; and that settled the matter. My father's attempt to marry Emma of Limoges had failed.

He seemed to regard this as another expression of God's displeasure and was sunk in melancholy. He continued feverishly to make plans for his pilgrimage. He was anxious for me to know that he still loved me dearly. I was sure that he did so more than he could any sons even though they possessed the magic quality of masculinity.

I was angry with him, and I should have been more so if I had believed he was going to achieve his purpose. First he had to make the pilgrimage, and that was going to take some time. He was not in especially good health, and the hardships he would have to endure would surely not act as a restorative. Then he had to find a bride and she must be fruitful. I was not one to anticipate disaster, and I think at that age I had an unshakable belief in myself and my destiny.

Preparations took some time. He explained to me that for a man in his position there was a great deal to arrange; and I was his main concern.

'I?' I cried, 'It would seem to me that I am your least concern since you plan to replace me with a more desirable heir.'

He was distressed. 'Eleanor,' he said severely, 'you will have to learn to curb your temper.'

'My temper, my lord! Have I not been extremely accommodating? I have helped you with your plans when, if they are successful, they will culminate in my loss!'

'Do not see it that way. You are my great concern. Much as I wish to go to the shrine of St. James, I am constantly plagued by my fears of what will happen to you.'

'The answer is simple. Give up the idea of the pilgrimage and sons. If I am worthy of your concern, surely a better fate should be found for me than to be packed off in marriage.'

'Packed off in marriage! My dear girl, your marriage shall be the most brilliant in Europe. That is what I wish to talk about. Louis . . .'

'The fat one or his son?'

'Both, my dear. Louis is a fine fellow. When his brother died, he stepped into his shoes with the greatest of ease.'

'Can that be true of one who was trained to be a priest?'

'Sons of kings have their duty to perform and they must take whatever comes to them.'

I wondered about Louis. I had for some time, for it was no news to me that, if all went well and we did not displease the King of France, there might be a match between me and his eldest son. I did not know how far my father had offended him over this matter of Innocent and Anacletus, but presumably

Aquitaine would be a big enough prize for such matters not to be an irrevocable handicap.

I had discovered all I could about the Court of France since I had heard that I might well one day marry into it. I was fascinated by the reputed size of the King. He had grown so large through excessive eating and drinking that it was difficult for him to move about. In his youth he had been tireless and excelled in all physical exercise. I suppose this had developed his appetite, which continued to be large when he was less active. In spite of this foolhardy indulgence, he was a wise man and a shrewd ruler. He had always been on friendly terms with Aquitaine until this unfortunate matter of the Popes had arisen. I think he probably wanted a match with us as much as we with him.

Now that my father had repented, friendship between the two was resumed. But I was not sure whether the union between myself and the heir to the crown of France would be so attractive if he discovered that my father was contemplating marriage. As the sister of the ruler of Aquitaine, I would be a much less desirable match than its Duchess would have been.

I had always imagined that my husband would be Philip but a strange thing had happened. He had been killed when out riding. It was so sudden that it was almost like an act of God. Philip had been riding through Paris when a pig had run under his horse's legs. He had been thrown clear, hitting his head on a stone wall; he had died instantly.

This was so unusual, so unexpected, that people said it was 'meant'.

Louis the Fat had several children besides Philip and Louis. There was Robert who became Count of Dreux, Peter de Courtenay, Henry and Philip and a daughter, Constance. She was later Countess of Toulouse, and the two younger boys became bishops. The second son, Louis, was intended for the Church and was being brought up to this until the pig changed the course of history. Louis was taken from his cloisters to become heir to the throne of France; and that meant that if I were to marry into France, Louis would be my husband.

My father went on: 'There is one great concern for me. I hesitate to leave you and Petronilla.'

I stared at him in amazement. 'What harm could come to us?'

'What harm indeed! There are those who might well take advantage of my absence. I shall talk to you very seriously. You are not ignorant of the ways of men. You are a very attractive girl. I have seen some of the men's eyes on you and I have heard their songs. They sing of romantic love, my dear, while they are planning seduction, perhaps even rape.'

'I understand well the nature of men, Father.'

'Then you will understand my concern. If I left you here alone . . . you and Petronilla . . . some brigand might come along, take possession of the castle and of you. He might even force his attentions on you.'

'Do you think I should submit . . . to that?'

'If his physical strength was greater than yours, you would be obliged to. Only recently there was the case of poor Emma of Limoges. You are especially attractive; you have exceptional beauty; but to some, Aquitaine would be even more desirable.'

'I would fight to the death.'

'But I do not want you dead, dear child. No, no, you have had freedom here at Court. You have been surrounded by young men and girls. You have made your verses, sung your songs, indulged in flirtatious conversations with young gallants. You have happily basked in their admiration. You revel in it. Some of these young men have been very handsome, very plausible. Sometimes I have feared . . . There must be no dalliance, Eleanor, neither for you nor for Petronilla. You must go to your husband completely pure . . . virgins . . . nothing else will do.'

I laughed aloud. 'You have no need to remind me of that, Father. I saw no reason why I should not be amused by these young men. Light amusement . . . that is all it has been.'

'I could not be at peace if I left you and your sister here while I was away. We shall all leave for Bordeaux, and I want you two to remain in the palace there until I return. I have spoken to Archbishop Geoffrey du Lauroux. He is a good man and he is one whom I can trust. He will watch over you and there will be none who dare flout his rule. He is a man of God and much respected.'

'Father, there is no need.'

'Daughter, there is every need, and that is how it shall be.'

I was not displeased. I loved Bordeaux and, in spite of the stern Archbishop, I intended to have a merry time there. I would discuss with Petronilla which members of our entourage we should take with us.

'I shall inform the King of France of my intentions,' said my father.

'Of your intentions to marry?' I asked quickly.

'No . . . no . . . that is in the future. I shall tell him that I am leaving for a pilgrimage to Santiago de Compostela. He will understand. He knows well what has happened and will realize the necessity for me to make my peace with God.'

'It seems,' I said, 'that it is all arranged.'

He nodded. 'We will make preparations to leave for Bordeaux without delay. I am eager to begin my pilgrimage and return to you.'

So we left for Bordeaux.

None would have believed that the man at the head of the little group of pilgrims was Duke William of Aquitaine. Dressed in sackcloth, a pilgrim's hat on his head, he resembled the humblest of his subjects. I thought that he must indeed be a worried man to contemplate such hardships as he would have to face.

But that was the object of the pilgrimage; it was a penance: if it were a pleasant journey, there would be no merit in it.

Petronilla and I stood in the Courtyard to say our farewells. There was a chill wind, and although we were wrapped in our fur-lined cloaks we shivered.

He embraced us with great emotion. 'I shall pray to God and all the saints to guard you,' he said.

'And we shall pray to them for you, Father,' I replied. 'You will need their help more than we shall.'

'I shall be returned to you . . . refreshed.'

But, I could not help thinking ruefully, as a prospective bride-groom.

'We shall eagerly await your return,' I told him.

We watched him leave and afterwards Petronilla and I went to the highest point of the ramparts and strained our eyes looking into the distance until we could see him no more.

'I wonder how long it will be before he returns,' said Petronilla.

'I wonder what sort of man he will be when he comes back,' I replied.

She looked at me expectantly but I ignored her. I did not want to explain my thoughts to Petronilla.

'Now,' she said, 'you are the ruler of Aquitaine.'

'Yes,' I answered slowly.

'You must be pleased about that. It is what you always wanted.'

I laughed and taking her by the shoulders kissed her.

'Yes,' I agreed, 'it is what I always wanted. And it is mine . . . for a while. Come. We'll make the most of it.'

'What shall we do?'

'You'll see. The Court at Ombrière will be as it was in our grandfather's day. Do you remember how we used to sit in the hall in the evenings watching the jugglers and listening to the singers? You were too young. But our grandfather used to take me on his knee and sing to me.'

'Tell me about it,' said Petronilla, for she could remember little.

So I told her of the songs they sang glorifying love and telling of the exploits of our grandfather and his knights.

'I remember some of it,' I said, 'but I did not understand it all at the time. They were a little risqué. Men were very daring in those days and they have changed little. They will sing songs of love and devotion and how they adore you and set you on a pedestal so that they can worship you, and all the time it is merely to lull your feelings into a sense of security, and when you are sufficiently lulled they will take advantage of you. And once that has happened they will tire of you.'

'Is that really true? Our grandfather did not tire of Dange-rosa.'

'That was because she was clever. We have to be clever . . . more clever than they are, Petronilla. That is what I learned in the Courts of Love.'

And during those months while we awaited my father's return I set up my own Court. In the evenings I would have the minstrels play for us; there were the story-tellers and the itinerant troubadours who were constantly arriving. It was becoming more and more like the Court of my grandfather's day.

I was the Queen of it all. It was in praise of me that they wrote their songs. They would sit at my feet, those handsome knights, and in their songs and in their looks they would proclaim their love for me.

I believe there were some who thought I would succumb. It was not that I should not have liked, on occasion, to do so. I was susceptible to their handsome looks and charming manners. I would pretend to waver. It was exciting to see the hope in their eyes. But I never gave way. I had learned my lessons. Whatever happened, I must be aloof. I must be the one they dreamed about, the one about whom they wove their fancies.

The Archbishop was dismayed. This was not seemly in his eyes. There was too much levity. There should be more time spent in devotions. I pretended to be contrite, but I did not change my ways. This was my Court and because my power might be transient, I was determined to enjoy it while I could.

I feared that, if my father came back a rejuvenated man with his sins washed away, he would marry, and if he had a son, that would be the end of my hopes. I threw myself into the enjoyment of those days when I was in truth Queen of my Court, the ruler of Aquitaine, and the days passed all too quickly.

There was no news.

Sometimes I went to the topmost tower and looked around. One day I must see the returning party. Surely he must come home soon, and this pleasant existence at Court must end.

Petronilla would stand beside me. 'He must soon come back,' she said. 'He has been gone so long.'

'It is a long way to go.'

'Then when he comes back he will take a wife, our step-mother, Eleanor. I think we shall hate her. She will have children, and if they are boys they will be more important than we are.'

'She may be barren.'

'I hope she is. No one but you should be ruler of Aquitaine.'

'If I marry the son of the King of France I shall have to go away.'

'I shall come with you.' I was silent and she went on: 'Please say I may. I should hate to be parted from you. I wouldn't. I should run away to where you were.'

I smiled, pleased by her devotion. 'You are always impulsive, Petronilla,' I said. 'You are a little like our father. You act without thinking what effect your actions will have.'

'Some say that of you.'

'Then we are a pair.'

'Promise I shall come with you when you marry and go away.'

'I promise.'

As we stood there one day, we saw a lonely figure riding along the road.

'He brings news,' I said. 'Let us go down and see what he has to tell us. It may be that he comes from our father.'

We were not the only ones who had noticed the arrival and when we went down a little crowd had gathered there.

A groom took the rider's horse. He was clearly exhausted and must have ridden a long way. He came to me and kneeling before me lifted woeful eyes to my face.

'I bring sad news, my lady.'

'You come from my father?'

'The Duke is dead, my lady.'

'Dead! No, that cannot be.'

'Alas, it is so, my lady. There were many hardships on the journey. The Duke developed a cough. It settled in his lungs. His legs became stiff. There were nights when there was no shelter. We could not travel fast.'

'He should never have gone,' I said. 'He should have stayed with us. There are other ways of expiating sins.'

'He became too ill to ride, my lady. We had to make a litter for him. It impeded our progress. It became clear to us all that he could not make the journey to Compostela.'

'Why did you not bring him back?'

'He would never have made that journey either; and he wished to go on.'

'And he did not reach the shrine.'

'He passed away when we were within a mile or so of it. We could see it in the distance. But he died contented. He knew that, although God had denied him the satisfaction of reaching the shrine, his sins would be forgiven and he would be received into Heaven. He talked of Moses, who did not reach the Promised Land. He wished to be buried at the shrine, my lady; and this was done.'

I felt dazed. I said: 'You are exhausted. You must rest. You should take some food. Come into the palace.'

This was a possibility which had not occurred to me. I had thought my father might return debilitated, for I knew his health was not such that he could endure hardship, but I had not thought of death. Never to see him again. Then one thought overwhelmed all others: Aquitaine was mine. No one could replace me now.

The Court was still in mourning for its Duke. Attitudes had changed. I had been admired by the courtiers as a beautiful girl; now I was their Duchess. They regarded me with a new respect.

I missed my father. When people have gone forever, one remembers so much that one wished one had done. I wished that I had let him know how much I had cared for him, that I had known, even when he planned to displace me, that his great concern had been for me. He did not want me to have to face difficulties such as those which had confronted him and given him great anxiety. I could have told him that I was different from him. I believed I would not have made the mistakes that he did. This was not so much conceit as conviction. I know now how wrong I was when I look back over a lifetime of mistakes; perhaps as great as any he made. But I wanted him back; I wanted to talk to him; I comforted myself with the thought that God had accepted his final sacrifice and given him absolution in return for his life, that he would be in Heaven and from there perhaps be able to look down on me and know that his fears for me were groundless.

I learned more from the messenger, of the hardships they had endured, and how when he became so ill he had sent a messenger to the King of France offering him my hand in marriage with the King's eldest living son. He had received assurances from Louis before he died, and I was told that because of this he died content.

That Louis intended to keep his promise was evident. Almost immediately emissaries from the Court of France arrived at Bordeaux.

The King's son, Louis, was on his way to visit Aquitaine, and I knew that he was coming to ask my hand in marriage. It was a courtly gesture—and typical of the French—for it was a foregone conclusion that I should accept him, since the marriage had been a possibility for some time. There was no fear now that any son of my father could claim Aquitaine from me. I was the best match in France for him; and as he would one day be King of France, he was the best for me.

Petronilla and I talked constantly of what would happen next. Perhaps it was rather soon after the death of my father for there to be all this excitement about a wedding, but the circumstances were unusual. I was a girl of fifteen and therefore in need of protection, and the King of France had decided to waive convention and act as good sense commanded him.

We were often at the tower from which we had a good view of the road. We expected to see signs of the French cavalcade at any moment. When I was Queen of France, Petronilla reminded me, she would be with me. I assured her that was a promise I intended to keep. She was too young as yet to be married and it was only to be expected that I should want to keep her with me and choose her husband for her.

So we talked as we watched and waited, and one day our patience was rewarded, for we saw in the distance a glittering company approaching. Pennants waved in the wind and from far off came the strains of music.

As we watched, a messenger came riding up. It was the Archbishop Geoffrey du Lauroux, whom my father had made my guardian while he was away. I went down to greet him, Petronilla beside me as usual.

'The French are approaching, my lady,' he told me. 'We must welcome them. The Prince is with them and I think I should bring him to my palace. A meeting between you must be arranged without delay.'

I agreed that this should be and he went off immediately.

Petronilla and I could not contain our excitement. Soon I should see my prospective husband. We went up to the top of the tower from where we could see the French camped close by. Their tents and pavilions made a colourful show with the banners displaying the fleurs-de-lys. It was as though an army was encamped there.

It is a never-to-be-forgotten moment when one is presented to a man never seen before and who is to be one's husband.

Poor Louis; knowing him so well now, I realize he was far more nervous than I. I try now to analyse what I felt then. Was I disappointed? In a way. He was no bold knight like those of whom I had heard so frequently in the songs of the Courts of Love, and scarcely a romantic figure. There was something rather timid about him. While that irked me in a way, for perhaps I had dreamed of a masterful lover, in another way it pleased me for I knew at once that I should be able to lead him the way I wanted him to go.

He was tall, fair-haired and blue-eyed, with rather pale skin, and there was little animation in his face. I suppose he was about as different from me as any person could be from another.

I had discarded my wimple and wore my abundant dark hair loose about my shoulders; it was too beautiful to be hidden. I had dressed with care in a blue gown with long, wide, hanging sleeves, a little demure yet seductive. The colour suited my dark eyes and olive skin.

The Archbishop stood there like some recording angel. I was sure he disapproved of my flowing hair. But there was so much that good man disapproved of.

Louis bowed. I curtsied. I spoke first: 'Welcome, my lord, to Aquitaine.'

'It gives me great joy to greet you,' he replied. 'May I present my commanders, Count Thibault of Champagne and Count Raoul of Vermandois.'

I turned to the two men who accompanied him. Count Raoul was very attractive; his eyes betrayed his admiration for me in a manner to which I was accustomed, but it was none the less welcome for that. I had heard of him. He was the Seneschal of France and the King's cousin, a man of great importance at the Court of France. I thought how differently I should be feeling if he had been the prospective bridegroom instead of Louis.

And there was Abbot Suger—a little old man, another of those who frowned on all that was merry.

The Archbishop glanced at Suger and said: 'Perhaps the Prince and the Duchess would care to talk together.'

As Louis said nothing, I replied that we should.

The Archbishop nodded, and drawing the others to a far corner of the room, he invited them to sit down. They would not leave us. That would be quite out of the question. Did they think that Louis would attempt to rape me? I looked at Louis and wanted to laugh, but he saw no humour in the situation.

I took him to a window-seat and there we sat side by side. The whole room separated us from the other little party—and this was as near to being alone together that we should get before we were married.

'You had a long and arduous journey, my lord,' I said.

He stammered: 'Yes . . . we had. The heat was so intense that we were forced to travel by night.'

'And sleep by day?'

He nodded. I could see that he found it difficult to stop looking at me. I was pleased for I was sure that he found me attractive.

'It must have been slow progress travelling with so much. It is like an army.'

'There . . . there were the packhorses carrying the tents and provisions and cooking utensils. Yes . . . it was like an army. It has taken us most part of a month to get here.'

I leaned towards him smiling. 'I hope you will find the journey worthwhile.'

He stammered: 'Oh, yes . . . yes . . . indeed.'

Poor boy. He did not know how to pay compliments. But somehow I liked him for that. In fact I was liking him more every minute. There was a rather charming innocence about him.

He said: 'I . . . I have come to ask your hand in marriage.'

'I know. I was expecting you.'

'I trust that I shall be fortunate enough to please you.'

'And I you.'

'You . . . you are beautiful.'

'Oh, did you expect some horrid creature with bad teeth and a squint?'

'No, I had heard that you were beautiful.'

'And you thought that all prospective brides are said to be that?'

A faint smile touched his lips. 'That is so,' he said. 'But you are really beautiful.'

'Thank you,' I replied. 'I am sure we shall like each other.'

He looked very relieved.

I said: 'Tell me about the Court of France.'

'I hope soon you will see it for yourself.'

'I wonder if it is anything like our Court here. Do you like music?'

'Yes.'

'Then that is something we both like.'

'I . . . I have only been at Court for a few years. Before, I was with the Abbot Suger at St. Denis. I was going into the Church but my brother . . .'

'Yes, I know. He was killed by a pig.'

'It changed my life.'

'Think of that. But for a pig you would not be sitting here today.'

'It is God's will.'

'I suppose one could say that of anything.'

The Abbot Suger and the Archbishop had risen simultaneously. The tête-à-tête with my future husband had gone on long enough for propriety. I felt rather annoyed that I should be told what I might and might not do. That situation should soon be rectified, but this was not the occasion to show my irritation. I wanted to create a good impression on Louis, so I dutifully rose and said *au revoir* to him and the rest of the company.

Then I went to Petronilla, to tell her about my first encounter with my bridegroom elect.

'He looks mild,' she said.

'How do you know?'

'I peeped down when they arrived. I had a good view. He hardly looks like the man I should have expected you to marry. I thought at first that it was one of the others . . . and I quite envied you.'

'Which other?'

'There were men with him.'

'Do you mean the Abbot Suger?'

Petronilla was overcome with mirth.

'You know I didn't mean him. Abbot Suger indeed! He looks such another as the grim old Archbishop. I mean the handsome one who was presented to you.'

'Do you mean Thibault of Champagne or Raoul of Vermandois?'

'The attractive one.'

'They were both attractive.'

'One was especially so.'

'What a lot you noticed!'

'One would be blind and insensitive not to notice that one.'

'Are you sure you did not mean Louis?'

'Indeed I did not.'

'I think I know. It was Raoul of Vermandois. I must say, he did seem rather attractive.'

'Rather! He was overwhelmingly so. I hope I shall have the opportunity of meeting him soon.'

'Petronilla, you are getting frivolous.'

'I follow the example of my sister always.'

'You must show more respect. Remember, I shall be not only the Duchess of Aquitaine but very soon, they say, the Queen of France.'

'I am looking forward to being there . . . particularly if this Raoul is going to be in attendance.'

'I can see I shall have to watch you. And how did you like my Louis?'

'He seemed rather mild . . . and very young.'

'And you had eyes only for the charming Raoul. I daresay he is something of a rake.'

'Oh, Eleanor, how can you know?'

'I have a sixth sense about these things. You are a very young girl, Petronilla, and I can see that you have to be careful. And how can you talk frivolously about your preference for this man when your sister is soon to be cast up on the altar of marriage?'

'It won't be an unwilling sacrifice. You must tell me *all* about it. I think Louis looks quite nice in a way. I think you will not have any difficulty in handling him.'

'He is attracted by me. I think he was afraid they were going to present him with some monster.'

'Well, he must have had a pleasant surprise, and you have not been disappointed. This is a happy day for us all.'

She was smiling smugly and I was sure she was thinking about Raoul of Vermandois. I could see that I should have to keep a wary eye on Petronilla. She was growing out of childhood and, like myself, she had been brought up in the Courts of Love.

We had to entertain our guests in a royal manner and I was determined to show the French that we in Aquitaine lived as graciously as they. But though I arranged banquets and tournaments, Louis took little part, though the Counts of Champagne and Vermandois distinguished themselves. I watched Petronilla. Her eyes were on Raoul of Vermandois. I thought: I really do believe she has fallen in love with him.

I had discovered certain facts about Raoul. He was married to the niece of the Count of Champagne. Of course, I told myself, Petronilla was young and frivolous. I remembered my own infatuation for my uncle Raymond. That had been intense while it lasted. I believed Petronilla would be more reckless than I, and I guessed that she had inherited our grandfather's sensual nature. I had myself inherited that nature to a certain degree but I had always been imbued with the love of power, and I thought that would prevent my being carried away by my emotions.

Meanwhile I was interested in Louis. I had to be if I were to spend the rest of my life with him.

I was pleasantly pleased. Not that I was by any means in love with him. Perhaps I did not want to be. I wanted to be in command, and being in love might prevent that. I saw that I could make Louis my slave. He was inclined to be puritanical. Poor boy, fancy being in the care of Abbot Suger all those years! I could imagine what that had been like. He would have led the secluded life of a monk . . . prayers, austerity, discomfort . . . And suddenly to be snatched from that sequestered life and brought out into the activities of the Court . . . and not as an obscure member of it but as its future King. No wonder he looked bewildered half the time. If what I had heard of his father's health was true, it would not be long before the crown rested on Louis's head; and now he had to be a husband.

I was not sure which would be giving him the greater qualms.

But his shyness certainly endeared him to me and I was beginning to think that I liked him better the way he was than I should have if he had been a man of the world like Vermandois. I knew that gentleman's type well. I had seen so many of them at my grandfather's Court. They were exciting, true; but they were not to be trusted.

So, on the whole, I was grateful for Louis. I would look after him as I looked after Petronilla. I would mould him to my way of thinking. I would make him the husband best suited to myself.

Our wedding day arrived. It had been decided that there was no point in delay.

It was a hot July Sunday and Bordeaux was *en fête*. Even the smallest houses had banners hanging from them, and the people had been crowding into the streets since dawn. All over town bells were ringing.

Louis and I rode through the streets amid the cheers of the people. They shouted for me. I was their Duchess. For Louis they had curious stares. He was the son of the King of France, but what was France to Aquitaine? Still, it was a good marriage.

I was young and female and there should be strong men to protect Aquitaine now. They had to remember that France was the sovereign state and even prosperous Aquitaine was a vassal to its King.

So we stood before the Archbishop Lauroux and made our vows. The golden diadems were placed on our heads. We were Duke and Duchess of Aquitaine and heirs to the throne of France.

As soon as the wedding banquet was over we left Bordeaux for our journey to Paris. At Taillebourg we were to spend the first night of our marriage.

As a girl I had listened to many songs of such occasions, and this was perhaps an advantage for I was more prepared than Louis. I saw at once that it was I who must take charge and teach him. He was extremely nervous, having some garbled idea of what was expected of him, but he was in no way certain how he must go about it. I had to guide him.

I was rather proud of the manner in which I was able to do this. The act of love came naturally to me. As I suspected, I was meant to enjoy it and I did. I knew at once that, even with my stumbling Louis, marriage suited me.

Louis was extremely grateful. I had been tender and tactful. I was a year younger than he, but I might have been several years older and compared with him I was worldly. I think I had been born sophisticated. From the age of two I had been precocious, and of course those first five years in my grandfather's Courts had made a deep impression on me.

Louis changed overnight. He admired me. Not only was I beautiful beyond his imaginings, not only had I brought him rich Aquitaine, but I had made him see that marriage was not so fearful after all. There was even some enjoyment to be gleaned from it.

The marriage was a success.

We were in Poitiers for a few days, and there we were to be consecrated Duke and Duchess of Aquitaine at a very impressive ceremony.

It was pleasant to be in that castle which—much as I had loved the Ombrière Palace at Bordeaux—had always been my home. Dangerosa was there and it was wonderful to go into the Maubergeonne Tower and talk to her. She wanted to hear all about the wedding and I was able to talk to her frankly about my relationship with Louis.

She was amused. She said it was a pity that the fat King of France did not see fit to teach his son a little of the ways of the world instead of so much about those of Heaven. 'Time enough for that when you get there,' she added.

She was still the same Dangerosa who had delighted me in my childhood and my grandfather in the last days of his life.

We were now going to entertain the company at Poitiers and she must help me.

'We have to show the French that we can do better than they can,' I told her.

'We shall. What do they think of us so far?'

'We shock them a little. Our dresses . . . our gaiety . . . our women. They think we should be a little more demure. And what they think of our songs, I cannot imagine. I believe they think we should be more subtle.'

'We will shock them even more. I will tell the minstrels to sing our most bawdy songs.'

'I don't think my Louis would be amused by that.'

'What a pity your grandfather is not here to see this.'

'Louis is not like my grandfather.'

'Nobody on Earth ever was.'

'No. But I am rather pleased with my young Louis.'

'Then I rejoice with you. Let us plan how we shall entertain them. Does he love the chase?'

'I think he loves best meditation and prayer.'

'I hope he does not engage too much in those habits in the bedchamber.'

'I think he is just a little eager to be in bed with me.'

Dangerosa laughed. Then she looked wistful—thinking of my grandfather, I guessed.

While we were at Poitiers I arranged a hunting expedition for Louis and some of the men. An unfortunate incident occurred— or perhaps not so unfortunate, for it gave me a different view of Louis. One of the castellans of the duchy, a certain Lezay, who had often been in conflict with my father and was always stirring up some mischief, had refused to pay homage to Louis as Duke of Aquitaine, and when the party went out on the hunt, Lezay with a few followers waylaid them and set upon them. It may well have been that they planned to take Louis hostage. However, Louis, it seemed, had a side to his nature which I had not suspected. He had a violent temper and when it was aroused—which was rarely—he was quite unable to control it.

He turned on his would-be captors and slew several of them. Lezay, unfortunately, managed to escape. The party returned to the castle with the tale of how they had been attacked and how, largely through Louis, they had routed Lezay and his men.

Louis told me his version of the affair after. 'When they attacked us, I was seized with a fury which was uncontrollable. I just drew my sword and slashed at them. I am afraid I killed several of them.'

'They deserved it. I'm proud of you.'

'Such rage is not pleasing to God. I should have controlled my anger.'

'And stood by and let them slay you! No, Louis. It is no use your pretending you are not a hero. You are. And I intend to treat you as such.'

He was very pleased that I should admire him, but I could see that his conscience still troubled him, and he was on his knees for a long time that night before getting into bed, though I was there waiting, propped up on my pillows, looking, I knew, most alluring.

His upbringing could never be completely eradicated. Even I, with all my wiles, could not do that. But I did not give up hope.

It was a glittering ceremony which took place in the cathedral at Poitiers when Louis and I were consecrated as Duke and Duchess of Aquitaine.

Afterwards we went back to the castle for a banquet, and we were feasting merrily when Suger came into the hall.

He strode to where Louis was seated and fell on his knees.

Louis rose to his feet and I saw his colour fade. He knew what this meant.

'Long live the King,' said Suger, kissing Louis's hand.

Poor Louis! He had only just become accustomed to a wife and now a crown was being thrust at him—neither of these had he wanted, although he was becoming reconciled to his wife. The unwelcome crown was going to weigh heavily on his head.

As for myself, a great triumph was rising in me.

I had just been proclaimed Duchess of Aquitaine and now I had become Queen of France.

Queen of France

Paris is a fascinating city. I have never known one like it. When I knew it, it stood on a crowded island in the River Seine. Parts of the wall which the Romans had built round it remained, and where it had fallen away steps had been made down to the river, making a landing-place for the numerous craft. Two bridges connected the Ile de la Cité with the banks of the Seine and that extension of the city which was fast expanding.

The island city seemed to be divided into two parts—the west dominated by the Court and the east by the Church in which rose the grey walls of the Cathedral of Notre Dame. The eastern streets were full of churchmen, and those on the west side housed knights and barons. The sound of bells was ever present. Every little byway was crowded and boats of all description filled the river. Students flocked to the place to hear the monk Peter Abelard who had arrived in Paris to preach; there were scholars from many countries eager to hear him.

I had never seen such a motley crowd. There were quarters where the tanners lived—butchers, bakers and tradesmen of all kinds. They filled the streets, rubbing shoulders with the prelates and gentlemen of the Court. It was a city of vitality. Young students sat about in taverns talking of Life; traders shouted their wares. They joked with each other; they abused each other; everything was there—except silence.

Intrigued as I was, I felt homesick for Poitiers and Bordeaux.

I did my best to make the Court similar to those I had known all my life. I had brought many followers with me; I had my minstrels and my poets. I wanted to re-create the Courts of Love in Paris—and this with a King who was almost a recluse and a mother-in-law who disapproved of everything I did.

I was so sure of myself. My friends were there. I was frivolous; I was pleasure-loving and my success with Louis made me feel omnipotent. He was very much in love with me and I found I could bring him to my point of view with the utmost of ease because he wanted so much to please me. I could have my own way with him and, considering the difference in our natures, that was certainly an achievement.

I was gentle with him in those days. I suppose that was how I achieved my hold over him. I was often impatient with his pious ways. There were times when he seemed to be trying to turn the Court into a monastery.

He was constantly at church. He used to pray for what seemed like hours at night when I lay shivering in my bed waiting for him. I took a venomous delight in contemplating how cold he must be kneeling on the floor. But of course people like that enjoyed discomfort; they took a delight in it because they felt it must be good.

I enjoyed riding through the streets of Paris, for the people cheered us. When they considered what I had brought to France, they must have thought Louis had made a good choice.

But I had my trials—chief of which in the beginning was my mother-in-law, Adelaide of Savoy, and of course the Abbot Suger was always there in the background casting a shadow over any form of pleasure.

They were forever criticizing me. They objected to the way in which I was bringing the Provençal way of life into the Court. The songs my minstrels sang were about love, just as they had been in the Courts of my father and grandfather. My grandfather was referred to as a man who had lived immorally and died excommunicated, who had abducted another man's wife, living openly with her and actually allowing his son to marry her daughter.

And I was the child of this union! 'Bad blood,' said my mother-in-law, Adelaide.

Her disapproval was more obvious than that of Suger. His criticism was spoken in prayers directing God to be lenient with me, to remember my youth. I supposed old Suger thought he was important enough to give God instructions. I was always amused by the prayers of the saintly. 'God do this, God don't do that.' I thought God probably laughed at them too, unless He was a little annoyed by their temerity.

My mother-in-law began gently in the beginning. 'My dear Eleanor, you are so young . . . and so is Louis. Two children, in fact. Do you think that dress is just a little too revealing?'

No, I did not. I had always worn such dresses.

'What a colour you have, my dear. You haven't a fever, have you?'

'I find colour becoming, Madame.'

She was such an old hypocrite. She pretended not to know that I had put it on.

Petronilla and I used to laugh at her. I thanked God for my sister. She was enjoying life at the French Court, although my mother-in-law's disapproval extended to her.

I heard her murmur once to one of her ladies: 'Dear God, how were they brought up in that licentious Court? One must not blame them. They are only children.'

I think that to be referred to as a child annoyed me more than references to the family's licentious Court. It was not true in my father's case, but I suppose it might be an apt description of my grandfather's.

It was inevitable with one of my temperament that the little niggling annoyances which I suffered from Adelaide should eventually become more than I could endure.

One day she came unannounced to my apartments. Petronilla was there, and we were trying on new gowns. Petronilla was in her petticoat when Adelaide appeared.

She said: 'I heard you laughing . . . quite immoderately . . .'

I had had enough. I was bolder in Petronilla's company than I should have been alone. My sister was too. We gave ourselves courage. I said: 'Is there a law in France against laughing?'

'What a thing to say!'

'You seemed to object.'

'I was just passing. . . .'

'And listening to our discourse, I doubt not.'

'What do you mean?'

'Well, if you had not been listening, you would not have heard.'

Petronilla was looking at me with shining eyes, admiring, encouraging, urging me on.

'I prefer not to be spied on,' I said, 'and I ask you to desist from the practice.'

'You forget to whom you speak.'

'Do not forget that you speak to the Queen of France.'

'You . . . you . . .' she spluttered.

I drew myself up to my full height. 'You may go now,' I said haughtily.

She stared at me in amazement; her face turned white and then red. She turned abruptly and went from the room.

Petronilla collapsed onto my bed and covered her face with her hands, her body shaking with mirth.

I was not amused. I wondered what I had done. She was after all the Dowager Queen and I was a newcomer.

' "You may go," ' said Petronilla imitating me, between gusts of laughter.

'There will be trouble now,' I said.

'Oh, you only have to talk to Louis. He'll be on your side. He's madly in love with you.'

I wished I had been more dignified. What had taken place had bordered on a brawl.

Louis was upset. He said: 'My mother is unhappy. She says you don't want her at Court.'

'I have never said that,' I told him.

'She says she thinks she should go away.'

'Did she really say that?'

He nodded wretchedly. 'I have tried to persuade her to stay but she is adamant.'

It seemed too good to be true. But it was not. A few days later Adelaide of Savoy left the Court. She said she thought there was no place for her there.

What a triumph! If only I could always rid myself of all my enemies so easily.

Louis was sad for a while. He hated conflict of any sort. But in time he seemed to forget it; and he bore no malice to me because of her departure.

I was amazed by my power over him. It was wonderful to be so cherished.

About this time there were murmurings of discontent in France. It was hardly to be expected that there would not be some mal-contents. A king who had been much respected, and who, I know now, had been one of the best rulers France had ever had, had died leaving a young one in his place. Naturally there were some who believed they could take advantage of the situation.

Louis was panic-stricken. I felt annoyed with him. There were times when he seemed to forget that he was king. Much as I liked having a docile husband I did not want a poltroon.

'You will have to quell this revolt at once,' I told him.

'I thought of sending one of my generals with a few men.'

'One of your generals with a few men! Oh no! You must go yourself. You are the King. It is you who have to defend your realm. You must go at the head of your army.'

He looked dismayed. Poor Louis, he would much happier on his knees before an altar or praying in a monk's cell than leading an army. His early beginnings when Suger had moulded him into a churchman had formed his nature—just as my upbringing in the Courts of Love had moulded my character. He hated the thought of war, but he had to go. I insisted. France was my destiny now as much as it was his. If he did not put down this uprising, there would be more.

Because he could not bear that I should despise him he put on armour and went to Orléans.

I proved to have been right. The sight of him with the might of the army behind him settled the question. The people of Orléans meekly surrendered, gave up their leaders to the executioners and shouted: *'Vive le Roi!'* as Louis rode through the streets.

He returned to me triumphant. It had not been so difficult after all. He was sorry he had had to order that the leaders be executed, but that was what his generals had suggested should be done.

'They were right,' I said. 'If you had allowed them to escape, any little town which thought it had a grievance would rise up against you. Oh, Louis, I am so proud of you. This is your first real test since you became king, and see, you have come right through with shining honour.'

I kissed him and told him how great he was and that it was nonsense to think he was not a soldier at heart. It was the duty of every king to defend his realm.

'I have no real feeling for it, Eleanor,' he said. 'The thought of inflicting pain and death nauseates me.'

'You'll grow out of that,' I assured him. 'A king must be

strong. The death of a few trouble-makers is nothing compared with that of thousands which a war would bring about. You should rejoice in your action, for I do.'

So I soothed him.

One rebellion will often breed another. This one was particularly depressing because it took place in my own dominions . . . and in Poitiers of all places, which I had always considered my home.

I suppose it should not have been so unexpected. Their Duchess had become Queen of France and they—a proud people, who had always known independence—were now under the sway of a foreign land, for that was what they considered France to be. They decided they would have none of it. They would throw off the yoke of the foreigner to whom they had been casually handed just because of their Duchess's marriage to the King of France. They announced that they would rule themselves and set about forming a Poitevin government.

This seemed to me the height of disloyalty. I was very angry. I did not stop to consider how these people might be feeling. They had lived in a free and easy manner under their dukes. There had been the occasional riots but my grandfather and father had known how to settle them with the minimum of fuss. This was different. I was more than their Duchess now; I was the Queen of France, and when they rose in rebellion, it was against France as well as against me.

'They must be punished severely,' I said to Louis. 'You must not be so lenient with them as you were in Orléans. You see, because you were not harsh enough, these people believe they can behave with impunity.'

'I did have the leaders executed,' he reminded me.

'It is not enough. You have to show these people that you are their master. You father always did and people say he was a good king. The people appreciated him even though they did laugh at his fatness. You have to show them, Louis. It is no use being soft.'

That disastrous affair of the Poitiers rebellion, I can see now, looking back, was the beginning of the rift between us. Had I been older and wiser, I should have known that I could not hold him in thrall for ever, because there were too many forces working against me. I thought I could because of my victory over

Adelaide of Savoy, but she was of small account compared with Suger, that shrivelled-up little man of humble origins, who had somehow risen to be the power behind the throne.

Louis rode off with his army. It was as easy a conquest as Orléans had been. The Poitevins had not been expecting him to come in such force. No doubt they had thought there would have been negotiations and some plan worked out. When they saw Louis and his army arriving, they immediately capitulated.

Louis then remembered my words. I knew he was anxious for me to think well of him. He would remember that he could not just meekly accept their submission and ride off again. I had impressed on him that he had to show them that this sort of rebellion was no light matter. Someone had to suffer for it.

He hated bloodshed but he knew he dare not return to me and say that he had forgiven them, merely disbanded their so-called government and declared all was over. He had an idea that he would take as hostages all the young men and women of Poitiers. They should be taken to France as exiles from their native land; and if ever any others felt they might rebel against him, they could remember what happened to those who did.

He named a day when all the young men and women were to assemble in the square prior to their departure for France.

It was not a wise thing to do. He should have executed the leaders of the revolt, but doubtless he remembered how contemptuous I had been of his previous mild action and that was why he had devised this plan.

The Poitevins were loud in their lamentations. To be robbed of their young was more than they could endure. They sent messengers all over the country appealing for help against this cruel sentence.

Suger was at this time at St Denis, and it was not long before he heard what was happening. He saw at once the folly of this action and realized that it could bring the whole of Aquitaine to revolt against the King of France.

He immediately set out for Poitiers, where he was welcomed by the citizens, who knew he had come on their behalf.

I could imagine how easily he swayed Louis. He had been doing it all his life, and Louis was made for swaying, I thought contemptuously. I could hear that voice . . . with the hint of the peasant in it, but perhaps all the more forceful for that. 'This must be stopped, my son. This is folly. These people have suffered enough. Give them back their children.'

I understood Louis. The thought of separating parents from their children did not horrify him so much as bloodshed. Emotional ties did not touch him so much as the contemplation of violence. Taking life was breaking a commandment. Nothing had been said in the Scriptures about the sin of separating parents from their children.

He gave way. The revolt was settled and the only punishment which had been inflicted on the rebels was a few days of fear that they would lose their children.

He came back and said to me: 'It is over. The revolt is quelled.'

'I know what happened,' I told him. 'Suger came and countermanded your order.'

'He came and showed me the way.'

I snapped my fingers at him. 'You gave way just like that.'

'It was the right thing to do.'

'It is the wrong thing to give an order and then withdraw it just because a priest comes along and tells you to.'

'I had to do it. Suger explained to me.'

'Suger! Suger! It is all Suger. He runs this country . . . not you.'

'He was my father's trusted minister and he is mine.'

'He was your master when you were at St Denis. He still is now that you are on the throne.'

'He was right, Eleanor.'

'I don't care. You should not have done what you did in the first place if you had no intention of carrying it through.'

'But I had to do what I did. Suger made me see that I could not separate those young people from their families.'

'It was a foolish thing to contemplate in the first place. You should have made them deliver up the leaders and then had them executed in the square so that all could see.'

'I couldn't bear that. I hate bloodshed.'

'Oh, Louis. How can you be a king if you can't even be a man? And you will never be a man while you have Nurse Suger to feed you his pap religion.'

'He is a good man. He is a priest.'

'He means more to you than anyone . . . I know that. I am as nothing to you compared with him. My wishes are of no account. You were dealing with my country. It came to you through me. I know these Poitevins. They will be laughing at you. They will be singing songs about this, mark my words. And they will make you live in their songs—the lily-livered King of France.'

I turned and left him.

He was very subdued for days after that. He was deeply wounded. I did not try to win him back, which was foolish of me. I think he avoided me by day. At night he would pray for a long time and I would doze off while he was still on his knees. He slept at one extreme end of the marital bed, I at the other. I was getting very restive. I wanted a lover and I could see that my husband was failing me miserably in that respect. How could a full-blooded woman, reared in the Courts of Love, granddaughter of the roaring lover-troubadour, find satisfaction with a husband who looked upon physical contact as sinful? With him there was only one reason for cohabitation, and that was the procreation of children.

And we had had no luck in that direction so far. Louis was only just capable of performing the sexual act with a good deal of coaxing and encouragement, so perhaps he was unable to beget a child.

This marriage which I had thought I might turn to great advantage was already proving a disappointment.

I lay in bed thinking of all the handsome men at Court. And here was I with this one!

I wondered whether he slept. I had a feeling that he was not altogether displeased by the rift between us. It gave him an excuse to escape the arduous and faintly distasteful business of making love.

Gradually my relationship with Louis returned to what it had been before the disastrous affair at Poitiers. There was talk of my coronation.

I was delighted at the prospect of this and temporarily forgot my disappointments. There was little I liked better than such a show, particularly when I was at the centre of it.

Petronilla and I spent a great deal of time discussing what I should wear, what she should wear and what my attendants should wear. It was fascinating.

I was surrounded by young men . . . my attendants and those

who came to Court to learn the social graces. I could easily have imagined I was back in Poitiers or Bordeaux, but for the fact that Louis was there with Suger in the background. I tried to draw Louis into our entertainments but he did not fit in. He danced awkwardly; he could not sing; and it was quite clear that he did not enjoy the theme of the songs we sang. He was an outsider on all these occasions.

Some of the men took to them with enthusiasm; one of these was Raoul of Vermandois. What an attractive man he was—knowledgeable and worldly, by no means young, but widely experienced, I was sure. He could convey so much by a look. I often thought how easy it would be to fall into temptation with such a man.

He was not the only one, of course, but for special reasons he stands out in my memory.

I had my coronation at Bourges, and it was a great success. I know I looked very beautiful and Louis was proud of me; he had forgotten his disappointment in me. He knew how lucky he was. Several of the men spoke of this, and of course they sang of it constantly.

I had begun to fret over Suger's influence over him, but I could see how futile that was. It would not be a simple matter to remove him, and in any case I was not sure that that would be wise. Suger, for all his distrust of the good things in life, was a great minister and I knew he was necessary to the government of France. Moreover, I knew in my heart that Louis would not agree to let him go, and if it came to a conflict between Suger and me, I could not be entirely sure who would be the winner.

I wished that I could become pregnant. I was beginning to be a little worried about my barrenness. I could not believe that I was incapable of bearing children. The fault must lie with Louis. It was not that I had a great many opportunities of conceiving. Oh, how ironical it was that fate should have married a woman like me to a man who was more like a monk.

I was also disturbed by Raoul of Vermandois. He was a far-seeing man in matters like this. He had a reputation of being a rake. To me, having been brought up in my grandfather's Court, where I had known many such men, that was a mild enough failing. But Raoul did seem like a kindred spirit.

There was suggestion in his eyes as he lay at my feet with the others. He had the trick of almost creating a sexual encounter by willing it to take place, a kind of mental seduction. I found it amusing and stimulating; and with a husband like Louis I needed a little stimulation at times.

The months were passing. I took various trips into Aquitaine visiting my subjects. I was always greeted with enthusiasm and they were a success. I very much enjoyed these journeys. They made me feel that I was their ruler in very truth. This was what they wanted. They did not want the French yoke, as they called it. They were Provençal and would remain so.

I used to sit in the castle halls and there would be singing and dancing such as I had known in the Courts of Love. I could see how important these journeys were. They said to the people: 'All is as it was. The fact that I am Queen of France makes no difference. I am your ruler. I belong to you as I never can to France.'

There was, of course, a great deal to interest me in Paris. I loved to ride through the cobbled streets where there was so much going on. It was a city of great contrast which struck me forcibly after my sojourns in Aquitaine where people lived a healthier, cleaner life. There they were not huddled together in little dwellings in dark streets where the crowded buildings with their overhanging gables shut out the light. Paris is a muddy city. The Romans called it Lutetia for this reason, the city of mud. But there was such vitality there . . . noise everywhere, stalls, little shops, salesmen and -women shouting their wares.

What struck me most was the number of students who had come there to discuss and listen to the new opinions which were flourishing. One saw them wandering through the streets or along the river banks, deep in thought. Theories were thrashed out, opinions circulated.

I could not fail to find it interesting.

There was one who aroused my curiosity more than any other, and that was Peter Abelard, who, some said, was the most shrewd thinking and the boldest theologian of the day. I was first drawn to him because of his romantic history. His story was like one of those renowned in the songs I heard in my childhood. He could have been a gentleman of leisure for he was the eldest son of a noble Breton family, but he chose to be a scholar. His talent was soon discovered; he was a brilliant speaker and as he had new and startling ideas to express, he began to be talked of.

He became one of the Realist teachers at the school of Notre Dame. He was all set for a brilliant career.

But how easily one can fall! And since he fell through love, he seemed to me a romantic figure. He became tutor to Héloïse, the niece of the Canon Fulbert. She was seventeen and very beautiful; they became lovers. When this was discovered, the Canon used every means at his disposal to separate them but he could not do so. They fled to Brittany, where Héloïse bore a son. They were married. Héloïse, having been assured that she had ruined Abelard's career, agreed to give him up. How stupid lovers can be! But if they were not, there would be no story. Abelard was brought to the judgement of the monks, who, in order that he might not be tempted again, castrated him.

That seemed to me a very tragic story—and to others too, for Abelard's misfortune was talked of throughout France. For a while he lived in a hut but so many disciples came to him that the hut became a school known as the Paraclete. Then he was invited to become abbot of St Gildas-de-Rhuys in Brittany. As for Paraclete, nuns came there and Héloïse was put in charge of them. Abelard remained in the abbey for some time but he was persecuted, and the chief of his enemies was that Bernard of Clairvaux who had, indirectly, been the cause of my father's death, for I was convinced that if he had never set out on the pilgrimage—which he would not but for his encounter with Bernard—he would be alive still.

Abelard now and then was in Paris, and when he was there people flocked to his rooms to hear what he had to say.

I often thought about him. He could have been another Bernard, another Suger, but love had stood in his way; and now, of course, for all his brilliance, he was something less than a man. I wondered whether he ever regretted it or, if he could have gone back, would have done it all again.

How much wiser were those who took love lightheartedly, as surely it was meant to be taken.

So the months slipped into years; and I was growing more and more restive, asking myself how a woman such as I was could go on living with a monk.

Four years passed in this unsatisfactory manner. There were times when I felt rebellious, but I had remained faithful to Louis. Not with a very good grace, I admit. I often railed against my fate. Yet I had to be careful. I was in a precarious position. I had always to remember that I was Queen of France. There were times when I was tempted to take a lover. There were so many attractive men at the Court and all eager. If it had not been for the fact that I must bear the heir of France, I think I should have overcome my scruples. But the French crown was a matter of the utmost importance. I dared not risk having a child who was not Louis's. It was something which, if it were discovered, could result in the most dire consequences.

So I kept my emotions in check and tried to reconcile myself to Louis. He still admired me, though at times he remembered one or two little things against me: my conflict with Suger, for instance, and the fact that his mother, a woman of considerable ability, who had worked well with his father, had left the Court because of me. These were matters which could not be entirely forgotten, and of course, when grievances appeared, they were remembered.

Like most people, Louis could at times act unexpectedly. I was amazed when I first discovered that he had a violent temper. Fortunately it was very rarely aroused, but when it was it seemed to change his character completely.

I shall never forget my surprise after the case of Lezay, the vassal who had caused trouble in the early days of our marriage. Lezay was a trouble-maker who would never bow to any form of discipline, and it was not to be expected that he would forget his grievances and settle down, particularly while there was an absent overlord. He refused the usual homage to his suzerain and, with a small party of men, to show his contempt for authority, stole some falcons from one of the royal hunting lodges.

One of Louis's rages overcame him then. He had the culprits brought to him and with his own sword cut off their hands.

This was so unlike Louis, who was thought to hate violence in any form, that all were amazed. But that was how he was when one of his violent rages overtook him. He suffered terrible remorse afterwards. 'It was as though some devil possessed me', he said, and that was exactly how it seemed.

Then there was the case of Marcabru, the poet-singer, who was so highly thought of in Aquitaine. I invited him to Paris. He had an exquisite voice, but unlike most troubadours he was no lover of women. His verses were cynical, which gave them an unusual and amusing quality. When he came to the French

Court, however, he wrote songs dedicated to me. I have to admit that I was gratified to have the admiration of such a misogynist so openly expressed.

Louis took exception to it. I supposed it was because he believed this man meant what he said, and he was jealous of Marcabru's ability to express his feelings. One day when Marcabru was singing Louis stood up and shouted: 'You will leave this Court at once.'

Everyone was astounded to see mild Louis in such a mood. He even looked unlike himself. His face was set in stern lines; his eyes blazed with fury; but those who had witnessed Louis's sudden rages before knew that he meant what he said. In that moment he was the King who must be obeyed.

I could see I had to be careful in my dealing with him. So for those four years I lived unsatisfactorily, indulging in fantasies as I could not in realities, listening to the protestations of love, through the songs which were sung, and dreaming dreams as I listened.

I was becoming more and more dissatisfied. I felt that, if I could turn Louis into a man, a king, I could find some contentment with him. I set myself the impossible task of trying to change him. I see now how foolish I was. But in those days I believed I was capable of anything.

If only he could have been as enthusiastic about the things which I cared for as he was over ecclesiastical concerns, all would have been well. He was at heart a churchman. When there was a conflict between Bernard of Clairvaux and Peter Abelard, he presided over the disputation with the clergy and the papal legate, and for this he received a great deal of credit.

But it was not as a member of the Church that a king should excel. A king was a ruler in his own right, and everyone knew that on occasion there had been conflict between Church and State. Louis must be a fighter, a conqueror, and I never gave up hope of trying to make him the man I wanted him to be. I should have liked to see him marching with his army, conquering, adding to our domain. France and Aquitaine were now joined by marriage, and had events turned out differently, Toulouse might be with us, because, after all, it had belonged to my grandmother Philippa.

Why did we not claim Toulouse? I was excited by the notion.

When I mentioned it to Louis he received the suggestion without enthusiasm.

Toulouse was now in the hands of Alphonse-Jourdain, the son of that Count Raymond, my grandmother Philippa's uncle, who had taken Toulouse before she had had time to claim it. She had regained it when Raymond was killed in the Holy Land, but then my grandfather had sold it back Raymond's son, and Alphonse-Jourdain was now in command.

They had no right to it, I declared.

Louis was certainly not of that opinion, in view of the fact that my grandfather had handed it over in order that he might be able to pay for his visit to the Holy Land.

But I insisted that it belonged to me because my grandmother had brought it to Aquitaine.

Louis did not want to listen, but I accused him of cowardice, of turning his back on the matter, not for reasons of logic but because he was afraid to go into battle.

He was very anxious for my good opinion and after some months I wore down his resistance. Once I had done that he seemed quite eager to go ahead with the plan.

It was necessary to raise an army, and for that we needed to bring all our vassals together, so we sent messages throughout the country calling them to Paris. There was a response from most but there was one notable exception.

When Thibault of Champagne came to see Louis, I insisted on being present. I was rather attracted by Thibault. He was a very important man and had strong opinions. He never offered me that blatant flattery which I expected from most and I felt a little irritated because of this, but perhaps it helped to stimulate my interest in him.

He told Louis quite frankly that he had no desire to join in a campaign against Toulouse.

'And why not?' asked Louis.

'Because, sire, I consider it would be doomed to failure and even if you succeeded in winning Toulouse, it would soon be taken back. The people of Toulouse are content with the way things are.'

'But,' I said, 'Toulouse belongs to me. It is part of my inheritance.'

Thibault bowed. 'I crave my lady's pardon. I thought it was

sold to the present family by your grandfather when he went to the Holy Land.'

'It belongs to me,' I said stubbornly.

Thibault inclined his head once more and made no further comment.

Louis said: 'I shall expect you with your company. We leave a week from today.'

Thibault replied: 'My lord, I think I could not expect my men to follow me in such a cause.'

'I shall expect you,' said Louis.

Thibault then retired.

'A contentious fellow,' I said. 'He forgets you are his liege lord.'

I could not believe that he would dare disobey Louis's summons but he did, and on the day we left he simply did not arrive.

Louis said: 'Perhaps one could not expect him to join in a fight for which he has no heart.'

'Vassals obey their liege lords,' I said. 'If they do not, it should be the worse for them.'

'When this campaign is over, you will not expect me to wage war on Champagne, I hope,' said Louis, a little testily.

'We can do without the help of Thibault of Champagne,' I said.

It was thrilling to ride off with pennons flowing in the wind. There is something magnificent about an army on the march.

I did not intend to accompany Louis into battle. I was going to my beloved Poitiers, there to await the triumphant return of his army.

We said goodbye to Louis, and Petronilla and I with our little company rode on to Poitiers, which would always be home to me.

Such memories came back. It had changed little. The people would always be the same. They had no great interest in conquests; they did not care that we were now bound to France by marriage. It was only when their easy way life was threatened that they could be roused to anger.

Petronilla indulged in memories of the past as we rode through the forest, hunting, hawking. Our evenings were spent in singing and reading poetry, and each day we watched for Louis's victorious armies.

Alas it did not happen that way. Why had I ever thought that

Louis could be a conqueror? He and his army arrived in Poitiers just as they had left Paris. They were an army in retreat.

Louis explained to me. 'They were prepared for us . . . waiting for us.'

'And you turned back.'

'There was nothing else to do. The army would have been cut into pieces. Alphonse-Jourdain had his men everywhere. They were on the castle battlements . . . arrows ready. Our men would have been mown down if they had attempted to advance.'

'So you just turned and came away?'

'It was the only thing to do, unless I wanted to see my army destroyed.'

Why had I thought he would make a soldier! There was nothing to be done but disband the army.

Louis remained at Poitiers with a small company and, despairing of him, I said: 'We could at least make a tour of my cities in Aquitaine.'

So, although the expedition was a failure in one way, in another it was a success. I loved Aquitaine. Never could any other country have the same place in my heart; and to be with my own pleasure-loving people was a great joy.

In the various castles we were lavishly entertained. I loved to sit in the great halls listening to the songsters, watching the dancers and remembering the past. I could almost see my grandfather seated there, putting out a hand now and then to caress his beloved Dangerosa. How different from the Court in the Cité Palace in Paris presided over by a puritan!

Louis was with us, aloof, uneasy, shuddering at the implications in some of the songs. I felt more frustrated than ever. I longed for a dashing lover who would carry me off and force me to obey him so that I could not be reproached for what happened.

The troubadours were handsome, their voices so soft and appealing, their eyes brilliant with desire.

Petronilla was languorously excited by it all. I thought: It is time she was married. We must find a worthy husband for her. I had watched her often. She was too much like myself for me not to understand her. I had seen her laughing and flirting with a score of men, and she had not my responsibilities to consider.

I was most attracted by Raoul of Vermandois. The fact that he was not young was an asset. I was sure he was a very expe-

rienced man. How different from my poor, inept, bumbling
Louis. Raoul was married to the niece of Thibault of Champagne, a very virtuous lady, I believed. I wondered how she felt
about being married to such an attractive man. I had heard rumours that he was by no means a faithful husband.

Raoul was always in the group nearest me. He would sing
with his eyes on me. He was a reckless man, I knew, and there
was no doubt what he was suggesting. Would he dare, I wondered, even if I would?

I could imagine Louis's falling into one of his rages. Raoul
must know that he was on dangerous ground. But still he continued in his unspoken courtship.

Louis was becoming aware that I despised him. I think he felt
humiliated by what had happened at Toulouse. A soldier would
have gone on and fought. Alphonse-Jourdain might not have
been such a formidable foe as he appeared—who knew? Louis
had simply lost his nerve; so he had turned away. Any man
would be ashamed of such an action—and even Louis was no
exception.

I did not refer directly to the subject, but I suppose I did taunt
him in many ways, and I was sure that it was because of this
that he acted as he did about the election of the Archbishop of
Bourges.

When the archbishopric fell vacant, the man most capable of
filling the post was a certain Pierre de la Châtre. Louis, however, had decided otherwise and had put in one of his ministers
called Carduc. He consulted Suger who assured him that he had
a right to elect his own Archbishop but there was no doubt that
Pierre de la Châtre was the best man for the post. Louis was
obstinate on this occasion. The Church stood against his candidate. It was always unwise to stand against the Church. I had
learned that through my father and grandfather; yet often there
was an irresistable urge to do so. Louis now felt such an urge.
The Church was strong and in spite of the King, Pierre de la
Châtre was made Archbishop and before Louis could protest
Pope Innocent had accepted the decision and consecrated Pierre
de la Châtre.

This was one of those occasions when Louis was the slave of
his temper. I was always amazed by these, and sometimes I
welcomed them. They did relieve the monotony of my existence
with my usually spineless monk.

'I'll not have it. I'll not have it,' he cried. 'When he comes to Bourges, the gates of the city shall be locked against him.'

I did point out to him that he was playing a dangerous game, that the Church was against him. I watched with interest to see how he would extract himself from this dilemma.

The Pope, like most people, was amazed at the stand Louis was taking. He thought he was under some influence—and what influence could that be but mine? He announced publicly that Louis was a child. He must get schooling and be kept from learning bad habits.

When Louis heard this his rage really exploded. He took a solemn oath that Pierre de la Châtre should never enter Bourges, and this of course had the inevitable result. Louis, who had been brought up in the Church, who was devoted to the Church, was now being denounced by the Pope himself, who passed the sentence of excommunication upon him.

Louis was bewildered. He could not believe this was happening to him. There was little which made a king so unpopular as this Edict, for it was not only the king who suffered from it. In every place he visited the churches would be closed and it would be as though the Church did not exist.

It did not please either of us to hear that Pierre de la Châtre, having been denied entry to Bourges, had gone to Champagne, where he had been welcomed by Thibault.

This made it clear that Thibault had ranged himself on the side of de la Châtre against the King.

Louis was deeply distressed. His prayers were intensified; he was nervous. I was constantly in fear that he would commit some weak action which would make the whole world despise him.

Then another matter drove all those from my mind.

I had been so concerned about Louis and this unfortunate trouble over the Archbishop that I had not seen as much of Petronilla as I usually did. Normally she was constantly in my company. We liked to be together and although we did not discuss affairs of state, we shared memories of the past and had always been the best of friends.

I noticed now that she looked a little pale, and there was a secretive expression on her face. A suspicion came into my mind which I immediately dismissed. Of course it could not be!

Something had happened and I decided to tackle her, but I

had to wait until we were quite alone; this was a subject entirely between us two.

I made the opportunity and I said: 'Petronilla, you had better tell me.'

The colour rushed into her face. I began to think: It is so. Oh no! Impossible!

'Come on,' I said firmly. 'It would seem that you are keeping me in the dark.'

She said almost defiantly: 'I am . . . so happy.'

'Well then, let me share your happiness. Are you with child?'

She did not answer. I was dumbfounded for, although the idea had occurred to me, it seemed so incredible that I could not seriously believe it. Petronilla pregnant . . . the sister of the Queen in such a condition . . . like some serving wench!

'We can be married,' she said.

'I should hope so. Who is this man?'

She was silent for a few seconds. I took her by the shoulders and shook her.

'Tell me,' I cried. 'Tell me.'

'It is Raoul of Vermandois.'

I could find no words. I had expected it to be some humble squire . . . some *mésalliance*. This was far worse.

At last I said: 'But . . . he already has a wife.'

'There is going to be a divorce.'

'A divorce? On what grounds?'

'Consanguinity.'

'And who do you think will grant that?'

'Raoul's brother is the Bishop of Noyon. He can get two other priests to support him.'

'So you have arranged all this?'

'When I became . . .'

'Petronilla, you fool! I could have arranged the grandest marriage for you.'

'Raoul is one of the most important men in France.'

'And already a husband.'

'I have told you that can be overcome.'

'And then you will marry. Oh, how could you? How could he?'

'I have always loved him . . . from the time I first saw him. Do you remember? He came with Thibault of Champagne before you were married.'

'Thibault of Champagne! Holy Mother of God, Vermandois's wife is his niece.'

'What of it?'

'What of it? Do you realize that we are on the worst possible terms with Champagne? Do you think he will meekly stand by and let his niece be cast aside?'

'Raoul says it will come out right in the end.'

'He is a philanderer . . . so to take advantage of an innocent girl.'

'He didn't have much chance, poor man. I forced him.'

Petronilla laughed suddenly and I laughed with her. 'You are an idiot,' I said.

'I know, but a very happy idiot. I shall have the best man in the world for a husband.'

'Not yet and I would challenge that statement.'

'And I have the dearest sister in the world. None could challenge that, Eleanor. You'll help, won't you?'

'I am most displeased.'

'I know. But you do like him, don't you? You do agree that he is the most fascinating man at Court?'

'At least that is one matter on which you and he will agree. He is conceited and arrogant.'

'And so very attractive. Admit it Eleanor.'

'I suppose he would appeal to some.'

She looked at me archly. She would have heard those honeyed compliments which had come my way. She knew that I liked the man myself. I could not hide such things from Petronilla.

She cried: 'I am so glad that you know. I wanted to tell you before. We always shared things, didn't we? But Raoul thought you would not approve. He was afraid you would try to prevent us. But now . . .'

I said: 'I see this has gone so far that there is only one thing for you, and that is marriage. But I do not think it is going to be as easy as you appear to think, sister.'

'But you will help us, won't you?'

I nodded slowly.

I wanted to be alone to think about him. I was deeply shocked. For so long I had thought that I was the one who mattered to him. I was the one for whom he was singing his songs. The looks had been directed at me, and all the time he and Petronilla were lovers!

It was a great blow to my self-esteem. I began to wonder how sincere any of the men were who cast desirous eyes on me. I wondered what they said to their mistresses in moments of intimacy.

But of course there was nothing to be done than to get Petronilla married as soon as possible. The sister of the Queen of France could not produce a bastard. What a scandal that would be! I could imagine how the Pope, Bernard and Suger would receive such news. To get them married quickly was common sense, and face whatever came of it after that.

I sent for Raoul of Vermandois. He came at once, bowed low and lifted his eyes to my face. They were full of the yearning which I had come to expect from him. That angered me.

I said: 'So, Monsieur, you are a monster. My sister has told me of this matter between you and her.'

'I await your pleasure, my lady.'

'I have not yet told the King. He will be even more displeased than I. I am surprised and shocked.'

'My lady, mortal man cannot go on yearning for the impossible for ever.'

'So he takes the next best? I think my sister should hear this.'

He smiled at me ruefully. 'My great sorrow is that I should cause you concern.'

'Did you think I should not be concerned to find my sister in this condition?'

'I will marry her at once.'

'You have yet to learn that the laws of France allow a man to have only one wife.'

'I no longer have a wife. I hope soon to remedy that when Petronilla honours me.'

'And when will that be?'

'Now. I have the annulment. I am a free man. It was granted to me this very day.'

'Through the good grace of your Bishop brother.'

'Families should always stand together. Do you not agree, my lady?'

'It is fortunate for some that they do. Well then?'

'I shall soon have the inestimable honour of calling you my sister.'

'I wonder how much good that will do you when you have to

face the wrath of the Count of Champagne . . . not to mention the Pope.'

'I am a man who will face his difficulties when it is necessary to do so and not before.'

'Sometimes that is not a very wise policy.'

'So I have your approval of our marriage, my lady?'

'I can do nothing else but approve when I am faced with such a situation. Please go now.'

He bowed and left me.

I was very angry. What a deceiver he was! To think that I might so easily have given way. It had been in my mind. He was very attractive and would be a skilled lover, I was sure, for practice makes perfect, they say, and he would be a very practised man.

And Petronilla had been his mistress! Of course, she was beautiful and more feminine than I. There was something helpless about Petronilla and men like Raoul of Vermandois were attracted by that sort of thing. I was more handsome than Petronilla but of a stronger and more forceful nature; I lacked that helpless femininity which I suppose was irresistible. And all the time he was pretending to long for me he was making love with Petronilla!

Moreover she had become pregnant, a state which eluded me although I had been longing for it intensely since my marriage.

This liaison between Petronilla and Vermandois would make trouble, I was sure. I dreaded to think of the action Thibault of Champagne might take. But what in the first hours upset me was the conduct of this man who had aroused such strong emotions in me.

I had anticipated the effect this would have on Louis. He could not belive it, and when I was able to assure him that it was true, he was overcome with shock.

'But it is so . . . immoral.'

'All men do not care to spend half the night on their knees,' I told him tartly.

'It would perhaps be better for all concerned if they did,' he retorted.

He was looking at me with the faintest of criticism in his eyes. This is your sister, he was thinking. It is to be expected considering the family from which you come. Your grandfather's antics were the talk of Europe . . . and your father was in perpetual conflict with the Pope.

I came at once to Petronilla's defence.

'She is in love with Vermandois and he with her. There is such a thing as love in the world, you know . . . real love . . . not the tepid variety which some have to put up with.'

He was too bemused to take in what I was saying. 'With child,' he kept murmuring. 'But this is impossible. We cannot have a scandal at Court.'

'It would seem we have that already,' I said. 'Louis, listen to me. This is regrettable but it has happened. Petronilla is my sister . . . yours now. Raoul of Vermandois is your kinsman. Let us face facts. There is only one thing to do. We have to accept this marriage. After all, Vermandois is divorced from his first wife. These things have happened before. It is of the utmost importance that we stand with them in this. If you give your approval, who can raise his voice against that?'

'I can imagine there are some who will.'

'Louis, you have to remember that you are the King. Your will is law.' I went to him and put my arms about him. 'You only have to stand firm, Louis. All must obey you.'

He said: 'You are right. There is nothing else we can do.'

When the marriage was announced there was a great deal of gossip throughout the Court. What of Vermandois's first wife? What was to become of her? Was this a precedent? When a man wanted to be rid of his wife, did it mean that all he had to do was to arrange for a divorce through obliging relatives? Of course, everyone did not have such relatives. Everyone was not related to the King and Queen.

I was astonished by Raoul and Petronilla. They were quite blissful, seeming oblivious of the storm they were raising.

I heard that Raoul's first wife had taken her children to her uncle Thibault of Champagne, and I knew then that it could not be long before there was real trouble.

I was right.

He did what I expected. He took the case to the Pope. His niece had been cursorily cast out by her husband because he wished to take a younger woman to be his wife. There had been a bogus annulment arranged by a relative of the Count of Vermandois, and two priests had been bribed to assist in this. Moreover the whole dastardly scheme had the approval of the King and Queen, whose sister was the new wife. Thibault begged the Pope to intervene on behalf of his wronged niece.

Louis was, of course, still in trouble with the Papacy, so we could expect Innocent to come down heavily on the other side. This he did. He answered Thibault's plea by sending his legate to judge the case. A verdict was soon arrived at: Raoul was still married to his first wife, and he and Petronilla were living in sin. They were excommunicated and so were the bishop and the priests who had granted the annulment.

I was furiously angry with Thibault of Champagne.

'There lies our enemy,' I said. 'You are too lenient, Louis, with those who work against you. This man should have been punished long ago for refusing to send troops to Toulouse.'

Toulouse was an unhappy subject with Louis. He knew he had behaved in an unkingly manner, and if ever I wanted to get my own way I could do so by subtly referring to it.

'He is our enemy,' I persisted. 'He has done this to discountenance us.'

'Well,' murmured Louis, 'one would have expected him to be angry, Raoul's first wife being a close kinswoman.'

'I would she had been anyone else.' That was a point on which we could agree. 'But it is as it is,' I cried. 'And now he has done this. What a scandal! What when the child is born? There will be those to say it is a bastard.'

'Which it will be if the marriage is invalid.'

'We are not going to accept this, Louis.'

'I do not see what can be done.'

'Something has to be done.'

He looked at me fearfully.

'We could march,' I said.

'March?'

'On Champagne.'

'You mean *war*?'

'What else is there to do? Sit meekly here and accept their insults?'

He was silent. I could see the fear of war in his face. I despised him. Raoul was a rogue, but at least he had courage to act as he wished and face up to the consequences.

'You will have to take up arms against him,' I insisted. 'You cannot allow him to flout you in this way. People will laugh at you. They will say you are not worthy of the crown.'

'I shall pray that God will settle the matter for us.'

'He will expect *you* to do something about it, Louis. It is your affair . . . not His.'

'All matters are for God's judgement.'

'I think God expects His servants to act for themselves. That is what you must do, Louis. In my mind, you have no alternative. You must take an army into Champagne. You must ravage the country. You must let him see that he is but a vassal of the King of France. If you do not act, *he* will be calling himself the King of France . . . for that is what the people will say he is.'

Louis was silent, grappling with his thoughts, trying to find some good reason why he should not go to war against the Count of Champagne.

He could find none.

And I knew that in time I should wear down his resistance.

Once I had made Louis see that war was inevitable, he began to grow enthusiastic about it. I reminded him again and again of how many times Thibault of Champagne had flouted him. He should take no more insults from him. Drastic action was necessary. Thibault had to be taught a lesson, and this was an opportunity to do so.

We discussed plans together and when that Christmas was over he set off with an army for Champagne.

This was no Toulouse. The last thing Thibault had expected was war, and he was not ready as Alphonse-Jourdain had been. Marching through Champagne taking towns was an easy matter.

I was delighted by Louis's victories. Champagne was fast falling into our hands.

Then there was to occur an event which scarred Louis's conscience for the rest of his life and which I believe was responsible for widening the rift between us.

It happened at Vitry-sur-Marne.

Louis himself was never in the forefront of the battle, war being so alien to his nature. He loathed violence and it was only when spurred on by one of his violent rages that he was guilty of it. He knew that his soldiers had ravaged the towns through which they passed, taking provisions, burning what they thought fit, ill-treating the women. Knowing him, I realized that he would have grappled with his conscience telling himself that it was all part of war. It was the soldier's reward for coming to the help of his lord. Why should they leave their homes, risk their lives, if not for the spoils of war, the warriors' perquisites? It shocked Louis, but he realized it was inevitable. It was one of the reasons why he hated war.

Truly he should never have been a king. It was an unkind act of Fate to send that pig running wildly under his brother's horse's hoofs.

At Vitry Louis suffered the supreme horror. He was encamped on the La Fourche hills with a few men while the army went in to storm the town. He could see what was happening from his vantage point.

The people of the town were unprepared. There was no defence, and Louis's soldiers went through the gates to the town with ease. Louis could hear the lamentation of the people, their cries for mercy. He covered his face with his hands because he could not bear to look. He had wanted to call a halt. I knew exactly how he felt for he told me afterwards. In fact he could not stop talking of it. He talked at odd moments during the day and in his sleep he woke from nightmares shouting about it.

He saw the blazing town. He knew that people were suffering. But what upset him most was when he learned later that women and children and old people had crowded into the church for sanctuary and the rough soldiers had lighted the roof of the church with their torches and had flung others through the door so that in a few moments the whole building was a mass of flames.

Not a woman, child or old person who had sheltered in the church survived. They were all burned to death.

When Louis heard what had happened he was overcome with remorse.

I think what upset him more than the deaths of the people was the fact that his men had burned them to death in a church.

Louis had little stomach for war after that. He had been successful for once and almost the whole of Champagne was in his hands. Thibault was once again speaking to the Pope. This time Bernard took a hand.

The terrifying man wrote to Louis in a forceful manner. What did he think he was doing? He was waging war on an innocent man who had done nothing save protest at a wrong done to a member of his family. What devil's advice was Louis taking?

Was I that devil? I think Bernard regarded all women as such, and I was the chief demon. Louis was being used by the enemies of the Church for their own ends, he said. He believed that if Louis would give up the lands he had sequestered, Thibault would do all in his power to get the sentence of excommunication rescinded.

Louis, of course, was eager for peace but I urged him to be cautious. It never occurred to him that Bernard and the Holy Father could be capable of duplicity; but this was proved to be possible, for when he eagerly called a halt to the war in Champagne it was only to find that the sentence of excommunication was still in force.

A certain antagonism was building between Louis and me. I think he partly blamed me for Vitry, remembering that I was the one who had urged him to go to war; I had tried to persuade him against giving way to the demands of Bernard and Rome. Bernard then had the temerity to suggest that when Raoul of Vermandois returned to his true wife the ban would be lifted.

'This was not what was promised,' I cried in fury.

'They say that all will be forgiven if Raoul will take his wife back.'

'But we shall have gained nothing. All that expense . . . all these victories and . . . nothing!'

I do not know what would have been the outcome if Innocent had not died suddenly in the midst of all this. It was a happy release . . . for us.

Celestine II was elected Pope and no doubt because of the pleas of Suger was persuaded to lift the ban of excommunication from Louis. Louis's relief was great. But I was furious because nothing was done about that on Raoul and Petronilla. They must remain outcasts. Not that they seemed to care. They appeared to be satisfied with each other. They now had a son named after his father. I could feel almost envious of Petronilla. She had a man and a child. I had neither.

I was now twenty-one years of age and barren. Yet in my heart I knew that the fault for this did not lie with me. But the matter concerned me deeply and I gave a good deal of thought to it.

Life was becoming intolerably dull. Louis was turning more

and more to religion. There was hardly any intimacy between us. I might have been living in a nunnery. I had little desire for him, Heaven knew, but desperately I wanted a child.

In a way he was still in love with me. Sometimes I would find him watching me furtively, but in his mind was the thought that I was the temptress urging him to acts which although he might indulge in them with mild relish, were repulsive to him in retrospect. I understood him well. It was ironic that such a man should have come to the throne. I often thought of that pig as one of Heaven's jokes.

He was growing rather haggard. The nightly prayers were longer than ever. There we lay at our respective ends of that cold, cold bed from which he would often start up in nightmares, shouting: 'The town is burning. Save them. Leave everything. Save them. Save the church.'

Vitry lived on in his tortured mind.

And I lay there thinking: I must get a child. What a temptation to give up to my impulses. There were so many handsome, virile men at Court, so many in love with me . . . if one could trust their words. But could one? All the time Raoul of Vermandois had been singing his love for me, he had been meeting Petronilla. The thought maddened me, but it cautioned me, too.

There must be a way.

It was said that Bernard was a saint and as such might have the power of miracle working. I believed that he wished France well. France was his country and he had always kept a paternal eye on Louis. I was sure he believed that Louis was meant for the Church, and no doubt he regretted that sudden appearance of the pig as much as Louis had. I felt an irresistible desire to laugh at the thought of Bernard's admonishing God for letting that fateful animal run out at the crucial moment.

An idea occurred to me. What if I went to Bernard? What if I talked to him of my predicament? What if I begged him to intercede for me with the Almighty, as he seemed to be on such good terms with Him? Could he influence God to make me pregnant?

An opportunity occurred which made me feel that God was watching over me. For some time Suger had been building a cathedral at St Denis. This was now completed and was to be opened with a brilliant ceremony which Louis and I were to attend with the leading churchmen. Bernard would most certainly be there.

If I could speak to him at the time, it would be more diplomatic than visiting him or asking him to visit me. So this was what I proposed to do. He would understand the need to give France an heir, I was sure. He might possibly be able to help me.

It was a beautiful day when we set out for St Denis. There were crowds everywhere to cheer us. The people were happy on this occasion. They loved a ceremony. There were so many people making their way to St Denis for the opening and dedication that there was no room to accommodate them all. Tents had been set up in fields, and there were crowds of all sorts and conditions of men and women. The inevitable pedlars called their wares, and there were apprentices, religious sects, the infirm looking for a miracle, and a smattering of pickpockets, I had no doubt.

Suger came out to greet us and to take us to those apartments which had been prepared for us. I asked if Bernard of Clairvaux was present and was relieved to hear that he was.

'I wish to speak with him,' I said. 'Would you arrange a meeting between us?'

Suger looked surprised but rather pleased, I thought. No doubt he believed that, if I wanted to see the saint, it might be a sign that I was reforming. I had never shown any desire to speak to him before.

I was left alone in the apartments. Louis had gone to the chapel to pray. I could imagine his pleas for forgiveness. Vitry, Vitry, Vitry. I was heartily sick of the name.

But I would not waste my thoughts on that. I had to prepare myself. What should I say when I found myself face to face with Bernard? How should I best approach him? He would be aloof, I knew. He cared not that I was the Queen of France. He was one of those who saw themselves above all others on account of their saintliness and their special relationship in heavenly circles. I had always found the saintly arrogant.

There were many stories about him, and I began to build up a rather terrifying picture.

I remember conversations I had with my women about him.

'He thinks it is sinful to eat. They say he was very handsome when he was young, and he hated his body because it was strong and virile, so he starved himself and nearly killed himself until some doctor made him see that if he did not change his ways he would die. Then he realized that God had sent him to Earth for a purpose and it was necessary for him to keep himself alive.'

'He never washed himself,' said another. 'He thinks that would be vanity. He wears a hair shirt . . . and the more full of lice it is the better he likes it, for he feels it is saintly to be tormented.'

'He never speaks to his sister. He has cut her right out of his life because she married and has a large family. He thought she should have gone into a convent.'

'He hates all women because he thinks the Devil has put them on Earth to tempt men to perdition.'

I had grown angry at that. 'Why do you regard this man as great?' I cried. 'If everyone were like him, there would be no people on Earth in a very short time. Of course people must marry. It says in the Bible "Be fruitful and replenish the Earth." I do not believe all these stories of this man.'

'He does hate women, my lady,' insisted one of them. 'I heard that when he was a young man he broke the ice on a river stream and plunged into the water because he had felt desire for a woman. He was only discovered just in time and nearly lost his life. But they revived him.'

'What silly tales,' I said. 'I do not believe any man would behave so.'

'My lady, this is a saint.'

'Surely a man could do God's work without going to such extremes. God put women on Earth surely for the purpose of procreating the race. It was He who arranged the relationship between men and women, and He presumably made it enticing so that there would be no lack of children. So all this seems nonsense to me.'

They smiled. They were accustomed to my forthright views.

I was rather disturbed though to contemplate the man I had to face.

The ceremony, led by Louis, was most impressive. He was in his element there among the clergy and the monks. He looked ecstatic. I felt almost sorry for him. What a tragedy that he had come to the throne when he would have been so much at peace in the Church.

I was impatiently awaiting the meeting with Bernard, which

was to take place immediately after the ceremony. He would be waiting for me in a small room.

We stood for some seconds regarding each other. There could not have been a greater contrast in two people. Perhaps he had expected me to come in sombre robes, but I did not. I was not going to make myself out to be what I was not. I knew I looked splendid in my velvet and my jewels, with my gown close fitting at the waist to show off my perfect figure, with the skirt flowing extravagantly to the floor. I wore a jewelled band about my hair. I wished to look my most seductive in defiance perhaps of this man who, when he was young, may have been ready to stifle his desire by plunging into icy water.

He was so frail that he looked as though he were not long for this world. They had exaggerated a little. He was not exactly dirty but I kept wondering about that lousy hair shirt. He had an unhealthy pallor; his hair was white and thin but there was a hint of blond in his beard and I wondered what he had looked like as a young man before the self-inflicted torture of his body had begun.

He was all that I disliked in men and I could see that I was all that he feared in women. Surely this could not augur well for our meeting.

I was remembering words I had heard attributed to him in which he stated his opinion of women. He had deplored their use of ornaments. 'Fine clothes and paint might seem to adorn the body,' he had said, 'but they are used to the detriment of the soul.'

I sat down and lifting my head high said: 'Pray be seated.'

He regarded me in silence for a few seconds and then took one of the chairs. I did not wish to be too close to him, for although the women had exaggerated it was obvious that he had no great regard for cleanliness.

'I wish to speak to you on several matters,' I said.

He bowed his head. I noticed that he did not look at me directly. Did I perhaps turn his thoughts in sinful directions? I hoped so.

I wanted him to work a miracle for me and I had to discover whether this man could help me to have a child. He had prophesied the death of Louis's brother, Philip; he had held the Host before my father who had crumpled before him. I had to face the truth. There was some spiritual quality in this man. If I did not think so, I should not be here at this moment.

I felt a certain awe which I tried to suppress. I was not sure whether it was due to the man himself or what I knew of him. I thought I would not speak immediately of my problem but of other matters on which I wanted to consult him.

I said: 'My sister and her husband are still under the ban of excommunication. It was promised that if we withdrew from Champagne that ban would be lifted.'

'Your sister has no husband. He who calls himself so is the husband of another.'

'The marriage was annulled.'

'By sinners.'

'Men of the Church.'

'Alas,' he said.

'I would ask you to use your influence. You of all men could do so if you wished. You have the power to subdue those about you. You have been chosen by God.' I could see that he was unimpressed by flattery. A different approach was necessary. I went on: 'Our troops have been withdrawn from Champagne.'

'The land must be given back to the Count.'

'It will be when the ban on my sister and the Count of Vermandois is lifted.'

'That cannot be until the Count of Vermandois returns to his lawful wife.'

I looked at his thin, austere face and saw the stubborn purpose there, and I knew in that moment that it was no use pleading for my sister. She must continue to pay for her pleasure; and indeed she was less disturbed about the consequences than I. I was in the presence of an extraordinary man and I was aware of the power which came from him. I had come here to plead my own cause not that of Petronilla. I decided to change my mood. I would try to be a little humble.

'I know that you are favoured by the Lord God,' I said. 'I would have you know that I have a great respect for you and for all you have done and are doing.'

'I am surprised to hear that.'

'Perhaps I have not appeared as appreciative as you might have thought necessary. The King, my husband, holds you in great regard.'

'The King, is a good man but often misguided. He is led by

evil influences.' The steely eyes bored through me. I was that evil influence he implied. He went on: 'He has been led into wars. He has offended God. He has taken up arms in evil causes. That must stop. I am sure the King is penitent. It is necessary for others to follow his example.'

I said: 'I wish to ask your help. In all the time of my marriage there has been no child.'

'Then it is God's will that there should be none.'

'I believe you could intercede for me.' I raised my eyes to his face pleadingly.

Bernard was having an effect on me. I could believe there was something holy about this man. There came into my mind a vivid picture of my father, standing before him in the church and then falling to the ground. Yes, there was a certain power about him. I believed he could work miracles.

So great was my faith in him that I was sure he was aware of it. His attitude changed subtly.

'So,' he said, 'you wish for a child.'

'It is necessary,' I answered. 'France must have an heir.'

'It is in the hands of God,' he said.

'You could help me.'

'It will be God's will.'

'But if you could intercede for me. Please . . . I beg of you.'

He was silent. He stared above my head as though he were in communication with some spirit above me.

'If you were to change your ways,' he said, 'if you were to dispense with sinful thoughts, if you listened to the voice of God, there might be a child. It is for you to change your ways.'

'I will do anything,' I said.

He bowed his head and folding his hands began to pray, and I was praying with him.

I said: 'If you would speak to my husband . . .'

'He also wishes for a child.'

'But,' I replied, 'he does little to help us get one.'

'Then let us pray.'

I had never thought to find myself on my knees with this strange man, who was so different from everything I had hitherto admired. Yet I believed in him.

'There would have to be peace with Champagne,' he said.

'Yes,' I said, for I knew it must be so and that our object in attacking Champagne would come to nothing. Petronilla and

Raoul would remain under the edict. They must fight their own battles. I had one object in mind. I must have a child.

So there was peace between us and nothing gained from that futile war.

This was unimportant, for Louis, no doubt primed by Bernard, returned to my bed and at last I became pregnant.

Great was my joy. I was ready to accept Bernard as a miracle worker. I had kept my part of the bargain. I had refrained from meddling in state matters. I had spent my days with the women, embroidering, reading good works. This was not as irksome as it might have been, for during the months of pregnancy I was naturally less energetic. I was determined to do nothing that would harm the baby, and I was in a state of exultation because that which I had so much desired was soon to be mine.

And in due course the baby appeared. A girl.

There was disappointment throughout the Court. A boy would have been so much more suitable. Not for me. My child was perfect; and I had never accepted the idea that a boy was more important than a girl.

Motherhood changes women . . . for a while. I had my nurses and attendants, but I was eager to be with my child during those first months. I marvelled at the miracle which that unsavoury old man had been able to perform.

Life was wonderful when such things could happen. I had my baby whom I called Marie.

It was not to be expected that I could become the sort of woman who was content with motherhood alone. I loved my child; I was proud of her; but I was not of the stuff of which doting mothers are made; and although I delighted in her, I needed stimulation, exciting adventure. I felt I was becoming stultified in my husband's Court.

Now that we had a child, he appeared to assume that he had done his duty and could dispense with the mating process which always left him with a sense of guilt. The prayers grew longer. I was very restive in my cold, unwelcoming bed. He still had nightmares about Vitry. I thought: He will never forget it.

I told myself that a woman of my nature could not be expected to spend her life in a Court which was more like a cloister. Petronilla and her husband were not often at Court. Oddly enough they seemed content with each other, and the fact that they were excommunicated did not seem to bother them very much. They shrugged it aside with such nonchalance that people were beginnning to forget about it. Never devout, they did not care that they were banned from the Church. I was a little envious of Petronilla.

Then news from the East set France in a turmoil. The town of Edessa had been captured by the Turks and all the inhabitants, many of them French, had been brutally massacred. All Christians should spring to arms. It was time to take another crusade to the Holy War.

At first I was not very interested. Nor was Louis. War had no charm for him and he was still humiliated by the affair of Toulouse and worse still by Vitry.

But it soon became clear that this was a matter to which we must give some attention. There was a grand assembly at Bourges, where the possibility of getting together men who would be ready to fight for the Holy Cause was discussed. There was another at Vezelai and yet another at Etampes. Louis was beset by doubts. He hated war, so might this not be God talking to him! It was not likely that he could expiate his sin by doing something he wanted to. He became morose; in his prayers he asked for guidance.

One day he said: 'A king who led an expedition to the Holy Land would surely wipe away his sins.'

Louis to go on a crusade! I considered it. I should not miss him—that much was certain.

Louis consulted Suger as he always did on important matters, wishing no doubt that he had discussed Champagne with him instead of me. Suger was not enthusiastic.

'You have your kingdom to govern,' he said. 'It would be a great glory to save the Holy Land for Christianity, but that is for others. Your duty lies in France.'

Louis by this time was growing very undecided. He was more obsessed by Vitry than ever, and his one great aim was to expiate that sin; he had to shut out the cries of those people in the burning church who continued to haunt his dreams. And seeing how deeply concerned he was, Suger implored him to take no steps without consulting the Holy See.

There was yet another Pope by this time, Eugenius III, and

he believed that people's indignation should be aroused against the Turks and that it was time to go into battle.

Someone was needed to preach with this purpose, and the Pope's thoughts went to one who had more influence in France than any other: Bernard of Clairvaux.

The Pope wrote to him asking for his help, and so fired by enthusiasm was Bernard that he replied at once, promising that he would go forth without delay. He was sure he could raise a worthy company of crusaders, who would go off to fight for God. So he came to Vezelai to preach the cause.

If Bernard gave his support to it, it must be right, reasoned Louis. He was growing more and more determined and Suger, who had at first raised his voice against the enterprise, no longer did so as it was supported by the Pope and Bernard.

It seemed a certainty that Louis would go on this crusade. And what would happen to me? If I could have been appointed Regent, I should have been content, but I knew that would not be. Suger, of course, would be in charge, and I should have even less power than I had at this time. It was a dismal prospect.

Then an idea occurred to me. Why should I not go with Louis? It would not be the first time a woman had gone on a crusade. The more I thought of it, the more I liked it. Visiting strange places, bringing a little comfort into the lives of valiant crusaders, was an excellent thing to do. I imagined my ladies singing to them. We would take wardrobes of beautiful gowns with us. We could lift the spirits of the warriors and make a great contribution to the enterprise. Men needed comfort after a hard day's fighting.

I became obsessed by the idea and when Bernard came to Vezelai to whip up enthusiasm for the cause, I accompanied Louis to hear him.

There was a unique power in that man. The frail little creature, looking more dead than alive, could inspire an audience, he could seize them and hold them; he could weave a spell about them. Sceptic as I was, I could believe there was some divine power in Bernard.

There was absolute silence in the square as his voice rang out: 'If you were told that an enemy had taken your castles, your cities, your lands, ravished your wives and daughters, desecrated your temples, would you stand by and let him continue or would you take up arms? My children, greater harm has been done to your brethren in the family of Christ. Christian warriors, why do you hesitate? Christ, who gave His life for you, now asks you to risk yours for Him. Defenders of the Cross, remember your fathers who conquered Jerusalem and who are now happy in Heaven. God has charged me to speak to you. Fly to arms. It is God's will.'

There was a deep silence when he stopped. He stood there, his arms raised to Heaven, and I think that all in that square felt the presence of divinity.

Suddenly there was a shout from the people: 'God willeth it. God willeth it.'

The King came to Bernard and kneeling took the cross from him. I followed. Bernard's eyes rested on me momentarily and there was approval in his glance.

Then the people were pressing forward. There was scarcely a man who did not want to pledge himself to the cause.

Adventures in Strange Lands

There followed months of preparation during which I grew more and more excited. The boredom of the Court was over. I could look forward to the months ahead with sheer delight. I could think of nothing but the Crusade. It was wonderful to feel such excitement about a *good* cause. I was taking a company of my most favoured ladies with me, so there was constant chatter in my apartments, as we discussed what clothes we should need. We were going to bring grace and refinement to the camp. That would be our main duty.

Louis was happier. He felt he was going to expiate all his sins in this venture. There were fewer nightmares and Vitry was hardly mentioned during those exciting days. He still spent a great deal of time in prayer. But he was content.

The country was to be left in the charge of Suger. He and Louis had had their differences, but in his heart Louis knew that the minister his father had bequeathed to him was a man to be trusted completely. Suger was for France. It was true that Louis was more influenced by Bernard, but he knew that Bernard was the emissary of the Pope and worked solely for Rome, while Suger thought first of France. Suger was without any doubt the man to take over the reins of government.

However, some in the country were not happy. A great deal of money was needed to finance the expedition, and that meant higher taxes to be borne by the people. There were some mur- murings about that. But not as many as might have been expected. People had a feeling that God had commanded this crusade and they did not want to offend Him.

Petronilla was sad. She would have enjoyed coming so much and I should have liked to have her with me. It was at times like this that the ban of excommunication could make itself felt.

Poor Petronilla, she must stay at home and console herself with her attractive husband.

We heard that Bernard's campaign in Germany had been as successful as that in France. The Emperor Conrad would be setting out with his army and we should all meet somewhere along the route to Jerusalem. Dispatches had been coming in from various places on the route. We had permission to pass through certain countries on our way where we should be given an honoured reception.

We were to leave Paris in June of that year 1147 and from there make our way to Metz, where men from all over the country would join us.

I had said goodbye to little Marie and tried to explain to her that her father and I were going away on a mission because God had asked us to.

There was to be a ceremony at St Denis before we left, and Pope Eugenius had come to France to bless the enterprise. It was a magnificent sight. From the cathedral hung flags and banners. Everywhere were men with red crosses emblazoned on their tunics; the streets and squares were crowded. People had come from miles round to witness the impressive ceremony.

We assembled in the cathedral. I caught a glimpse of Adelaide of Savoy. My mother-in-law eyed me with dislike and disapproval. I expected she was thinking me bold and brazen to accompany her son on this expedition. But I cared nothing for her.

The Pope was offering the chest containing the relics of St Denis for Louis to kiss and this he did with solemnity. Then Eugenius took the banner of France, the oriflamme shimmering with red and gold, and presented it to Louis, who as he took it, looked inspired, ready to fight for God and the glory of France.

So we rode out of Paris on our way to Metz for the meeting of the men who would come from all the four corners of France. I had rallied those of Aquitaine and was proud that so many of them had answered the call. I rode at the head of my ladies. They looked beautiful. I had insisted that there must be nothing drab about them. Their task was to bring beauty and relaxation

to the men. But we were crusaders none the less. Our soldiers
would feel refreshed and inspired because of our company. This
we firmly believed.

At first everything was idyllic. We put up our tents each night
and as the weather was good we sat in the open. Fires were
made; we cooked; we sang and told stories. Those who liked
such things enjoyed them while the more pious spent the time
in prayer.

And so we passed into Germany to learn that the Emperor
Conrad had gone on ahead with his army. We should meet up
with him, we believed, in Constantinople, where the Byzantine
Emperor Manuel Comnenus, we hoped, would offer us hospitality.

The euphoric atmosphere waned a little. Food became scarce.
There was trouble in one of the German towns when hungry
crusaders seized food which was being unloaded, and a fight,
which was scarcely a holy one, broke out; that caused a great
deal of unpleasantness. These peaceful towns would not tolerate
a marauding army descending on them and stealing their provisions even if they did call themselves holy crusaders.

Louis was distressed when the citizens of Worms refused to
trade with the crusaders and the shortage of food increased. This
was Germany, not far from home, and many were asking themselves how they would fare in really hostile countries. It became
clear that some of the enthusiasm for the crusade was beginning
to wane.

After that fracas some men left the army and returned to their
homes.

It seemed best to go on as quickly as possible, and so we set
out, trying to forget the unfortunate incident which had resulted
in a number of desertions.

So we pressed on to Constantinople.

We were greatly relieved to arrive there. I was attracted at once
to the Emperor Manuel Comnenus. He was young and full of
fire and ambition, indeed a man whose company I could enjoy.

He came to meet us surrounded by a glittering cavalcade. He
had an easy charm but there was a watchfulness about him. He
was particularly charming to me and told me that an apartment
should be prepared for me which would naturally be unworthy
of me but which was the best he could offer.

He told us that the Emperor Conrad had already arrived and was on the point of departure for the next stage of his journey.

What a joy it was to live in a palace after months of being on the move! I and my ladies revelled in it. Our saddle-bags were unpacked and we dressed ourselves in a manner suited to such a Court and we were very merry.

We talked together a great deal about Manuel Comnenus, whom we all agreed was a singularly attractive man. He gave us all his rapt attention. He was serious with Louis and his advisers, a little frivolous with the ladies, and his looks and gestures expressed his admiration for me. It seemed to me that he was the sort of man who knew how to be whatever everyone wanted him to be. That needs a great deal of shrewdness and I was sure Manuel was not lacking in that quality.

To be in Constantinople stimulated my imagination. It was a wonderful city, founded by Constantine the Great, from whom it derives its name—the City of Constantine who had been baptized in Rome by Pope Sylvester in the year 326. Small wonder that riding through the streets of this great historic city, with its Emperor beside me, I felt inspired. I told myself that whatever hardships lay ahead I should always be grateful for the opportunity to join this crusade.

We were greeted warmly by the Emperor Conrad and had many interesting conversations comparing our journeys. He had suffered less hardship than we, although he did admit that it was the army which had been treated with respect and when some of his men had gone off alone they had encountered hostility.

I realized that an army descending on a town could provide difficulties for the inhabitants, even though they made a peaceful transit.

In due course Conrad departed. We were not quite ready to do so yet and Manuel continued to treat us as honoured guests, talking a great deal about himself and his country and the continual watch that had to be kept for the Turk whose covetous eyes were always on Constantinople.

I found Manuel of great interest and this was due, in some measure, to the fact that I was unsure of him. I knew he felt insecure and his main aim was to protect his territory. He had unexpectedly become Emperor four years earlier. He had been the youngest of four brothers, but so clever had he proved himself, and so hazardous was the position of the empire that, when two of his brothers died, his dying father had insisted that his youngest son inherit after him, taking precedence over the remaining elder brother. The villainous Turks consistently threatened them, and a very astute and wily ruler was needed to keep them at bay. I was not surprised that Manuel attempted to turn every situation to his advantage.

He told both Louis and Conrad that if he helped them he would expect them to return any of the cities they took which had previously been his, and captured by the Turk. Both Louis and Conrad felt that they were not in a position to promise this and they replied that there would have to be consultations. So the matter was left in abeyance.

We continued to be entertained after Conrad's departure. We were taken to Constantine's Palace and there saw many holy relics—the cross and crown of thorns among them, which impressed us greatly.

Then a disquietening incident occurred. It began when Manuel said he had something to tell us which would cheer us. A messenger had come to the palace with the news that Conrad had had a resounding victory and had defeated the Turkish army. The way was clear now for us to go ahead.

It was disconcerting to discover by chance that it was quite the reverse when a member of Conrad's army found his way back to Constantinople. He was bedraggled, weary and half dead from exhaustion. He begged to see the King of France. Louis was always accessible and the man was brought to us. He told us how utterly Conrad's army had been defeated. It seemed that they had been led into a trap where the Turks were waiting for them. Taken by surprise, they had been overwhelmed and were now a defeated army.

The Bishop of Langres assembled the commanders together, with the King, to discuss this matter. I insisted on being present. I was, after all, the Queen of France and one of the leaders of the expedition, even if it was a band of women I was leading.

The Bishop said at once: 'There is treachery here. Conrad's men were cut to pieces because the Turks were lying in wait for them. How did they know the road the Germans would take? Depend upon it. They were betrayed.'

'By whom?' asked Louis.

'Need you ask, sire? By the Emperor Manuel Comnenus most certainly.'

'How could he, a Christian, lead Christians to the Infidel?'

'With the utmost ease, my lord. He is no friend to us. Of that I am sure.'

'But the Turks are his enemies.'

'He needs to placate them. No doubt they had offered bribes.'

'I find it hard to believe that of any man,' said Louis, 'and especially a Christian. Manuel has been a good host.'

'My lord, that does not prevent his being an enemy. Conrad's army is in retreat. The Turk will be awaiting the coming of ours.'

'What shall we do?' asked Louis. 'Confront Manuel? Ask him if this be true?'

The Bishop raised his eyebrows to the ceiling, as well he might. My poor Louis was no diplomat. One of his greatest weaknesses was to believe all men were like himself—a trait of the innocent, perhaps. I thought: Save me from good men.

I was not sure about Manuel's treachery but I could well believe it existed.

'We are among traitors,' went on the Bishop.

'We must act with great care,' said Louis. 'Until we are sure of Manuel's good faith we will tell him nothing.'

'He already knows a good deal. We could beat him at his own game.'

'How so?'

The Bishop's next words made me catch my breath. 'We have a well-equipped army here. We could capture Constantinople.'

Louis stared at him.

'Our plan is to go to Jerusalem, to make the Holy Land safe for Christian pilgrimage.'

'That is why we should make sure that this is a safe haven for them, and not ruled by a traitor who has just sent a fine army to destruction.'

'I would engage in no war but a holy one,' said Louis.

The Bishop sighed.

Several of the others spoke.

'My lord Bishop,' said one, 'you are not sure of Manuel's treachery.'

'Did he not tell us that Conrad was victorious? Surely that could only have been so that he could lead us into the same trap.'

'He could have been misinformed.'

I knew how these men were feeling. They wanted to move on. They wanted to go to the Holy Land. They wanted the glory that would come with the capture of Jerusalem. No one at home would understand the importance of taking Constantinople.

As I listened I began to see that the Bishop might well be right. Although I was attracted by Manuel, I knew an ambitious man when I saw one, and I was fully aware that he would sacrifice everything to gain his own ends . . . the German army . . . our army . . .

Had I been the commander I should have said: Let us take Constantinople. But of course they would not listen to me. I shrugged my shoulders. The inevitable would happen. We should leave Constantinople and march on. But at least we could be wary of any traps Manuel might set for us.

We took our farewells of Manuel and listened with scepticism to his protestations of friendship. None of us betrayed our doubts of him—not even Louis, who did not really believe in them, which was the only reason why he was able to deceive Manuel. The rest of us were more subtle and some of us could put up as good a front of deception as Manuel himself.

We crossed to Asia Minor and when we were encamped there Manuel's treachery was proved without a doubt when we came upon Conrad with the remains of his shattered army.

The sight of him saddened us. He was no longer the confident warrior wielding the sword of righteousness; he himself had been quite badly wounded; he was a defeated man.

He sat in the royal tent with a very few of us—myself and some of Louis's most trusted advisers. I was sorry to see among them Thierry Galeran, a man I detested and who, I was sure, reciprocated my feelings. He was a eunuch chosen, because of his immense strength, to be Louis's bodyguard. He was more than that; he was also a diplomat and considered to be brilliant. He always slept in Louis's tent that he might be ever alert for the King's safety. He seemed to have become one of Louis's chief advisers. I suppose a woman such as I was would feel a natural anathema to such a man. But he was ever-present and I knew that Louis paid great attention to what he said. He would stand there, often silent, listening, and I was sure he missed nothing. He was alert as Conrad told the story of his betrayal.

'Our guards were led up through a ravine, and as we came into the open stretch of land they were waiting for us. Our men could only emerge in threes and fours, so we were an easy target. The Turks are fierce fighters. Even in fair battle an army needs all its skills to equal them; but when one is led into such a trap . . . My gallant army . . . we came out with such high hopes . . .'

'Then there is no doubt,' said Louis, 'that Manuel is a traitor.'

He had at last accepted what the rest of us had known for some time!

Conrad decided that his army could not continue in its present state. He would perhaps go by sea to Palestine. He was unsure and we decided that we would go on without delay.

Louis and his advisers had a plan of action. They were now on dangerous land where they could encounter the enemy at any moment. They must be prepared and act with the utmost caution. At least they had learned something from Conrad's experiences.

There were the usual prayers and exhortations to the Almighty.

'We have God on our side,' said Louis. 'We cannot fail.'

'Conrad was set on a course of righteousness just as we are,' I reminded him.

'God works in a mysterious way. He tries us . . . He tests us.'

'I hope He will remember that we are fighting in His cause and not forget as He did with the Germans,' I said.

Louis was shocked at what he called my near-blasphemy.

'But,' I went on, 'we shall never win through if we do not face the facts. We are fighting a dangerous enemy and we have to rely on ourselves rather than divine help. No doubt the Musselmans are praying to their god. So perhaps this is a war of the gods.'

'You talk in such an unseemly manner and you should not,' said Louis.

I laughed and turned away.

However, when they did meet the Turks our army was ready and with righteousness on their side put up a magnificent fight. This was at Phrygia close to the Meander River. I watched the battle from a point of vantage on a hilltop. Our men were dedicated, but so were the Turks. I had never seen such fierce fighting. It was quite terrifying—particularly when one could not be sure which way the battle was going.

My relief was intense when I began to see that our men were gaining the advantage. The carnage was terrible but the Turks suffered more than our army; and at last the battle was won. It was a great victory. We had lost few men comparatively. This was just what our army needed, for many of the men had become dispirited by the sight of Conrad's bedraggled army and I wondered how much more would be needed to set them thinking longingly of home and the quickest way to get back to it.

Now they were victorious and glowing with the triumph of conquerors, rejoicing in the spoils of battle, for they had gained not only a victory over the Infidel but some of his treasure.

There was feasting and revelry in the camp that night.

The Bishop of Langres commented that such an army could have taken Constantinople.

'Nay,' countered Louis. 'We came here to expiate our sins, not to stand in judgement or punish the Greeks. When we took up the cross, God did not put into our hands the sword of His justice. Sinners such as Manuel Comnenus will face God on Judgement Day. We are here to fight the Infidel, and our aim is to set up Christianity throughout the world.'

Much as Louis hated war, he was triumphant on that night. 'God is telling us that He is pleased with what we are doing in His cause,' he said.

There were songs of rejoicing in the camp—many of them glorifying the battle and the bravery of the men.

'This is what they need,' I told Louis. 'You see how wise I was to bring the minstrels with us.'

He was not sure. He thought the time should have been spent praying and giving thanks to God.

I laughed at him. I knew I was right.

If only our triumph could have continued; but the fortunes of war change suddenly.

We were on the march again. We knew that very soon there would be another encounter with the enemy. They would have gathered together their scattered forces, and those proud people would wish to avenge their recent defeat.

There was a conference among the advisers.

Thierry Galeran pointed out that the saddlehorses which were necessary to carry our finery were an encumbrance. This was a reproach to me. I did not think it necessary to explain my reasons to such a man. He said that, as we were such an unwieldy cavalcade, it would be a good idea to split up and that I with my ladies should go on ahead.

'We will need soldiers to protect them,' said Louis.

'We can send a small force with them.'

'Our best troops will have to go to defend the ladies,' insisted Louis.

Galeran replied that we had exposed ourselves to danger by coming and if the best troops must accompany us, they should take us to a plateau which overlooked the land through which the army would have to pass. They would therefore be in a position to view the advancing army and if the fight was going against us they could hasten to the rescue of those fighting below.

This was agreed and at Pisida we split up and I, with my ladies and a troop of the best guards in the army, went on in advance.

The countryside was so beautiful as we came into the valley of Laodicea. The sun was warm and we were all hot and tired. I had rarely seen such an enchanting spot. Waterfalls gushed from the hillside, and exotic flowers bloomed among the grass. There was a certain amount of shade from the bushes.

'We will tarry here for a while,' I said.

The commander of the guards came to me and respectfully pointed out that the King's orders had been that we encamp on the plateau where we could have a good view of the surrounding country.

I could see the plateau in the distance. It looked stark and uninviting.

I said: 'I insist that we rest here for a while. Let us have a song to while away the time.'

So we sang and the time passed so pleasantly and sudden that—it seemed without warning—darkness came upon us. I could see no reason why we should not encamp there; it would give us a restful night and we could go to the plateau at the first light of dawn. The commander was uneasy but he could scarcely disobey my orders.

After a good deal of head-shaking and consideration of the fact that it would not be easy to move in the darkness, it was agreed that we should stay.

The decision proved disastrous.

Louis, some way behind us with the army, was being attacked by the enemy. At first they were harassed by small parties, and then the Turks were descending on them in force. Encumbered by the packhorses, the French fought back furiously, but they were no match for the Turks. Louis told me afterwards that his great concern was for me and the ladies, but he believed that we would be on the plateau by that time with the picked troops who, when they looked down, would see what was happening and come down and deliver an effective attack on the enemy.

Desperately he fought his way through to a spot where he could look up to the plateau and to his dismay realized that the troops were not there. Of course they were not. They were in the beautiful valley of Laodicea.

Louis almost lost his life on that occasion and probably owed it to the fact that he looked more like an ordinary soldier than a king, so no one noticed him particularly. He said afterwards that God did not intend him to die then. His horse had been killed and he was on foot believing that his last moment had come, not knowing which way to turn to escape the slaughter, when suddenly he saw a high boulder beneath a tree. He believed God had put it there for him. He stood on this and hauled himself up into the tree. The leaves were thick and he was completely hidden. From there he watched the terrible disintegration of his army.

We did not realize immediately that something was wrong. We reached the plateau and waited for the army to catch up with us. Scouts were sent back to find out what had happened and it was only when the poor wounded remnants of our army—Louis among them—came to our camp that we were fully aware of the disaster.

I had never seen Louis so distraught. He was like a different person. He was haggard; there was blood on his clothes; no one would have believed this poor creature was the King of France. His army had been overcome; all the baggage was stolen; we had lost countless horses and, worst of all, many of our men. We hardly had an army now, and as the dreadful truth swept over me I felt we could not long survive. I was filled with remorse, blaming myself. If we had not delayed in the valley, would the outcome have been different? The Turks were a ferocious enemy, determined to avenge their recent defeat but, if the guards had been in a position to go to the rescue of the rest of the army, surely it would not have been such a disastrous defeat.

In spite of my guilt, Louis was overjoyed to see me safe. Despite his lack of desire there was no doubting his affection, and as far as he could love a woman he loved me. It seemed strange to me that I, who appeared to have such a strong sensual appeal to most men, should attract him. I often thought that he would have been happier with a pious woman, one who could have shared in his devotions. I was grateful that he did not blame me, although it would have been quite reasonable for him to have done so.

He said: 'It was horrible. All the time I was wondering what had happened to you. I dared not think what might have been your fate if you fell into the hands of those barbarians.'

'I should probably have ended up in a harem,' I said.

'Don't speak of it. The thought sickens me.'

But this was no time to brood on past disasters; he had to act quickly. Here we were in a hostile land far from our objective. We had lost not only my fine clothes and jewelry, our musical instruments and all that was going to make the journey worthwhile for me, but the litters which at times had been necessary for my ladies and me, essential food and most important of all a large proportion of our army.

We were in a sorry condition.

I cannot recall that time without horror. We thought we were in a bad state but we had no notion of what was to follow. We dared not stay where we were, yet we feared to move. We knew that the country we had to traverse was over-run by Turks. Many of our survivors were wounded. They needed rest, which was impossible; they needed food, which we lacked. What could be done?

Louis took on a certain dignity. Perhaps he was better in adversity than in triumph. He prayed more than ever, which was to be expected; but he did act.

'We must go on,' he said. 'We must make for Antioch. The Prince of Antioch will surely help us.'

Antioch! The name had a magic ring for me, for my uncle Raymond was now the Prince of Antioch. I remembered how he had impressed me when he visited my father's Court long ago. I tingled with pleasure at the memory. He had then seemed to me the most handsome and enchanting man I had ever seen. Of course I had been a child, but I remembered telling him and myself that I should never forget him. Now the prospect of seeing him was like a beacon in a dark night. I believed that if only we could reach Antioch in safety all would be well.

'There,' said Louis, 'we should be amongst our own. Raymond is the Queen's uncle. He could not refuse to help us. Yes, we must make our way as best we can to Antioch.'

There followed one of the most wretched periods of my life. The hazardous journey had begun and when we set out, in spite of all that had happened, not one of us had any notion of what we should have to endure.

The weather was cruel. There was torrential rain which flooded the rivers. Many of our tents were washed away—as were our horses and even some of our men. There was mud everywhere. We were cold and hungry. The men were grow-ing more and more disillusioned, and there was murmuring among them. Surely, if they were in truth following God's will, He would not allow this to happen to us. There were long terrifying days when we were harassed by Turkish sni-pers. One never knew when an arrow would come whizzing one's way. These turbaned barbarians would suddenly dart out on fast ponies, shooting as they rode. One could bear that as long as they kept their distance. The horrifying moments were when they descended on us, their *yataghans*—swords with a single-edged blade—flashing in their hands, and to know that there was murder in their hearts and that our men were exhausted, angry and disillusioned.

Every day when I awoke after a fitful and uncomfortable sleep, I would ask myself: Shall I live until this day is out? Is this my last?

I said to Louis: 'We should have listened to Suger. He was right. We should never have come.'

'It was God's will,' said Louis.

'So said Bernard. But he was wise enough not to accompany us.'

'He believed it was not his place to do so. He could serve God better where he was.'

'He could certainly serve Him more comfortably. So could we all.'

Louis did not like such comments. After all, Bernard was reckoned to be a saint and very close to God. I did not share his reverence. All I could think of was that we should have listened to Suger.

Gone were my beautiful garments—no doubt adorning some harem woman. All my beautiful jewels . . . gone. And here I was, unkempt, with nothing with which to beautify myself. If the Infidel had allowed me to keep my gowns, I felt I could have borne anything else. Now I was getting desperate. I wanted to go home.

What was the use of wishing that? We were a long way from home and from Jerusalem and we had no alternative but to continue with the journey.

The horror of those days lives with me still—a nightmare from which it is impossible to escape. I had never imagined I could be in such surroundings. What were we doing here? I would cry to Louis and myself: Why did we ever embark on this fools' mission?

Louis could only say that it was God's will, and if we should die in His service we had the comfort of knowing we should go straight to Heaven. I wished I had his faith.

Meanwhile we had to go on; we had to live through those days of wretchedness and fear. There were occasions when I almost hoped that a Turkish arrow would provide me with a way out of this torment.

There was not enough fodder for the horses; many of them died. We lived on their flesh. I hated the smell of roasting meat when we lighted our campfires. We baked bread in the ashes of those fires—and somehow we managed to survive.

If we could reach Pamphilia, we might find shelter and provisions and perhaps guides to take us to Antioch.

Antioch. I said it over and over again to myself. If only I could see my uncle Raymond, I was sure everything would be well.

So the days passed, never without a fear that the enemy would destroy us. We laboured on until, exhausted beyond description, we saw in the distance the walls of Satalia, a little port in Pamphilia.

A shout of joy went up from every throat. Never could any traveller who had been almost without hope have felt such overpowering relief.

We spurred on our tired horses—those of us who had them still—and even the animals seemed to have acquired fresh vitality. The long march was over. We were there.

As we came into the city, we were surprised to see how few people there were. Many of the houses seemed deserted. We made our way to the governor's palace.

He came out to greet us. He was welcoming but melancholy. He would have been delighted to treat us as we deserved, he said, but there had been so many raids on the town that many of the people had left. He could give us a little food but he was not sure whether it would be enough for our needs. We had come at a difficult time.

He took Louis and me with some of the commanders into the palace, where food was prepared for us. There was not enough shelter for all our soldiers. Some of them went to the deserted houses and stables, fending for themselves as best they could. At least we had roofs over our heads.

The governor was anxious to help—as well as he could. He advised us that our best plan was to get to Antioch as soon as we could.

'That is what we propose to do,' said Louis.

'How far is it?' I asked.

'My lady, it is forty days' march and the country is infested with Turks. It would be a hazardous journey.'

I cried: 'It will be similar to that which we have already suffered. Oh no. I do not think I could endure that.'

'You could go by sea,' said the governor.

'And how long would that take?'

'Three days.'

'Then by sea we must go,' I said.

'What of transport?' asked Thierry Galeran, who was as usual at Louis's side.

'I will do my best to find boats to carry you there.'

I felt greatly comforted. In three days we should be in Antioch.

But it seemed that God was determined to try us. With the memory of the cries of the burning victims of Vitry in his ears, Louis could endure hardship. I could not. And when I saw the vessels which were to carry us on this journey, I knew that our troubles were by no means over.

In the first place there was not enough transport to carry us all; and those boats that would were only just seaworthy.

There were many conferences as to what must be done.

Clearly some of us would have to undertake the forty days' march to Antioch. This caused great consternation. Louis was distraught. How could he sail away and leave his men behind? Yet how could he take them with him?

'There is only one thing to do,' he said. 'We must take everyone with us.'

'The ships would sink before they were a mile from the shore,' he was told.

'How can I leave my men behind?'

Galeran said: 'They will just have to continue with the march. They have come so far. They have endured great hardship but they knew that the crusade was not a pleasure trip. They are expiating their sins. They will have to march.'

'While I sail in one of the ships!' cried Louis. 'Never! I shall place myself at the head of them.'

Galeran reasoned with him. He was the King. He was the leader of the expedition. He must not expose himself to unnecessary danger. There was only one thing to do. Sail to Antioch with those who could be accommodated in the ships.

'How can I do this?' wailed Louis. 'How can I?'

'It is clearly God's will,' was the answer. 'If He had intended all the men to go He would have provided the ships.'

Louis was at length convinced that this was so, and he and I, with the ladies and principal knights and commanders, boarded one of the ships and set sail for Antioch, after Louis had left all provisions behind for the men who must march.

He was greatly distressed by this and fretted continually as to the fate of those left behind for the long march.

And so we left. We had lost three-quarters of the army.

Three days, we had been told. It was more like three weeks . . . three weeks of abject misery. I wondered how I survived them. There were times when I should have been happier to die than go on. No sooner had we left the land than storms beset us. We were driven miles off our course. Antioch seemed father away than it had when we were on the march. I longed to be back on land, riding along through the mud and slush, beset by the fear of Turkish arrows—anything but this fearsome pitching and tossing, fearing at any moment that this was my last, and hoping that it was.

The winds tore at us, throwing our flimsy vessel hither and thither on that dark and angry sea. There were days and nights of despair when I thought we were never going to reach Antioch. But one morning I awoke to find the ship steady and the sun shining. We had sailed up the River Orontes to the harbour of St Symeon.

A great joy came to me when I heard the shout, 'Antioch! Praise be to God! We are there!'

My joy was soon replaced by horror. I should see my uncle soon and what did I look like? My hair was unkempt, my face pale, my gown tattered and dirty. Oh, this was cruel! To meet him again thus.

He was waiting to greet us—Prince Raymond of Antioch. I thought I had never seen anyone so handsome as my uncle. He was tall and blond, a prince in every way. As we came ashore, his eyes were searching for me. I learned very soon that one of our ships had already arrived so he knew of our misfortunes and was prepared for us.

And there he was standing before me. I felt ashamed. I was so accustomed to men's eyes lighting up with admiration, and now I had to appear before the most charming of them all in my present state.

He said: 'It is Eleanor, my little niece.' He took me in his arms and kissed me. 'I should have known you anywhere. You are as beautiful as you promised to be.'

I touched my face and laughed uneasily.

'You have suffered a great deal,' he said, his voice soft and tender, his eyes alight with compassion. 'Well, you are here now. You are safe, praise be to God. You are going to rest and all will be well.'

He turned to Louis to greet him, and soon we were on our way to the palace.

When I think of the Court of Antioch now, I think of paradise. In the first place it bore a strong resemblance to the Courts of Aquitaine. Raymond and I were of a kind—products of Aquitaine. He loved luxury and soft living as I did. Yet he was ambitious. He had come far since my childhood when he had visited my father's Courts as a penniless younger son who was going to England to make his fortune. Well, he had made that fortune. He was the ruler of Antioch, and he had made it like part of Aquitaine.

During those idyllic days which followed I was to discover Antioch. It was here that I began to know myself and to see how I was wasting my life. I was to see that Raymond was all that Louis was not; happily could I have lived the rest of my life in Antioch.

Raymond's Court was the most civilized I had ever known. It had its origins in the distant past, having been developed by the Romans. It had passed through many hands since then and, it seemed to me, had preserved all that was good from them. Because its climate was so fertile, fruit and flowers grew in abundance; I was not surprised that in the East it was known as 'Antioch the Beautiful' and 'Crown of the East'.

I learned later that Raymond's was an uneasy possession. Antioch was too strategically placed to be safe; it had passed through too many hands—the Arabs, the Byzantines, the Turks and now the Christians held it. 'For how long?' must be the question forever in the minds of those who lived the luxurious life within its walls.

Raymond had beautiful apartments prepared for me. I was to bathe, for he had hot and cold baths as the Romans had; he had carpets on the mosaic floors; and there was that rarity, scented soap. How I loved the comforts he had prepared for me.

I found laid out on my bed a robe of purple velvet, and no

garment has ever given me so much delight. I took off my stained and filthy clothes; I lay in my scented bath; and when my hair was washed and I wrapped the velvet robe about me, I felt wondrously happy.

Everything about the palace was perfection. There was glass in the windows and from them I could see the beautiful gardens surrounding the palace—the fountains, the lush green grass, the brilliantly coloured flowers—beauty everywhere. I was constantly reminded of my beloved Aquitaine.

A banquet was prepared for us. Raymond sat at the head of the table, Louis on one side of him, I on the other; and it was to me that he gave his attention.

How gracious he was! How charming and sympathetic! He listened to our account of our sufferings; he applauded our piety in making this dangerous journey. Jerusalem must be made safe for pilgrims, he said. We must stay in Antioch until we were quite refreshed; he would do everything in his power to help us.

I was in a daze of happiness. It was not only due to the fact that we had emerged from our ordeal to this paradise; it was not only the prospect of a stay in such surroundings: it was Raymond. I was sure that there was no man on Earth who could combine his fine qualities with such handsome looks and overwhelming charm.

And what was so gratifying was that he seemed to find the same joy in me as I in him. He understood me so well. His first act was to send bales of material for me to choose from, and with them came seamstresses who would carry out my instructions with all speed. Beautiful silks and velvets . . . all magnificently woven. He presented me with jewels.

And there in his Court were the minstrels . . . the poets just as there had been in my grandfather's. He had the charm of my grandfather, which was not surprising since he was his son.

Raymond's wife Constance, through whom he had inherited Antioch, was very gracious to me. I thought she was lucky to have such a husband and I wondered if she was a little jealous of the attention he paid me. She would tell herself, though, that I was his niece; I remembered it too; but for that fact, it would seem that he was wooing me, so tender was the attention he bestowed on me.

What happy days! He arranged banquets and tournaments for us. He was determined to please us. Such things, of course, were little to Louis's taste, and all the time he was yearning to continue the journey. It was only because of the persuasion of Galeran and his knights that he consented to stay. We must all recuperate, they told him. We were all in a poor state of health and in no condition as yet to face further hardships. All needed a stay in such a place; they needed good food; many of them had been wounded; they needed rest.

I had apartments separate from Louis in the palace. Thierry Galeran slept outside his door. The man irritated me more than ever. I knew he regarded me with dislike, and I had no desire to have him near me. Louis was nothing loath. In fact, I think he was relieved not to have me in his bed, complaining about those long prayers and being a continual reproach to him and perhaps a temptation. All I knew was that I was glad to be away from him.

I spent a good deal of time with Raymond. When we rode out with a party to hunt he contrived to be alone with me. (It might have been that those in attendance were aware of his desire and helped to further it.) We had many interesting and illuminating conversations.

He talked a good deal about his coming to Antioch and the days of our childhood in Aquitaine.

'I have tried to make this place a little like it,' he said. 'Does one ever forget one's native land? And I have you here with me . . . Queen of France but still the Duchess of Aquitaine.'

'That is what I like best of all,' I told him.

'And Louis, of course, only shares it with you. If you two parted, he would lose Aquitaine and you would still be its Duchess.'

It was the first time I had thought of leaving Louis. Often I had been exasperated and wished myself free of him, but Raymond spoke of it as though it were a possibility.

'Why?' I cried. 'Do you think I could leave Louis?'

He gave me that dazzling smile of complete understanding. 'You, my dear Eleanor, you, the Queen of the Courts of Love, married to such a man! How incongruous it must be! Oh, I understand how the marriage came about. Do not marriages of such as we are often happen in this way? They are affairs of state and should be treated as such.'

'Before my father died he made this marriage for me.'

'Indeed he did. He found you a crown. What a pity he did not find you a man to wear it.'

'Louis exasperates me,' I said.

'I can understand it. I marvel. There he is, with the most beautiful woman in the world, he who should have been a monk.'

'He was brought up to go into the Church, as you know. But for a pig . . .'

Raymond laughed. 'What a sobering thought! Our destinies left to the judgement of pigs!'

I laughed with him. 'But for a pig I should have married Louis's brother. Would he have been a better proposition, I wonder.'

'He could hardly have been worse.'

'And your marriage, Raymond?'

'It is not unsatisfactory. It was necessary, as you know.'

I nodded. 'All those years ago I remember so well your coming to our Court. You had everything then . . . but lands and money.'

'A very sad lack, I do assure you.'

'But one which you were determined soon to remedy. You were going to England to the Court of King Henry.'

'So I did and he was good to me. But I was just a landless youth . . . son of William of Aquitane, it is true, but a younger son.'

'Determined to make his way.'

'And the opportunity came with the death of Bohemund I, who was slain by the Turks in '30. Bohemund was a great fighter. He came out on a crusade as you and Louis have. Antioch was then in the hands of the Mohammedans, and it was necessary to take it from them to make the road to Jerusalem safe for Christians, so Bohemund fought to free it; and when he had done so, instead of continuing with the crusade, he settled in Antioch, made himself its Prince, and kept the city safe from marauding Turks. On his death his son, Bohemund II, became Prince of Antioch.'

'And when he died?'

'There is where I came in. He left only one daughter, Constance, his sole heiress, and an ambitious widow, Alice. She proposed to marry Constance to the son of the Byzantine Emperor, and there was great consternation throughout Christendom, Antioch being a place of great importance on the way to Jerusalem. There was I, at the Court of King Henry, looking for a way to fortune. Why should I not be sent to Antioch to marry the girl? I was unmarried. I was young and strong. They thought I had the qualities of a ruler. It was my great opportunity.'

'And you took it.'

'It was not so easy. There was Alice to be confronted. I guessed I should have trouble there. I came to Antioch. Alice received me. She was very gracious and seemed to have some affection for me.'

'That does not surprise me.'

'But she wanted the Byzantine for Constance.'

'And you for herself?'

'You have guessed.'

'What a difficult position you were in!'

'I had had a long and arduous journey to Antioch. There were many who knew my purpose and were bent on stopping me. I was in disguise most of the time . . . as a pedlar sometimes, at others a pilgrim. Having managed to overcome all those hazards, I was not going to miss that for which I had come—which was marriage to Constance . . . and Antioch.'

'I am sure you were very resourceful.'

'I had to be. My future was at stake. Alice insisted that I marry her, and there was nothing I could do but appear to submit, so preparations for our wedding went ahead. But before the wedding day I quietly married Constance, who was then nine years old. It was not difficult, for it was what the people of Antioch wanted and they helped me in this. They had chosen me as their leader, and the only way I could become that was through marriage with their heiress.'

'And Alice?'

'It was a *fait accompli*. What could she do? The people were for it. They wanted a Prince and they had chosen me.'

'And how wise they were! I knew, when I was a child, that one day you would be one of the great rulers of the world. And you see I was right.'

'You see me thus at this moment, my dear one, but I am

most insecure. If the Turks came here to attack me in their hundreds of thousands, I should be lost. I should be unable to stand against them. The occasional raid . . . the general harassment . . . that can be dealt with. The people are loyal to me. They enjoy life here. They would fight with all they have to retain it. But the Turks are a ferocious people. They fight for their religion as we do and there is no greater cause than that.'

'I am surprised to hear you talking thus, Uncle. You seem so content here.'

'I live in the present. I fancy you are like me in this. Indeed, have you ever known anyone who understands you as I do? I share your thoughts, your emotions.'

He had come close to me and was looking intently into my face.

'No,' I said vehemently, 'I never have. When I am with you I feel I am right back in my own beautiful country. I have missed it so much . . . ever since I left it.'

He kissed me with passion.

I was delighted and startled. I said: 'That was scarcely an avuncular kiss.'

'What are such relationships,' he said, 'when people know they are as close as you and I? What matters anything . . . race, creed, blood ties?'

My heart was beating very fast. I said slowly: 'I suppose that is so.'

He held me against him. 'I have never known this feeling for any other,' he said.

I replied: 'Nor have I felt for any other what I feel for you. It is because you and I were brought up in the same country. There we spent those early and important years. Aquitaine will always be home to us. You have made another Aquitaine here. How wonderful it is to be here! After all I have suffered . . . you cannot understand the hardships.'

'I can, my beloved. I have suffered something like them myself. That is why I want to stay here . . . make this my Heaven upon Earth. Could I have a more beautiful setting?'

I agreed vehemently that he could not.

'Out there . . .' He waved his arms to indicate the world outside Antioch. '. . . there is strife . . . everywhere, it seems. In England, where I was helped by King Henry when

I was more or less a boy and starting out on my adventures, there has been trouble since his death. Stephen on the throne, Matilda claiming it. Stephen Matilda's prisoner . . . Matilda reigning. What sort of a country is that to live in?'

'Two claimants to the throne is certain to cause strife. Who is the better ruler?'

'Neither is good, and coming after Henry it is even harder for the people to bear. Matilda wants the throne for her son. It's natural. After all, she is the grand-daughter of the Conqueror and Henry's direct heir. Stephen only comes through the female line. If he were a strong man it might have worked for I do not think the people want Matilda.'

'Well, all that is far away.'

'And our concerns are here . . . in Antioch.'

'It is so wonderful to be here. Everything is so cultured . . . so gracious. And to hear people speaking our language as we speak it—moves me deeply.'

'I have brought many Poitevins into Antioch.'

'The poets and the musicians . . .'

'I wanted to make it as much like my father's Court as possible.'

'What an outstanding man he was.'

'He lived his life fully, did he not? He obeyed no rules. Who else but my grandfather could have carried off Dangerosa and lived with her at his Court as he did?'

'She came very willingly.'

'One would expect that with such a man.' He turned to me. 'Eleanor,' he went on, 'since you have come here I have been so happy.'

'And I . . . Uncle. It is still like a dream to me . . . after all that suffering to come to a place like this . . . and you. It was like dying and then finding oneself in Heaven.'

'Pray do not talk of dying. You have much living to do yet and why should we not create a Heaven here on Earth?'

'That is what you have already done.'

'Now that I have you here, yes. I never want you to go. I want you to stay here . . . with me . . . for as long as we both shall live. You are silent. Does it seem so impossible to you?'

'I fear so, though it enchants me.'

'There has always been a special bond between us.'

'I know.'

'Then we must accept what Fate has given us.'

'You mean . . .'

He held me tighter.

'There should be complete intimacy, complete understanding between us. I love you.'

'But . . . you are my uncle.'

'My dear, what of that? Why should an uncle not be in love with his niece? Who can decide where love shall come? I love you. I need you to make my contentment complete. I am planning now to keep you here. I live in fear that Louis is going to suggest moving on. I am going to do my utmost to prevent that . . . and you will help me.'

'I never want to leave you.'

'Then you feel for me as I do for you?'

'Yes . . . yes . . . I do. I should be the most desolate woman on Earth if we were parted.'

'Then I am happy. I will show you a little arbour in the grounds of the palace. I will see that we are undisturbed. There we shall be alone and we shall discover how much we need each other. Will you come, Eleanor? Will you?'

I did not hesitate for a moment. 'Yes,' I said eagerly. 'I will come.'

And that very day Raymond and I became lovers.

He was my uncle. He was married to Constance and I to Louis. But I did not care. I was happy. At last I knew what it was to love and be loved by a man. I could see nothing wrong. It was the shameful fumblings of Louis which disgusted me. This glorious emotion, this unbounded happiness which now uplifted me, made me happy beyond guilt.

I had changed. My women noticed. They said I was more beautiful than ever. Raymond continually told me that. We were in each other's company whenever we could be.

It was impossible to keep a relationship such as ours secret. When he was present I could not keep my eyes from him. Even he, a man of the world and, I have no doubt, hero of many romantic adventures, must betray his feelings. I was aware of the love in his eyes; the ardent desire must be evident to all.

I knew this was what I needed in my life. It was ironic

that I should have found it in this oasis in the heart of the most cruel country I had ever known and with my own uncle.

Louis had become quite repulsive to me. I told myself I could never share his bed again. What a mercy that he was the man he was! I was already thinking of how I could escape from him.

'You could ask him for a divorce,' said Raymond.

'And even so we could not marry.'

'Popes are very amenable to a bribe.'

'And Constance?'

'Ah,' he said. 'There is Antioch. But you could stay here. Divorce Louis and you will still be Duchess of Aquitaine. You and I could return now and then to our native land.'

I pictured it. Raymond and I together at the Court of Poitiers, lying on cushions, entertained by *jongleurs*, singing our songs to each other.

It was an impossible dream. And those visits to Aquitaine? We should have to make the long journeys across hostile country. The idea of doing that again filled me with horror: And how could I go back with my uncle as my lover . . . and would Constance, the heiress of Antioch, allow us to?

But it was pleasant to dream. Sometimes, when I look back, my stay in Antioch seems like a dream . . . a dream from which I had to wake inevitably in time to harsh reality.

In between our bouts of fierce love-making we talked. Raymond took me completely into his confidence and was as frank as he would have been with his most important ministers. He told me of his concern for Antioch and how he planned to strengthen the city. It was the gateway to Jerusalem. Christendom should remember that.

He said: 'I am going to put a proposition to Louis and his advisers. Soon he will be talking of moving on. There is no doubt that the whole company is in better health than it was when it arrived. Those who plan crusades do not always realize the need for safe havens on the road to Jerusalem where crusaders can stay for a respite, to deal with their sick and wounded, to replenish their packhorses. It is nonsense to raise such money—much of which is lost on the way and falls into the hands of the enemy—and to ignore the ports of call. Louis should have taken Constantinople.'

'It was suggested by the Bishop of Langres, but Louis was so eager to proceed with the journey to Jerusalem.'

'As I say, there is a lack of foresight.'

'He would believe the best of Manuel Comnenus. Louis believes the best of everyone until something is proved against them. He would not accept the fact of Manuel's treachery until he saw Conrad himself bleeding and wounded, and heard what had happened from his lips.'

'He must be made to understand. Even here in Antioch we live in habitual fear. We are surrounded by the enemies of Christianity. It is known that Christians find refuge here. The Saracens have their headquarters at Aleppo. From there they send out their men to harry the Christians. What we need is to take Aleppo and make it a safe haven for Christians. What a missed opportunity not to take Constantinople. The French army was in a good condition then. They could easily have taken it. It would have been a great victory for Christendom.'

'You would like to see Manuel Comnenus defeated?'

'I would indeed. That Greek is as much our enemy as the Saracens themselves. Of course he betrayed the Germans. He would have been delighted if they had all been destroyed. We of Antioch are his vassals. He could take us tomorrow if he were minded to. Why cannot people see that if we are going to hold Jerusalem we must make the route safe? I should like to see a string of cities all along the road to the Holy City . . . all in the hands of the Christians.'

'In France and Europe generally they have no conception of what travelling is like. They think it compares with taking a journey across France . . . and even that can be dangerous. But they have no idea what it is really like.'

'Louis should have. He has experienced it.'

'Are you going to suggest this to Louis?'

'In due course. Perhaps you could prepare him.'

'I think there will be little hope of convincing him. He is determined to go to Jerusalem. He thinks that only when he is in the Holy City, when he kneels at the shrine, will his sins be washed away and he be able to forget Vitry.'

'Nevertheless, speak to him. Make him see that we must make the way safe for Christians.'

'What do you propose? That you join forces with him and march against Aleppo?'

He nodded. 'It is essential that we destroy the Saracen stronghold. You have some wise men among you. The Bishop of Langres, for instance. He saw the need to capture Constantinople.'

'If you were successful in capturing Aleppo, he would want to march on to Jerusalem. What then of us?'

'You could stay behind.'

'If only that could be!'

'My dearest love, one does not say "If": one knows what one wants and says "I will".'

I could believe that with my powerful lover. I was sure he was capable of achieving anything. The only thing I could not bear to contemplate was parting from him.

I sought out Louis.

'What are your plans?' I said.

He replied that we were to leave Antioch in the very near future.

'Did you know that at Aleppo, not very far from here, the Saracens have their stronghold? It is from there that parties are sent out to attack Christians. When we leave Antioch, we shall have to endure what we did before.'

'We knew the road was not easy. You should not have come. It is no place for women.'

'From what I have seen it is no place for men either. The way should be made safe for Christians.'

'Life is not meant to be easy.'

'What nonsense. Life is meant to be enjoyed, and if the way to Jerusalem can be made easier, it is folly not to make it so. There should be more places where pilgrims and crusaders could be sure of a haven. It should be our aim to make it so.'

'My aim is to go to Jerusalem and kneel at the shrine . . . to confess my sins and ask for absolution.'

'I am sure it would please God more if you helped to make the way safe for those who go to worship Him. There should be more places like Antioch on the way.'

A look of derision curved Louis's lips. 'Places like Antioch!' he cried. 'What is this place? It is given over to pleasure. Life is soft and easy here. That is not the good life.'

'Why then did God make such a place where living is easy

and comfortable and the fruits of the Earth grow in abundance?'

'You are bemused by this place.'

'Who would not delight in it after all we have suffered? It seems sensible to me to make the way easier for those who come after us. We should have taken Constantinople.'

'It was not what we came for.'

'We allowed the treacherous Greek Manuel Comnenus to destroy Conrad's army. If we had gone first, it might have been ours.'

'Our plan was to go to Jerusalem.'

'But for the hospitality of my uncle we should all be dead by now.'

'We should have died in a holy endeavour.'

I sighed impatiently. 'Can't you see that God is showing us what to do?'

'I doubt God would show you.'

'He showed the Bishop. Remember how he urged you to take Constantinople?'

I noticed Thierry Galeran in the room. He sat so quietly that one was hardly aware of him. I was irritable suddenly. 'Can I never be alone with you, Louis?' I said.

'You are alone.'

'What of that . . . er . . . person?'

'Galeran is always here.'

Galeran rose and bowed. I could see the dislike in his eyes. 'My lady, it is my duty to protect the King on every occasion.'

'What do you think he has to fear from me?'

He lowered his eyes as though he were afraid to meet mine.

'You may leave me with the Queen,' said Louis. 'Wait outside the door.'

Galeran bowed once more and left.

'That creature . . . one can hardly call him a man . . . annoys me.'

'He is a good and faithful servant.'

'You take too much notice of him.'

'Not only is he noted for his strength but his intellect.'

'To make up for his lack of manhood, I dare swear. I do not trust such. Louis, do think about what I have said. Consult with your advisers. I am sure they will agree that the way to Jerusalem must be made safe.'

'Has your uncle been talking to you?' I remained silent. 'I know,' went on Louis, 'that you are frequently in his company. The whole Court knows that.'

'He is my uncle, Louis. It was years since we had seen each other. Has he not treated us with lavish hospitality?'

'Lavish indeed. We do not need singing and dancing to beguile our evenings.'

'Perhaps you do not, but others might. All of us do not want to spend our evenings on our knees.'

'We are on a sacred journey.'

'Which we could not have continued without my uncle's hospitality.'

'He owes that to God.'

I was exasperated but I knew it would be no use talking to Louis.

On the way out I saw Galeran. He was standing close to the door. I was certain that he had listened to everything Louis and I had said.

In the arbour, when I told Raymond about Louis's responses, he said he might be able to arouse in Louis's advisers an understanding of the need to protect the route and he would appeal to their logic.

'Louis is after all the King,' I reminded him. 'If he did not agree that it was wise, they would doubtless do what he ordered.'

'He is stubborn indeed.'

'It is true that he relishes suffering. He has never complained. He even wanted to march overland to Antioch because his men had to. It took some persuading before he joined the ship. Raymond, I don't know how I shall endure living with him . . . after this.'

'You need not. You must ask for a divorce.'

'On what grounds?'

'Consanguinity. After all, there is a close relationship. That can usually be found even if one does have to go back some way.'

'I must speak to him, Raymond. I will not be dragged away from you.'

'That is something we must avoid at all costs,' he replied.

We always left the arbour separately. Sometimes I went first, sometimes Raymond. Although the whole Court knew that there was a very special relationship between us, we had to observe certain proprieties. Lovers are generally so bemused by their love for each other that they have little thought for the impression they may be giving to others. They hide their faces and think they cannot be seen. Perhaps we deluded ourselves into thinking that the outstanding tenderness and love we obviously had for each other was that which naturally existed between an uncle and his favourite niece.

On that day I left after Raymond, and as I did so I thought I heard a movement in the shrubbery close by. I stood listening. Not a sound. I thought I had been mistaken. Few people ever came this way, and certainly not at this hour.

It was fancy. So I thought then. But of course I was lulled into that sense of security which is often found in lovers.

Raymond called a conference with his advisers and Louis's. I was present.

Raymond stated his case with clarity. He was a vassal of the traitor Manuel Comnenus. They knew that the Emperor Conrad, as fervent an upholder of the Christian Faith as they themselves, had suffered at the traitor's hand, his forces annihilated, his mission ended. And why? Because he was yet another of those Christians betrayed *en route*. It had happened in the First Crusade. Would they help him prevent its happening again? Logical reasoning would show such intelligent men that there was need for action.

I watched earnestly, willing them to agree with him.

Some of them—certainly the Bishop of Langres—saw the point. He said: 'If we could have these safe places at intervals along the route, Christians would be able to fight off the marauders with confidence, knowing they were on their way to a respite. I would agree with the Prince.'

Louis spoke and I hated him at that moment. 'We have not come to fight wars,' he said. 'We have come to worship at the shrine of Jerusalem. I shall never allow myself to be led in another direction.'

'This is a fight for Christianity,' insisted Raymond.

'Christianity is for peace,' replied Louis softly.

I could see the fanatical look in his eyes. He was seeing Vitry burning; he was hearing the agonized cries of the victims. I knew that Raymond was pleading a lost cause.

We met later in the arbour.

'Louis is a fool,' cried Raymond.

'A fool and a monk.'

'How could they have married you to such a man?'

'That is what I ask myself.'

'You will not stay with him.'

'I feel that I cannot.'

We made frantic love. We were both disturbed and afraid, although Raymond did not admit it. We knew we were approaching a climax and were unsure what would happen next. It was easy to talk of leaving Louis, of spending the rest of my days in Antioch and Aquitaine—but how possible was that!

I left first on that occasion. And as I passed the shrubbery, I was aware of a shadow there.

I halted and cried out: 'Who is there?'

To my horror Thierry Galeran emerged.

'What are you doing here?' I demanded.

'I saw you go into the arbour, my lady. I knew you would tarry there some time. I came to protect you on your way back to the palace.'

I felt the hot colour flooding my face.

'Are you . . . spying on me?'

'My duty is to serve the King.'

'And how can you do that prowling about the grounds?'

'I thought it my duty, my lady.'

He was insolent. There was one thought hammering in my mind: He knows.

Perhaps I should have been aware that the whole Court knew. Neither of us, I thought on reflection, had been exactly reticent.

'You alarmed me,' I said. I wanted to humiliate him. My women said that he was very sensitive about his condition. I had never heard why he had been castrated. I wondered if some enemy had done this to him. 'At first,' I went on, 'I thought you were going to assault me. Well, never mind . . . That is something you could not understand.'

It was his turn to flinch.

I held my head high and walked ahead of him towards the palace. I was very disturbed. Had Louis set him to spy on me? Hardly. It was not Louis's way. No. Thierry Galeran had taken it upon himself to do so; but I was certain that what he had discovered would be reported to Louis.

I decided that I would confront Louis before Thierry Galeran could do so.

I went to him. He looked rather embarrassed to see me. So perhaps he knew. He would have been aware of my fondness for Raymond but it would never have occurred to him that we could be lovers.

I had changed. Love had changed me. I knew now what I wanted. Before, I had been vaguely dissatisfied. Now I was entirely so. I would not stay with Louis.

I found him at his devotions which irritated me further.

'Louis,' I said. 'I must speak to you . . . alone.'

He nodded and signed to those about him to leave him.

Before I could speak he said: 'We shall be leaving Antioch in a few days' time. I have been discussing this with those concerned and they believe we can make the necessary preparation, and in, say, three days resume our journey.'

'It is folly,' I cried. 'It is going to begin all over again . . . all the hardship and misery . . .'

'We all know that our goal is Jerusalem. There has never been any doubt of that, and however hard the road is we must take it.'

'Louis,' I insisted, 'you have already lost the bulk of your army. Do you intend to lose the rest?'

'We came for a purpose. God will look after us.'

'He has been a little remiss in that direction so far,' I said wearily.

'We are here now. We have come through so far.'

'And what of those who have not? What of those who have died either from the sabres and arrows of the Turks or from very revolting illnesses? Do you call that looking after?'

'Eleanor, you frighten me sometimes. I fear that God will take some terrible revenge on you. You talk blasphemy.'

'Perhaps He might like those of us who speak the truth. After all, what is in my mind has been put there by Him. But enough of this theology. If you are foolish enough to leave, I shall not come with you.'

'You cannot mean that!'

'I do, Louis. I am not leaving Antioch.'

'How can you stay behind?'

'Perfectly easily . . . as my uncle's guest.'

'Your place is with your husband and the French army. Have you forgotten that you are the Queen of France?'

'That is a matter about which I want to speak to you.' He looked puzzled.

'Louis,' I said, 'let us be frank. You and I are not suited, are we? I believe there are times when you regret our marriage. As for myself, I regret it all the time. We cannot go on. I want a divorce.'

'Divorce! How can you suggest that? You are the Queen of France.'

'Queens have been divorced before. I shall not be the first.'

'But . . . why? It is impossible.'

'Why?' I asked. 'Because you are not meant to be a husband. You know it is the Church to which you give your devotion. I might want to marry again. I want a divorce.'

'You would renounce the crown of France!'

'Yes, I would. I should no longer be Queen of France and you Duke of Aquitaine. But it would be better for us, Louis. We should be so much happier without each other.'

His face puckered as he looked at me. He was bewildered and unhappy. I was amazed. In spite of everything, he loved me in his way. It was not a passionate desire such as I had for Raymond, but it was a steady affection, an admiration for my beauty, I supposed, though it was difficult to believe that Louis was susceptible to that. He had really been very patient with me. He found a wife embarrassing. He was continually trying to avoid physical contact; and yet, all the time, in his way, he loved me.

I felt a little touched, but it did not prevent my determination to get away.

'I believe you have not given this matter enough thought,' said Louis. 'My poor Eleanor, you have suffered a great deal on this journey, and here you live in luxury provided by your uncle. You have always been too fond of pleasure and you should pray for help to conquer that. I think perhaps you are a little overwrought.'

'No,' I cried. 'I do really believe we should be happier apart.'

'We have taken solemn vows. On what grounds could we break them? It would be a terrible sin in God's eyes.'

'Consanguinity is a sin.'

'Consanguinity? What consanguinity?'

'Families like ours always have links with each other. There must be close blood ties between us.'

'Eleanor, what are you saying? I think you are tired. You have suffered a great deal.'

'I am tired of a marriage which is no marriage.'

'What do you mean? What of our daughter?'

'One child in all these years! Why? Why? Because you are more of a monk than a normal man. How can a woman get children in such circumstances? You are not meant to be a king, Louis. And you would not have been . . . but for a pig.'

Louis said: 'It is God's Will that I am as I am. It was God who put the crown on my head. It is His Will that you are my wife. This is something I accept and you must needs do the same.'

'Louis, will you consider this matter of a divorce?'

'No,' he said vehemently.

I thought I saw the beginning of one of his violent rages which could spring up like a storm at sea.

'Think of it,' I said, and left him.

It was not long after that when he came to me. He dismissed my women. I thought: He has seen Galeran. He knows the truth now.

I was right.

He was staring at me in horror. I imagined he was picturing me writhing in Hell fire for which he was now sure I was destined.

'A most disturbing suspicion has come to my mind,' he said.

'I know what it is,' I retorted. 'Your spy did his work well.'

'Spy . . .'

'Galeran. He has been very watchful of me.'

'I cannot believe him.' He was almost pleading. 'If you tell me it is a lie, I will believe you.'

'If it is that Raymond and I are lovers, it is no lie.'

He looked completely taken aback. He stammered: 'The man is your uncle.'

'And so?'

'You and he. This is more than adultery. It is incest as well.'

'Have done,' I said. 'Raymond and I love each other. That is something you cannot understand, Louis. I know that full well. But we love each other and I am going to stay in Antioch. For the first time in my life I know contentment. You may be a monk, Louis, but I am no nun. I have done with the old life. I have endured it too long. I want to be free.'

'I am astounded. I could not have believed this of you.'

'Which shows how little you know me.'

'To break your marriage vows . . . and with your uncle!'

'He is a man, Louis, and you and your spy could not understand that. I have endured this life too long. I will no more. You can go, as you plan to, with those poor men who must follow you to their misery and possibly death. But I shall stay here.'

'You cannot do this, Eleanor.'

'I can and I will. It is finished between us, Louis. No more of that reluctant intercourse. You should be rejoicing for I am sure you hated it as much as I did. Just think of it! You can pray all night if you wish and none to reproach you. See the good sense of this. We are not for each other. You want to spend your life in prayer and meditation. I want to live mine. Two such people cannot live together in harmony.'

'It is indeed time we left this Court of sin.'

I laughed. 'You were glad enough to come when you were starving and sick. You are ungrateful, Louis. If I were my uncle, I would turn you out at once.'

He was tight-lipped and controlling his rage.

'We shall leave at the earliest possible moment and you will be with us,' he said.

'No,' I cried. 'Never.'

And I left him.

* * *

I told Raymond of that interview. He said he had guessed Louis would not agree to a divorce.

'I have told him that when he leaves he will go alone.'

'Perhaps in time then . . . Who knows?'

'He could not believe it when I told him, although that snake Galeran has been spying on me for a long time. But now Louis knows.'

'The marriage could be annulled on grounds of adultery.'

'I do not care on what grounds as long as I am free.'

Raymond was thoughtful. I supposed he was worried about the effects this would have on Constance if it became generally known that he was my lover. I imagined that there had been love affairs in his life before. Perhaps Constance—married to one who must surely be the most attractive man in the world—was ready to accept his infidelities and look on them as a necessary evil.

'Louis has said nothing to me of his departure,' said Raymond.

'He is determined to go.'

'We shall have to see what happens.'

'But I shall stay here with you, Raymond.'

'I could endure nothing else,' he said fervently.

A mood of wild recklessness came over me. Raymond had made me realize what I was missing in life and I had no intention of going back to the old ways. I wondered at myself for allowing my youth to have been frittered away with a man like Louis. Time was passing. I must begin to live my life as it must have been intended that I should.

I was longing for Louis to be gone.

There seemed to be tension throughout the palace. It was only natural, said Raymond, that a man like Louis should be completely bewildered to discover that his wife was in love with another man—and that man her uncle. He was as one who did not know which way to turn.

'He will accept the inevitable,' said Raymond. 'I think perhaps he wants to get away from a place which has been the scene of his rejection.'

So it seemed.

I had retired for the night and dismissed my women. I was in no mood for sleep. I sat at the window looking out onto the beautiful gardens and wondering what would be the outcome of my dilemma when I heard a gentle scratching on the door.

I went to it and opened it. A page stood there.

'My lady,' he said, 'the Prince wishes to see you at once. Without delay, he said. It is of the utmost importance.'

'Where is he?' I asked.

'He awaits you in the arbour of which you know. I am to escort you there.'

Excitement gripped me. It seemed natural that he should choose the arbour for our meeting-place. I wrapped a cloak about me, put on stout shoes and went out with the page into the night.

The scented air, the soft darkness made my spirits rise. What a lover he was! What I had missed all those years!

I was close to the arbour when a tall figure emerged from the bushes.

'Raymond!' I cried.

But it was not Raymond. To my dismay I recognized the craggy features of Thierry Galeran.

'What . . .' I began. I could see that he relished the situation and that added to my fury. 'What do you want?' I cried.

'You will see, my lady.'

'Raymond,' I called.

'Alas, for you, my lady, I do not think the Prince will hear. It may well be that he sleeps in his apartments with his wife.'

A terrible fear came to me. I had been trapped and to my dismay I saw that Galeran was not alone. Several men loomed up from behind the bushes, and a cloak was thrown about me.

'What are you doing?' I cried.

'You will soon discover. Come . . . we are going now.'

I struggled. 'I shall not . . .'

But Galeran had picked me up in his arms. The strength of the man was amazing.

'Quick,' he ordered. 'This way.'

And so I was taken. I struggled, trying to kick, but my arms and legs were bound and I was placed on a horse. We went on through the town, which was deserted for it was well past midnight. I wanted to cry out, but it was no use for no one would hear me.

Outside the town Louis and his army had gathered.

My hands and feet still bound, I was placed in a litter.

And so, in the quiet early hours of the morning, I left Antioch—Louis's prisoner.

How I hated Louis during that journey! I was incensed by the indignity of my abduction and I blamed myself for so easily falling into the trap. I was hoping all the time that Raymond would come and rescue me. What a forlorn hope! As if he could muster an army from those pleasure-loving subjects of his! As if they would agree to come and snatch the Queen of France from her husband!

I felt trapped and embittered.

It was not until we were several days from Antioch that I was allowed my freedom.

My hatred for Galeran was even greater than that I had for Louis. He was the one who had actually carried me off. There was an inborn animosity between us.

But when the first shock began to wear off, I could not hate Louis. He was so ineffectual. Everything he did seemed to end in failure. And he did love me . . . at least enough to plan my abduction.

But what a sorrowful journey it was! I could not stop thinking of those beautiful gardens, the hanging flowers, the richness of the palace. Every comfort known to man was in that palace. It was a paradise and I had lost it. I asked myself when I should see Raymond again.

I soon realized how futile it was to waste recriminations on Louis. He apparently did too, for he did not refer to my affaire with Raymond. I suppose we both tried to appear as normal as possible in the circumstances because we were aware of the gossip which must be circulating.

The journey, too, was arduous, although we did not suffer the hardships we had before. I thought a great deal about my future; and there was one point which I did feel determined on—that I was not going on living the life Louis expected me to. I must, in due course, when we had both had a chance of getting used to the idea, discuss with him the matter of divorce.

And finally we reached Jerusalem. A shout went up from the men when the stone walls of the Holy City came into sight. Waiting to greet us at the Jaffa Gate was Queen Melisende, who was Regent for her son Baldwin, who came with his mother.

The people of Jerusalem welcomed us waving palms and olive branches.

'Blessed be he who cometh in the name of the Lord,' they sang as we walked with them to the Holy Sepulchre. I thought how uneasily they lived in this city, constantly expecting attack. No wonder they were delighted to see the crusaders—even though it was such a depleted and forlorn-looking army.

So we arrived at the Rock of Calvary and the Tomb of Jesus.

Louis flung himself onto his knees. This was the moment for which he had been waiting. I knew that to him everything he had suffered had been worthwhile. He had reached his goal; the crime of Vitry was forgiven; his sins were washed away. Louis's faith was complete. He was in a mood of exultation as he laid the oriflamme on the altar.

He prayed there for a long time, and after that he was led by Melisende and Baldwin through the city to walk along the Via Dolorosa and to visit all the shrines. There was a look of ecstasy in his face. He showed no sign of exhaustion and was almost reluctant to be taken at last to his lodgings in the Tower of David.

I missed Raymond's lavish hospitality; and how I missed *him*. There were times at night when I wanted to cry weakly in my bed. What would become of me? I wondered. Of one thing I was certain. Something must happen. I could not go on in this way.

I think Melisende and even young Baldwin were aware that I was under some cloud. They did not treat me in the way I was accustomed to be treated. I knew my own attendants—so many of whom I had brought with me from Aquitaine—were shocked at the way I was treated. To have been roughly handled by the eunuch Galeran was most demeaning. They were quite outraged on my behalf.

I thought: As soon as we leave this place I shall take some action. I must be free of Louis.

Could I go back to Antioch? Would that be possible? And what of Constance? What would her action be? She had accepted the manner in which Raymond had treated me, the attention and the gifts he had showered on me, but she had thought that was as an uncle to a beloved niece. Now she would probably know that I had been her husband's mistress. Would she be shocked as others had been?

The future looked bleak.

It was not easy to talk with Louis. Now that he was in the Holy Land, he was like a man bemused.

A few days after we came to Jerusalem, Conrad arrived. He had sailed from Constantinople, to which he had returned after losing his army. But he did not go Manuel Comnenus, of course. He was fully aware who had betrayed him. He no longer had an army. He came as a humble pilgrim.

He was embittered. To have been led into a trap by one in whom he had placed his trust was one of the greatest blows he had ever suffered. All he had left of a great army was a band of ragged pilgrims. But at least he had reached Jerusalem.

I thought how foolish these men were. They risked their lives—which was all very well if that was what they wanted; but they risked the lives of others too. They were inspired by preachers like Bernard—who had the good sense not to accompany them; they set out with hope and glory in their hearts and suffered privation, degradation and often death. For what? To pray at a shrine? Could they not live the lives of Christians more fully by carrying out the teaching of Christ in their homes?

I was impatient with them, with the world and most of all with the cruel fate which had married me to Louis and deprived me of my lover.

Having reached Jerusalem, Louis was in no hurry to leave it. He was in his element visiting the shrines, spending hours at them on his knees. But he must render some service to the Kingdom of Jerusalem. Even Louis realized this. There were conferences with Melisende, Baldwin and Conrad, and it was decided that they must make an attack on one of the cities of the Musselman princes who were harassing Christians on their way to the Holy City.

They decided to lay siege to Damascus.

The largest and one of the most beautiful cities in Western Asia, Damascus was prosperous and set in a plain bounded by the Black Mountains in the south and the Anti-Libanus range in the north-west. They chose it because to capture that town for the Christians would redound to their credit throughout Christendom.

Louis needed such a victory. The crusade had shown little

but disaster so far—but then I had a feeling that anything he undertook would end in disaster.

I scarcely listened to their plans for conquest. My heart was in Antioch. Every morning when I awoke I would wonder what Raymond was doing and whether he was thinking of me as I was of him. What had his feelings been when he arose on that morning and discovered that I had been taken away from him?

How could I be interested in this foolish dream of conquest which these little men were concocting?

They had an initial success and were soon encamped about the walls of Damascus, calculating how long the inhabitants would be able to hold out without food and water.

How trusting Louis was! He believed that those about him who professed to be Christians were as guileless as he. He was no warrior. He was fully aware of this, as he hated war. But this venture, he would assure himself, was in the name of Christianity. The truth was that he could not bear the thought of returning home with his depleted army and nothing achieved except prayers at the shrine of Jerusalem and the expiation of his own sins. His people would say he was saving his soul at the cost of all those lives which had been lost on the way. Wives and mothers would revile him for taking their men away from him. All those fine words, all that waving of crosses . . . what was that now? He had to have a victory to make the project worthwhile and to make those at home proud of their country.

Alas, poor Louis. He was surrounded by dishonest men. None of them appeared to have any heart for the battle. We learned afterwards that young Baldwin himself accepted bribes from the governor of Damascus for messengers to be smuggled out of the besieged city who could reach Nureddin, the Emir of Aleppo and Mosul. Nureddin was a fierce fighter; his name was dreaded throughout the area; he was a legend, as fanatical a Mohammedan as Louis was a Christian, as determined to maintain his religion throughout the land as the Christians were to uphold theirs. He was even more dedicated than his father, Zengi, and his had been a name to strike terror into his enemies.

Word came to the men who lay outside Damascus: 'Nureddin is coming.'

The thought of the bloodshed which would inevitably ensue was too much for the besiegers. They dedicated to return to Jerusalem and ignobly retreated and when the people of Damascus saw that they were retreating—frightened at the mention of Nureddin's name—they sent out cavalry to chase them away.

And so ended the attempt to take Damascus.

A feeling of lassitude spread through the ranks. What was left of the army had lost its enthusiasm for the crusade. The men were nostalgic for France. Of what use was it to stay in Jerusalem? They could not spend their days visiting shrines. How many times had they traversed the Via Dolorosa, halting where Jesus had halted with his cross, praying, singing hymns of praise. They had done it—and they wanted to go home.

Many of them left, Conrad with them. He had lost his army and was nothing but a humble pilgrim now.

I said to Louis: 'It is time we left.'

He nodded gravely, but he made no attempt to leave. Each day he was at the holy shrine; he said he found great contentment in prayer.

I wondered whether he had no wish to return home because he would return defeated. Moreover he knew that I was waiting to take up the matter of our consanguinity. Perhaps he feared to return to a people who might despise him—a poor king who had lost an army and was on the point of losing a wife.

Months were passing and still Louis would not go home. Few of those who had come out with him remained.

I was relieved when letters came from Suger urging him to return, reminding him that he was a king with a kingdom to govern.

I saw the letter he sent back to Suger. 'I am under a bond,' he wrote, 'not to leave the Holy Land save with glory and after doing somewhat for the cause of God and the kingdom of France.'

'How,' I demanded, 'are you going to achieve these feats of glory when you have no army now?'

'I must do something. We should have taken Damascus.'

'You should have taken Constantinople when you had a fine army. You could have done that with ease. But you did not see that and so . . . you have lost your army and what have you to show for all the expense paid for in taxes by the people of France and Aquitaine? Nothing! Nothing at all.'

He covered his face with his hands and I knew by the way his lips were moving that he was praying.

I wanted to castigate him with words, but somehow I could not do so. He was such a pathetic figure.

Suger wrote again. 'Dear Lord and King. I must cause you to hear the voice of your kingdom. After having suffered so much in the East and endured such evils, now that the barons and lords have returned to France, why do you persist in staying with the barbarians? There are those who would ravish your kingdom. We invoke your piety, your majesty and your goodness. I summon you in the name of the fealty I owe you to tarry no longer. If you do, you will be guilty in the eyes of God of a breach of that oath which you took when you received your crown.'

I think that letter of the worthy Suger really shook Louis out of his complacency and brought home to him the fact that he must delay no longer and begin the journey home.

He wrote to Suger: 'I am coming now.'

It was a relief to me to take some action at last. We had been more than a year in Jerusalem—a year since I had seen Raymond. I still thought of him constantly, remembering so much that was precious to me, reliving those enchanting moments, wondering if I should ever again set eyes on his dear face.

Easter was celebrated with much ceremony in Jerusalem and when it was over we were ready to go. It was two years since we had left France—two years during which I had faced hardship such as I had never imagined, and ecstasy too. They were the strangest and most illuminating years of my life so far, and I was quite different from the young woman who had left France at the head of her Amazons, setting forth on the great adventure.

I remembered that time when our depleted army had prepared to leave for Antioch. What had happened to those who did not sail? I could not bear to contemplate what the answer might be. But how tragic it was that now we needed only two ships, for there were no more than three hundred people left of that great assembly which had set out two years before.

I chose which ship I should sail in and ordered that the baggage be put aboard. I had some beautiful Eastern silks and brocades. All the wonderful garments and jewels which Raymond had given me had been left behind when I had been abducted, and everything else had been picked up later. Some of the fashions interested me, and when I was in Jerusalem I had had to do something so I searched for attractive items.

There was a question of how we should divide ourselves, and I told Louis that I refused to travel in the same ship with Thierry Galeran. I could not endure the man and he had shown me so clearly that he was my enemy. I knew that he would be close to Louis all the time, that Louis listened to him, took his advice and relied on him.

'I do not wish to deprive you of your bodyguard,' I told him, 'so I shall travel with my ladies in one ship and you and he may go in the other.'

Rather to my surprise Louis made no objection. He knew that when we reached France my first concern would be to set negotiations for divorce in progress.

So we set sail for Acre.

I had not imagined that our troubles would be over. I had learned what an uncomfortable and dangerous venture sea-travelling could be. Nor was I wrong.

There were the usual hazards of weather to contend with, but at least it was summer. There was one great danger which we suddenly realized. Manuel Comnenus was at war with Roger of Sicily, and ships of those two rulers roamed the Mediterranean in search of each other. Being neutral, we had not feared trouble from either, and it was an unpleasant surprise when we encountered ships of Manuel's navy. They surrounded us and boarded us and we were told that we were prisoners of Manuel Comnenus and were ordered to follow them back to Constantinople.

Once again I thought of Louis's folly in not teaching Manuel a lesson when he had been in a position to do so. I wondered what he and his familiar, Galeran, were thinking now.

What would have been our fate I have no idea but, as we were preparing to obey orders, several ships of the Sicilian navy came on the scene. Learning what had happened, they fought off the Greeks and soon Manuel's ships were in retreat. The Sicilian sailors behaved most courteously towards us and eventually we were able to continue our journey.

It had been an alarming experience. I wondered what would have become of me if I had been taken to Manuel Comnenus.

Now there was the sea to face.

We sailed on, never losing sight of the other ship and just as I was beginning to believe that we were nearing our destination and would soon be on the last lap home, we ran into a heavy mist. It lasted for a day and a night and when it lifted there was no sign of the ship in which Louis was sailing.

The mist was followed by a storm which drove our ship along the coast of North Africa. We were forced to land and were given some hospitality by Berber chiefs and were able to stay while the ship was repaired and stores were loaded. Then we set sail again.

I was beginning to feel that this ordeal would never end. We were becalmed for several days and I lost count of them. Food was running low and there was little water; and there we were motionless on a sea without a ripple to disturb its glassy surface. I began to think that this was the end.

Then one day I was aware of movement. The blessed wind had come at last to relieve us. I heard the sailors shouting. We were indeed moving.

Days passed. I was too ill, too tired, too listless to move, and still we sailed on. At last we were in sight of land, and that day we came to Palermo.

It was fortunate that we had landed on friendly territory. King Roger, whose navy had saved us on the high seas, was now our host, and when he heard that my ship had put in at Palermo he sent word that I was to be royally entertained.

What bliss to lie in a bed, to eat delicately presented food, to know the comfort of waking on land! I never wanted to be in a ship again.

There I learned that Louis's ship was missing and that in France it was believed that we had both been lost at sea.

For two weeks I lived quietly in the lodgings which King Roger had ordered should be put at my disposal. Most of my ladies were too ill to attend me, and there was nothing we wanted to do during those weeks but lie in the shade and watch the brilliant sunlight dancing on the water, which was now as benign as it had been malevolent when we were at its mercy.

There was news. Louis's ship had arrived in a port near Brindisi in Italy. I heard that he had been very anxious, fearing what might have happened to me, and that when he was told of my safe arrival at Palermo he was overjoyed.

I must come to him, he said. The Bishop of Langres was very ill and he dared not move him.

I was relieved to hear that he was safe. My feelings for Louis were so mixed that although I wanted to be rid of him, I would have been very sad to hear that he was dead. I knew he was a good man and that his motives were of the best, but he had failed me in all that I looked for in a husband and, having experienced love with Raymond, I could not live the rest of my life with such a travesty of a man as Louis.

In due course I joined him in Calabria. He was delighted to see me and reiterated that his greatest concern had been for my safety, telling of his almost unbearable anxiety when the mist had lifted and he found that our ships were separated.

I said I too had suffered anxieties on his account.

He looked at me pleadingly and I knew he wanted me to say that we should forget our distressing talk of divorce and try once more to be content with each other. But I was unmoved and as determined to leave him as ever.

There was no point in staying in Calabria. Now we must make our way home.

'We should,' said Louis, 'visit Roger who has done so much to help us. It would be most discourteous not to do so.'

I agreed. I had heard that the Court of Roger, who called himself King of Sicily, was luxurious; and I felt I needed to rest awhile in such surroundings before beginning the rest of my journey.

Roger was at Potenza and he received us royally. He was gracious, and it was pleasant to be in the company of an attractive man who made no secret of the fact that he admired me.

But it was at Potenza that I heard the tragic news which made me wish I had not survived.

Soon after we left Antioch, Nureddin had attacked the city and Raymond had successfully routed the enemy's armies. Nureddin would have accepted a truce which would promise Antioch freedom from harassment for a number of years. Raymond was a proud man, I knew that well. How he would have laughed at Louis's retreat from the walls of Damascus at the mere mention of Nureddin's name. Instead of a truce he decided on a further attack. I knew he was impetuous. He had not stopped to think, in his desire for me, what effect our relationship would have on Constance and Louis. He was like his father, I supposed. He had all the charm, all the good looks, everything that makes an ideal man . . . in peace time; but he could not have been a shrewd warrior otherwise he would not have gone forth to attack the mighty Nureddin with so small a contingent.

It was King Roger himself who told me about it.

'Of what could he have been thinking? To go out and attack such a man with a small force! Did he think he was going to frighten Nureddin and make him believe reinforcements were coming up? Nureddin is not the man to know fear, and there were no reinforcements. Raymond fought bravely, but he was doomed. He must have known it.'

He was slain. I could imagine with what rejoicing the news must have been received in the enemy's camp. He was the bravest of the Christians, their most respected leader. The Musselmans respect bravery. They put his head in a silver box and carried it to Nureddin.

I could scarcely bear to listen. I thought I was going to faint.

'The Queen is overcome,' said Roger.

'Raymond was her uncle,' explained Louis. 'There was great affection between them.'

My uncle! My lover! And the most handsome, the most perfect man in the world. And they had killed him. Why did they wage their senseless wars? Why must they always kill what was good and fine in life?

I said I would retire to my apartment. I wanted to be alone. I wanted to remember every moment of our time together.

Raymond, my love, so alive, so different, the one I had been waiting for all my life—and now he was dead.

In spite of my sorrow, I was more determined than ever to leave Louis. I should never see Raymond again; my hopes of returning to Antioch and living there in luxury, Duchess of Aquitaine and beloved of Raymond, had gone forever. Raymond had died and Louis, in spite of all the hazards he had faced in the last two years, still lived.

I said to him: 'Louis, I must have a divorce.'

'You have not given enough thought to what this would mean,' he replied.

'I have thought of little else . . . for months.'

'Your lover is now dead and you could not have married him had he lived even if he planned to divorce his wife on some trumped-up charge.'

'This is a matter between ourselves,' I said firmly. 'I want a divorce.'

'We are in Italy,' said Louis. 'We should not leave without visiting the Pope.'

I considered this. If I were to get my divorce, I would need the help of the Pope. It seemed to me a good idea to have a meeting and if possible discover what his attitude would be.

When I was presented to Eugenius, my hopes were raised, for he was benign to both of us. True, he treated Louis with especial respect. He said he had found favour in the sight of God for all he had endured and, although the result had not stored up treasures on Earth, it certainly had in Heaven.

Louis was delighted and there were plenty of opportunities for prayer.

When Eugenius heard that it was our matrimonial difficulties we wished to discuss with him, he was mildly perturbed. But he was one of those men who believe himself equal to any situation and for that reason almost always was.

He said that in such matters there were usually two sides, and it would be an advantage to all, he was sure, if he heard us separately.

I thought that was good sense, for there was much I would not want to say in the presence of Louis. I looked forward to our interview but I knew it was no good trying to explain to a celibate such as Eugenius was—or should be—how I could no longer endure Louis's inadequacies.

Eugenius had already talked to Louis, and he received me with a show of great kindness as though telling me that, although he disapproved of divorce, he was ready to listen to what I had to say.

First he told me that Louis did not want a divorce, that he loved me as dearly as he had on the day he married me and that he was ready to forget all differences between us and would try to make the marriage the success it had been in the beginning.

I had thought about this a great deal ever since I had known I was to have this meeting with Eugenius.

I knew that is was useless to say that my nature was such that I could no longer endure to be married to a man who lived like a monk. Louis had presumably most gallantly refrained from mentioning my adultery with Raymond, which I am sure the Pope would have deplored and perhaps most certainly then might have agreed to the annulment. I was not sure that I wanted it on those grounds as I wondered that, if it were and I were condemned, would my possessions have been in jeopardy? I was not sure on that point; but I thought it would be unwise to bring up the matter. I had to admit that Louis was not the man to take advantage of such a situation. But perhaps he thought that if my affair with Raymond was brought to light it would reflect unfavourably on him. How could I be sure what was the reason for his silence; but I did believe that Louis would always be an honourable man.

I decided to use the line most likely to win approval from the Pope and at the same time protect myself from scandal.

'Holy Father,' I said. 'I have been anxious for some time about my close relationship with the King. We are third cousins and as you know through all the years of our marriage we have been blessed with only one girl. It is the only time I have conceived, and I ask myself, is this due to God's displeasure because of that close relationship forbidden by Him?'

Eugenius was thoughtful. 'The relationship . . .' he murmured. 'Yes, there is a degree of consanguinity.' It *was* the right course to take.

'But,' went on the Pope, 'I do not think it insurmountable. There could be a dispensation. It would give me great joy to see you and the King living in harmony.'

'I should always be concerned regarding this closeness between us.'

Inwardly I was smiling. I thought of that entirely intimate relationship with one who was indeed close to me in every way . . . my own uncle. But I dared not think of him now. I had to try to forget him, for thinking of him could only bring me sorrow.

I could see that Eugenius was a little impressed by my suggestion. It *was* extraordinary that a youngish and fertile woman should have failed to conceive during so many years, and when she did to produce a girl when the country needed a male heir for in France a girl could not inherit the throne. Any other point which I could have brought forward would have carried no weight, I could see. On consanguinity my hopes rested.

Eugenius was thoughtful. 'You need children,' he said. 'You need a son who will be heir to France. France needs an heir.'

'That is true, Holy Father. You will understand, I know, that my husband is a man who spends more time in prayer and religious contemplation than most men.'

'He is a good man of the Church.'

'But it needs more to be a good King of France. Holy Father, I need children. I need to give France its heir. Yet how can I when my husband is hardly ever in my bed?'

'It is of course necessary for him to be there . . . on occasion.'

'He has no desire to be.'

Eugenius looked grave. 'I must ponder this matter,' he said. I bowed my head and left him.

There was something innocent about Eugenius; I honestly believed he wished us both well and that he had a great regard for Louis was obvious. Louis was at heart a churchman such as Eugenius himself.

Perhaps I had given him the impression that if I could have sons all would be well. I had been obliged to do that, for the only excuse I could give for wanting a divorce was the fear that our close relationship displeased God. Louis, I gathered, had said that he longed for us to be in harmony together, that he loved me and never wanted another for his wife.

What happened would have been farcical if it had not been so distressing for me, because it put me into a situation from which I could not escape.

Eugenius behaved like a nurse to two bewildered children. He thought he knew what was necessary to make us happy and he determined to do his best to give it to us.

He had a room prepared in which there was a great bed. This room he hung with relics and he sprinkled the bed with holy water. First I was led to it, then Louis. We were to share it.

We all knelt down and Eugenius prayed to God to bless us and to give us proof of His goodness and mercy towards two children who had lost their way. He saw us in bed together and then left us. I was both amused and despairing. I could see no way out of this. I thought cynically: I wonder he did not wait to see the act and to have anthems sung while it was being performed.

Louis was in earnest. He did his best. I was passive. What else could I do?

In the morning Eugenius greeted us with immense satisfaction. He thought he had solved our problem and saved us both from the ignominy of divorce. He was so pleased with himself for having dealt as he believed so satisfactorily with the matter, and with us for supplying him with a problem which enabled him to show his skill. He showered blessings on us. He told us how high the kingdom of France stood in his esteem. He prayed there would always be complete harmony between us.

And then we made our journey to Paris. There was no great welcome for us. Our crusade had done nothing for France. It had cost too much in lives and property. There was murmuring throughout the realm.

Suger, however, was delighted to see us back. He had, as we had known, ruled the country well during our absence; but it would take the people a long time to forget husbands and sons who had set out full of zeal and met death on the way to Jerusalem.

I had my own troubles. The Pope's bed had proved fruitful and I was pregnant.

That winter was harsh. I had little to comfort me except my daughter Marie, now a child of five. It was wonderful to see her again and to find her charming and intelligent. She scarcely remembered me but we were soon good friends.

It was difficult to go on with my plans for divorce now that I was expecting Louis's child. The Pope had been rather clever after all and I had to admit to a certain awe and uneasiness that perhaps God had concerned Himself with our affairs as I had actually conceived among the relics and holy water. I had less respect for those symbols than most because I had been brought up in my grandfather's Court where they had been of little account. But I did wonder now.

I was desolate and, strange for me, listless. I half wanted the child and half did not. I had some maternal instincts, as Marie had shown me; but on the other hand this new child was an impediment to my divorce, of which I was thinking more and more.

The Seine was frozen over; people were saying it was one of the coldest winters in living memory.

So I lived through that dreary time, and in the early summer of the next year my child was born. To the dismay of Louis and his ministers I produced another daughter. For myself it mattered not. I loved little Alix just as much as I should a boy . . . perhaps more. I did not care for the future of France.

My great desire was to escape from it.

I continued to think of the divorce.

A Royal Divorce

Life continued to be unsatisfactory. I had two children now, and if I separated from Louis I should lose them for they were 'Daughters of France'. For a time my maternal instincts battled with my desire to be free, but I discovered that above all things I wanted to escape from Louis, to live my own life, to find someone who would be to me what Raymond had been and stifle this yearning for him which beset me. I knew I could only escape from it if I found someone to take his place.

Louis was disappointed by the cool reception he had received from his subjects. We learned that there might have been a rebellion but for the wisdom of Suger, who had kept a firm hand on affairs and had reigned cleverly during his term of regency. Some anxious moments had occurred when Louis's brother Robert had decided to make a bid for the throne. It naturally seemed to him that Fate had been unkind in making him a younger son when, in his own estimation, he would have made a much better king than his brother. Perhaps he would have. While we were facing death on our crusade, he had gone about the country trying to rally people to his banner. His case was that the King had been brought up in the Church. It would be well for him to go into a monastery when he returned and let Robert take the throne.

It might have seemed a sensible idea to some. Not, however, to Suger. God had made Louis King and, if he had been unfortunate, he was a man of God, the chosen of the Lord, their anointed King, and so he must remain. When Louis returned, although the people of France did not welcome him warmly, they made it clear that they wished him to remain their King, and Robert's hopes foundered.

Suger was against the divorce. I believed his reason might be that it would remove Aquitaine from France, for Louis owned it only through me, and if I went, I would take it with me. It was that thought which had sustained me ever since I made up my mind that I must leave Louis.

So we went on. Louis had brought some cedars from the Holy Land, and these he himself planted in Vitry on that spot where the church had been, thus he believed laying the ghosts of all those people who had perished there. I think he felt a relief from guilt after that.

We had reverted to our old pattern of life. I rarely saw Louis at night. We had separate bedchambers. He found it embarrassing to share one with me. I kept assuring myself that divorce was the only answer, and whatever the Pope did or Suger wanted, I must be free to live my own life.

After a while I think Louis was beginning to realize this. He was undoubtedly anxious because there was no male heir. He would do his duty but I guessed he was reluctant to endure more of those embarrassing couplings when perhaps he imagined what my torrid love-making with Raymond must have been like. But it might be that his imagination would not stretch so far, as he had had little experience. There were people who could bring forth children of one sex only, and what if, after the unpleasant intimacy, I did the same again? I wondered if it occurred to him that he might have better luck with another partner and the offensive ritual need not be performed very often.

He was a man who would regard duty as a serious matter. It was God's will that a king should bring forth heirs. There could be civil war if, on his death, he did not leave a son to follow him.

I really believed that Louis was growing a little more responsive to the idea of divorce.

If we both wanted it, the Pope could surely give it for reasons of consanguinity.

I was hopeful. Then a situation arose which drove all thought of divorce from Louis's mind. It was the prospect of war.

It came from Anjou. Geoffrey of Anjou interested me. I had seen him on rare occasions when he had come to Court. He was an extremely handsome man. In fact, he was known as 'Geoffrey le Bel', as well as 'Geoffrey Planta Genesta' because he made a habit of wearing a sprig of the plant in his hat. The soldiers called him 'the Plantagenet'.

He had become important through his marriage to Matilda, the daughter of the King of England, because she had brought him Normandy. Her grandfather, known as William the Conqueror, had taken England in the year 1066 and as Duke of Normandy and King of England had made himself as important as—and perhaps more so than—the King of France. The second William, who had followed him on the throne, had not been the ruler his father had been but, fortunately for England, he had soon been followed by another son of the Conqueror, Henry, who was now seen to have been a very wise ruler. He had had, and this was *un*fortunate for England, only one son and a daughter. This son, another William, had at the age of seventeen been drowned in the wreck of the White Ship, a tragedy which would never have happened but for the drunken state of the sailors who were manning it. It was a great sadness for the King for he had lost his only legitimate son—although he had several who were illegitimate, for he was a very sensual man; and the matter of inheritance was immediately of the utmost importance. But for the accident to the White Ship, the strife which comes from civil war would have been avoided.

When his daughter Matilda had borne a son, King Henry must have been delighted, for if he took after his mother, he would be a very forceful character. It was soon after the boy's birth that the King died, through eating too many lampreys, so they said. Poison was not suspected for, though he had been a stern ruler, he had been a wise one. His people had called him 'the Lion of Justice' for he had brought back law and order to the land which it had not known since the days of the Conqueror.

But on the death of the King trouble started. It was an indication of what happened when kings did not leave a male heir. Now there were two claimants to the throne of England: Matilda, wife of Geoffrey of Anjou, and Stephen, son of Adela, the Conqueror's daughter. So it was a question of the late King's daughter or his nephew. There should have been no doubt, for Matilda was in the direct line, but because she was a woman, before she could claim the throne, Stephen swooped down and, with the support of many of the barons, took it. Matilda was not the woman to stand aside and let someone else take what was hers by right. Hence the trouble.

Stephen was affable and pleasant of manner but, it turned out, a weak king. Not that Matilda would have been much better. She was a formidable woman, strong-minded, very arrogant and over-bearing—characteristics which made her unpopular while the easy-going Stephen, ineffectual as he was, won the people's affection.

Strife had continued on and off in England over the years. At one time Matilda was in the ascendant, at another Stephen.

It was at this time, while I was wondering how I could obtain release from my intolerable marriage, and just as I was beginning to think that Louis might agree that it was best for us both, that trouble with Geoffrey of Anjou arose.

It was always a matter for concern when one of France's vassals began to gain too much power. The people of England might reject Matilda for their monarch, but Matilda had a promising son. He had joined his mother's forces in England and had already shown himself to be a good soldier. If this boy was ever King of England—and he could be and, incidentally, Duke of Normandy as well—he would be far too powerful for Louis's comfort. Stephen was the younger brother of Louis's one-time enemy Thibault of Champagne but those old grievances had been forgotten now. Petronilla and Raoul were no longer at Court. The ban of excommunication had never been lifted, but as it did not seem to worry them, no one thought of it now. They had three children, a son and two daughters, and were quite resigned to the quiet life. Poor Raoul was very ill and not expected to live. I saw very little of them now. The affair had made a rift between us.

Louis was growing more and more worried about Geoffrey of Anjou. The man with his aggressive son seemed to have little respect for anyone; and Matilda, though she despised her husband, doted on her eldest son—she had two others—for it was on young Henry that she pinned her hopes. If she could not have the throne of England for herself, she was determined that it should be bestowed on her son.

Trouble was brewing and matters came to a head when Geoffrey of Anjou captured a castle on the borders of Poitou and Anjou which belonged to Gerald Berlai, whose duty it was to guard the frontier. Not only did Geoffrey take the castle but he made Gerald and his family his prisoners, treating them with some severity.

It was sufficient provocation for Louis to take up arms. He was ranging himself beside the Count of Champagne, who naturally supported his brother Stephen and wished to see Stephen's son, Eustace, inherit the crown after his father. And that was something which Geoffrey of Anjou and his son Henry were determined should not happen.

I was surprised that Louis allowed himself to be drawn into war. Suger was against it, and although Suger was getting old, he still influenced Louis more than anyone. But Louis could not, even now, forget Vitry. The planting of cedars, the building of a new church on the site of the old . . . none of these things could expunge that terrible memory from his mind. He still thought of it. The crusade which had been meant to lay the ghost forever had not entirely done so—probably because it had been such an outstanding failure.

I talked to him about the proposed campaign. The situation between us was growing more and more embarrassing. He knew I desperately wanted that divorce and was ready to face anything to get it. He was wavering, but the subject was unpleasant to him. But I did discuss this conflict with him.

I asked him why he, who so hated war, was now ready to undertake it again.

'It is my duty,' he said, with that stubborn look which I knew so well. 'The Plantagenet has ill-treated Berlai. I cannot allow that. Moreover, these Angevins have to be taught a lesson. They are the Devil's breed. That is a well-known fact. The Devil came to them in the shape of a beautiful woman who bore them sons and who would never go into church until she was forced to. Then, when confronted with the Host, she turned back into the spirit she had always been—and was never seen again.'

'Louis, you don't believe such a tale!'

'I believe it,' he said.

I would have laughed him to scorn but I remembered what had happened when my father had been confronted by Bernard carrying the Host.

'Vitry belonged to Thibault of Champagne,' he said. 'I want to help him now.'

'Will you never forget Vitry?'

'Sometimes I fear not.'

'So you are going to war. Is this a further penance?' Louis was silent.

'Suger thinks it unwise,' I went on. 'He says you are fighting King Stephen's battles for him.'

'Suger does not understand.'

What a fool he was! How I longed to be rid of him.

He had another grievance. Young Henry Plantagenet had not, as his vassal, sworn fealty to him for Normandy. It was almost as though he were saying: I owe no fealty to France. I am the heir to the throne of England.

Such arrogance, Louis had decided, must be curbed.

Thus it was that he found himself marching to the borders of Normandy.

Louis's war-like efforts were almost certain to come to nothing. He had not even made camp when he was overcome by a fever, and it was necessary for him to return to Paris. He did not come alone. He brought his army with him. I thought the fever might have been brought on by his extreme distaste for the action he was about to take. But he was certainly ill when he returned and the doctors said he must rest in bed.

Suger was quite pleased. He visited the palace and told Louis that this was God's way of preventing a war which should never have been contemplated. What had he hoped to do? Wrest Normandy from Matilda's son? He would never have done it. The English would never have allowed it, and even though that country was busy with its own problems the thought of losing Normandy would have aroused them to action.

Suger said he would ask Bernard to come and they would summon Geoffrey of Anjou and his son to Paris, where a truce could be arranged.

Louis was quite pleased about this. It was a great relief to him when his doctors said he must keep to his bed. So the conference had to be conducted by Suger and Bernard.

Bernard arrived. His antipathy to me was obvious. He would know about my desire for a divorce. I had a sneaking feeling that it would not displease him. He was different from Suger. For all Bernard's saintliness he lacked Suger's single-minded devotion to France. Suger thought a divorce would not serve the country well. For one thing France would lose Aquitaine. Suger

believed that, if Louis and I would continue together, God would
relent in time and give us a son.

Bernard felt differently. Bernard was a man of the Church. I
wondered if scandal concerning myself and Raymond had
reached his ears. If it had, he would feel I was unworthy to bear
the heir of France. He would, I was sure, like the King to have
a more amenable wife. Bernard believed I had put a spell on
Louis and that spells came from the Devil. Bernard might well
help me in achieving my ends. As the days passed, my desire
for release from this intolerable marriage grew greater.

Geoffrey of Anjou arrived in Paris with his son. I was mildly
interested to see these two about whom there had been so much
talk.

Geoffrey I had seen before and I remembered him vaguely.
The son I had never seen. He was very young—seventeen, I had
heard. I wondered what it was about him that made him so often
the object of people's attention.

I was told that they had brought Gerald Berlai with them—in
chains.

'It is a most ignoble way of treating a noble lord,' said one
of my ladies.

'They want us to know that he is their prisoner,' said another.

'What has he done . . . but defend his castle?'

'They say he sent forays into their land and made a nuisance
of himself. They would tolerate it no more and have taken his
castle and made him their prisoner.'

I had been feeling so bored and listless that I was quite looking forward to the confrontation.

I was seated beside Louis who had left his bed briefly to be
present. He looked pale and wan. There was no doubt that he
had been genuinely ill, but I was sure the illness had been
brought on through his hatred of war. In any case, it had stopped
that, so doubtless it was a blessing in disguise . . . certainly to
those men who would have been killed in a foolish cause.

It was an amazing scene. The man in chains before them and,
on either side of him, his captors. Geoffrey of Anjou stood there,
legs apart, defiant. He was still a very attractive man, though he
was reaching for forty. But it was the son who caught my attention. So this was Henry Plantagenet . . . the young man who
was astonishing everyone with his military gifts. He was by no
means handsome—quite the reverse, in fact—but one was aware

of an intense vitality. He was not tall—stocky rather; he had reddish hair and a very high colour; he looked excessively healthy. He did not seem to be able to stand still; he looked as though he found that irksome; his legs were slightly bowed as though he had lived most of his life in the saddle. I noticed his hands were red and chapped.

I could not stop looking at him. It was his overwhelming vitality which attracted me. There was an air of restlessness about him, as though he was straining his patience to the limits in order to stand there.

Now he was aware of me. He stared at me somewhat audaciously. I returned his gaze and for some moments he appeared to be assessing me. Insolent! I thought—and, oddly enough, I liked his insolence. I saw admiration in his eyes. They were warm, almost suggestive. I felt a pleasant excitement. I had heard he was a lusty young fellow and had, at the age of seventeen, already fathered two bastards.

A mere boy, I thought. I was eleven years older than he. But nevertheless, he interested me.

Bernard had taken charge of the proceedings. Geoffrey was an old enemy of his whom he disliked intensely and on whom he had already pronounced the ban of excommunication.

I liked these Plantagenets; there was a recklessness about them; they reminded me of my grandfather.

Bernard declared his horror to see Berlai in chains and demanded that he be immediately released, to which Geoffrey replied that he would not be told when to release his prisoner and he would decide what his fate would be.

Bernard then said that if Geoffrey would release Berlai, he would attempt to have the ban of excommunication lifted.

'I do not regard holding my enemy as a sin,' retorted Geoffrey, 'and I have no wish to be absolved on such an issue.'

Bernard was outraged. He called upon God to witness the blasphemy of this man.

'God hears you,' he said. 'You have offended against Heaven. Your fate is sealed. Very soon you will be called upon to face your Maker, and then you will be forced to repent your sins. You will be dead in a month.'

There was a hushed silence. Then Geoffrey and his son, taking their prisoner with them, walked out of the room.

They did not leave Paris immediately and, when the furore

had subsided a little, it was agreed that there should be more talks.

The next day I saw Henry Plantagenet again. There were several people present but he came close to me. His hand touched mine as if by accident. His was rough but in spite of that I felt a certain thrill at the contact. He smiled at me, his eyes seeming to take in every detail, travelling over my throat and beyond.

'You are very beautiful,' he said almost mockingly. I bowed my head in acceptance of the compliment.

'So accustomed to praise, I doubt not,' he went on, 'and so it should be, for you are worthy of it. I would I could speak with you somewhere . . . alone?'

I raised my eyebrows. 'Matters of state should be discussed with Abbot Suger,' I said.

'I would rather discuss them with you. Come, my lady, you will be safe, I promise you.'

'It did not occur to me for one moment that I should not be.'

I should have turned away. I should have said that the insolent boy was not to approach me again. But I hesitated. There was something about him which made me want to tarry.

I said: 'I cannot imagine what you would wish to discuss with me.'

'Then give me an opportunity to tell you.'

'Come to my apartment,' I said, 'in an hour. One of my women will bring you to me.'

He bowed.

I was feeling absurdly excited. There was something unusual about him. He had said I was beautiful, but he had spoken in a matter-of-fact way as though stating an obvious fact. There was no note of wonder in his voice, as I had heard many times before. And what was he suggesting? I could hardly believe I had assessed him correctly. He was the sort of young man who would walk into an inn, take a fancy to a serving girl, summon her to his bed as though he were ordering a meal, seduce her and then be off. What games did he think he could play with the Queen of France? It would be amusing to see.

I was waiting rather impatiently for him.

'Young Henry Plantagenet,' I had said to my women, 'has some request to make. I have promised to see him. When he comes, bring him to me.'

He stood before me. It was obvious that he paid little attention to his appearance. I saw why they called him 'Henry Curtmantel', for he wore a very short cape quite unlike the usual fashion. He was, I discovered, the kind of man who does not care what he looks like but dresses always for his own comfort.

'Well, sir,' I said, 'what would you have of me?'

'I think you know,' he replied with a smile.

'I am quite unaware.'

He raised his eyebrows. 'Perhaps it is too intimate a matter to be brought up just at this moment.'

'I do not understand you.'

'I think we are going to understand each other very well.'

He was having an extraordinary effect on me. I had to admit to myself that I found him exciting and very attractive. It amazed me that I should, but I was starved of excitement. Ever since I had lost Raymond I had been looking for another to replace him, never hoping to find that perfection which I had enjoyed, but perhaps someone who was slightly less handsome, slightly less charming. And now this young man, so different from Raymond in every way, was arousing in me those emotions which I had shared with my uncle.

I tried to think of other matters. 'Your father must be very uneasy after Bernard's curse,' I said.

'He does not care for the old man.'

'His prophecies have been known to come true. He prophesied the death of my husband's brother.'

'He who was killed by the pig?'

'Yes, the same.'

'We are of the Devil's brood, you know. We are immune from curses.'

'You are bold . . . you and your father.'

'To be bold is the only way to live. I am sure you will agree with that.'

'Perhaps I do.'

He came closer to me and took me by the shoulders. I began to protest but he seized me and held me against him. He laughed and then suddenly he pressed his lips down on mine.

I made a pretence of protest, but I knew this was what I had wanted from the moment I saw him. He had known it, too. It had been one of those cases of spontaneous attraction.

He drew away from me, still holding me by the shoulders.

'You are the most exciting woman I have ever known,' he said.

'And you are the boldest young man and the most insolent.'

He drew me to him and kissed me again.

'Do you realize . . .' I began, in half-hearted protest.

'I realized from the moment I saw you that you were going to be mine.'

'That is nonsense.'

'No, sound good sense. Why not? When I looked across that room I said to myself: "There is the woman for me." '

'You have forgotten you are talking to the Queen of France.'

'I never forgot that for a moment.'

'And you here . . . a vassal of the King.'

'We don't take kindly to the term.'

'I have seen that. You have offended the King . . . and now Bernard.'

'As long as I please you, I do not care.'

He took my chin in his hands and I was again aware of their roughness. What was I doing with this uncouth young man? I did not understand myself. I was surprised and delighted and found myself yearning to be closer to him.

'I want to be with you . . . alone,' he said. 'Where can we meet?'

'For what purpose?'

'That we may give expression to our feelings.'

'You must be mad.'

'Mad with desire for the most beautiful woman on Earth. And you, my lady, what do you think of your ardent suitor?'

I said: 'I think this is a joke.'

'Your responses belie those words. It is serious. Did you not know it when we looked across that room at each other? Old Bernard thundering away with his curse and poor Louis sitting there looking as though he thought the roof was going to fall in on us . . . and you and I just looked at each other . . . and we knew.'

'I do not know why I listen to you. You omitted to swear fealty to the King. You come here with one of Louis's seneschals in chains. You invoke the curses of Bernard. And most brazen of all you make advances to the Queen.'

'I am not sure that the Queen has not made advances to me.'

'Nonsense.'

'When we looked at each other, something passed between us . . . some understanding. I knew that you felt for me what I felt for you, and when two people such as we are agreed on such a matter, there is nothing that can stand in our way. Let us be frank. I believe that you and I could bring great joy to each other.'

'We do not know each other.'

'I have heard much of the Queen of France. Doubtless you have heard my name mentioned. So we knew each other before we met.'

'We have just met face to face.'

'At last Fate has been kind to us. Tell me when I may come to you. If you don't tell me, I shall find a way, rest assured.'

'I need time.'

'Time? Time passes too quickly. My father and I cannot stay indefinitely in Paris.'

'What of your prisoner?'

'What has Berlai to do with us?'

'I understood you were coming to see me on state matters.'

'No, on something far more important.' He gave me another of those bewildering kisses.

'Come,' he said. 'We waste time. When can I be with you . . . alone?'

I hesitated and betrayed myself. I wanted to be with him. I knew what he was suggesting and I felt reckless. The longing for Raymond would not diminish until there was another to take his place. Was it possible that that one could be this brash boy? He was the only one who had aroused these wild emotions in me since Raymond.

I said I would see him again . . . alone . . . that very day.

There was no finesse about Henry. I was glad. I was realizing how foolish I had been to try to replace Raymond with a pale shadow of himself. Henry was quite different. Henry was himself, and there was no one like him. He was without grace, frank, not exactly crude because he was, I discovered to my delight, highly educated; but he dismissed with contempt the graceful maneuverings of the courtly lover. I could match his rampant sexuality with my own, and for the first time since I had lost Raymond I was fulfilling my needs.

We delighted in each other. Two sensual people, each of whom had found the perfect partner.

When he said he had never enjoyed an adventure more, he meant it. When he said I was more beautiful than any woman he had ever known, he meant that, too. He was not one for pretty speeches. It was very refreshing.

For a few days I lived in a dream of contentment—not thinking beyond the next encounter. I could not have enough of him, nor he of me. He had no qualms about seducing the wife of the King of France. Perhaps he knew it was not the first time I had been unfaithful to Louis. Such as Henry would have no respect for Louis.

I was delighted to find that he was not merely the virile lover for whom I had been searching. He had a great respect for learning, and both his parents had wanted the best tutors for him. Master Peter of Saintes had been his first tutor, and when his uncle, Earl Robert of Gloucester, had brought him to England to join his mother, he had made sure that he had been given the best instruction. Soldier-adventurer that he was, Henry had taken to learning. I had known from the start that he was unique.

After our first wild rapturous encounter I felt alive as I had not since I lost Raymond. I was happy. I felt as though I was going to live again.

Every moment we could, we spent together. It was not easy for people in our position to escape alone. We had good friends, both of us, and recklessly we took advantage of that. Sometimes I used to marvel at what had happened. I was passionately in love with a man eleven years younger than I, who was not at all handsome, who was bowlegged, whose hands were red and weatherbeaten, who hardly ever uttered a compliment, who did not sing songs in praise of my beauty—in fact, he was entirely different from any man who had interested me before. It was amazing, but all the more exciting for that. I could think of nothing but Henry, and I was dreading the day when he would leave.

He talked about his childhood, of his overbearing mother, of her tempestuous life with his father.

'She is a very handsome woman,' he said, 'determined to have her own way. She never forgets that she is the daughter of the King of England and the widow of the Emperor of Germany. I think she greatly regretted having to give up the title of Empress and then having to fight for her rights and failing to win them. All her hopes are on me now. I have to go on and win the crown of England.'

'And there is Stephen's son, Eustace,' I said.

'Yes . . . and the King of France would send aid to him.'

'Louis has no stomach for fighting. It is only because of Vitry. He cannot forget that. He wants to help Stephen's brother, the Count of Champagne . . . and that means Stephen's son.'

'He will not succeed. I tell you this: I am going to be King of England one day.'

'I know you are. England and Aquitaine . . . they could be ours if we married.'

He was slightly taken aback and was silent for a few moments contemplating this glittering project.

I was the richest heiress in France. He was the Duke of Normandy, and his sights were set on the crown of England. Matilda had failed to grasp that crown, but he could succeed. How could weaklings like Stephen and his son Eustace hope to defeat such as Henry Plantagenet?

'What a prospect!' he said slowly. 'England and Aquitaine and nights like this together in holy wedlock. Alas, my Queen, you have a husband.'

'I have long been wanting a divorce.'

'And failed to get it.'

'I shall, though. I am determined.'

'On what grounds?'

'Consanguinity.'

He burst out laughing. 'And you and I? I doubt not we are as closely related.'

'We will forget that.'

'Yes, let us forget it. All the noble families are connected by blood. It is a good thing. It makes a divorce that much easier when it is wanted. Of course, the marriage could be annulled because of me.'

'We do not wish for that.'

'No, no.' He laughed again. 'Consanguinity is best. And do you think it possible?'

'Suger is against it. I know that is because he does not want Aquitaine to slip out of France's hands.'

'He's a clever old man.'

'Louis takes his advice on everything, but Bernard hates me. I think he would like to see me leave Louis.'

'He is more formidable.'

'Yes, but Suger is strong and constantly beside Louis. I have been trying for years and I cannot bring him to the point. But I do believe he is beginning to relent. He is a monk at heart and has no feeling for love.'

'Poor fellow! What he misses!'

'He does not think so. He prefers to spend his nights on his knees.'

'But this divorce . . . You and I. I like it. England and Aquitaine . . . together with the most exciting woman in the world. What more could a man ask?'

'Do you think it possible?'

'Of course it is possible.'

'And if I were divorced?'

'You and I would be together. No longer would you be Queen of France. Shall you mind that?'

'I shall rejoice in it.'

' "Duchess of Normandy" is not such a bad title. What think you of "Queen of England"?'

'That would make me the happiest woman in the world.'

And so we plighted our troth.

Negotiations continued and to the surprise of all Geoffrey of Anjou released Gerald Berlai. He said he had intended to do so from the beginning and that was why he had brought him to the Court of France; but when Bernard had made threats against him, he had become incensed and acted as he did.

Moreover, Henry swore fealty to Louis for the fief of Normandy and was acknowledged as Duke; so what had begun in such a stormy fashion ended in peace.

Louis was very satisfied with the proceedings. He believed that Bernard's threats of the dire consequences had subdued Geoffrey but I knew differently. The Plantagenets had what they wished for, and that was a truce with Louis which would prevent his taking up arms on Stephen's behalf.

Meanwhile Henry and I were spending each night together. So deeply was I immersed in our relationship that I did not care if I did betray my secret to those about me. They would discover in any case. It was impossible to keep secrets from one's ladies. But they would not dare to tattle even among themselves for fear of my wrath, so at night Henry would come to my bedchamber, and there we would indulge in that which had become of the utmost importance to us both.

We were the more desperate because we knew that we should soon have to part. But it would not be for long, I assured him. I was more determined than ever now to have my divorce and I would. Louis would be more intolerable to me after this interlude.

I wanted to be with Henry; I needed him. I was passionately in love with him and he with me. Perhaps he was also a little in love with Aquitaine, and perhaps I did cast covetous eyes on another crown, this time to be shared with the man of my choice. The crown of France—the crown of England. What did it matter? It was the man who was important to me.

It may have been that we each liked what the other had to bring, but that was no deterrent to our passion; and I think that perhaps my nights with Henry were even more exciting than those I had spent with Raymond, for with Henry there was hope of a lasting relationship which there could never have been with Raymond. Henry had brought me to a new life; he had taken me away from the nostalgic past; and I was deeply in love with him. I *must* get my divorce.

When I was alone with Louis, I asked him once more.

He shook his head. 'It would not be good for France.'

'You listen to Suger.'

'He is the wisest man I know.'

'But surely he cannot wish you to continue with a marriage which is no true one.'

'It is a true marriage to me.'

'Louis,' I said, 'you know that you were not meant to marry. You should have gone into the Church.'

'God decreed it should be as it is.'

'Yes . . . yes. God in His Heaven commanded a pig to kill your brother, I have heard it many times. You should give your country a male heir.'

'You wish to try once more?'

'God has shown clearly that he does not intend us to have a male heir. You must divorce me and marry someone who can give you what you need . . . what the country needs.'

'Suger does not believe it is God's will.'

'Suger fears the loss of Aquitaine.'

Louis looked at me sorrowfully. 'I have heard rumours of you
. . . and the young Plantagenet.'

'Yes?' I said.

'It grieves me.'

'You could have the marriage annulled.'

'For adultery.'

'It is the most conclusive of all reasons.'

'Do you want so much to leave me?'

'I believe it would be best for us both. We have never been
suited to each other.'

'I am sorry I have failed you.'

'We have failed each other. Louis, it is clear to me that we
should never have married. We are too close in blood.'

Even as I spoke I shivered. I was as close if not closer to
Henry Plantagenet.

'That,' I went on vehemently, 'is the best of all reasons. If
you divorced me for adultery you would not be able to marry
again, and you must marry again. Suger must realize how badly
France needs a male heir.'

'He believes we could get one through prayer.'

'It is not the usual method.'

Louis ignored my remark. 'If we were truly penitent, He
would grant our request.'

He seemed uncertain. No doubt he was thinking there was
much to forgive. Vitry for him, adultery for me.

I said: 'Bernard would advise a divorce, I believe.'

I was sure that was true. Bernard thought I was a devil incar-
nate. I thought: If it were not for Suger, it would not be so
difficult.

Impatiently I left Louis. He would waver constantly. Suger
on one side, Bernard on the other. He would never come to a
conclusion.

The Plantagenets had left, and life was inexpressibly dreary
without Henry.

Not long after their departure there came startling news.

They were riding with their party when, overheated after hours
in the saddle, they decided to halt for a rest near the river. They
sat for a while watching the cool river flow by. Geoffrey announced his intention to have a dip in the river. It would cool
him down, he said. So he and Henry divested themselves of
their clothes and went in.

They swam and sported together for a while, then came out and dressed. After that they made their way to the spot where they would encamp for the night. There was a cloudburst and they were drenched to the skin, but it was a warm day and they were not bothered by this, hardy warriors as they were.

I heard in detail what had happened later.

That night Geoffrey developed a fever. He was fearful, remembering Bernard's prophecy: 'You will be dead within the month.' There was still time for that to come true. He called his son to him and spoke to him as a man does on his death bed. Henry laughed the idea to scorn.

'Do you attach importance to the words of an old man spoken in anger?' he demanded.

It seemed that Geoffrey did, and as the night wore on, Henry began to believe that he might be right. He tried to convince his father that he was frightening himself to death just because a so-called prophet had made a pronouncement. But at length it was necessary to send for a priest, and by the morning Geoffrey was indeed dead.

There was a great deal of talk about Bernard's spiritual power. People remembered that he had prophesied the death of Louis's brother. Bernard it seemed could lay a curse on a man and that was what he had done to Geoffrey.

There would be new responsibilities for Henry now, but I had no doubt that he would be able to deal with them.

And then . . . Suger died. Louis was desolate. He had loved the old man, and I doubt a king ever had a better servant. He was buried with great ceremony at St Denis. When I attended the funeral, all I could think of as they laid him to rest was that the great obstacle to my freedom was removed.

There was Bernard now, and although he was my great enemy—and Suger had never been that—I believed he would help to get me what I wanted.

Suger had had a kingdom to hold together; Bernard had a soul to save. I was sure he thought I was descended from the Devil when he considered my grandfather and father; and I really did believe that he wanted to see me separated from Louis.

I went to work on Louis once more. I pointed out the need for divorce, for him to marry a woman who could give him sons, as I clearly could not. Why not start afresh with someone of whom God—and Bernard—could approve?

Bernard arrived in Paris, and Louis discussed the matter with him.

There was a degree of consanguinity, said Bernard, and it might well be that that did not find favour in God's eyes. Moreover my reputation would no doubt have offended the Almighty. When Bernard came down in favour of the divorce, I knew the battle was won.

Bernard worked his will. Very soon he had the barons believing that the best thing that could happen to France was that its King and Queen should be divorced.

At length it was decided that the case should be heard at the church of Notre Dame de Beaugency under the jurisdiction of the Archbishop of Bordeaux.

I took up residence at the nearby château after having given instructions that when a decision was reached it should be brought to me immediately. As soon as I had it and it was favourable—which it must be—I would make my way to my own dominions and there wait for Henry to join me.

There was only one matter which saddened me. I should have to part with my daughters. They must be declared legitimate. I had no fear on that point. Bernard was on excellent terms with the Pope, and they both favoured Louis; but of course as Daughters of France they would have to stay with their father, and I should lose them. I did love them, but my life had never been entirely dedicated to them. At that time I was not a woman to live only for my children; and the sexual hold which Henry Plantagenet had on me was greater than anything else. So I should have to reconcile myself to losing my daughters; but I had always known that if there was a divorce that would be an inevitable outcome.

I sat in the tower watching the church for the first sign of a messenger.

At last I saw the two bishops—one of them the Bishop of Langres—accompanied by two gentlemen, coming into the courtyard and I hurried down to meet them. The bishops were getting ready to make a long pronouncement but I said impatiently: 'I can wait no longer. Tell me, what was the verdict?'

'May we come inside?' one of them asked.

'No,' I said vehemently. 'No more delay.'

Seeing that I was determined the Bishop of Langres said: 'My lady, the Court has declared that the marriage is null and void on account of the close relationship between you and the King.'

I was overjoyed as I took them into the château.

Louis was near to tears when he said goodbye to me, and so was I when I took my farewell of my children. I promised them we should meet again and I hoped not before too long.

I told Louis he should marry again and this time he would get a son. It was his duty to do so, and it was what Bernard and the people wanted. He would have to do his duty towards them.

He shook his head miserably. The last thing he wanted to do was marry again.

Poor Louis! What a pity they would not allow him to go into a monastery.

But it was all over. There was no need for me to stay. I was free.

Now I could return to Poitiers. First I must send a message to Henry to tell him the news and that I would wait in my capital city for him to come to me.

And so I set off.

It was springtime, it was Easter, and the weather was perfect. I wondered how my people would receive me. They had always had an affection for me, but they might have heard of the somewhat scandalous life I had led. But what would they expect from my grandfather's grand-daughter? They had not been very pleased about the union with France. Perhaps they would be glad to welcome me back, but should I stay with them? How could I know what my future life would be with the man whom I had chosen to be my new husband? It was gloriously obscure, which was perhaps what made it so attractive.

I was all impatience to reach my destination and I urged my little party to move with speed. We spent the nights at various châteaux where we were given hospitality. Many of our hosts were as yet unaware that I was divorced from the King of France. I doubt whether it would have made any difference if they had known, but I felt it was a good idea not to mention it. They would know in due course. Such news travels fast, as I was to discover.

We were passing through the territory of the Count of Blois when we saw a party of horsemen approaching, led by a very good-looking young man. He leaped from his horse and almost prostrated himself before me.

'This is the greatest good fortune, my lady,' he said. 'I heard that you might be passing through my land and I prayed that I might discover you and your friends before you left. My castle of Blois is close by. The afternoon is drawing on. I shall deem it the greatest honour if you will rest under my roof.'

This was charming and I bade him rise. I thanked him for his offer and said we would be delighted to accept it. He was soon riding beside me, and his excited glances were an obvious indication of his admiration. I was accustomed to this of course and not greatly surprised to receive it; but I was no innocent, and it occurred to me that the young man might have some ulterior motive.

'I knew your father,' I said.

Memories came back, for this young man was the son of Thibault who had caused so much trouble at the time of Petronilla's marriage to Raoul of Vermandois.

We talked a little of the past and he told me he thought I should have more protection. I should have a bodyguard. 'Such an illustrious lady,' he said, 'should not ride with so few to care for her.'

'I am guarded enough,' I assured him. 'I am near my own home, and one feels safe among one's own people.'

He shook his head. 'I am glad I came upon you, for it gives me this chance to be your protector.'

I smiled and replied that I had always believed I was a woman who could look after herself.

'In so many ways, yes, but a strong arm and a loyal heart are good to have beside even the bravest of us.'

By the time we reached the castle I realized that he was aware of the divorce, and I imagined there would be one thought in his avaricious mind: Aquitaine. This was a lesson to be learned. There would be suitors—not so much for me but for Aquitaine. I must not forget that once more I was the richest heiress in France. I had emerged from my marriage with my lands intact. His talk of protection made me pensive. I thought of all the women who had been carried off by certain bold men. Dangerosa had gone willingly, others might not have done so.

What was in the mind of this young man? Would he take me to his castle? Would he attempt to seduce me? That I fully expected, but he was going to be disappointed there. But what if he held me prisoner? What if he forced me? Was that possible? I should be in his castle, surrounded by his minions. He would have an advantage over me, for in his own terrain he would have the means of keeping me captive.

I was not exactly alarmed but alerted.

At the castle a great welcome was given us. It was an interesting place and had been in the possession of the Counts of Champagne since the year 924. I had heard songs in my grandfather's Court about it. The first Thibault had been a fierce baron who had ravaged the countryside, taking all he wanted, including the women, and the whole neighbourhood went in fear of him. He was known as 'the Black Midnight Huntsman'. The present Count seemed mild in comparison but even with him I must tread warily.

The emblem of the place was a wolf. I thought it apt in view of the reputation of the first Count. The name 'Blois', I learned, comes from 'Bleiz' which means Wolf in the Carnute and Celtic languages. I had wondered why the first Count had adopted the name and called his castle after that most rapacious of animals, and whether the present Count was trying to follow in his ancestor's footsteps.

As he led me into the great building, his words sounded ominous. 'I shall do everything I can to make your stay here a long one.'

And I thought: I shall do everything I can to make it brief.

I said to him: 'You are indeed kind, Count, but I am in great haste to reach my city of Poitiers, and I shall be able to take advantage of your wonderful hospitality for only one night.'

He smiled wistfully but there was a gleam of something I did not quite like in his eyes.

He ordered that the finest bedchamber in the castle be prepared for me and he set them in the kitchen making a meal worthy of me.

So far so good. It was what was to be expected for the Queen of France.

One of the saddlebags containing what we should need for the night was unpacked, and I changed from my riding habit into a velvet gown, and wore my long hair loose about my shoulders. I was rather pleased with the result, for although I was determined to teach the Count a lesson, that did not mean I wanted to diminish my allure in any way.

I quite enjoyed the evening. I was seated at the table in the place of honour. My women, watchful, aware of the situation, were entertained graciously by the knights of the castle. Young Thibault gave all his attention to me. I was gracious to him and accepted his compliments with assumed pleasure. I allowed him to serve me with the food, which was excellent. The minstrels were pleasant, and I really felt I was close to Aquitaine and the old days.

He told me that my visit was the greatest honour which had befallen his castle.

'Oh come,' I said, 'you exaggerate.'

'Never,' he declared passionately. 'This is the happiest night of my life.'

He was drinking a great deal of wine and pressing me to do the same. It was something I never did, and I was certainly not going to on this occasion for as the night began to pass I grew more and more suspicious.

I told him how I admired his castle and how interesting it must be to remember his ancestors who had lived in it for so many years, especially the founder of the family, the Black Midnight Hunter.

'Oh, he was bold,' he said. 'He took what he wanted.'

'There are some like him today. I wonder if you are one, my lord.'

A sly glint in his eyes! Oh, yes, he had plans. And he thought he was getting on very well with me. I let him believe it, the arrogant young fellow. I compared him with my Henry. Surely he could not believe that I would consider him as a husband! His eyes were greedy . . . thinking of me in his eager hands . . . and Aquitaine to follow.

He said he would gladly lay his castle and its contents at my feet.

'You hold Blois lightly, my lord,' I told him.

'Nay, I treasure it beyond my other castles. It is why I would lay it at your feet. Only the very best would be good enough for you.'

'You should be grateful that I do not accept your offer.'

'Ah . . . if you would . . . I should be the happiest man on Earth.'

He is growing a little muzzy from the wine, I thought. He is going too fast. I decided to let him trip himself up.

'Well, Count, have you anything else to offer?'

'This hand,' he said. 'This heart.'

I laughed. 'That sounds like a proposal of marriage.'

Yes, indeed he was far gone. I saw the light in his eyes. He actually believed that I liked him. His arrogance angered me.

'I have never seen a woman as beautiful as you are, my Queen,' he said.

'I am Queen no longer. You know that, do you not?'

'I know it and rejoice in it . . . for myself, and condole with poor Louis.'

'That is charmingly said. I am also ruler of Aquitaine. You had not forgotten that, had you?'

'I can think of nothing but your beauty.'

'But Aquitaine is beautiful, too. Surely you will agree with that?'

'I daresay it is. But I had not thought of it.'

'Oh, had you not? It is not very clever of you to forget Aquitaine.'

'What I mean is that I am so deep in love with you that it would not matter to me if you were the lowest serving maid and not a great lady.'

'Then you are a man without discernment. One who does not see the advantages will not get very far in life, I fear.'

'You are laughing at me.'

'Forgive me. I thought you were laughing at me. Laughter is good for us. Let us enjoy it.'

'If I could realize my dearest dream and marry you, I should be the happiest man on Earth. I beg of you be kind to me. Tell me you will consider this. There is nothing I would not do for you. Please, please think of it.'

I did think: This has gone too far and is quite absurd. The man must think I'm a fool, and I could not forgive anyone for thinking that.

I said coolly: 'Let us have done with this farce, shall we? Of course I will not marry you.'

He looked quite taken aback. Oh yes, he was very drunk but there was a certain shrewdness in his eyes.

'I will never give up hope,' he said.

'Hope sometimes comforts even when the goal is quite out of

reach. And now, if you will indulge us, I should like to hear your minstrels once more before I and my ladies retire for the night.'

His tongue ran round his lips at my mention of retiring. Indeed he had plans and I must countermand them. He called for the musicians and I watched him as he listened to the songs of love. When it was over, I rose, my women with me.

'And now, my lord, I shall say good night to you.'

'I shall conduct you to your bedchamber.'

I bowed my head and we went, my ladies and I, the Count leading the way.

And there was my chamber with the ornate bed, the sight of which made his eyes glisten.

I turned to him. 'My thanks to you, Count. Your hospitality has been all that I could have expected.'

He put his face close to mine. 'If you should need anything . . .'

'I will remember,' I told him.

He went reluctantly and I immediately called my women to me.

I said: 'I do not trust the Count. He will attempt to come to this room tonight. Four of you will sleep here—and where is my esquire?'

They brought him to me—a fresh-faced young man, earnest and eager to excel, the sort who would be immune from bribes and therefore completely trustworthy.

'I am relying on you,' I said. 'You see me here, not exactly alone but with a small company compared with that which the Count could muster. I believe he wishes me ill and I would be prepared. Lie outside my door, across the threshold, all through the night. Let no one pass. If anyone should come, shout and draw your sword, threaten to slay him, no matter who he is. Tell him my orders are that you shall let no one pass. No one is to enter my room without my permission. Shout. Make a noise. Wake the whole castle.'

'I will defend you with my life, my lady.'

And I knew he would. How right I was. It must have been just after midnight when we heard the commotion outside the door.

My young esquire was declaring: 'On the Queen's orders no one passes this threshold.'

Then came the Count's blustering voice. 'You young fool, do you realize that this is my castle, my room? Everyone under this roof is either my servant or my guest.'

'My orders are, my lord, that no one passes.'

The Count must have realized that he was awakening the household. He was just sober enough to see that his best plan was to return to his own apartment. The silly young fool, if he wanted to make such plans, he should give them more consideration and above all keep a cool head. He should have studied my grandfather's methods.

I was temporarily safe but I must not stay another night in his castle. Perhaps even during this night the Count might sober up and the first thing such a bombastic young man would want to do would be to justify himself in my eyes and his own. He had means at his disposal; here in his castle he could easily subdue my little band. I must act promptly.

As soon as he had gone, I sent the esquire down to the stables to tell them they must make preparations to leave as soon and as quietly as possible. My ladies and I would make ready and join them in half an hour. We were in acute danger.

So, during that night, quietly we left Blois.

I often wondered what young Thibault thought when he awoke to find we had gone and that all his grand schemes for capturing Aquitaine had come to nothing. It would be a lesson to him— as it was to me.

The sooner I was married to Henry, the better; only then would I be safe from ambitious men.

We made our way out of Champagne to Anjou.

Anjou must be friendly territory. I surveyed it with pleasure. Anjou, Normandy . . . they were Henry's, and soon Aquitaine would be with them, and, in time, I was certain England. What a brilliant prospect! I was not only going to marry the man I loved but acquire great possessions as well. We were completely suited to each other in every way. What a happy conclusion this would be to all my tribulations.

We were riding along merrily when in the distance I saw a figure—a lonely one this time.

'It seems,' I said, 'that we have little to fear from one rider. I wonder who it is and why he rides with such urgency. I believe he is looking for us.'

This proved to be the case. The young man pulled up his sweating horse, leaped to his feet and knelt before me.

'My lady,' he stammered, 'I come to warn you. You are riding into danger.'

'From whom this time?' I asked.

'From one who calls himself my master—Geoffrey Plantagenet.'

I cried: 'The brother of the Duke of Normandy!'

He nodded. 'There is an ambush a mile or so from here. Because of your friendship with my true master, I was determined to warn you.'

'Who is your true master?'

'The Duke of Normandy. I served him well and would do so again. He gave me over to the service of his brother and I have never been happy since.'

'I see. So Geoffrey Plantagenet would waylay us. For what purpose?'

'He plans to marry you, my lady.'

'Indeed? They say these Plantagenets are the spawn of the Devil.' I smiled. That applied to Henry, too. So his little brother Geoffrey thought to trap me, Geoffrey the ne'er-do-well, the brother whom Henry despised.

I looked at the young man. I had learned to judge people and I trusted him. The recent experience with Thibault had sobered me considerably. There would be other upstarts who thought they could abduct me, perhaps even rape me and force me to marry them, just to give them possession of my rich duchy. It was the well-worn way in the past for gaining coveted lands. But these little men had not the gift for it.

I said: 'I believe you. You will ride beside me and lead us away from the ambush.'

So he did, and it was a pleasant experience for me because not only had I foiled the ambitions of Geoffrey Plantagenet but I was able to talk of my lover to one who knew him well.

There was no doubt that he idealized Henry. I was to discover that Henry had a certain quality which bound men to him. He was a born leader and never in the years to come did I doubt that.

The young man had been heartbroken when he had been assigned to the weak brother. He did not wish to serve Geoffrey Plantagenet, who was jealous of Henry and hated him. Their father, realizing the worth of Henry and the worthlessness of Geoffrey, had left the younger son only three castles.

'His father was a wise man,' I said.

'So I think, my lady, and when I heard that there was a plot to abduct you and force you to marry Geoffrey, I knew that was not what my lord Duke of Normandy would wish.'

'How right you were! I am grateful to you. I promise you that you shall stay in my household, and I think it very likely that I shall be able to persuade the Duke to give you back your place in his.'

How fortunate I was in that loyal servant of Henry's. When we reached Poitiers in safety, the first thing I did was to send the young man with a message to Henry to tell him that I was in my capital city, awaiting the coming of my bridegroom.

What joy to be home! I should never feel towards any other place that which I felt for my native land. The people welcomed me. They rejoiced in the divorce. They had never liked to feel they were under the yoke of France.

They shouted their greetings; they cheered me. 'Now Aquitaine will be the land of song again,' they said.

It seemed the whole world knew of the divorce. That troubled me not at all, but I did realize that my marriage to Henry must take place soon, for I had an idea that Louis would do everything he could to prevent it. The last husband he would have wanted for me would have been Henry. He would think, as all his ministers would: Anjou . . . Normandy . . . Aquitaine . . . that would make Henry almost as powerful as the King of France; and if he succeeded in taking the crown of England, he would be one of the most powerful rulers in Europe.

Louis, therefore, would be urged to prevent our marriage, which he might be able to do, because until Henry was King of England he was Louis's vassal.

I wanted no hindrances. There had been enough of those. What I wanted was the ceremony to be over quickly. I wanted to be Henry's wife at the earliest possible moment.

How wonderful it was to be once more in the Maubergeonne Tower. Memories of my grandfather came back to me. I thought: This will be once more the Court of Love.

I was a little pensive, for somehow I could not imagine Henry sitting on a cushion singing ballads. He never sat when he could stand; he was restless, a soldier, not a poet but a man of action. He was not gallant like my grandfather who had always known how to turn the gracious phrase; after all, he had been a poet of some standing. Henry was curt almost to the point of brusqueness; he did not pay compliments; one deduced from the intensity of his love-making that he found one desirable.

I would have to adjust my ideas to suit this most exciting of men, and this was what I would do. But even in the very depth of my obsession for him, I knew that I should always be myself, and that could not change for anyone . . . not even Henry.

There was a great deal to do. The French officials had left now, to the joy of the people. Aquitaine was mine to rule, and I must set about the task without delay. It was good for me to have so much to do, for the waiting was irksome. I appointed my advisers; there were many meetings with them. They must all swear fealty to me once again for I was now solely Duchess of Aquitaine in my own right and not Queen of France under the King.

I knew Henry would come as soon as he could. He would understand the need for speed. He wanted this marriage as much as I did. I would not allow myself to ask the question: Is it me he wants or Aquitaine? She was my rival, this beautiful country of mine. No one could assess me with her; but together we were the most desirable *partie* in Europe. I told myself I would not have had Henry indifferent to my possessions. He would have been a fool if he had been, and I was not a woman to tolerate fools.

Do not question, I admonished myself. Accept . . . and you will be the happiest woman on Earth.

At last he came. What a day that was! I saw his party in the distance, for I was ever watchful. So I was in the Courtyard to greet him. He leaped from his horse and lifted me in his arms, and I thought: This is the happiest moment of my life.

We must be alone together. We must make love. It had been so long that I had forgotten how exciting it was. He had arranged the wedding, which must take place without delay. He would not delay in any matter, I was to discover; and the wedding was no exception.

He was amused, guessing what a storm it would raise.

'At last you are free,' he said, 'because of your close relationship with Louis. What of our relationship, my love?'

'I know,' I answered. 'We are both descended from Robert of Normandy.'

'And not so far back! You and I are more closely related than you and Louis. There is a joke for you.'

'I know. I know.'

'And what will the King of France say when he hears you are married to me?'

'He will say . . . or his ministers will: "Anjou . . . Normandy . . . Aquitaine and possibly England".'

'That is just what they will say, and they will be wrong with their "possibly England". It is going to be "certainly England".'

'Of course.'

'I care not two bad pears for what Louis thinks.'

'Nor I. So why do we concern ourselves with him?'

'We shall not, though he could stop us if he tried. It's this matter of suzerainty. So let us get the deed over with . . . quickly. That is my wish. Is it yours?'

'It is. Oh yes, it is.'

'Then so shall it be. We do not want a grand ceremony. I should not in any case. I hate prancing about in fancy costume like a play-actor. You will have to take me rough like this.'

'I'll take you as you are,' I said.

'And you, my love, will have to be the elegant lady . . . but you are that without effort so I will accept it."

And so we talked and planned; and on that May day of the year 1152 in my native city, without the pomp and ceremony which is usually such an important part of the proceedings when people like Henry and myself are united, we were married.

It was a wonderful day—less than two months after the divorce for which I had so craved—and I was happy.

We had a little respite before we should be caught up in what must inevitably follow. They were exciting days which passed all too quickly. I had been carried away by the magnetic and overwhelming personality of this man; I had thought of little else but him since I had first seen him. I knew he was a great man, and my instinct told me that his life would be eventful and triumphant. I had known soon after I saw him that, above all things, I wanted to spend the rest of my life with him.

During those days I began to learn something of the man beneath the façade, and gradually the true Henry began to emerge.

Henry's Wife

The two weeks which followed my wedding were the most exciting, surprising and revealing I had ever known. I was idyllically happy. I had the man I wanted. But it became clear to me during the days after our wedding that I had a great deal to learn about my husband. When there is such an all-consuming physical passion as there was with Henry and myself, although one seems to grasp in an instant that there is complete sexual harmony, one can be quite ignorant about the person involved. Blinded by physical demands, one ignores characteristics which would be obvious in others.

When I looked at him, with his square, thick-set figure made for agility rather than grace, his bow legs, his wide, thick feet, his close-cropped sandy-coloured hair, his bullet-shaped head and his rough red hands, I marvelled that I, who had been brought up in the most elegant of Courts, could have this feeling for him. His eyes were grey and rather prominent but they were quite beautiful in repose; but I was to see them raging in fury, and then they had quite a different aspect.

He was different from anyone I had ever known. He conformed to no pattern. He hardly ever sat still. He would wander about a room as he talked; there was no refinement in his speech; he never couched his expression in soft words; what he meant to convey came out bluntly, right to the point. He did not care to sit and eat in a civilized manner. He seemed to think it a waste of time. Food did not greatly interest him. It was something one must take for nourishment, and that was all it meant

162

to him. I did not then ask myself why he had captivated me; during those two weeks when we were together every minute of the night and day I was obsessed by him.

He was well educated—his parents had taken care of that—and he was fond of learning. He had read a great deal, which amazed me in one so active. But as long as he was doing something which seemed to him worthwhile he was contented; and reading must have seemed that.

He had little admiration for poets and minstrels and regarded them with a certain contempt. When I look back, it seems to me that, if I could have chosen someone as completely different from myself as possible, I might have chosen Henry.

How we talked during those blissful days. He told me a great deal about his parents. There was no doubt that he had a great affection and admiration for his mother, the forceful Empress Matilda. He was proud of her although she did fail so dismally to regain her kingdom.

'It was hers by right,' he said. 'Was she not the daughter of the King? Stephen had no right to take England from her. She should have been Queen.'

'I should have thought the people would have rallied to her,' I replied. 'Was it because she was a woman that they turned to Stephen?'

'No. Stephen is as weak as water . . . but he has charm. He is affable. He is approachable. He smiles on them and they like him, in spite of the fact that he is ruining their country. Matilda . . . well, she is a haughty woman. She cannot forget that she was Empress of Germany. The English do not like her manner.'

'Did she not see that she was spoiling her chances?'

'My mother is not a woman to take advice. Her life has not been easy. She was five years old when she was sent to Germany to marry the Emperor. He was thirty years older than she. There she was made much of, spoiled for discipline for evermore: and when she was a little older, she became the Emperor's petted wife. She was unprepared for what was to follow; and when he died and she was brought home, she was twenty-three years old. She clung to the title of Empress—indeed, she still calls herself Empress now and insists that others do. She is a very forceful woman, my mother; and when at the age of twenty-five she was married to my father, she considered him far beneath her. She was ten years older than he, and she despised the boy of fifteen who was descended from the Counts of Anjou—who in their turn were descended from the Devil. Imagine it. Poor Mother.'

'Since she is so forceful, the daughter of a King and the widow of an Emperor, I wonder she did not refuse to marry him.'

'Her father was even more forceful. Matilda wanted the throne, so she was obliged to submit. For years she would have little to do with my father. She despised him and let him know it. Then after about six years she decided to do her duty and I was born. A year after me there was Geoffrey and after him William. So at length she produced the three of us.'

'You are fond of her and were fond of your father too.'

'They both did their best for me, but we boys were brought up in a Court where there was continual strife. I have never known two people hate each other as they did.'

'Perhaps it has made you strong.'

In turn I told him of my childhood, of those first five years spent in my grandfather's Court. I told of the *jongleurs* and their songs which enlivened the long evenings while the fires glowed and the light was dim. I told him of my bold grandfather and Dangerosa, and the miracle which Bernard had conjured up to show my father the error of his ways.

He told me of the beautiful woman who had wandered into his ancestor's castle and so charmed him that he married her, and how sons were born to her, how she always made excuses why she could not go to church and one day when she was prevailed upon to do so, she was confronted by the Host and suddenly disappeared and was never seen again.

'This is the story which gives rise to the legend,' he said. 'They say the woman came from Satan and that we Angevins are the spawn of the Devil.'

'Am I to believe that?'

'You will discover,' he replied.

They were wonderful days which I wanted to go on forever, but of course they could not. He was restless; he had lands to conquer. I should have to wait for these periods when we could be together. I told myself that they would be the more precious because I had to wait for them.

Henry had placed people all over France and England. He said that if one was going to take the right action one must know what the enemy planned. He must have as much information as possible. It was from one of his men that we heard about the reaction to our marriage at the French Court.

Louis had rarely been so startled.

How blind he was! He had seen me with Henry. Had he not noticed that overwhelming attraction between us? Of course he had not. What did Louis know of such emotion?

He was incensed. He and I had been divorced because of the closeness of our relationship and I had immediately married someone who was even closer. It was a blatant disregard for decency, the Church and the crown of France. Why, when it had been suggested that my elder daughter should marry Henry Plantagenet, this had been rejected because of the closeness of their blood, and now I, the mother, had the effrontery to marry the man myself.

The marriage must be dissolved at once.

Henry and I laughed at the idea. In our eyes, we were ideally suited and nothing on Earth was going to separate us.

We heard that, shocked beyond measure by the 'incestuous union', many of the French nobles were assembling at Court. Naturally, rejected suitors such as Geoffrey of Blois and Geoffrey Plantagenet raged in their indignation—although why the latter should complain of the blood tie between his brother and me when he was ready to commit the incestuous sin himself needs a little explanation.

The fact remained that they were gathering against Henry.

A messenger arrived at Poitiers. As Louis's vassals, Henry and I were to present ourselves to him to answer the charges against us.

Henry snapped his fingers at that. 'Louis will have to stop thinking of me as a vassal,' he said.

But when he had news from his spies that Louis was planning an attack, he was alert. He was not sure where the attack would come from. Aquitaine would be faithful, we knew; but Normandy was less secure. His brother Geoffrey was a traitor and there was nothing he would like better than to see Normandy wrested from Henry, of whom he had always been intensely jealous.

'I must go to Normandy without delay,' said Henry. 'You will be able to hold Aquitaine.'

I knew he was right. The honeymoon was over.

This was the kind of life to which I must become accustomed.

I must not complain. Now it was my task and great desire to prove to him that he really could rely on me in all things.

So we said goodbye and Henry rode away. I must fortify my castle and make my people aware of the French threat.

They were loyal to me—the more so because Henry was not here. They made it clear that they would fight for me, their Duchess, for I was their ruler, but they did not owe the loyalty to my consort that they owed to me.

I accepted that. In a way I was pleased by it. I had learned enough of Henry to know that he considered himself the master of all about him, and that included me. That was something I should have to teach him was not the case. I would do it gently, of course, but no man, not even Henry, was going to subdue me.

In our passionate moments he had murmured that he had never known a woman like me. He would have to remember that. No matter what power he had had over members of my sex in the past, no matter if it was the way of the world that men should rule, it should not happen with Eleanor of Aquitaine.

So in my fortress I waited while a watch was kept for the approach of the French.

Nothing happened. I knew Louis's reluctance to go to war and I am sure that a war against me would have an even greater repugnance for him. I heard he had turned his forces towards Normandy and there was no sign of hostility towards Aquitaine.

I thought a great deal about Louis's campaigns. Had there ever been one which was successful? It was hard to remember. Poor Louis, doomed to failure. What hope had he against a shrewd strategist like Henry?

News came of the progress of the battle. Henry was winning everywhere. I was amused to hear that his truculent little brother Geoffrey had now lost the three castles which had been left to him and caused such a grievance.

It was not long before Louis and his pathetic attempts at war were completed routed. Henry was victorious: Normandy was safe; and Henry returned to Poitou.

How happy we were to be together!

'It is good that this happened,' said Henry. 'It will teach

Louis a lesson. He will not wish to meddle in my affairs again in a hurry.'

He was delighted with all I had done. I could see that he thought our marriage a great success since we could work so well in unison.

I told him that Aquitaine must be wooed. The people were completely loyal to me, but they had never taken kindly to Louis and I wanted them to feel differently about Henry. He saw that I was right.

I said: 'We should make a tour of the country. We should stay in the castles. You must get to know them and let them see that this marriage of ours is a good one for them as well as us.'

He told me that England was very much on his mind. Stephen might not live much longer and when the time came he must be ready.

'Eustace will not meekly stand aside.'

'I do not think the people will want him.'

'Let us talk of these things while we are making our journey through my country.'

And this was what we did.

My people were wary of him, but it was heartening to see the enthusiasm with which they greeted me. They loved me. When I rode among them in my silk and velvet gown, with my hair flowing about my shoulders, they were enchanted. Henry, however, square and stocky, somewhat inelegant, was not their idea of the romantic lover; he did not match the heroes of the ballads they loved to sing; he was not the kind for whom lovesick maidens sigh.

Moreover, he was impatient. The nights we spent at the various castles brought no joy to him. He found it irksome to have to sit still so long. I was disturbed because I knew that, in spite of our passionate relationship, he wanted to be away in England.

The fact was that my people did not take to this uncouth man who had married their Duchess, but I did not know how greatly they resented him until we came to Limoges, where I saw a side to his nature which gave me twinges of alarm. We did not go into the town but encamped outside. This was a pity for if we had not done this, the trouble might not have arisen.

We had had a long day and were hungry. The cook came to me and told me in great distress that the town would provide no food for us.

Henry was present. 'And pray why not?' he demanded. 'And who has said this?'

'It was one of the servants of the castellan, my lord.'

'Bring him here to me this moment.'

The man was brought and stood trembling before Henry's wrath.

Henry had changed. His eyes were bulging; they were wild. I had never seen him like that before.

'What does this mean?' he demanded.

'My lord,' stammered the man, 'my master has said that the town of Limoges is not obliged to supply food to those encamped outside its walls.'

'Does your master know who comes?'

'Yes. It is the Duchess and her husband.'

That added to Henry's rage. Not the Duke and the Duchess, but the Duchess and her husband. It was how they regarded him. He thought this a slight to him—which it was probably intended to be.

I could well believe in that moment that he had the Devil's blood in him. His face was purple, his bulging eyes blazing with fury.

He strode out of the tent. I heard him shouting orders. I did not know at once what those orders were but when I did I was appalled.

The walls of the town were to be razed to the ground and the newly built bridge destroyed. In future when the *Duke* and Duchess of Aquitaine visited the town of Limoges there would be no insolent men to deny them hospitality because they had encamped *outside* their walls.

I suppose I could have countermanded the order. What if I had? What would have happened? What would he have ordered *me* to do? I was too stunned to act. I did nothing to stop the orders being carried out.

I thought afterwards: Suppose I had given orders that it was not to be done. There would have been war, I was sure . . . war between my people and my husband, and I should have stood with *them*.

It was the first time I was aware of those black rages of his. This was when I knew that there was a great deal to learn about my husband.

We left Limoges and continued our journey. It was not the same.

The news of what had happened spread through the duchy, and I noticed some sullen looks. My people would accept me and all my sins, for they were the sort of peccadilloes which they understood. The burning of the walls of Limoges was quite another matter.

Henry was very shrewd. He quickly assessed the people's attitude towards me and he was too clever to resent it. I realized that he was planning to leave me in control of Aquitaine while he looked after Anjou and Normandy—and of course his eyes were on England. There was nothing petty about his feelings. Everything about him was larger than life—even his rages.

During those first months of our marriage he endured those evenings when we sat and listened to the minstrels, but I knew he thought it all a waste of time. He was, though, studying those about us, deciding whom he could trust and of whom he would have to be wary. He was assessing the value of my property, considering what would be wanted for its defence if need be; and all the time he was noting the people's love and loyalty to me.

If I had ever thought of him as a malleable boy, I was rapidly learning my mistake. I might be eleven years older than he and that must give me some advantage, but it also meant that I had the understanding to know this man I had married and how I must act if I wished to keep him. An uneasy thought had occurred to me: that my feelings for him were stronger than his for me. I was as deeply sensual as he was; we were matched in that; but it did occur to me to wonder what happened when he was far away from me. He was hardly the man to put himself under restraint. I learned in those first few months that it was not going to be easy to keep such a man entirely mine. He had always had a reputation for promiscuity before marriage. He was lusty, looking all the time for conquest no matter in what direction. I was beginning to feel a little uneasy as I emerged from my first flush of passion.

But I was no weak woman. I was sure I would be able to deal with any situation which presented itself to me. In the meantime this wandering life had to come to an end. He was thinking of England.

I knew that he had to go and that I had to let him go. It seemed to be my fate to marry men who were absent from my bed. Louis had stayed away from choice; it was different with Henry. He was lusty, but ambition came first—so I thought then. I had to learn that this husband of mine was the sort of man who did not set great store by love when lust would suffice. For him the parting would not be such a wrench for he would casually indulge in sexual relationships whenever the opportunity arose— and such opportunities were strewn in his path. That had always been a way of life, and his marriage would not alter that. This I had yet to discover, and fury possessed me when I did.

I should have known, of course. I should have been more worldly. He did care for me in a way. He admired me as he did his mother, recognizing that both of us were exceptional women of intelligence and experience. He was not one of those men who thought of women as naturally inferior. Only when they were did he think so. He respected me as he did his mother, but I was to discover that the idea of remaining faithful to me had never occurred to him.

At this time I was still living in a romantic glow, although the affair at Limoges had opened my eyes a little and set warning bells ringing in my mind. I had begun to understand that he was not quite what I had thought him.

He talked to me glowingly of his plans. He could not rest idly anywhere, and there was a task to be completed. He had to wrest his heritage from the supine Stephen and his useless Eustace, as he called then. For this he needed an army, and armies cost money. He needed a great deal of money. I could supply some but not all that was necessary. He had to set about finding it without delay.

He was going to Normandy, from where he would doubtless cross the Channel. His mother would do all she could to help, and she would guard Normandy while he was in England. My task was to keep Anjou, with Aquitaine, safe for him during his absence.

He discussed this at length when I should have preferred to hear his protestations of fidelity and undying love, and his sorrow because of our enforced parting. But Henry would not waste time on such trivialities. The preliminaries to love-making did not appeal to him. They were a waste of time. We both knew what we wanted; there was no need for wooing. He wanted to talk of plans.

I was to go to Anjou, for my presence would be needed there more than in Aquitaine, where I could rely on the loyalty of my subjects.

I agreed with all this. I did suggest that it might be better if he tarried until the spring, for if he went now he would arrive in England in the winter. Would that be wise?

He said he would have preferred the spring but must perforce make do with the winter. And that was an end of the matter.

So he went to Normandy and I to the castle of Angers, where I settled down to wait for his return, praying that it would be a triumphant one.

To my joy I found that I was pregnant. I laughed inwardly, thinking of all the barren years with Louis. So it *was* his fault. I had always suspected that it was; there was bound to be something less than a man about Louis. But a woman does get uneasy feelings when she wants desperately to conceive and cannot; and it is only natural that she begins to wonder whether the lack of fertility is in some way due to herself.

I was happy; this was the best time for pregnancy, with Henry absent, and it brought with it a certain serenity which made life very pleasant.

I filled the castle with troubadours so that it resembled the Court of my grandfather. Petronilla, a widow now, came to join me and we were as close as ever. A mother herself, she had a great deal in common with me; and we both loved those evenings of song. We would sing together and talk of the old days.

I was very interested in one of the troubadours, Bernard de Ventadour, who reminded me so much of the old days. He was a fine poet and had a wonderful singing voice. I was very glad that he had come to the Court—and his coming itself had been quite romantic.

He had been wandering through the country looking for a castle where he might rest for a while and ply his profession of poet and musician. I supposed he had heard that I was in residence, and so, knowing how I cared for poetry and music, he presented himself at the castle. He had a certain arrogance which I found not displeasing. He dared to ask if he might see me.

Always interested in musicians I allowed him to be brought to me. He behaved in a manner to which I had become accustomed in my father's Court and which I had missed since I married Louis. He prostrated himself and when I bade him rise he gazed at me, his eyes blinking as though he were in a very bright light.

I was amused.

'Forgive me, my lady,' he said. 'I am dazzled.'

He was implying by my beauty, of course. I smiled. It was so reminiscent of the old days.

'You wish to sing for us here?' I asked.

'It is my great desire to do so.'

'Are you a good musician?'

'I have been told so, my lady.'

'How is it that you have no place to go to?'

'I had, my lady, until I was turned adrift.'

'Did you displease your master?'

He put his hand to his heart. 'It was a misunderstanding, my lady.'

'Between you . . . and a lady?'

'Between me and a lady's husband.'

I could not help smiling at the audacity of the man. 'Let me hear you sing,' I said.

His voice was exquisite, and the words of the song were romantic and poetic. I was enchanted.

'Your own words?' I asked.

'My lady, I write my own songs. Then only can I express what I feel.'

He was one of those troubadours who would have been welcomed at my grandfather's Court, and I made him welcome in mine.

How glad I was. He fulfilled a need in my life. All through those months while I was awaiting the birth of my child I listened to his songs—and they were all written for me. Every word, every gesture expressed his admiration for me. I liked it. It comforted me and in a way compensated for Henry's absence.

It amazed me how a man of such humble beginnings—he was said to be the result of a liaison between a soldier and a serving maid—could be endowed with the soul of a poet; but Bernard de Ventadour undoubtedly was. There was an exquisite refinement about his verses which was the very essence of romance. They made me feel precious, cherished, high above all other women.

There was no question of physical love between us. I just luxuriated in his admiration and the beautiful use of words which

soothed the longing for Henry; and I thought the perfect existence would be with two men close to me—one to satisfy my
physical needs, the other to assuage that inherent longing for
romantic and unattainable love. So I dreamed of Henry's return
and listened nightly to the songs of Bernard de Ventadour.

In August my child was born—a son. I was delighted—not
that I would denigrate my own sex in any way but I did know
that Henry would want a son, and when all was said and done,
it did please the people to have a male heir. When I thought of
all those wasted years with Louis, and Suger's eagerness and
certainty that if we went on trying we would succeed, and St
Bernard's grim disapproval, I laughed out loud. And here I was
soon after my marriage with Henry producing the longed-for
boy. St Bernard had died a short time ago. It was a pity that
neither he nor Suger would know what had happened.

I was devoted to the child, more so than I had been to Louis's
girls. I suppose it was because this one was Henry's and when
Marie was born I was already heartily tired of Louis. I had had
no joy in my marriage. But this was different. I longed for the
news to reach Henry that he had a son.

There was some news of Henry during that winter. Occa-
sionally someone would arrive at the castle who had a little to
tell. I knew he was in England. I heard of some success, but
there was nothing definite.

It was spring before I saw him. Little William was then eight
months old, not as sturdy as I should have liked him to be, but
I was assured that children were often frail for the first months
of their lives.

Henry went first to Normandy and then came on to Anjou.

It was wonderful to see him. We embraced fiercely and gave
way to all the longing of the past months. Our desire for each
other had not abated; rather had it intensified after our absence.

He was delighted with little William. Here was another side
to his nature. I was amazed to see how tenderly he picked up
the child and lifted him high in the air . . . laughing happily. It
was wonderful to see him thus.

He was very eager to tell me what was happening. That was
really what was uppermost in his mind.

He had had the most amazing good fortune. It really did seem
as though God were on his side.

'I landed at Wareham,' he said, 'which is on the coast of

England, with 140 men-at-arms and 3,000 infantry. I went straight to Bristol. Far-sighted men have seen that Stephen is not good for the country. He is affable and charming, but affability and charm do not necessarily make good rule. A king has to be strong . . . and it is being seen what is happening to the country over the years of this man's rule.'

'There must have been a great deal of disruption when your mother was at war with Stephen,' I said.

'It is not good for the country. In my grandfather's day, England prospered. The English are seeing what a difference a strong ruler makes. My great-grandfather, the Conqueror, and my grandfather, King Henry, were strong; they introduced good laws which the people obeyed. There is anarchy throughout the country now because of Stephen's soft rule. And there are those who believe in me. They know that I am made of the same stuff as the Conqueror and King Henry, and they are right, by God. So they acclaimed me at Bristol. They were for ousting Stephen and making me their King.'

'This is most heartening.'

'You have not heard all. We marched to Malmesbury and laid siege to the castle. We took the outer fortifications with speed, but the keep was too strong so we had to fall back on the siege. Stephen was by this time alerted and he came with his army to the relief of Malmesbury Castle. Now listen to this. This is like Divine Providence. There is a little river there, the Avon. It became so swollen that Stephen could not cross it. The rain started to fall in torrents; the wind was strong and it drove the rain right into the faces of Stephen's men while we had it on our backs. They simply could not march forward or even stay where they were. Stephen is not the most resourceful of commanders. To him there was only one thing to do. He turned his army round and marched back to London. So the castle fell into our hands.'

'What great good fortune.'

'It was a sign.'

'I did not know you believed in such things.'

'I do when they are in my favour.'

I laughed with him. It was so good to have him back.

'What then?' I asked.

'We had to go to Wallingford. That was one of the main purposes of our visit to England. Brian FitzCount of Wallingford has been a loyal supporter of mine for years. He was my mother's, and when she retired and left the field to Stephen and there was comparative peace in the country, he carried on the war . . . he and a few others. He has been doing good work for me, and Stephen's men had reached the stage when they were besieging him in his castle. He sent word to me that he needed help; I had to go to his aid. So after our success at Malmesbury we marched to Wallingford.'

'Looking for further help from Heaven?'

'If we needed it, yes. I knew that on equal terms we were a good match for Stephen. He might have an army but an army needs a commander, and I did not think Stephen had much heart for the battle.'

'He sounds like Louis.'

'Not quite like that, but nevertheless he is not a man designed for war. The two armies faced each other. Our men were ready for the fight. But to my amazement word was brought to my camp that Stephen wished to parley with me. So we met face to face. He had his advisers with him and I had mine. There was a strong feeling that a battle when we might be killed and our armies decimated could do no good to the country. We were both being rash. It might well be that some compromise could be worked out. Why did we not agree to a truce while we both considered our rival claims, and perhaps some solution could be found? To tell the truth, I was not averse to a little respite, and I certainly got the best of the bargain, for Stephen agreed to withdraw his garrison from Wallingford and raise the siege. So I had achieved what I wanted without a battle.

'Now this is where he had another sign from Heaven. Eustace has always been a fool. As ineffectual as his father, he lacked his charm and his goodness. That is something for which we have to be grateful. He was furious when he heard of the truce. He thought his father was playing into my hands. He has always been jealous of me. I am sorry for Stephen. He has two sons—Eustace one of them and the other young William who is without ambition and would not take the crown if it were handed to him. Eustace is—or was—the only bar to the throne. But for him it could have come to me naturally.

'Now listen. Eustace went off on a little war of his own, ravaging the countryside and the castles of all those whom he suspected of being favourable to me. His little adventure took him to Cambridgeshire, where he began plundering the lands which belonged to the monastery at Bury St Edmunds. The monks naturally protested. He then went to the monastery itself and demanded that the monks give him the treasure that he might pay his soldiers. They replied that they would offer him hospitality, as it was the rule of the monastery to give that to all travellers, but they had no intention of parting with their treasure. Eustace demanded of them whether they knew who he was. He was the son of the King—their King-to-be. If they did not hand over the treasure he would plunder their harvest and the corn should be taken to his castle. The monks quietly bowed their heads and he believed they would give up their treasure. They said they would prepare a meal for him which they did.

'But scarcely had Eustace taken a mouthful of the dish of eels which they set before him than he fell writhing to the floor. He was dead within an hour.'

'It does look like Providence.'

'Those monks have done a great service to their country. Eustace is no more. William does not want the crown. You see?'

'And Stephen?'

'I could find it in my heart to be sorry for him. He is a mild man. He lost his wife recently and she meant a good deal to him. And now he has lost his elder son and heir. Perhaps the reason why he felt he must go on fighting was to retain the throne for Eustace.'

'So the way is clear. But there is still Stephen.'

'We have had a meeting. This is an end of war. He has named me his heir and is very affectionate towards me. He is to be King of England until his death, and then I shall be accepted as his natural heir.'

'It is wonderful . . . but he could live for ten years.' He nodded gloomily. 'Heaven has been kind to you so far.'

'There is a great deal to be done in England. It has been ill-governed since the death of my grandfather. I am to have a say in affairs while Stephen lives. He will listen to me.'

'A great task awaits you. Let us hope you will not have to wait too long. And now you will stay here with your wife and son?'

'I must go to Rouen,' he said. 'I have business there.'

'You are surely not going away again!'

'I must. I shall shortly be going back. Why do you not join

me in Rouen? My mother wishes to know you. She will want to see the child.'

I was overjoyed. So we were not to be parted so soon. And one day I should be beside him when he claimed the crown of England.

Henry had gone to Rouen and I was to follow as soon as I could make arrangements to do so. I was very excited and faintly apprehensive at the prospect of meeting my notorious mother-in-law, Matilda. I remembered another mother-in-law, Adelaide of Savoy. I had been only a very young girl when I had first been confronted by her and she had greatly resented me. She had deplored the influence I had had over Louis and we had been enemies from the day we met. It was true the final victory had been mine and she was the one who had found it expedient to leave Court. Matilda, I felt, would be quite a different proposition.

I both longed and dreaded to meet her.

I was very much aware of the strong bond between Henry and Matilda. He admired her immensely; he liked to hear her opinions, and I knew he took her advice now and then. I felt she would be almost like a rival, and if I was prepared to resent her, how did she feel about me?

I was extremely anxious when we stood face to face, but almost immediately I began to feel more at ease. She was very handsome still; she must have been about fifty at this time; and there was great dignity about her. I drew myself up to my full height, determined to let her see that I was a match for her. I need not have done so. Her shrewd eyes surveyed me with approval, and suddenly it struck me that we were two of a kind. We understood each other, and that meant we appreciated each other.

A certain hauteur disappeared and she took my hands and smiled at me.

She said: 'You are a beautiful woman. I am glad for Henry.'

Then she kissed me.

Henry was watching us and I was delighted to see how pleased he was by the rapport between his mother and me.

She had arranged that there should be a great welcome for us at the castle.

Those were happy days with Henry, basking in his approval

because his mother liked me, showing my son to his grand-mother and enjoying the delights of family life. It would not be for long though. Henry would never stay in one place. His do-minions were too far flung. There was trouble from one of the vassals. There were always rebels seizing opportunities for mak-ing trouble.

Henry was at this time deeply immersed in the affairs of England, for when Stephen had sworn that he should have the throne after him, he had made him co-ruler, so that Henry needed to know exactly what was going on, and was indeed preparing for the time when he would be King. Stephen knew that his own rule had been weak, and Henry was trying to rem-edy that. Not that he could do a great deal until the crown was actually his, but his mind teemed with possibilities. Messengers were constantly going back and forth between Henry and Ste-phen. Therefore to hear of trouble in those dominions over which he already had sway infuriated him.

It was at this time that I saw him in one of those rages which amazed and alarmed me and which later I was to dread. I really believed the story of the devil woman who was the ancestress of the Counts of Anjou when I saw him writhing on the floor, his ruddy face purple, his eyes bulging, shouting blasphemies and rolling about biting the rushes. He was like a man possessed.

I really thought he had gone mad.

Fortunately Matilda explained to me.

'He has these fits of temper,' she said. 'He always has had. He is so enraged that he has to give vent to his feelings.'

'He is wasting his energy.'

'He has plenty to spare. He will recover quickly and take action. Then he will give all his energy to teaching these men a lesson.'

I remembered the walls of Limoges. There was yet something else I had to learn of him.

Matilda was right. In a short time the fit was over; his energy was unimpaired. Within a few hours he had gathered together his men and was riding off to deal with the recalcitrant rebel.

Matilda and I were often together. She heartily approved of the marriage. She was without sentimentality and I doubted she would have welcomed me into the family circle but for my pos-sessions. But she liked my good looks and good health.

'You will have many children,' she prophesied.

'One needs opportunities,' I reminded her. 'I have never had a surfeit of those.'

'Henry has the energy of ten men and you, my dear, are no frail flower. There will come a time when you and he will be together more often, although of course a king is always roaming far and wide if he looks after his country as he should. There is lusty blood on both sides of Henry's family and on yours too if I have heard aright. It will be one of the happiest days of my life when I see Henry on the throne of England.'

'There may be many years before that comes to pass.'

'Who knows?' said Matilda.

I was very amused to hear that Louis had married again. His bride was Constance of Castile. Poor Louis, one thing I could be sure of—he would be a reluctant bridegroom.

I wished him luck and I wondered what Constance would be like, and how she would relish those nights in a cold bed while he was on his knees praying . . . for what? Courage to approach his wife? I could never feel anything but a mild and slightly contemptuous affection for Louis.

Matilda and I grew close during that period. She liked to talk of the past. I recalled mine, too—life at the Courts of Love, marriage with Louis, my adventures in the Holy Land. We had both lived dangerously.

I learned much about her and grew fond of her, but I could see clearly why the people of England had rejected her. Her life was a lesson to us all—but then I suppose most people's lives are.

She talked vividly of herself and I think she was glad to have an audience of a kindred spirit. She made me see how alarmed she must have been when, at the age of five, she was told that she was going to Germany. What effect would that have had on a child of her age to be told that she was going to be sent away from her home and all that was familiar to her, to be the wife of a great man—an Emperor who was thirty years older than she?

'I was lucky,' she said. 'Like you, I had good looks. What a boon they can be! Henry, my husband, was a kindly man and he liked the look of me from the start. But he sent all my English attendants away—they always do. They want to make you one of *them*. So I was German, my upbringing, my outlook. I spoke in German; I thought in German; I was the little German my husband intended me to be. But the English do not like the German ways, it seems. I was crowned almost as soon as I arrived—that was when I was betrothed to Henry. I remember how the Archbishop of Trier held me reverently in his arms while the Archbishop of Cologne put the crown on my head. And when I was twelve years old Henry married me and once again I was crowned. He was kind to me; he seemed to me a very old man. Thirty years is a great deal—particularly when one is very young. But I was happy with him, and it was a great blow when he died.'

'Were you with him when he died?'

'Yes, I was. It was in Utrecht. He wanted me at his bedside when he was dying and he put the sceptre in my hands. He wanted everyone to know that he left his dominions to me. How strange it is that one is so greatly loved at certain times of one's life and then . . . the whole world turns cold towards one.'

'You have your son Henry,' I reminded her.

'Yes, we are close, my son and I. I want for him all that I have missed.'

'And it seems he is going to get it.'

'I have never doubted that he would succeed. He is made for distinction.'

We could agree on that.

'Tell me of your marriage to Geoffrey of Anjou,' I said.

Her face hardened. 'How I hated him! And he hated me, too. How different he was from my Emperor. I thought I should be loved in England as I had been in Germany. My father made the barons swear fealty to me. He was afraid, of course, that as I was a woman there might be a dispute about my taking the throne when he was gone.'

'And he was right.'

'I was furious when he married me to Geoffrey of Anjou.'

'Could you not have refused?'

'You did not know my father.' A gleam of admiration came into her eyes. 'He was quite different from Stephen. That is why Stephen shows up as such a weakling. There was nothing weak about King Henry. He was determined to have a law-abiding country and he had one. He made stern rules. He had to, after Rufus who was no good at all and undid a good deal of the work which his father, the Conqueror, had set in motion. It is very important for a country to have a strong King.'

I nodded vigorously, thinking what had happened in France because of a mischievous pig.

'I protested,' she went on. 'But it was no good. And they sent me to Anjou. I hated him on sight. He was a boy of fifteen.'

'He was exceptionally handsome.'

'I did not care if he were Adonis. I had no wish to marry a foolish boy. It was an indignity. Ten years younger than I. I was not a little girl any more. I was a young woman. I had been an Empress. I had been treated with the utmost respect by my husband and all those about me. In fact, they had implored me not to leave Germany. I could have stayed there. I was their Empress.'

'I think I should have done so.'

'My father would have insisted that I return. You cannot know the power of that man. But even he realized the marriage was a mistake. He might have made Geoffrey marry me but he could not make us live together. We quarrelled all the time. He hated me as much as I hated him. He drove me out of Anjou and I went to Rouen and then to England, but for political reasons we had to be together again. I realized the need for heirs and so did he, and in spite of our dislike for each other we lived together, quarrelling incessantly, of course, but at least giving us the chance to produce a child. I have never regretted that.'

'It gave you Henry.'

'And he has been the most important person in my life ever since.'

'What of the other children?'

'Geoffrey was born a year after Henry. You have already heard of him.'

'Yes, it was his idea to capture me and force me to marry him, but that was just after my divorce from Louis.'

'He will never succeed in anything. And then there is William. But for me, Henry is the one.'

'For us both,' I said.

'I realize that he has married a woman who is worthy of him.'

'It makes me happy that you should approve of the match,' I said honestly.

'I could do no other. I would not be so foolish as to say that your lands do not count. They do . . . enormously. You have made him mightier. He now owns more of France than the King of that country. That is through you. And now, of course, there is England.'

'You must regret after all your efforts that you did not succeed in taking it from Stephen.'

She nodded. 'It was mine by right. I was the daughter of the King . . . his only legitimate direct heir.'

'It is this infuriating prejudice against women.'

'Which we have both had to overcome. Never mind, my dear, it is a fact that we rule far more than is generally realized. But people will always choose a man rather than a woman. When my father died and I heard they had chosen Stephen, I was mad with rage. I appealed to Rome . . . but like everyone else the Pope decided in favour of a man. I did have my half-brother, Earl Robert of Gloucester—one of my father's illegitimate sons and a good brother to me—to help me. He came to Anjou and later, with him, I landed in England, with 140 knights who were ready to support my cause. People began to rally to my banner.' Her eyes shone at the memory.

'And you were successful?'

'Oh yes, I was successful for a while. They accepted me as the true heiress. The late King was my father. I was the closest to the throne. They had to admit this was so, so I captured him. Eleanor, Stephen was my prisoner! I sent him in chains to Bristol Castle. How well I remember that triumphant progress through England. The people acclaimed me. They wanted me then.'

I looked at her steadily. She was staring ahead, reliving it all. I saw the haughtiness in her face: Matilda, Queen of England.

'I came to London. I did not wait for my coronation. I declared myself Queen. I was determined to rule as my father had. I told myself that I must show no weakness. The very fact that I was a woman meant that I must display my strength at every turn. I must not allow any one of them to take advantage of me. I know now that I was too proud. They did not like me and I did not understand them. They are not disciplined like the Germans . . . and I was a German.

'I did not know these people whom I planned to rule. They did not protest. They appeared to accept what I did. And then suddenly they rose against me as one. They turned me out of London. There was only one thing I could do . . . hasten to Oxford. I reached there in safety but I did not stay there. I had to get to Winchester to talk with the Bishop there. He had supported me but I had heard he was considering turning back to Stephen as the people had shown so clearly their rejection of me.'

She turned to me and gripped my hands.

I said: 'Would you rather not speak of it?'

She shook her head, and a look of scorn came into her eyes. She was a woman who would always despise weakness, most of all in herself.

'I think that stay in Winchester was one of the most horrifying experiences of my life. I had forced my way into the city, and no sooner had I taken possession of it than it was stormed by Stephen's followers. He was still a prisoner in Bristol Castle but his wife—another Matilda—had rallied an army to fight for his cause. She was one of those good, gentle women who surprise everyone by their strength when it is necessary to show it. Sometimes I think they are really the strong ones. She was with the army which besieged the city.

'Have you ever thought what it would be like to be within the walls of a city when the foodstocks are dwindling daily and everywhere people are dying of sickness and starvation? I hope, my dear, that you never experience it. I knew that we could not continue much longer, and when the city was taken I should fall into the enemy's hands. I should take Stephen's place. I should be their prisoner. I would rather face death than that. Humiliation . . . indignity . . . they are something I could never endure.

'Stephen's wife, Matilda, was a humane woman. All she wanted was our surrender and the release of her husband. She did not want revenge. I thought then what a fool she was, for out of the kindness of her heart she allowed us to take our dead out at night, passing freely through the guards, so that the corpses might be given a Christian burial. One day I was watching one of these sad ceremonies—the bier, the rough coffin, the body wrapped in a winding sheet—and an idea came to me.'

She smiled at me, her eyes sparkling. She was a woman whose face betrayed her feelings. I could well imagine that she had not been able to hide her contempt for her humble subjects, and this was the main reason why she had lost her throne.

'I saw my way out. I should be a corpse. I should be wrapped in a winding sheet and placed in a coffin, and so I should be borne out of the city gates and through the guards to safety.'

'What a daring plan! And it worked?'

'I remember it clearly . . . even now. I awake at night thinking of it. It seemed an unending journey through those guards.
I could hear their voices and I lay, still as Death, in my rough-
hewn coffin, the sheet over my head, scarcely daring to breathe,
and I thought what a fool the saintly Matilda was, to have made
such a procedure possible.'

'And when you had passed the guards were there horses waiting for you?'

She shook her head. 'No, there could not be. All I knew was
that I could get help at Wallingford, so there was nothing to do
but make our way there on foot.'

'And you did that?'

'It is surprising what one can do when one has to.'

'But what a triumph!'

'Shortlived. From Wallingford I went to Oxford. There I
hoped to rally help and continue the fight. Unfortunately, in
attempting to escape from Winchester my half-brother Robert
of Gloucester was captured by the Queen's men. This was a
bitter blow to me because he was my greatest general, one of
the few in whom I could have complete trust. Queen Matilda
bargained with me. The release of Stephen for Robert. I stood
out for a long time, but at length I saw that I had to have Robert
back and I gave way, so Stephen was freed.'

'And so was Robert.'

'Oh, my good brother! He came to Oxford. He said we could
not continue without help. I had sent messengers to Anjou asking Geoffrey to come to my aid, but my husband ignored my
request. Robert said he would go to Anjou himself. He would
impress on Geoffrey the urgency of the situation and see if he
could induce him to come to my assistance. I was loth to lose
Robert but at length I agreed, and he went. It was then that
Stephen—now freed—came against me and the castle was
besieged. Can you imagine my feelings?'

'Indeed I can. You had escaped in a shroud only to find yourself in a similar position.'

'And there is nothing more depressing. Moreover, it was winter, for the siege had lasted three months. It was the same as it
had been before . . . lack of food, sickness and what looked
like inevitable surrender. "I will not fall into Stephen's hands,"
I said. "I will not. I will not." And those about me just looked

at me sadly and shook their heads. They did not understand my fierce determination.

'I sat at my window. The wind was blowing a blizzard, and the river below my window was one thick sheet of ice. It would be weeks before it melted even though the weather changed tomorrow. Then I had an idea. There was no moon. Clad in white, one would not be distinguished from the scenery . . . and on the other side of the river was freedom.'

I caught my breath in admiration for this woman. I was not surprised that Henry admired her so fervently. She was indomitable.

'I sent for a dozen men I trusted,' she went on. 'I told them the plan. We should wrap ourselves in white furs and let ourselves down from the window onto the ice, and silently we would cross it to the bank. And that, my dear daughter, is what we did.'

'And when you had crossed the river?'

'Then we walked . . . in that bitter wind, we walked. But my spirits were lifted because once more I had had a miraculous escape. It was six miles to Abingdon. It seemed more like forty. But at last we arrived. There we found horses and made our way to Wallingford.'

'I suffered great hardship during our crusade, but I think you suffered more.'

'I had a cause to fight for and that buoys up the spirit. It carries one through adversity.'

'But you had so many defeats.'

'Yes, but I always thought that in the end I should succeed. I was not sure how, but I was the rightful heiress of England and I believed that justice would be done in the end.'

'Tell me what happened at Wallingford.'

'We were exhausted. We took food first, I think, and then we slept and slept . . . and I had the most wonderful awakening. When I opened my eyes, standing by my bed was the one I loved best in the world: my boy Henry. I thought I was dreaming. I struggled up and stared at him. He flung himself into my arms. "I am here, Mother," he said. "Uncle Robert brought me. I am here to fight for you." It took me some time to realize that he was actually beside me. But there also was my good brother Robert. He had been to Anjou. He had not been able to bring Geoffrey, that wastrel husband of mine, but he had brought my beloved son.

'What a joyful reunion that was! What a day! After that night of adventure to come to this. I shall never forget that descent on ropes down to the cold ice; and then to come here and find my boy waiting for me . . . it was wonderful.' She smiled and the softening of her face was remarkable. 'Just a boy . . . but ready to fight. You know the power of him. He only has to appear to make you feel that because he has come all will be well. Do you feel that too, my dear?'

I nodded, feeling too moved to speak.

'I think you know the rest. It is common knowledge. Robert brought up my boy to be a soldier, but my cause was a lost one. The people of England had rejected me . . . and they would continue to do so. I might be the King's daughter, but to them I was a German and they do not like Germans. Stephen, for all his weaknesses, was preferable.

'My brother Robert was very wise. He knew that further fighting could only bring us defeat, and I could not hope for more miraculous escapes. I had been lucky to have achieved that twice. It would be tempting fate, said Robert, to hope for more. But he had great belief in Henry. ''One day,'' he said, ''he will take what is his but we must wait for that day.'' I knew he was right and I believed that although the people of England would not accept me, when the time came they would take Henry.

'There was nothing vindictive about Stephen . . . nor about his wife. They wanted peace. She was a deeply religious woman; he was easy-going. That was well for us. I stayed in England for five years after that, living mostly at Gloucester or Bristol. And meanwhile Henry was growing up . . . learning to become a soldier. Robert took charge of his education, too. I have Robert to thank, in part, that Henry is the man he is today.'

'And it has all worked out well. England will one day be Henry's.'

'With no more fighting. When Stephen dies . . .'

'That cannot be very long now,' I said.

'Five years . . . ten years. In the meantime Henry has a great deal to look after here. There will always be vassals ready to seize opportunities to rebel. But I thank God that in time he will be King of England.'

The bond between us was growing stronger. She had shown me a vulnerable side to her nature which few saw. In her turn she understood my feelings for Henry, and each day she let me know in many ways how contented she was with the match.

She was delighted when I was able to tell her that I was pregnant once more.

'You will be the mother of many sons,' she said, and she embraced me warmly. 'Sons,' she went on. 'Although I deplore this denigration of our sex, what power they bring to a family.'

'I wish William's health was better.'

She nodded gravely. 'You will soon have others, my dear. The only way to guard against sorrow in one's children is to have a quiverful.'

Now our talk was all of babies. I often smiled to think of two women such as we completely absorbed in this domestic talk.

It was October. Henry had not yet returned when a messenger arrived at the castle. He came from the Archbishop of Canterbury.

Stephen had died unexpectedly of a flux. Henry, Duke of Normandy, was now King of England; and it was imperative that he cross the sea at once and lay claim to his kingdom.

Messages were immediately sent to Henry. He came to Rouen without delay. There was no time for anything but intensive preparation. He was taking an army with him, for how did he know what he would find on the other side of the Channel?

'You must come with me,' he said. 'You must be crowned with me. A king is not a king until he has been crowned.'

Matilda's eyes were shining with triumph.

'It is the moment I have been waiting for,' she said. 'Everything will be worth while now.'

'You must come with us,' cried Henry. 'You must see me crowned.'

'And what of Normandy? Because of this great prize, are you going to forget your lesser possessions?'

He threw back his head and laughed.

'Is not my mother a great general? Let me tell you this: there is not one that I value as I do her.'

So she must remain in Normandy and we should set sail.

It was with emotion that I bade her farewell.

'Alas that you are not with us,' I said.

'My place is here,' she answered.

'It is sad that after all you have done you cannot see him anointed.'

'I shall be happier here knowing that Normandy is safe.'

So we left, my baby William with us and the other in my womb. Petronilla was in my suite. It was comforting to have my family around me.

And so to Barfleur to embark for England.

Queen of England

The waves were lashing the coast; the wind shrieked a warning to all mariners; and we were drawn up at Barfleur contemplating that menacing sea and thinking of our new kingdom which lay on the other side of it.

It is impossible to cross in such weather, was the general verdict. No ship could be sure of doing it. It would be thrown about and all on board drowned.

Henry could never bear delay. He looked at the angry sea and gnashed his teeth. I thought he was going to fall into one of those rages which I dreaded. I had seen only a few of them but they were terrifying. No. Surely he would not dare show his rage against the heavens at such a time.

He gritted his teeth and said: 'We sail.'

Sail in this weather! We were all aghast.

They tried to dissuade him. Perhaps by tomorrow the sea would be calmer.

He shouted at them. We were not waiting until tomorrow. We were sailing that very day. The ships were seaworthy. He could not wait. Rough seas could go on for months. December was not the month he would have chosen to set sail, but Stephen was dead and England without a ruler. It was a hazardous situation for any country to be in. He was not going to risk disaster just for the sake of a trip across the water. It happened to be a time when he had inherited a kingdom for which he had waited many years, and he was not going to allow a little wind to stop him taking it.

Never shall I forget that crossing. I do not know how we survived it. I was pregnant too, and in any case suffering certain discomforts. I should have demanded that we wait for more clement weather; but not even I argued with Henry when he was in his present mood.

He could not stand still. He strode about the deck, ever watchful. I remained below. I could not face the terrible pitching and tossing of the vessel. My condition made me feel really ill, and I knew that Henry would not care to have sick females about him. He never would, and certainly not at such a time. He was in a fever of impatience to claim the throne.

It seemed that we suffered this torment for hours; and then one of my women told me we were in sight of land. I staggered onto the deck. There was no sign of the rest of the convoy.

Henry wanted to get ashore at once. He would not wait for the others. He would go straight to Winchester.

As we rode along, people came out to look at us. I realized that they had not been expecting the arrival of their new King, for they could not believe that any could cross the Channel in such weather. Already they were recognizing him as a man of power since he defied the elements and with a jaunty nonchalance.

He acknowledged their greeting with obvious pleasure and so we rode into Winchester to be greeted by Theobald, the Archbishop of Canterbury.

We were in due course joined by the rest of the company who had reached England, and Henry, having satisfied himself that that portion of the treasury which was kept in Winchester was intact, made arrangements to set out for London.

He was insistent that his coronation should take place without delay, for he firmly believed that a king was not accepted by the people until he was anointed.

So we came to London. I had never seen anything like this city. The sky was overcast and there was a light drizzling rain in the air. There was activity everywhere; the river was crowded with craft of every description; I saw the great Tower which Henry's great grandfather, the Conqueror, had built. It dominated the landscape. The cobbled streets were full of people. Everywhere there were shops and stalls; and the great purpose of these people seemed to be to buy and sell. There were two great market-places, I discovered later, one near the western gate by the Church of St Paul, where the folkmote was held; the other in Eastcheap. I was amazed to see what goods were offered; they seemed to have come from all corners of the world. There were taverns and eating-houses. No, I never saw a city like this one. It seemed as if the streets must be crammed full of life as compensation for the leaden skies.

In Paris I had missed the clear brilliance of my native skies; but here, in spite of the weather I felt an uplifting of my spirits. An excitement gripped me. This would be my country. I had noticed the brilliant green of the countryside as we passed on our way to the capital, but this city filled me with anticipation. I was surprised that I should be contemplating living here with pleasure.

I saw from the glint in Henry's eyes that he was feeling a similar emotion. Of course, it was not new to him. He had lived in this country for several years. But now it was his and I believed he was going to love it with an intensity which neither Normandy nor Anjou could arouse in him.

First we went to Westminster Palace, which was in such a state of disrepair that we could not stay there. Alternative accommodation was found for us at Bermondsey Palace which, though somewhat primitive compared with those to which I was accustomed, was at least an improvement.

Henry said that the coronation should take place without delay. Until he was crowned King he could not be contented.

I doubt whether there had ever been such a speedy coronation.

'These people will expect a grand display,' he said, 'and even though there is little time for the preparation we must give it to them.'

Fortunately I never travelled if I could help it without as splendid a wardrobe as I could muster. I was seven months pregnant, but that must be no deterrent. I intended to be crowned beside Henry, for if he was King of this country, I was its Queen.

I was determined to impress the people of England. I wanted to give them the sight of fashions they would never have seen before.

My kirtle was of blue velvet with a collar of the finest gems; over it I wore a pelisse, edged with sable and lined with ermine, with very wide sleeves. It was not unlike the pictures I had seen of the costume worn by the wife of the Conqueror. I thought it would be a good idea to look a little like her, to remind them of the stock from which their King had come. I wore my hair flowing with a jewelled band about my brow.

Even Henry had taken some trouble with his appearance on this occasion. His dalmatica was of brocade and embroidered with gold, but he clung to the short cape which had earned him the nickname of 'Curtmantel'. In spite of his rather stocky figure and his contempt for fashion, he looked quite impressive with his leonine head and close-cropped tawny curls. A King they could be proud of.

The people had crowded into the streets to see us as we went back to the Palace of Bermondsey. They cheered but they were not over-enthusiastic. It was as though they were waiting to see what would come from this new reign.

They had suffered civil war, and that must always have a sobering effect. But now the succession was settled. This was the grandson of that great Henry, and they knew, now that he was dead and they had experienced life under a weak monarch, that he had been a great King.

The new reign had begun and Henry was eager to put right those wrongs which had been perpetrated during the reign of his predecessor and to introduce his own rule.

Our coronation had taken place on 19 December, and although he was impatient to be off on a journey which would take him to the important places throughout the country, he did realize that the people would expect Christmas to be celebrated in a royal manner—he must not make the mistake his mother had. As soon as the Christmas celebrations were over (and he warned me they must be lavish, as I would know how to make them), he would set out to discover what was wrong with the country and what he was going to do to remedy it.

With Petronilla's help I devised some entertainment for Christmas. I would send for some of my minstrels but of course there was no time for that now. I thought of the pleasure it would give me to see Bernard de Ventadour again. I would create a Court under these gloomy skies which would equal that of my beloved Aquitaine.

But now the time was short. We planned feverishly. We must not disappoint Henry. Nor did we. It might well be that he would not have wanted anything bearing a resemblance to the Courts of Love, but later I should make my own Court to suit myself.

One memory which stands out very clearly from those Christmas revels is that of Thomas à Becket, because I first saw him there.

I did not see any great significance in the meeting then; it was only afterwards that it became of such importance. But I could not fail to notice him. There was something distinguished about him, and that was obvious in the first moments of meeting him. He had great presence. He was very tall and good-looking, with a somewhat hooked nose which gave him a patrician look, and one of the most compelling pairs of dark eyes I have ever seen. He must have been about fifteen or sixteen years older than Henry.

I had rarely seen Henry take to anyone as quickly as he did to Thomas à Becket. He had charmed Archbishop Theobald equally, it seemed, for he had spent several years in the Archbishop's household and had been favoured by him, which of course had aided him in his career.

Henry brought him to me and, almost before the usual pleasantries had been exchanged, he would have him tell me of the romantic love affair of his parents.

'It will please the Queen,' he told Becket. 'Doubtless she will make a song of it, or get one of her minstrels to. She has a great fancy for poets, and she is one herself.'

Becket and I took each other's measure steadily, and I knew in that moment that there was some special quality about this man; I was not sure whether I should be wary of it.

'I am honoured,' said Becket, 'that my gracious Queen should wish to hear the story of my humble beginnings.'

Henry gave the man an affectionate push. I wondered why it was that they had become on such familiar terms so soon; he could not have known the man long. We had arrived in England only a few weeks before. Henry, of course, was open in his dealings with people. If he liked them, he did not disguise the fact; nor did he if it were otherwise. He had no time for subtlety.

Becket was learned and well read. So was Henry. I had gathered that. They made allusions to classics with which they were familiar and which the others might not understand. The difference in their ages was great, but Henry was mature beyond his years; he was not the sort of man who would suffer those about him who bored him.

He urged Becket to tell me the story. It was certainly strange. It went something like this:

His father, Gilbert, had been a native of Rouen, but after the Norman invasion of England, like so many, he decided to seek his fortune there. When he was a boy, in his little village of Thierceville, in Normandy, Gilbert had played with Theobald, who was determined to go into the Church. Theobald was a very ambitious man; he followed the Conqueror to England and in due course became Archbishop of Canterbury. Like many men of his generation, Gilbert decided to make a pilgrimage to the Holy Land and, taking with him one servant, he set out. He reached Jerusalem without any great mishap but on his way home the party with which he was travelling was captured by the Saracens.

Becket continued: 'To my father's horror, he heard that he was to be taken to the Emir Amurath, who was a sadistic man whose favourite pastime was torturing Christians. My father in due course was brought before him. Now, I must tell you this: my father was a man of unusually dignified bearing and outstanding good looks. The Emir admired beauty in men as well as women, and he could not bring himself to impair such beauty, so he sent my father to a dungeon. My father must have been blessed by God for his gaolers were also struck by his appearance and showed him some kindness. He responded and they became so friendly that he learned their language.'

'He certainly was fortunate,' I said.

Henry said jocularly: 'Naturally so, good Becket. Providence was determined to put no hindrance in the way of your entry into the world.'

'I thank you, sire,' said Becket, bowing with mock irony.

Yes, I thought, they are certainly on unusually good terms.

'In time,' went on Becket, 'the Emir remembered my father and sent for him. He was amazed to see that the only effect prison had had on him was to make him understand their language. My father told him that he had learned it from his gaolers. The Emir asked him questions about London. My father knew how to talk entertainingly and he amused the Emir with stories of that part of the world which the powerful ruler had never seen, but of which he had heard much. He was given fine garments, for the Emir made a companion of him; and soon my father had apartments in the palace, and the friendship between them grew so much that in time he was invited to dine at the Emir's table.'

'Now,' said Henry, 'the romantic story begins. This is what you will want to sing about.'

'The Emir's daughter dined with her father, and she was impressed by Gilbert's fair looks as well as his talk.'

'You know what is coming,' said Henry to me.

'There was love between them?' I asked.

Thomas à Becket nodded. 'Of course he was a Christian and she was of another faith. For all his friendship with my father, the Emir would never have agreed to a marriage between them. She was very determined. She insisted on my father's teaching her to become a Christian. He gave her a name . . . a Christian name. He called her Mahault—which is another name for Matilda—because that was the name of the wife of the great Norman, Duke William, who had conquered England. My father was fully aware of the dangerous game he was playing. If the Emir discovered how far this matter with his daughter had gone, he would be put to death . . . very likely crucified, a favourite punishment for Christians. They were always singing the praises of One who died in such a manner, so it seemed logical that they should die the same way. My father was prepared for that, for he was a deeply dedicated Christian.'

I cannot remember his exact words, but he went on to tell us how the Christian prisoners planned to escape and Gilbert, of course, was to escape with them. His position had made it possible for him to help them, and this as a Christian he was committed to do. But there was Mahault. He could not take her, of course; but his duty lay with his fellow Christians. The escape was well planned and succeeded.

'And the poor girl was left behind?' I cried.

'She was heartbroken. They thought she would die. Then suddenly she began to recover, because she had decided what she would do. She was going to England to find Gilbert. She planned with care, sewing priceless jewels into her garments, and when she was ready she stole out of the Emir's palace and set out. There were many pilgrims on the road and she joined a party of them. She found some who could speak her language and told them what she planned to do. She knew two words in English: London and Gilbert. It seemed that God was watching over her, for in time she arrived in England.'

'Now comes the end of the story,' said Henry. 'I like it.'

'Yes,' said Becket. 'She went through the streets of London calling Gilbert. That was all. She became a familiar sight. People talked of her—the strange woman with the Eastern look who knew only two words—Gilbert and London. She called for him, sometimes piteously, sometimes hopefully. It was my father's servant who saw her, for he had been in captivity with my father. He took her to him. The quest was over.'

'There,' said Henry, 'is that not a tale of true romance?'

'It is indeed. I never heard the like.'

'It was God—making sure that we had a Thomas à Becket.' Henry slapped the man on the back.

I certainly was intrigued by the story but most of all perhaps by the quick friendship Henry appeared to have formed with this man.

Later I spoke of him.

'It is not surprising that this Becket is an unusual man,' I said, 'with such a father and an Eastern mother.'

'A woman of great purpose.'

'And a noble gentleman.'

'Yes, that is what produced Becket.'

'I wonder what his childhood was like in such circumstances.'

'He has told me parts. He was brought up in a very religious way. His mother was a convert to Christianity and, remember, they are often the most intense. Both his parents wanted him to go into the Church. A nobleman who had visited the house was interested in their story of the strange marriage and naturally his attention turned to Thomas. He took him to his home in Pevensey Castle and brought him up as a nobleman's son.'

'Ah yes, there is certainly a touch of the nobleman about him. His tastes would appear to be expensive.'

'I tell him he is too fastidious for a commoner,' said Henry.

'He could scarcely accuse you of being too fastidious.'

'Becket did not want to go into the Church. He fancied business. He did well—which was to be expected. Then disaster struck. His mother died and his father's house was burned to the ground—and soon after that Gilbert died. Becket was melancholy. His parents had meant a great deal to him. Theobald, who had become Archbishop of Canterbury and remembered playing with Gilbert as a boy, persuaded Thomas to join his household. Thomas was twenty-five then. Of course, there he was noticed immediately.'

'Yes, he is a man who would be. He is so tall . . . and those dark eyes of his, which he must have inherited from his mother, are very handsome. His very thinness makes him look taller and he seems to stand about four inches above other men.'

'He did not stay in the Archbishop's house. There were those who were jealous of him and made his life difficult, and although Theobald was aware of Thomas's brilliance, he let him go for the sake of the peace of the household. He sent him to his brother Walter, who was the Archdeacon of Canterbury. After Walter's death, Becket took that post.'

'He hardly seems like a man of the Church.'

'No, he is far too amusing. I think he considered for a time which way he should go.'

'He seems to have taken your fancy.'

'I verily believe he is the most interesting man I have met since coming to these shores.'

I suppose I should not have been surprised when shortly afterwards Henry told me that he had made Becket his Chancellor.

I was now heavily pregnant. Henry had left London and was travelling through the country. I missed Matilda and wished she were with me. But I had Petronilla, now a sober matron, mother and widow, quite a different person from the frivolous girl whose hasty love affair had created such consternation.

Eagerly I awaited the birth. From the palace I could look across the river to the Tower of London, that great sentinel which guarded the eastern side, and from there to the west, dominated by the spire of the cathedral, and beyond to Ludgate. I could see the strand along the river, with the wharves and the houses of the nobility with their fine gardens and their boats staked to the privy stairs which ran down to the river. I knew the strand led to Westminster Palace where we should have taken up residence, of course, if it had been fit for habitation. This would have to be remedied. There would be so much for me to do. But first I must give birth to my child.

It was not a difficult birth, and there was great rejoicing throughout the palace when it was over and I had another boy.

I said: 'This one shall be called Henry after his father.'

* * *

After the birth of the child, I took my place beside Henry in his journeyings round the country. I was enthralled by my new realm and wanted to learn as much about it as possible. The people were very different from the natives of Aquitaine, but I liked them none the less. They marvelled at me and I felt that they were by no means hostile. They had taken to Henry; his ways suited them. They liked his careless way of dressing, his rough and ready style. I suppose he made them feel he was one of them. On the other hand they did appreciate my elegance and they were obviously delighted and rather over-awed by my appearance. They were very interested in my clothes and seemed to like their Queen to look attractive.

So that was a happy time.

One could not expect it to continue. We were both back in Bermondsey for a brief respite when we were disturbed by a visitor, Henry's brother Geoffrey.

We made much of him, but I could see he was envious and bent on making trouble. That irritated me. Did he think he would have had the wit and courage to win this crown? People like Geoffrey wanted everything to fall into their hands with no effort from themselves.

I guessed that he had come to see what he could get, and he soon made it clear that I was right about that.

'Now you have England,' he said, 'Anjou should be mine.'

'I think not,' retorted Henry.

'It was what our father intended.'

'You could not hold on to Anjou.'

'Why should I not?'

'Because you lack the experience to do so,' Henry told him. 'I cannot throw away my father's inheritance. He left you three castles.'

'And you took them from me.'

'I might restore them.'

Geoffrey was furious. He left us in a huff.

Henry snapped his fingers. 'Young fool,' he said. 'How long does he think he would hold Anjou?'

'He has a very high opinion of himself,' I replied. 'What a lucky escape I had. The young fool had the temerity to make a bid for me. Of course, it was doomed to failure—as all Geoffrey's projects would be.'

Henry dismissed his brother from his mind but I did not think the matter would end there.

Then Matilda announced her intention of coming to England. Henry was delighted and great preparations were made to receive her.

'She will want to see you in your crown,' I said. 'She has dreamed of that for so long.'

'And worked for it,' said Henry soberly.

She was indefatigable in his service. No sooner had she come than I realized she had a purpose in doing so.

'I think it is necessary for you to come over,' she told Henry. 'Geoffrey is intent on trouble.'

'He has been here, you know,' said Henry.

'I do know it. He came back with grievances. You are brothers, he says. Why should you have everything?'

'It was as my father left it,' said Henry. 'But I have been thinking I should do something for Geoffrey.'

'Not Normandy,' said Matilda.

'No. And not Anjou either. I don't intend to throw away my dominions.'

'He is preparing an army,' went on Matilda. 'How I hate this warfare in families.'

'To give him Anjou would be tantamount to throwing it away. How long do you think he would hold it?'

'Not long,' said Matilda.

'There is Ireland.'

'What of Ireland?'

'I had thought of conquering it and giving that to him.'

Matilda was very serious. 'You have Anjou, Normandy and England. My dear son, your resources are going to be stretched as far as they can go with those territories. Do not add to that, for the love of God. You could lose them all by taking one more bite. Besides, the Irish are a troublesome race. They would need a constant army to subdue them. And how do you think either of your brothers would like that?'

'I suppose they should have something.'

'Geoffrey has shown that he cannot even hold his own castles. You must come back to Normandy with me. Eleanor can look after matters here. She has good men around her, has she not?'

'She has. There is Becket, my Chancellor, in whom I have great trust, and there are Robert of Leicester and Richard of

Luci. Yes, that is what we must do. I will come back with you and settle this brother of mine once and for all. And Eleanor will make sure that all is well here. My two generals . . . I am lucky to have you both.'

'You can put your trust in us—can he not?' said Matilda to me.

I agreed that he could.

I was sad that he was going away so soon, but I was reconciled that this would be our way of life. And at least he did me the honour of respecting me to such an extent that he could leave me in charge.

He and Matilda departed. The matter was urgent and once he had decided on a course of action, Henry could never delay.

I was very busy. I had conferences with the Earl of Leicester and Richard of Luci. I liked them both and we understood each other well.

Then one night the nurses came to me in great distress. Little William was fighting hard for his breath, and they feared that he was very ill indeed.

We had had many alarms with William and I was constantly anxious about him. I called in the doctors but, alas, there was nothing they could do. My little William, the boy of whom I had been so proud, passed away while Henry was in Anjou fighting his brother.

I was very sad. I had loved the girls I had had from Louis, but Henry's boys were especially dear to me.

It was while I was mourning for William that I found I was once more pregnant.

Henry returned from Anjou. He was triumphant. Naturally Geoffrey's pathetic little revolt had been put down. He did have a certain conscience though, for it was true that his father had said that, when Henry came to the throne of England, Anjou should go to Geoffrey.

Henry explained to me. 'To give it to him would be to throw it away. If my father had really known what he was like, he would never have agreed to that.'

'But he had done so.'

Henry went on: 'I have told him he cannot have Anjou . . . or Normandy. I must make sure that they are safe. I have compromised with him and I think he is satisfied. An income for life . . . a handsome income . . . on condition he leaves Anjou to me.'

'That should suffice,' I said.

'My mother will look after Normandy, and if there is any trouble and I have to leave England, you will look after this country for me.'

'We are a close triumvirate,' I replied.

'That is so, my love. You and my mother are my two most trusted generals, as I have told you.'

He was delighted that I was once more with child.

His friendship with Thomas à Becket was growing in a manner which surprised not only me. The two were becoming inseparable. They hunted together, hawked together, rode, walked and talked. Like others I could not understand this attraction. They were so unlike each other. Becket was meticulous in his dress; he always wore the finest clothes. He had a love of luxurious living which ill accorded with his calling but which I have often found a characteristic of those who come to gracious living rather than were born to it. True, at Pevensey Castle, where he had spent many years with Sir Richer de l'Aigle, he had developed a fondness for easy living which stayed with him. There was a natural elegance about him; I could understand Henry's regard for him; but this intense friendship was strange indeed.

Becket was a man of the world, churchman though he might be. That he was unusually clever, I had no doubt. He gave the impression of one who had no regard for ambition. He made no concessions to royalty whatsoever; he treated the King as his equal and had no hesitation in disagreeing with him if he thought fit. It might have been that which Henry found so refreshing. There was no doubt that the man had an unusual charisma.

Henry set him to organize the refurbishment of the palace in the Tower of London, a task which Becket performed with great competence—and extravagance.

Henry was amused and chided Becket about the cost, asking him how he, as a churchman, could spend so much on luxuries for the King when the money might have been spent in helping the poor.

'And what do you think his answer was?' said Henry to me. ' "Better to have a well-housed King than leave him so uncomfortable that his temper frays from time to time." '

Henry slapped his thigh, indicating how the remark had amused him. Becket was, of course, referring to the King's rages.

'I pointed out to him that my temper frayed no matter where I was housed, and when I was provoked my rages overcame me.

' "You admit to weakness," he said. "That is one step along on the road on which God will guide you." What do you think of that?'

'That this man takes great liberties with the King.'

'He cares not for kingship. I am a man. He is a man. That is how he sees it. Becket says what is in his mind. That is why conversation with him is so interesting. He is such an amusing fellow in a quiet and witty way.'

'He should take care that you do not fly into one of your rages with him.'

'With Becket? Never!' He laughed. 'Though it would be amusing to see his reaction. I know what he would do. He would stand looking on in silence, watching, and then ask God to forgive me my waywardness.'

'And you would merely say, "Thank you, my good and faithful servant, for interceding with your good friend the Almighty on behalf of your humble sovereign." '

He laughed aloud.

'You must admit he is a great man.'

He went on smiling, evidently thinking of some aspect of their conversation which amused him.

It certainly was a most incongruous friendship, and there was hardly a day when they were not together.

In due course I brought forth a daughter. We both wanted to call her Matilda after Henry's mother. She was baptized in the priory of the Holy Trinity at Aldgate, which was appropriate, as the priory had been founded by Queen Matilda, the wife of Henry's grandfather.

I still mourned William, but little Henry had consoled me, and this one was an added comfort. But soon after her birth I began to grow restless. It is probably a state in which women find themselves after childbirth. There is so much preparation before the child appears and one is carried along on a tide of serenity, but when the child is there, life for a time seems lacking in purpose and one feels the need to take some action.

I found the grey skies depressing. I saw the sun too rarely and I felt a longing for my native land.

Henry was in France at this time. There was more trouble over Anjou. I knew that Geoffrey would never be content. He was a born trouble-maker.

Suddenly I decided I would consult no one. I would go and visit my own country, taking the children with me.

A great excitement possessed me. I was going home . . . perhaps only briefly, for I should never forget that I was Queen of England. I could leave the country in the good hands of Leicester, Richard de Luci—and Becket, of course. So I gave orders to make ready for the journey.

I joined Henry in Anjou. He was pleased to see me and, having settled matters there, agreed that we should take the opportunity, being on the spot, to make a progress through Aquitaine to remind the people that we were their rulers.

I was delighted at the prospect. Alas, I was less contented as the tour proceeded, for, although I was welcomed warmly by my people, it was not the case with Henry, and they did not hide the resentment they felt towards him.

Henry had declared that the government of Aquitaine was inefficient. It was not good enough, he said, to have the province defended by the individual castellans who looked after their immediate surroundings. There should be a head of government, and of course that must be Henry, and deputies appointed by him to take charge in his absence according to his wishes.

I knew them well enough to realize that they were asking themselves: Who is this upstart who has married our Duchess and now thinks he owns us? He is worse than the King of France.

It was not as it had been. Alas, life does not stand still. Change comes . . . a little here, a little there, and soon the whole picture is different.

I tried to make my Court at the Maubergeonne Tower what it had been in the past, but it was not the same. I had my troubadours, and I was delighted to see Bernard de Ventadour, who had earlier graced my Court with his verses and his rendering of them in exquisite music.

Henry had his life—his rough riding, his forays into the countryside, his journeys, his friendship with Becket. I would have mine. I did not care for the outdoor life. I longed for those days when I had my poets round me singing of romantic adventures. And I was going to have it.

I kept Bernard de Ventadour with me. He raised my flagging spirits. It was wonderful to be courted and loved through his music. I had been brought up in such an atmosphere, and it was natural that I should re-create it.

This was Aquitaine, not England.

I had a notion that Henry had something on his mind and that it concerned me. I would catch him watching me covertly, as though he were assessing me.

He came to the hall one evening when Bernard de Ventadour was lying at my feet singing one of his love songs. My ladies and the gentlemen of the Court were listening intently. The song was about the beauty of the loved one, who was too high and noble for the singer to reach.

Henry stood, legs apart, head thrust forward, glowering at Bernard, who went on singing unfalteringly and perhaps putting more expression than ever into his voice, while his warm southern eyes rested on me.

'By the eyes of God,' cried Henry, 'what nonsense!'

Then he turned and strode away.

Bernard went on singing.

When he had finished there was half-hearted applause from those who did not know what action to take. I knew it was no use ignoring the incident, so I said: 'The King did not like your verses, Bernard.'

'If the Queen liked them, that is all I ask.'

There was a breathless silence. I was asking myself, could Henry really have been jealous?

I was a little afraid for Bernard, knowing how violent Henry could be. Indeed, I had been astonished by his restraint. He might well have commanded Bernard to stop singing, even ordered him to leave. I did not want that to happen. I would try to placate him, and perhaps it would be better if Bernard were slightly less prominent for a while.

When I was in our apartment, Henry came in. He looked at me, his tawny eyebrows raised a little. He was not going to wait for me to comment. He was coming straight into the attack.

'That insolent fellow will have to go.'

'Are you referring to Bernard de Ventadour?'

'Bernard de Ventadour! A fine name for a serving wench's bastard.'

'Oh, come,' I said. 'We are talking about a great poet.'

'Poet!'

'Indeed yes, and recognized as such by people who know of such matters.'

'Which I don't, eh? I have better use for my time than listening to such jibbering. Insolent dog.'

'Insolent! He has never shown me anything but the utmost respect.'

'And he has shown me something, too. He is your lover.'

'What nonsense!'

'That stuff he was singing . . .'

'You must know it was just poetic imagination.'

'Imagination! Tell him he can go back to the kitchens from which he came. They can find a place for his imagination down there among the spits and pots.'

'I thought you liked those who are intelligent.'

'I could have his tongue cut out. That would put an end to his licentious drivelling.'

'Do you think my people would allow that? Already you are no favourite of theirs. This is my country, Henry. You would do well to remember that.'

I saw the colour coming into his face. He tore off his cloak and flung it from him. He lay on the floor and kicked at the wall. He gnashed his teeth, biting the flounces about the bed.

I watched him. I had seen these rages before, but there was something not quite the same about this one. The thought flashed into my mind: He is staging this. There is something behind it. He is performing for my benefit.

On other occasions when I had seen those senseless rages I had been alarmed . . . for his health, for his sanity. I had indeed thought he was possessed by devils and there was something in that story about his ancestry. But this was different.

He was shouting obscenities about Bernard and me.

I drew in my skirts and walked past him, out of the apartment.

Henry said no more about Bernard de Ventadour, but I advised the troubadour not to sing when he was present. I told him I feared the King was jealous and when he was enraged he could be terrible.

Bernard was no fool. He might say that he only cared for me and that the opinions of others mattered not to him, but Henry was formidable, even in Aquitaine where he was unpopular.

I was once more pregnant and was beginning to wonder whether my life was to be spent bearing children. It was true that I had wanted them and that I now had only one son, but I did feel that the pregnancies were too frequent, and a little respite in between would be desirable.

My sojourn in Aquitaine had been a disappointment. It was no longer the same, for while the people loved me and accepted me as their Duchess, they could not forget that I had a husband and that he was trying to force his rule upon them. They did not like it. He did not understand them and they did not understand him. He thought that what was successful in England could be successful here. We were a different people. We had lived too long in the sun; we did not care for discipline; we liked to go along smoothly, effortlessly. Henry was quite alien to these people. They could not understand his restlessness, his love of law and order, his immense energy.

I wanted to go back to England. I found life too depressing in the sunshine of my native land.

It was February when we arrived in England. Henry had gone to Anjou. He was still concerned about troublesome Geoffrey. Matilda was as good as a general, and Normandy was in excellent hands; he trusted those in England. But I knew he would be with me as soon as possible.

He would be missing Becket, I thought ruefully.

I was feeling well in spite of my pregnancy. I was getting used to that state now.

An uprising on the Welsh borders brought Henry back to England before Easter. This was what we had to expect from life, I supposed. As soon as one little corner was safe, there would be trouble in another.

With his unbounded energy he set about getting his army together. The Welsh campaign was not a great success. The Welsh were fierce fighters, and the victory Henry had expected had not come. Instead he was all but defeated and shrewdly he quickly made a concession to the Welsh which would confine them to their own country and make the border safe.

He came back less triumphant than usual. We had an affectionate reunion, but again I had that feeling that he had something on his mind.

We were alone in the bedchamber when he looked at me steadily and almost defiantly said: 'We shall have another in the nursery.'

I naturally thought he was referring to the child I was carrying and I replied: 'I wonder if this one will be a boy.'

'It is a boy,' he said. 'His name is Geoffrey.'

I stared at him. I saw the defiant look in his eyes and I knew. He had been preparing me for this. His mock rage over Bernard de Ventadour was when he was wondering how to broach the subject. He had been hinting at my infidelity to excuse his own. And now he had decided to exert his rights and to let me know he was the master. Hence his arrogance.

'Geoffrey?' I said. 'And who might this Geoffrey be?'

'He is my son.'

'Your . . . bastard?'

'Yes, of course. Since he is not yours he must be.'

'And you want to bring him into the royal nursery?'

'I *am* bringing him into the royal nursery.'

'Without consulting me?'

'I am telling you of my wishes now.'

'And you think I will consent to this?'

'He is coming tomorrow.'

'No!'

'But yes. It is good for him to be with his brother and sister.'

'I do not understand how you can behave like this.'

'There is much you have to learn of me then.'

'These are *my* children.'

'Mine too, I hope.'

'How dare you!'

'Why so outraged? Your reputation is not exactly chaste.'

'And yours, my lord?'

'Not chaste either. I have never questioned yours. Why should you mine?'

'How old is this boy?'

'A little older than Henry.'

'Then . . . so long ago . . . you were unfaithful!'

He looked puzzled. 'Madam, I was far from home. Do you expect me to live like a monk? There are women, of course. They mean nothing . . .'

'And this one . . . the mother of the boy . . . she means nothing to you?'

'Nothing at all.'

'Yet her bastard . . .'

'Is mine also. I care about the boy.'

'How do you know this child is yours?'

'I know.'

'Men can be fooled, you understand.'

'I understand that in him I am not mistaken. He will arrive tomorrow. He is to be treated as the others.'

I was speechless with rage—not so much by the prospect of having the child in the nursery as that almost immediately after our marriage he had been unfaithful to me.

He went on: 'He will be brought here and he will come straight to the nursery. He is a pleasant child.'

'Are we to have a succession of your bastards invading the nurseries?'

'It is only this one whom I wish to have here at the present.'

'What a lecher you are! I suppose when you are with your armies you take any woman you fancy as you pass through the towns. You sport with the camp-followers.'

'It is the way of men on the march. And I am surprised that you are surprised it should be so. I believe you had certain adventures when you were on the march. I have heard some spicy scandals about you and your uncle. I always went outside the family.'

'How dare you speak to me thus.'

'I speak as I will to you, as to any of my subjects.'

I had been a fool. I should have known. I remembered the days when we had first met and that immediate attraction between us. It had been nothing but what might have happened with a tavern wench. I felt humiliated and angry with myself.

I said: 'I married you when you were a mere duke, Duke of Normandy, and hard pressed to keep the title.'

'That is past. Now I am King of England.'

'And I am the Queen and Duchess of Aquitaine.'

'Queen because I made you so, remember?'

'You are insulting *me* by bringing this child into the nursery.'

'As I see it, I am doing my duty by *him*.'

'Could you not put him into some nobleman's household?'

'I want him to be in mine.'

'And you will disrupt your family to do this?'

'I command that he be brought up here and that there shall be no prejudice against him.'

I felt beaten. I knew him well by now. I could imagine those journeys of his, the nights he spent with women . . . any woman who happened to be available. Why had I thought it could be otherwise with such a man? He was lusty and licentious; this was the life he had led before his marriage and he saw no reason to discontinue it. This was how it had always been. I had to get used to it.

I turned away from him but he caught my arm and pulled me around to face him.

'Have done with fancy songs from fancy troubadours,' he said. 'Face the real world. Men will be men and if the woman they would have is not there they will take another. It is always so with such as I am and always will be. You must needs face the truth.'

'You have been trying to tell me this for a long time. You wanted this boy brought in. You were going to ask me to take him in. You have been steeling yourself to do it. Then you decided on this arrogance . . . this insistence.'

'My dear Eleanor, you are too clever by half.'

Then he laughed and held me against him. He was knowledgeable about women—having had so much experience of them, I supposed. He thought that if he made love to me, made me believe that I was still more desirable to him than anyone else, he could bend me to his command. But my feelings had changed towards him. I wrenched myself free and left him.

The boy came. There was no doubt that he was Henry's—the tawny hair and eyes, the confident manner; he was the lion's cub. He was a pleasant creature. Young Henry took to him right away. Matilda liked him. He quickly became a favourite in the nursery.

8 September of that year 1157 was a day I have often thought of as the happiest in my life because on it my son Richard was born. He was beautiful from the moment he appeared. Not for him that period which most little babies go through when they look like old men of ninety. He was fair-haired and blue-eyed with a skin like milk and pale pink roses. I loved him dearly

from the moment I saw him, and for the rest of his life he became the most important person in mine.

It may have been not only because of his unusual beauty but because my relationship with Henry had undergone a change. There had been times before he brought young Geoffrey into the nursery when he had irritated me, but he had never failed to charm me. I had seen those violent rages which had appalled me and I had realized that some of them were performed for effect, because he liked people to be in awe of him, simply because he wanted to be able to do with them what he wished. But still he had remained the man I loved. Now I looked at him through clearer eyes. Why should I, a fastidious woman, have become so besotted about a man who did not care for his appearance, dressed in a slovenly manner, ate his food walking about—not caring how it was served, had no great good looks, was bow-legged and weatherbeaten with rough red hands? He had power, yes, great power, but he was devious, crafty and unscrupulous. He had never paid his brother Geoffrey the amount he had contracted to in exchange for Anjou. True, he had read a great deal. He would read while he was in church.

He was a great King; he did know how to rule. But he was greedy. He wanted to take as much land as he could. He chafed that anything should belong to anyone else.

I was growing out of love with Henry, and all my affection had been transferred to my golden-haired child.

Even at an early age Richard responded. His smiles were for me. He was contented only when I was near. There had been a bond between us from the moment he was born. He was a blessing. He soothed those wounded feelings engendered by Henry's disloyalty. I now faced the truth. He must have bastards all over the country. He would pass through a town taking women as it pleased him and thinking no more of it.

I often wondered about Becket. They were so much together. Was Becket around when Henry was wenching? And if so, did he share in the sport? He seemed to in everything else.

Once I asked Henry this.

'Did you know,' he said, 'that Becket has taken a vow of chastity?'

'People do not always keep to their vows,' I pointed out.

'He does. He's a churchman, remember.'

'A very unusual churchman,' I commented.

I was annoyed that Becket should take up so much of his time and charm him so obviously. Before I had Richard I should have been jealous. Now I could shrug it aside. I said I thought it was rather odd for a chancellor-churchman to be so frequently in the company of a king-rake. That amused Henry.

'I'll tell Becket that,' he said.

I could imagine how Henry teased Becket, how he would try to lay him open to temptation. Becket, of course, would go his own way. I was sure that one of the holds he had over the King was due to his independent outlook and his indifference as to whether he offended Henry or not.

Accounts of their adventuring were brought to me from time to time. There was one incident which rather amused me and about which there was a good deal of talk.

They made such a contrast when they went riding out together: Henry in his plain Angevin jacket and short cape, his red hands unencumbered by gloves and the Chancellor, elaborately clad in scented linen and a fine embroidered sable-lined cloak.

One day, as King and Chancellor rode together through the streets of London, they came upon an old man shivering in his rags. Henry pointed out the man to Becket and asked if it would not be an act of charity to give him a warm cloak. Becket agreed that it would indeed, at which Henry leaned towards Becket and attempted to take the magnificent fur-lined cloak from his Chancellor's shoulders. Realizing what was about to happen, Becket tried to save his cloak, and the two of them tugged at it. Their followers thought there had been a disagreement between them and stood back amazed. The King was triumphant. He won the cloak and shouted to the shivering man, who must have looked on with amazement, that the Chancellor wished to make a gift of it to him. Poor old man, I daresay he could not believe his good fortune. But I wondered how Becket felt to lose such a garment, which he must have treasured. I liked to think of Becket cloakless against the cold, joining in the King's amusement, for I was sure he was too clever to have done anything else.

People talked of the incident and that was how it reached my ears. It really was amazing—the terms those two were on. Henry seemed as though he could not have enough of the man's company. It was almost like a love affair.

There was a strong vein of humour in Henry's character. He

liked to make a bizarre situation. This was apparent when he came up with an idea for young Henry's betrothal.

He said to me: 'It is time young Henry was betrothed. I have the very bride for him.'

'Who?' I asked.

He looked at me slyly. 'Louis has a daughter. It is clear to me that he will never have a son. He couldn't get one with you, could he? And look you, you manage very well to get them with me. But he does have a girl through this new marriage of his . . . Marguerite. I want her for Henry. And then . . . as there will not be a male heir, in due course Henry could have the crown of France.'

The audacity of the suggestion so took me aback that I could find no words.

'I think he might be persuaded,' went on Henry.

'*His* daughter to marry my *son*!'

'There is no blood tie between them, although you and he were once husband and wife . . . apart from that remote one which you used to get free of him. It is a piquant situation.'

'He would never agree.'

'I believe he would. His Marguerite has a chance of being Queen of England, our Henry of being King of France. Why, it is irresistible.'

'It seems vaguely incestuous to me.'

'That is because you have such stern morals in these matters, my love.'

I recognized this as an oblique reference to Raymond of Antioch, but was too astounded to resent. I was trying to contemplate what Louis would feel when confronted with such an outrageous suggestion.

'It is a good idea,' went on Henry enthusiastically. 'I can see a union between France and England. Between us, in the family, we already have a large part of France. I see no reason why we should not take over the whole country.'

'Louis would not even see us if we went to France. Think how embarrassing that would be.'

'I have already thought of it and I have made up my mind how I will start this matter. I shall send an ambassador to Louis. I shall choose someone who can present the case in all its reasonableness, who can charm and persuade in the most graceful manner possible.

'Who could do that?'

'Becket of course.'

'Becket! Would this be the task of a chancellor?'

'It would be if I made it so.'

'And do you think Louis would for a moment entertain such an idea?'

'He will . . . the way Becket will present it.'

I could not stop thinking of the audacity of the idea. I wondered what Louis would think of his daughter's marrying my son. How he had longed for a son. And no sooner had I left him than I produced one. It must have seemed ironic to him, hurtful too. People must say that he was incapable of getting sons. How disappointed he must have been when, after all his efforts in his new marriage, the result was only a girl.

No. He would never agree. At first I thought Henry was joking. But no. He was very serious about the matter.

Becket came to see me. He told me he was to go to France on this very delicate mission of which I would be aware. I was well acquainted with the French Court and he would be glad of my advice on certain aspects of his visit.

I explained to him that the French Court was more elegant than the English; the French would not be impressed if he travelled without some state. This seemed to please Becket. I had an idea that he was rather fond of ostentation. He liked to assume grandeur. Understandable, I thought, in one who came from humble beginnings.

He asked me about Louis, and I thought back to the days which I had spent with my former husband.

I said: 'Louis is a good man at heart. He is timid, no great soldier, no diplomat; there is nothing subtle about him. He should have been a man of the Church, so it may be you have something in common, my lord Chancellor.'

I smiled to myself. I could see no resemblance between them whatsoever.

I went on: 'He is as unlike our King as any man could be. You will need to be earnest and show that you are deeply religious. That would win his respect. He will be shocked by your mission. I can hardly believe it will succeed.'

'I shall do my best to make it.'

'He is a man who hates war and cares for his people. He ought to be a good king; but good kings are made of different stuff, for it does not seem necessary for a good king to be a good man.'

He agreed with me and thanked me.

I was interested to see what he made of my advice, and it was with amusement and wonder that I watched the procession depart. Becket was certainly going to make an impression.

It was June and, to my chagrin, I was pregnant once more. Henry was an indefatigable lover. I understood now that I had been foolish to expect fidelity from him. Women were a need in his life. Although I could now regard him dispassionately, he still attracted me physically more than anyone I had ever known . . . even Raymond. I found him irresistible, as I believe he found me. But it was different from those early days when I had loved him. I did not any more. I just had need of him; and that this intercourse should have led to another pregnancy, and so soon, was a source of irritation to me. It was ironic that during the first years of my marriage to Louis I had longed to conceive; now I could not stop doing so.

I had three months to go and was getting unwieldy.

Becket's entourage was very grand indeed. The procession was led by his servants, who walked in groups of ten or twelve singing as they went; then came his huntsmen with their greyhounds and other dogs, and after that six waggons containing his bed and other furnishings, and two waggons which had been packed with flagons of the best English ale, which he proposed to present to the French. Each waggon was drawn by five horses, all of them magnificent, with mastiffs to guard them. There followed the packhorses on each of which sat a monkey to create a comic effect. Then came the squires with their falcons and hawks, followed by the gentlemen of his household; and finally, in all his glory, the Chancellor himself.

And how he revelled in it.

I wondered what effect he would have on Louis. It might not be the way to win him over, but I was sure the French would be impressed by all the show. Accustomed to Louis's sombre appearance they would say to themselves: If this is the Chancellor, what must the King be like?

I wished I could have seen Becket's arrival in Paris. I should so much have enjoyed seeing him riding through the streets. I heard later that Louis entertained him in royal fashion and that Becket retaliated by giving an even grander banquet for Louis.

Years later I heard the visit referred to, and one item remains in my memory still. It was that Becket paid 100 shillings for just one dish of eels.

Once again I marvelled at this intimacy between him and the King. They were so different—Becket revelling in that ostentation for which Henry had no desire whatsoever.

But there was some magic about Becket for he achieved what I had thought to be impossible. He made Louis see that a marriage between my son and his daughter could be feasible.

Henry was delighted. He came to me in a state of enthusiasm.

'He has done it,' he said. 'I knew he would. Only Becket could have brought this off. I shall leave for France at once. I shall get this thing settled.'

His eyes were shining. I could see that he believed the crown of France was within his grasp.

While he was away my child was born. I had three sons now— Henry, Richard and this new one, Geoffrey.

I recovered quickly but I had made up my mind that I was going to have a respite from childbearing. I was tired of all those weary months, and then, when the child was born, almost immediately I was expecting another.

Here I was confined to my apartments while exciting events were taking place in the world. Then I hated to be in one place for long. I started to pine for Aquitaine and knew that it was not good for me to be absent for so long. *I* was the ruler of Aquitaine; they would not accept Henry. They were even more suspicious of him than they had been of Louis. At least Louis had been ineffectual. None could say that of Henry.

I had made my son Richard heir of Aquitaine. The eldest, Henry, would, of course, have England, the new Geoffrey I supposed Anjou. There was territory enough for them. And if everything went as Henry planned, young Henry would have France as well.

I knew how Henry's mind worked. He would wring the utmost advantage from this match. He had talked to me often of the Vexin, that buffer state between Normandy and Louis's kingdom; and I had seen the acquisitive gleam in his eyes. If he could get control of the Vexin he could feel that Normandy was considerably safer than it was at this time. He longed for the Vexin and I knew he was going to ask for it as Marguerite's dowry.

I imagined Henry's meeting with Louis. Louis must have schooled himself. I wondered whether the thought of Henry and me together came into his head. The puritanical often suffer from acute imagination in these matters, I believe. He would be most uncomfortable and obsessed by his visions. Poor Louis. Did he in his heart feel reproachful towards God for not making better arrangements for the procreation of the human race?

Henry would go to Paris in a manner entirely different from that employed by his Chancellor. I pictured him in his short cape and simple jacket—no concessions from Henry—riding his horse magnificently—he and his horse always looked as though they were one—his gloveless, chapped hands unashamedly exposed. 'Is this the King?' the people would ask. 'How different he is from his Chancellor.' But there would be no mistaking the regality. Henry could not hide that if he tried. I imagined that proud head, leonine and tawny—a King to respect and fear.

Louis and his Constance received him graciously. Henry of course could put himself out to be charming when there was much to be gained. He would show his erudition; his conversation would be witty and very much to the point. Perhaps I should not have been surprised that, between them, he and Becket should manage to get what they wanted from Louis.

On the marriage of Marguerite and Henry, the Vexin should form part of her dowry. The poor child was only a year old, so Louis had a long time before he need relinquish his hold on that important territory.

Henry remained in France. He would not leave it until he was sure it was safe to do so. Meanwhile he was stabilizing his friendship with Louis.

He sent messages to me. I was to join him in Cherbourg with the children.

England was peaceful, and Robert of Leicester and Richard de Luci were capable of firm governing. So I went.

Henry was delighted with the new baby.

'There is nothing like a bevy of sons to strengthen the throne,' he said.

'Perhaps too many could make trouble,' I reminded him. 'Think of your brothers.'

'There you have a point,' agreed Henry. 'But my sons will be different. I shall bring them up the way I wish them to go.'

I looked at him steadily and said: 'They are my sons also. I shall have a hand in their upbringing.'

He laughed. 'Our interests must be as one,' he said. 'I would not care to have you as my enemy.'

'Nor I you, my lord.'

Then he kissed me and I was rather afraid that this might lead to the usual encounter, but I eluded him, saying that I had much to which I must attend.

I was all eagerness to hear about his meeting with Louis, and he was only too pleased to tell me.

'Louis does not appear to have changed much since he was your devoted husband. Constance . . . well, she is meek and mild. As different from you, my dear, as one woman could be from another. I'll swear she does not plague him as you used to.'

There was grudging admiration in his voice and I did not resent his words.

'Did he mention me?' I asked.

'By no means. He skirted over the subject. I saw his eyes on me and I guessed he was thinking "What can that fastidious lady see in this coarse creature?" He seemed to have forgotten that she has a coarse side to her nature. Think of all those adventures in the Holy Land.'

'So you read the thoughts of others?'

'Such as Louis, yes. He would not allow me to bring Marguerite to England, and do you know why? Because he did not want his little daughter brought up in *your* Court . . . even though she is to marry your son.'

'Did he say this?'

'I told you your name was not mentioned. When I reminded him that a bride is brought up in her husband's country, his mouth tightened and I'll swear he was murmuring a prayer under his breath. "Oh God, save my innocent daughter from that wicked woman." '

'I am sure he was doing no such thing.'

'Well, he said no most firmly. "No, no. My daughter stays in France." Now this, of course, was something which I could not allow. We might as well not have gone there . . . all that expense . . . it would be for nothing.'

'And Becket's trip must have been a costly one.'

'What Becket did was right.'

'You mean for him to travel like a king and you as a commoner?'

'Our own styles suited us best. And what matters it, since we achieved the desired result?'

'But you say Louis will not allow Marguerite to come to England.'

'That has nothing to do with Becket's ostentation and my humility. It was due to absent influences.'

'You mean because of me.'

'Exactly.'

'But you did not mention me.'

'Your presence was there . . . floating between us. You are not easily dismissed from people's minds, my love.'

'So she is still with her father, and your mission is unfulfilled.'

'By the eyes of God, what do you take me for? Certainly that is not so. You know my Chief Justice, Robert of Newburg. What a righteous man! His castle is so convenient. Right on the borders of Normandy, so that he can keep an eye on what goes on on the other side. He is very pious . . . a man after Louis's own heart. I suggested that the little girl be brought to his household. It would be safer than the perilous journey across the water. Louis had to give way. Not a breath of scandal concerning Robert of Newburg has ever passed any lips. In fact, all talk of his piety. So, that little matter was settled and the innocent child will be spared the evil influence and be brought up in a house of virtue.'

'I see,' I said. 'Well, I suppose it would have been somewhat ironic for Louis's daughter to be brought up under my care.'

'Incongruous indeed. But all is well. Louis and I have visited churches together. I have been a very virtuous man for his sake—and now we are the best of friends.'

'For how long?' I said.

'For as long as it is necessary, I hope,' he replied with a mischievous grin.

So we spent Christmas at Cherbourg, and Henry's delight in his son pleased me; it was a happy time.

There was a new development. Henry's troublesome brother Geoffrey died suddenly. Henry expressed no remorse for their quarrel; he was without sentiment and would have considered it hypocritical to feign grief he did not feel, which was honest, of course. It was typical of him that he immediately began to assess the advantages his brother's death could bring to him.

For one thing, it was the end of a trouble-maker. By great good fortune, two years before his death Geoffrey had been offered the county of Nantes which he had eagerly accepted. Nantes was one of the most important cities in Brittany and there had been unrest in the province for some years. It was hoped that Geoffrey would be able to prevent rebellion. Well, now he was dead and, said Henry, Nantes belonged to the family.

I was amazed by him. His resources were stretched to the limit. He was trying to rule England, Normandy, Anjou and Aquitaine. And now he was thinking of adding Brittany to his possessions. I recognized the acquisitive gleam in his eyes. Sometimes I believed it was a dream of Henry's to conquer the whole world.

He set about stabilizing his claim to Nantes and, because of his new friendship with Louis, he asked his permission to take over the city. It did not surprise me that Louis gave in to this. There had been trouble in Brittany for some time, and Louis was always seeking peace. He recognized in Henry a strong man, and although even he must have known that Henry had his eyes not only on Nantes but on the whole of Brittany, he agreed to his taking possession of the city.

Henry did not hesitate. He went in with his armies and set up his deputies to rule.

This visit to France, this friendship with Louis, was proving very useful to him.

It was I who first talked to him of Toulouse. It had always rankled in my mind that it had passed out of my family's hands. It had come to us through my grandfather's wife Philippa, and although my grandfather had sold it to raise money to go on his crusade, I had never felt that that justified our not bringing it back to where it belonged.

To add Toulouse to what he already had was a great temptation to Henry. I knew he was looking ahead a few years to when our son was King of France and almost the whole of that country was in our hands. England and France should be ruled by one king. Together they could stand against the world.

Henry believed he knew Louis. A man of peace would do anything in his power to avoid going to war. Yet even Louis must view with disquiet the prospect of Henry's acquiring more territory in France.

Louis had added to his stature in a way. He was no longer the tool of Suger and Bernard of Clairvaux; and this had made him more his own man. They were both dead and he had escaped from their influence long enough to have developed a little character of his own.

When Henry demanded the return of Toulouse in my name, Louis must have been overcome with shock. In his simple honest way he would have believed the King of England was his friend. I wondered that he had not yet learned that there is not true friendship between kings; there is only expediency. It was unfortunate that Louis's sister, Constance, was married to the Count of Toulouse. She was the widow of Eustace, King Stephen's son, and Louis would naturally feel that he must look after his sister's interests.

I felt strongly about Toulouse. I always had. I did remember Louis's abortive attempt to take it. But Louis's attempts would always end in failure. It would be quite different with Henry. He was enthusiastic for the campaign and set about raising an army. In due course he had with him the most influential barons of England. Becket was there, with equipment and followers more splendid than any. It seemed to me that he fancied himself as a conqueror; he certainly had great energy and the will to succeed. The Scots were there, with the Welsh, and it seemed certain that Henry could not fail to take Toulouse.

Louis, however, made an unpredictable move. He took a few troops with him and went to the aid of his brother-in-law. Consequently when Henry's army arrived to take possession of the town, Louis was inside it.

Henry was faced with a dilemma. To attack Toulouse meant attacking Louis, and Louis, while Henry was in France, was his feudal lord. I never thought that Henry would be over-plagued by such scruples. It may have been that he foresaw that if he made the French King his captive he might be catapulted into a war of gigantic proportions. England was docile at the moment but if anything went wrong there he would have to return at short notice. There were men in Normandy, Anjou and Brittany who would be only too ready to turn against him if they thought they had an opportunity of succeeding. I suppose that on reflection Henry acted in his usually shrewd manner; but the disappointment was intense.

There was nothing more frustrating for an army in perfect order than to come within sight of victory and have it snatched from them because of scruples.

I was amused to hear that there was discord between Becket and the King. Thomas, that holy man, was bent on war. He wanted to cut a fine figure on the battlefield. He wanted to take his splendidly caparisoned equipage into a battle which should have been won before it started.

Becket said the King was acting foolishly.

Henry told Becket to remember to whom he spoke.

Becket, so sure of himself, continued to tell the King that he was acting in an ill-considered way.

That was not true. Henry never did that. Even his rages were calculated to terrify people and remind them of their fate if they offended him.

Henry cried out that Becket had better have a care. He would do well to remember who was the master of us all.

Becket must have been nonplussed. I was rather pleased that the arrogant man had been taken down a step or two, but he apparently realized he had gone too far and that because Henry had shown him unusual favour he must not take advantage of that. The King had helped him rise. He could as easily put him down. I could not believe for one moment that Becket would want to lose all that magnificence by which he set such store.

Henry withdrew his army but he did capture a few strongholds and peace was concluded. Alas, Toulouse remained out of our hands. It was a terrible disappointment to me. I had always had a special feeling for Toulouse and I had believed that Henry would bring it to me. In a way, Louis had scored over him. It had been a masterly stroke to go to the city when he knew an attempt would be made to take it. It showed real courage and perhaps—though unlikely—shrewd reasoning. Had Louis guessed that Henry would not attack when he was there? He was of course taking a great risk, but Louis had never been a coward. The care of his own skin had never come first with him; as long as he was sure he was in the right, he was contented.

So . . . Henry had failed.

Perhaps he was not the mighty figure I had imagined him. In

fact, he was by no means the man with whom I had fallen passionately in love. Unfaithful . . . from the start of our marriage . . . slovenly, often ungracious, far from good-looking. In fact, with every year he grew less so. His skin was freckled and rough from the wind, his curly hair allowed to go its own way. He cared nothing for the gracious way of living.

Why had I married him?

Physically he was still exciting. It was, I suppose, that immense strength, that arrogance, that power. But I was beginning to think that I had been unlucky in both my husbands.

Events being as they were, he must stay on the Continent, but I must return to England. Both of us could not be away too long. I was nothing loth. I wanted no more children and I feared that if Henry and I remained together the inevitable would happen.

I enjoyed being in England with my children—particularly Richard, although I loved them all. I fancied they were all fonder of me than they were of Henry who had no idea how to behave with children. He over-awed them. They were suspicious of him when he tried to be jocular with them. I was the one to whom they rushed for comfort.

My little Richard grew more beautiful every day. He was a true Plantagenet and did not resemble my side of the family at all. He was golden-haired and blue-eyed, with a beautifully clear skin. He was going to be taller than the others.

I heard news from France, from Henry, who wished me to pack up and join him without delay.

Louis had been married to Constance for six years and had managed to produce one daughter, Marguerite, now betrothed to our Henry. But news had seeped out that at last Constance was pregnant again. I laughed to contemplate it, imagining all the efforts Louis must have undertaken to achieve this result. I pictured those nights on his knees beside the royal bed before he took the plunge and managed after an effort to perform his duty for France.

Now his efforts were crowned with success.

Henry was far from pleased. What if the child should be a boy? Young Henry would be cheated of the crown of France. There was only one thing we could do. We could betroth our little Matilda to the boy as soon as he was born, thus making sure that, if our son could not be King of France, our daughter should be Queen.

I laughed aloud. The man's mind was so devious. One had to admire him. He let no opportunity pass.

I prepared to travel with the children.

When I joined Henry in Rouen, he was in a mood of great excitement. The birth was imminent.

'Becket will have to persuade the King once more,' he said. 'We shall have to find some way of making the project agreeable to him.'

'It will not be easy,' I told him. 'Do you think he will want two of our children married to two of his?'

'He has to want it. We managed with one. We will with the other, and if it is a boy, it will be imperative.'

We were all in a state of nervous tension when Queen Constance was brought to bed. She produced another girl and, poor lady, died in the attempt.

The immediate threat was lifted. There was no boy to displace Marguerite. The throne of France was safe for Henry's son.

Then there was more cause for alarm. Louis proposed, with indecent haste, to marry again. It was for France, of course. He had not given up hope of producing that boy. There was no difficulty in finding a bride for the King of France. Adele of Blois and Champagne was chosen.

Now Henry was in a ferment of apprehension. A new marriage! A young woman! Even Louis might succeed.

Louis's daughter was named Alais. Henry told me that he thought as a precaution a marriage should be arranged between her and Richard; but that could hardly have been suggested at this stage.

His thoughts turned in another direction.

'Until Marguerite and young Henry are married,' he said, 'our position is very uncertain. You know how often these intended marriages are brushed aside. Trouble has only to blow up between Louis and me and all our efforts will come to nothing.'

'We must hope for peace between you. Toulouse has made no difference to the proposed marriage.'

'That was settled amicably.'

'Were you thinking of that when you did not take the city?'

He lifted his shoulders. 'What I plan is to get the young pair married.'

'They are little more than babies.'

'That is of no account. They can go back to their nurseries afterwards. I did not intend that the marriage should be consummated in their cradles.'

'Louis will not agree.'

'Louis will not know until after the ceremony.'

'You would do that?'

He grinned at me. 'Robert of Newburg has the girl. He could not withhold her from me. You know there is a little trouble in papal quarters. I don't think anyone there would want to offend me. Any consent we needed from them would be freely given. Everything will be done as it should be, and Louis will be presented with a *fait accompli*.' I could not help admiring him. 'And,' he went on, 'I shall get my hands on the Vexin, for once the marriage is performed the dowry must be paid.'

'Do you think all this is possible?'

'It will be if I decide it shall.'

Henry had decided, as he said, so it should be. Marguerite, aged three, was married to Henry, aged six. Poor bewildered children, they did not know what was happening to them.

Henry took possession of the Vexin and the rest of the dowry and was very pleased with himself.

Louis was less pleased, but he was as bewildered as our young bride and groom. He had just married and had to face those fearful bedroom ordeals once more. His one thought must have been, Let me get a son quickly, oh Lord—and nothing else matters.

We spent Christmas at Le Mans, and during that time, to my intense irritation, I became pregnant again.

We remained in France. It seemed necessary. Henry had acquired new possessions and he was very watchful of the King of France, fearful that at any moment he would hear that Adela had given birth to a son.

During that year, while we were so involved with the birth of the child who turned out to be little Alais, the Archbishop, our good friend Theobald, had died.

This was a blow to us. Theobald could be completely trusted. He was that rare creature—a truly good man. He had been deeply religious, generous to the poor, ever ready to help those in trouble. He had been learned and liked to surround himself with men of his own calibre but that did not mean that he had not had sympathy and attention to give to those less gifted than himself. He had remained faithful to Stephen throughout that King's troublous reign and had on Stephen's death given that loyalty to Henry, whom he considered the rightful heir. Henry was wise enough to know a good subject when he found one and Theobald had certainly been that.

During the last year he had been very ill, and it was known that death was not far away. He had written several times to Henry, begging him to return to England that he might behold 'his son, the Lord's anointed, before he died'. Henry could not, of course, allow sentimental attachments to defer him from protecting his lands overseas, so Theobald's request went unanswered. Theobald also asked that Thomas à Becket, his archdeacon, might be spared to visit him. But Henry would not send Thomas either.

They had patched up their quarrel over the action at Toulouse, but I imagined Thomas had learned a lesson. He could go so far and no farther—although that was a great deal farther than most men would dare go.

Theobald expressed the hope that the King would consider Thomas à Becket to fill the post of Archbishop of Canterbury which would fall vacant on his death.

Theobald died that April. Henry was upset that he had lost such a good man, but he said he was in no hurry to fill his post. He could very well do without an Archbishop of Canterbury.

I was surprised that Theobald had suggested Becket. That worldly man—whose vanity was clearly a part of his nature, for otherwise why should he always appear in such exquisite garments and surround himself with beautiful possessions and revel in the life of luxury—Archbishop of Canterbury! It must have been a joke.

'Of course,' said Henry, 'if he were my Archbishop I could expect to be on better terms with the Church than I and my ancestors have sometimes been.'

'Thomas is a man who has his own opinions. Remember what he felt about Toulouse.'

'Thomas comes round to my way of thinking when it is necessary to do so.'

'Have you broached the subject with him?'

Henry shook his head. 'Not yet. I am unsure . . . so far. There is another matter I have to discuss with you. It concerns young Henry.'

'What of him?'

'He is now a married man.'

'He is six years old.'

'Too old for a future king to be in his mother's nursery.'

'I have always watched over the care of my children.'

'Which you must admit is not quite expected for a royal brood.'

'I care not what is expected. These are my children.'

'But listen to me. Henry has to be brought up in the household of a nobleman where he can learn the manly arts . . . where he is not able to run to his mother when he hurts his little finger.'

'That is not how the nurseries are run. The children are taught to be strong and resolute.'

'I know your feelings for them and I applaud them . . . in a measure. But Henry has to get out into the world. It has always been thus.'

I pondered this. It was true. Henry was getting to an age when he must leave the family nest for a while. I should not lose him altogether. Like all my children he was especially devoted to me. Henry's relationship with his children was perhaps the one part of his life in which he failed. His attempts to show affection were often clumsy. They respected and admired me; they liked my beautiful gowns; they would stroke the material and I would explain to them what it was and how I had designed my gown myself. They were my children more than his.

Henry would have to go, of course. I was delighted that Richard had quite a long time to stay with me.

I said; 'Into whose household did you propose to send him?'

'Why, Becket's, of course.'

'Becket's!'

'Why not? I shall send him to England with the child very soon.'

'You have told Becket?'

'I have.'

'And what does he think?'

'He is delighted. He already loves the boy.'

I said: 'At least he will be brought up to have a pride in his appearance.'

That amused Henry. 'True,' he said. 'He will be turned into an exquisite gentleman who will please his mother. Becket will make a man of him as well.'

Of course the boy would have his riding masters, his archery instructors; he would learn the laws of chivalry and everything that was necessary to his upbringing; and with Becket he would be trained in art, literature, music and all those accomplishments which I thought so necessary. No, I was not displeased. If he had to go to someone, Becket was the best choice.

'And what,' I said, 'if Becket becomes the Archbishop of Canterbury?'

'I see no harm in the future King's being brought up in the household of an Archbishop, do you?'

'None whatsoever,' I replied.

'There is something else. I want to make sure that there is no strife after my death. I want Henry crowned King of England.'

'What . . . now!'

He nodded. 'I lead a somewhat hazardous life. Here one day, but who knows where I shall be the next. What if I were to die tomorrow?'

'God forbid!'

'Thank you for your heartfelt expression of love for me.'

'Why do you talk of death in this way?'

'Because it is all around us. I want to make the throne safe for the boy.'

'But he is the natural heir.'

'There would be some, I daresay, to cast doubt on that. I want to be sure that, when I die, there is a king on the throne. I want Henry crowned . . . soon.'

'But what of you?'

'There will be two Kings.'

'Two Kings! Who ever heard of such! And one a boy of six.'

'He shall be King before I die. He won't know it, of course. It will make no difference, but he will be crowned, and if I died tomorrow, he is the King of England. The English would be very loth to turn from the throne one who has been anointed as their King.'

'I wonder at the wisdom of it.'

'*I* am sure of the wisdom of it.'

'Would the lords agree?'

'They might have to be persuaded.'

'I expect you could do that.'

'With Becket's help.'

'You have discussed this with Becket?'

'Not yet. Of course if he were Archbishop of Canterbury he would crown the boy.'

This man amazed me. I felt I should never know him.

We travelled to Rouen to see Matilda, who received us with great joy. She had changed even in the time since I had last seen her. I wondered if I should alter like that when my life was nearing its end. She was no longer the stormy creature of her earlier years. I believe her rages had been as violent as Henry's, only more dignified. I could not imagine her lying on the floor biting the rushes. Now she was a lady of good works. The people of Normandy had always respected her; it was those of England who would not have her. She had completed a Cistercian house near Lillebonne, was very proud of it and pleased that she had lived long enough to see its completion for, she told me, when she had been in Oxford, just before she had sped across the ice, she had made a vow to God that, if he would allow her to escape, she would build such a place.

Now she felt at peace.

Henry talked to her as he always had. He really did regard her as one of his generals. He always remembered that he could rely on her loyalty as on few others, and in addition to that he respected her judgement.

He talked about the vacant See of Canterbury.

'Theobald was a good man,' she said. 'It is always a sadness to lose such as he was. He was never a friend of mine. He was always Stephen's man, but he was unswerving in his devotion, and being a man of some wisdom he must have known that Stephen was not good for the country. Then on Stephen's death he turned to you with great relief. But he would never have helped you while Stephen lived. That is the sort of man you want around you. As I grow older, I regard loyalty as the greatest gift.'

'We have to fill the vacancy,' Henry said.

'Which you must do with the utmost care. An Archbishop of Canterbury can have too much power for a monarch's comfort.'

'That is what I think,' said Henry. 'It is why I am considering putting Becket in it.'

Matilda put her hand to her throat and turned pale.

'Becket!' she cried. 'Oh no, you must not do that.'

'Why?' cried Henry. 'He is the very man. He will work with me . . . not against me . . . as so many churchmen would do. I want no one taking his orders from Rome.'

'I feel it would be wrong to appoint Becket,' she said quietly.

'You do not know him as I do.'

'He is not so much a man of the Church as a diplomat.'

'Why should not the two go together?'

'It would be wrong.'

'I tell you, you do not know Becket.'

'I know it would not work.'

'But why . . . why? Give me one reason why it would be wrong.'

I reached out and touched her hand. She took mine and held it fast. 'I spend a great deal of time in prayer and meditation now, Henry,' she said. 'I can only say that something tells me it would be wrong. If you do this you will regret it. It will bring you great sorrow.'

'To have my best friend in such a post!'

'He cannot be Chancellor *and* Archbishop of Canterbury.'

'Why not? Tell me why not.'

'He cannot,' she said.

'My dear lady Empress, you are not acting with your usual good sense. Tell me what you have against Becket.'

'Nothing—except that he must not be your Archbishop of Canterbury.'

'Why? Why? Why?'

'I know it. There will be pain and suffering . . . violence. It must not be. I know these things.'

Henry said: 'I have made up my mind.'

'Becket has not agreed yet,' I reminded him.

'Becket will do as he is told.'

I could see that opposition was strengthening Henry's resolve. Usually he listened to his mother but in this matter I feared his mind was made up.

When I was alone with her, Matilda said to me: 'Try to persuade him. It is wrong. I am convinced of it.'

'You know Henry. Can anyone ask him to change his mind once he had made it up?'

'Oh, he is obstinate . . . obstinate. I trust this will not come to pass.'

'If you know something . . . if you could give him some good reason, he would listen to you.'

She touched her heart. 'It is just a feeling I have here.'

And that was all she would say.

We took our farewells of her. Henry was as affectionate as ever towards her but he did not mention Becket to her again.

I said to him: 'She is very insistent. It was almost as though she had some spiritual knowledge.'

'She has become very religious. I would never have believed it of her. She thinks Thomas a dandy, an ambitious man—and of course that is not her idea of what a man of the Church should be.'

'She did not say that . . . just that she had a strong conviction.'

'She is growing old, alas. She was a great woman when she was younger.'

I said: 'I think she is a great woman now. Have you discussed this matter of Becket with your ministers?'

'The decision is mine.'

'Why not wait until you get back to England and take it up with Leicester and de Luci?'

'I don't need to. My mind is made up.'

'And you think Becket will accept?'

'I think he must when he knows it is my will.'

I knew then that Becket would become our next Archbishop of Canterbury.

Becket's reaction to the suggestion was one of dismay. Henry told me of his reluctance.

'He declares that it will be the end of our friendship.'

'Why so?'

'Because the Church has always been at variance with the State.'

'Did you not tell him that your reason for appointing him was that your being such great friends—one head of the State, one head of the Church—you could put an end to such variance?'

'I told him that, yes.'

'And what did he say?'

'That if the variance was there, our friendship would not change it.'

'I must admit it is a strange appointment for such an ambitious man.'

'All archbishops are ambitious. Otherwise they would be parish priests all their lives.'

'But a man who is known for his sumptuous hospitality, who lives like a prince, who spends most of his time hunting and hawking with his dear friend, the King . . . he is not the man for the Church. A strange choice indeed for such a post.'

'I want it,' said Henry. 'He will work for me. My Chancellor and my Archbishop. It is an excellent arrangement.'

'You hope to manipulate Becket.'

'He might attempt to manipulate me.'

'He will not succeed. No one would succeed in doing that.'

'Ah, you have confidence in me then?'

'Confidence in your determination to have your own way and brush aside all who attempt to stop you.'

'Then I will have my way in the Church.'

'And has he accepted?'

'He was persuaded at length by those prelates who were present. They knew my will and they wanted to please me. Thomas said he was uneasy and he told me privately that he would be deeply grieved if there was friction between us.'

'He was outspoken about Toulouse.'

'Thomas would always be outspoken.'

'We can only hope that this appointment will bring harmony between Church and State.'

Thomas returned to England, taking young Henry with him. I was relieved to see that there was already affection between them. Thomas would be kindly and gentle with the boy, and that eased my qualms considerably.

In due course I heard that the Canterbury Chapter, having been made aware by the justiciar of the King's insistence, elected Thomas Archbishop, and later the election was ratified at Westminster by the bishops and clergy there. By June he was ordained priest in Canterbury Cathedral by the Bishop of Rochester, and the following day he was consecrated by the Bishop of Winchester. Henry arranged for the pallium to be sent to him from Rome, so that he did not have to make the journey there to get it; and by August he had received it.

He was now Archbishop of Canterbury but Henry thought it wise to postpone that other scheme for crowning Henry for a while, although he intended to do it in time.

Our progress through our dominions had taken us to Choisi on the Loire, and it was while we were resting there for a short period that the first indication of what trouble might be brewing between Henry and Thomas was given to us.

A messenger arrived from Canterbury. Henry received him at once. I was with him at the time and eager to know what news there was from England.

The messenger handed Henry a package. He opened it and stood for a moment looking in astonishment at what it revealed. It was the Great Seal of England and could mean only one thing. I saw his face grow purple as he read the accompanying letter.

I dismissed the messenger for I could see that Henry was going to have one of his rages and it would be well for the innocent carrier of bad news to be out of sight of that.

I went to him and took the letter from him. It was from Thomas à Becket. It stated that he must resign the chancellorship as he could not do his duty to one master while he served another.

Henry was spluttering: 'The knave! What did he think . . . it was what I planned. Chancellor and Archbishop . . . his duty lying with me. Now he will be a slave to the Pope.'

I shook my head slowly. Now was not the time to remind him of how his mother and others had warned him against taking this step. I saw the foam at his mouth and the wild look in his eyes. He picked up a stool and threw it at the tapestried wall. He clenched his fists, and blasphemies poured from his lips.

I stood watching him quietly.

This was a genuine rage. He had thought to rule Thomas à Becket and he had thrust him into a position which he did not want; now he was realizing that even he could make mistakes. His rage was against himself as much as Thomas. He flung himself onto the floor and catching up bunches of rushes gnawed at them insanely.

I think I fell completely out of love with him in that moment.

I was uneasy. Instinct told me that this was the beginning of conflict between the King and his newly appointed Archbishop.

My daughter was born that year. She was named Eleanor after me. We were in Normandy at the time, at a place called Domfont. She had a ceremonious baptism conducted by the Cardinal Legate who happened to be there at the time, and she was presented at the font by the Bishop of Avranches and Robert de Monte, Abbot of Mount St Michael.

She was a healthy baby—as all my babies had been, with the exception of William.

I was very happy with my children but I did miss my eldest, Henry, and his absence brought home to me the fact that I could not keep my children with me all the time.

The Beloved Enemy

I was no longer young. At forty most women are resigned to old age. I was not like that. I redoubled my efforts. I adopted a discreet use of cosmetics; I was meticulous in choosing my clothes. I knew that I looked like a woman ten years younger.

Henry was twenty-nine and looked more than his age. He was the opposite of me and never made any attempt to protect himself from the ravages of time, spending long hours in the saddle, sleeping in any place which offered itself, sharing the discomforts of his soldiers. That was probably why he had their devotion.

Sometimes I looked at him, with his bow-legs, his rough skin, his earthiness, and I marvelled that I could ever have been as obsessed by him as I was in the early days of our marriage. Added to all this was his blatant infidelity. I had accepted that because it meant nothing to him; and for all that he must have been aware of my waning affection there persisted a certain bond between us. We admired each other in certain ways. I had to admit that he was a great ruler; any decision he made had reason behind it. I had never known him make one which did not have what he believed to be some advantage to himself. Sometimes he was wrong, as in the case of appointing Thomas à Becket to the Archbishopric of Canterbury, thinking to have a Chancellor-Archbishop whom he could control. It was a mistake but it had had logical reasoning behind it. He had miscalculated his man though—which was odd when one considered all the time he had spent with Becket.

He reminded me that he had been four years in France. I had been here a considerable time too, but not quite as long as that.

'Four years away from my kingdom,' he said.

'We are singularly blessed in Leicester and de Luci.'

'Yes. But it is time I went back.'

I agreed with him. I wondered whether the appointment of Thomas had anything to do with his wish to return. I think I had begun to question my relationship with him when I first knew of Thomas. In those days they had been almost like lovers. Henry's eyes shone when he looked on the man; he began to be amused in anticipation before Becket spoke. There was some indefinable attraction Becket had for him. Thomas had never been diffident. There was nothing of the sycophant about him; indeed he had been openly critical of Henry, who had taken from him what would have enraged him from another. Perhaps I had been a little jealous in those days when Henry had meant a great deal to me.

And now, did he want to go back to England because Thomas was there? True, it was time he returned. England was the most important of his possessions. He must not neglect it.

His avaricious acquisitiveness put a great strain on him. He could never resist seizing any possession which came his way; he seemed to forget they had to be protected.

So now we were to return to England and he planned to spend Christmas at Oxford.

We travelled down to the coast. The sea was at its most treacherous, the winds violent. It would be folly to put to sea in such weather. We waited and time passed. We should certainly not be in England for Christmas.

Instead we spent it at Cherbourg without a great deal of celebration because we were unprepared; and each day we waited for the wind to abate. I was longing to see my son Henry and wondering how he was faring in Becket's household. It was about eight months since I had seen him and, as before that we had been constantly together, I missed him very much. I planned to see him as soon as I returned to England.

As the weather did not improve and we remained at Cherbourg, Henry grew very impatient.

'I doubt not,' I said, 'that the first person you will wish to see when we get to England will be your recalcitrant Archbishop.'

'I shall need to see all those who hold posts of importance,' he replied.

'I hope you will be equally eager to see your son.'

'Oh, he is in good hands . . . the best possible.'

'In the hands of the man who refused the office of Chancellor which you wished him to keep?'

'Becket has a mind of his own.'

'It would be better if that mind was in accordance with that of his King.'

'You have never liked the fellow. I can't think why. I should have thought he would have been your sort .. cultured . . . pretty clothes . . . nice clean hands. I think, my dear, you are a little jealous of my affection for him.'

'It was rather excessive.' He laughed aloud.

'Perhaps it has diminished a little,' I went on. 'He angered you when he slid out of the chancellorship.' Henry's face darkened at the memory, and I could not resist adding: 'You made it very clear that you were displeased.'

'Thomas is too honest a man to deny what he thinks right.'

'I hope he is as honest in all his dealings. He did manage to accumulate a great deal of wealth. I wonder how.'

'He would have been a fool if he hadn't, and Thomas is no fool.'

'I can see,' I said, 'that you are looking forward to the reunion. I myself look forward with equal pleasure to seeing my son again.'

It was not until the end of January that the weather allowed us to sail. When we landed at Southampton, Becket was among the delegation waiting to welcome us; and, to my delight, with him was Henry.

My son and I embraced. I held him at arm's length and looked into his handsome face. How I loved those fair Plantagenet looks which came from his paternal grandfather. It was a pity Geoffrey le Bel had not passed on his good looks to his son, but at least they were there in my children, having slipped a generation.

'You have been happy, I see, my son,' I cried. 'How we have all missed you.'

'I missed you,' said Henry.

'And you have been happy?'

'Oh yes.' I saw him look at Becket, and there was something like adoration in his eyes. I felt a twinge of annoyance, but my maternal feelings were stronger than petty jealousy. I was glad he had found a good home and affection with Becket.

Thomas himself had changed. He was thinner. His features, which had always been of an ascetic nature, were more so. There was a look of serenity about him. He was still splendidly attired, but I learned later that under his fine garments he wore a hairshirt. I was surprised. I had always felt a certain contempt for those people who tortured their bodies. Why? I asked myself. What good were they doing to humanity? What satisfaction could such acts bring to God? And what sort of god would be impressed by such folly? The wearing of hairshirts seemed to me a form of self-righteousness which I despised. I was surprised that Thomas could have indulged in such self-torture.

I warmed to him a little because he had been good to my son. I was deeply conscious of the greeting between him and the King.

Thomas knelt before Henry and I saw the softness in the King's face. 'Get up,' he said roughly, and then they were clasping hands, Henry was laughing.

'Well Archbishop-now and Chancellor-that-is-no-more, how fare you? By the eyes of God, you *look* like an Archbishop. What have you done to yourself? Come, we shall ride side by side.'

And they did. I heard their laughter and some of their conversation, in which Henry referred to Thomas's rejection of the Great Seal.

'Thomas, I could have killed you.'

'I guessed you would be displeased.'

'Displeased! I was murderous. It was a mercy for you, Thomas, that you did not bring the Seal yourself. How dared you provoke me so?'

'Because, my lord King, I knew I could not remain Chancellor and be Archbishop at the same time. The Church is apart from the State.'

'Why should they not march together?'

'They cannot always see through the same eyes.'

'Why shouldn't we make them do so?'

'It may not always be possible.'

'Then there will be trouble between us.'

'I feared that if I took the post it would impair our friendship, and that is very dear to me.'

'To me also, Thomas. We will work together.'

'There may be battles between us.'

'Good. I like a battle. I'd rather do battle with you, Thomas, than live in peace with others.'

Besotted as ever, I thought.

But that was not quite true. I sensed that Thomas knew it and saw trouble ahead.

And how right he proved to be.

Looking back, it seems to me that for a long period after our return to England our lives were dominated by Thomas à Becket.

I believe that, of all his possessions, Henry loved England best. If he had been content to be King of England only, his reign would have been completely rewarding. The people were of a less fiery nature than those across the Channel. They wanted a peaceful existence and knew that Henry was a strong king. It was because of this that he was able to leave the country in the hands of well-chosen administrators. He had already shown his ability to rule rather in the manner of his grandfather, the first Henry. At the beginning of his reign he had put the financial working of the exchequer in order and had changed the debased coinage of Stephen's regime to a uniform currency; he had brought new laws of justice into the country and new forms of taxation. Henry himself did not live extravagantly; when he needed money, it was for the country or to build up an army, to provide arms for his wars, which he would say were for the good of England.

On our return Henry thought we should make a progress through the country, and after Oxford we travelled to Westminster, then through Kent to Windsor, to Wales and up to Carlisle in the north. Henry was very anxious to call at Woodstock and spend some time there. Later I was to discover why he was so attached to this place.

By this time there was a controversy about what was called Sheriff's Aid. This was a tax which those who owned land paid to the sheriff to compensate him for his work on their behalf. Henry was in need of money and it occurred to him that if this tax was paid to the treasury as an ordinary one would be, instead of to the sheriffs, it could be of use to him.

At the council meeting at Woodstock, Henry brought up this matter of Sheriff's Aid.

In the past Becket had given his opinion freely to the King, and their friendship had not been impaired by this. But he was in a different position now and perhaps he over-rated the King's affection for him, because he immediately opposed Henry's suggestion that the tax should be paid to the treasury and not the sheriffs.

Becket said it would be a mistake to take this money from the sheriffs, which was just a payment for the services they rendered to the people who paid it. If the sheriffs were not paid, who knew what devious practices they would indulge in, to make up for their loss?

Henry was angry to be opposed—and by Becket.

'By the eyes of God,' he cried, 'it shall be given to the treasury as a tax, and it is not fitting for you, Archbishop, to oppose me.'

Thomas ought to have seen Henry's rising temper. He wanted Thomas on his side, not always pulling against him.

Thomas's reply was: 'By the reverence of those eyes, my lord King, not a penny shall be paid from any of the Church lands under my control.'

Henry's rages were generally well timed, and the council meeting was not the place to indulge in one. Coldly he dismissed the subject. But I could imagine how Thomas's opposition rankled; anyone else who aroused such animosity in him would have to beware. I thought then that it might have been different with Thomas—but perhaps not.

I believed Henry was waiting for some chance to show Thomas who was the master, and it did not help that he was defeated on this matter. He should have remembered that the Church had its own laws outside the State.

Even when I heard it, I could not resist mentioning this to Henry. I wanted to impress on him the mistake he had made in insisting on Becket's taking the archbishopric. This was just a small matter of contention between them. There could be bigger ones.

I said to him: 'This is one of the occasions when, in certain quarters, the Archbishop is more powerful than the King, the Church more than the State.'

'That is not so. But the Church has too much power.'

'You may think it is time that was changed. A matter like this will lead people to think that the Archbishop of Canterbury is the ruler of this country, not the King.'

That did nothing to soothe his ruffled temper, but I could not prevent myself telling him what I thought. I just had to remind him how foolish he had been to make so much of Becket and then commit the final folly of creating him Archbishop of Canterbury.

He then began to look about him to find some way of making Thomas understand that, although he had scored over this matter of the sheriff's tax, the King was most displeased at this attitude and it was something he would not tolerate.

Shortly after the controversy about Sheriff's Aid, there arose the case of Philip de Brois.

When Henry had taken over England after Stephen's death, he had been appalled by the anarchy which prevailed throughout the country and he had immediately begun to reform the laws and the administration of justice. He had instituted judges who travelled round the countryside trying the cases against criminals so that these were not left to local courts. It had had an undoubted effect, and the country was considerably safer for law-abiding people than it had been in Stephen's reign. But if a member of the Church was accused of a crime, he was not tried by the King's court of law but by that of the Church. It seemed to Henry that, if these particular criminals had enough influence in high places, they escaped very lightly.

It was another example of the Church's taking precedence over the State.

Thus the case of Philip de Brois.

The man was a canon who was accused of murdering a knight. I think it was some trouble over the knight's daughter, whom the canon was said to have seduced. When the canon was threatened by the girl's father and realized that his villainy was revealed, he promptly killed him. De Brois had been taken before an ecclesiastical court, presided over by the Bishop of Lincoln, where all he had been required to do was swear to his innocence—and having done so, he was released.

Henry, seeking ammunition with which to attack the Church, thought he might have it here.

'All this man did,' he pointed out, 'was to swear he was innocent. Any criminal could do that. There was no submission of evidence, no witnesses called . . . and he goes free. Why?

Because he is a canon of the Church, and the Church protects its own. Well, I am going to protect my people.'

In this battle with Becket he turned more to me. He knew that from the first I had resented his friendship with the man and he supposed that I would certainly not be ready to support Becket against him. I was not entirely in agreement with him because I felt he was doing harm to the people's image of him as a wise king by taking up the battle against Becket. By making Becket Archbishop, he had also made him a holy man in the eyes of the people. Chancellor Becket had been the worldly sophistocate; as an Archbishop he had made a complete turnabout; his tall, spare figure and his ascetic, pale face were an indication of his abstinence; the rich garments he wore were only a concession to his former tastes, and under them was the hairshirt.

My fortunes were bound up with those of Henry, and although I liked to score over him in private, I did not want his position to be shaken in the smallest way.

I said: 'The man is said to be innocent because he swears before God that he is, and it is said that any churchman would prefer to take his punishment on Earth, rather than suffer eternal damnation.'

'That's all very well,' said Henry, 'but a great many of these churchmen are rogues and they should be seen as such. Philip de Brois is going to come before one of my judges and he can plead innocence there, but if he is found guilty, he shall suffer a just punishment. How can I keep order in my land if the crimes which are forbidden to some are allowed to go free in priests?'

'You are fighting against the Church,' I said.

'The Church must obey the laws of the land like anyone else. And if I wish to fight against the Church, I will.'

But, of course, he was fighting against Becket.

He had ordered the judges to bring him a list of the priests who had recently been accused and released after swearing their innocence before a Church tribunal. It was one of these justices, Simon Fitz-Peter, who had brought up the case of Philip de Brois.

He said that he felt there was a strong case against the man and, acting on the King's order, when he was holding his assizes at Dunstable, he ordered Philip de Brois to appear before him to stand trial. Philip de Brois promptly refused and, moreover, was insulting to Fitz-Peter who reported the matter to Henry.

Henry was enraged. He demanded that de Brois now appear on two charges—murder and contempt of court.

This was where Becket came into the battle.

I could not understand the man. He was recklessly exposing himself to the King's wrath. Why? I have never understood Becket. It was as though there were two men in one body. In the days of his chancellorship when he had played the affluent dandy, with his luxurious living, his sumptuous table, surrounding himself with valuable possessions, always adorned in the finest clothes, there had yet been something austere about him. In spite of his grandeur and love of pomp, those fine classical features of his had suggested an ascetic man. Now one side of his nature seemed completely subdued. The ascetic had come forth, the sybarite had retreated. I was appalled to think of that hairshirt beneath his magnificent robes.

Becket was a man who could not be half-hearted on any matter. Now he had determined to defend the Church against the State—the State being his one-time close friend Henry. He was going to stand for the rights of the Church no matter in what danger it placed him. He was a dangerous man. As I watched this battle between them, I was growing very uneasy, and I was turning more and more against Henry. He was acting foolishly. He wanted to proclaim to all that he held supreme power. But the Church had stood through centuries, and I believed that he did not completely realize the formidable nature of his foe, so sure was he of his own strength.

Becket pointed out that the law could not be changed over one case. Men of the Church were tried by the Church. That was Church law. Henry might rant and rage but he had to accept Becket's logic. This was the law; and Henry, who set such store by law, could not enforce it on others and disregard it himself.

It seemed to me that he was losing this battle with Becket.

They both had to compromise. De Brois could not be tried in a lay court because he was a churchman. On the other hand, since the King wished there to be a further trial, this would have to be before an ecclesiastical court.

The result was a foreseen conclusion. The murder case, said the prelates who were gathered together to form judgement, had already been settled. De Brois had sworn his innocence. No priest would lie before God, for to do so was to imperil his immortal soul and destroy all hope of a future life. Therefore de Brois was innocent of murder.

It was true that he had flouted one of the King's justices and that was due for punishment. He had been guilty of contempt of the King's Court, and for that he should be exiled for two years. In addition he should wear a penitential robe and go barefoot to Simon Fitz-Peter and make his apologies to him for his ill-mannered and ill-advised behaviour.

When Henry heard this, he was enraged. His eyes looked as though they would fall out of his head; he ran his hands fiercely through his cropped curls and brought his fist down on a nearby stool with such vigour that I feared he had harmed himself.

'By God's eyes,' he cried, 'I'll have an end of this. I am going to study this whole matter of Church judgement versus the State. I'll not have others ruling in my kingdom.'

I said: 'You are taking on a mighty enemy in the Church.'

He did not answer. I knew he was thinking about Becket.

Another matter had arisen which gave Becket a chance once more to flout the King's authority.

Some time previously, Henry had wanted to arrange a match for his young brother William. William was a docile young man; he had never caused Henry trouble as his brother Geoffrey had. William was without ambition. He was gentle and all he wanted was to live in peace. It was difficult to understand how Geoffrey le Bel and Matilda could have had such a son. He was so different from his ambitious brothers.

Henry was very attached to William. He had at one time thought of conquering Ireland to give to him, but Matilda, seeing the folly of this, had dissuaded him. Henry had some strange notions sometimes. The idea of expecting a young man like William to hold in check one of the most turbulent places in the world was astonishing. However, Henry did not cease to think of William and wanted to see him comfortably settled; and if he could not be a ruler of Ireland, he could at least be a man of great wealth and property, as was due to the brother of the King.

The opportunity came with a widowed Countess, heiress to large estates. Henry sent for his brother and told him that he had a fine match in mind for him. William responded characteristically. He thanked his brother warmly for his efforts on his behalf, but when he married he must marry for love.

Henry greeted such a statement with roars of laughter. 'Marry for gain, boy,' he said. 'Love and marriage do not always go together but that does not mean you need not find love.'

But William was determined; it is amazing how strong the seemingly weak can be at times. Henry was fond of the boy. It had always been a comfort to have a young brother who was not planning to rise up against him and who bore no malice but only admiration for his success.

He asked William if he would be prepared to meet the lady and perhaps get to know her a little. William replied that would be a pleasure, for he did want to please his brother who had taken such pains to get him happily settled. The outcome caused Henry a great deal of amusement and satisfaction. The pair met and in a few weeks William came to Henry, his eyes alight with happiness. He had fallen in love with the Countess and she with him; there was nothing they wanted more than to be joined in matrimony.

Henry was gleeful. He embraced his brother. He said William had never caused him a moment's anxiety. Everything was set fair. Henry had provided for his brother. He was going to have the love match which suited his temperament and ideals, and the marriage would bring money into the family in the most agreeable way. What could have been more satisfactory?

And then Becket intervened.

The marriage could not take place because the bride and groom were second cousins, and in the eyes of the Church it would be no true marriage because of consanguinity.

Henry was furious. He cursed Becket. Here was the Church meddling again.

I was alarmed. I was afraid that if this matter were pursued Becket might raise the question of the legality of my marriage to Henry as there was a close blood tie between us. Our position was vulnerable. I had had my divorce from Louis because of the closeness of our relationship, and I was more closely related to Henry. What if Becket worked this out?

Henry was going to fight the matter out with Becket, but I reminded him of our own position and he saw the point. We had our children to think of. We did not want queries to be made concerning their legitimacy.

At length, with much gnashing of teeth, he agreed to let the matter of William's marriage drop and the pair parted, for the bride's family would not hear of a marriage forbidden by the Church.

It was yet another mark against Becket. The Philip de Brois case still rankled and Henry had made an oath that he would change the law.

We were at Westminster and Henry decided to delay no longer. He called together a meeting of the leading churchmen and the most important barons of the country.

When they were all assembled, he told them that for long he had been troubled about the crimes which were committed in the country and that he had pledged himself to restore that justice and respect for the law which had been the order of his grandfather's day.

'It has been brought to my notice,' he said, 'that numerous crimes have been committed by members of the Church who, when apprehended, immediately fly to the shelter of the Church which protects them from justice. During the years of my reign there have been over a hundred murders committed by men who, because they are priests, have never paid the penalty for their sin. There has been rape and robbery, and if the man who commits these crimes is a priest, all he has to do is stand up before his ecclesiastical friends and say, "I am innocent." It will not do. It is for this reason that we have priests who think they have special immunity and can commit crimes for which the layman is severely punished. Now, I intend that, in future, any churchman, whoever he may be, if he is suspected of a crime, shall be deprived of the protection of the Church and be given over to the judges whom I shall set up to try criminals, and so keep this country safe for law-abiding citizens. All my subjects must obey the same laws.'

He paused for a moment and looked full at Becket.

'My lord of Canterbury,' he went on, 'I demand that you and all your bishops and clergy give your consent to the handing over to my courts of justice any of your churchmen who are caught committing crimes, as was the law in my grandfather's reign.'

Thomas and his fellow churchmen were taken by surprise. They had thought they were called together to discuss other matters. Thomas must have forgotten what he knew of Henry if he thought he would let the matter of Philip de Brois be passed over easily. He should have been prepared for this.

He asked permission to retire with this fellow churchmen, for, he said, they must discuss this in private. Henry gave them permission and they filed out.

When they came back, Thomas announced that it was not fitting for the King to make such a demand, nor was it fitting for the clergy to grant it. They must obey the law of the Church.

Henry shouted angrily that the laws had worked well in his grandfather's day, and in those days archbishops who had been dedicated servants of the Church—holier men than some he could name today—had not questioned the rights of the King's Courts to try criminals.

Thomas replied that the clergy would be obedient and ready to obey the King in everything they could, saving their order.

Henry cried out that he wanted to hear nothing of their order. He demanded that they obey the King. He wanted their obedience to the old laws which had worked well for the country under the first Henry.

He turned his back on Thomas and demanded one by one of the others if they would obey their King. They all gave the same answer which Becket had. They would obey the King, saving their order.

Henry talked to them, cajoling them, threatening them. They stood firmly with Becket.

They had already sworn an oath of allegiance from which they would never swerve, said Becket. They would obey him in all things . . . saving their order.

Saving their order! How he hated the phrase. It meant they would serve him unless the Church wanted them to do otherwise.

Frustrated, angry, unable to keep his rage under control, Henry left the hall. He came to me and told me exacty what had happened.

''Saving our order'': they kept repeating it . . . one after another. It was Becket. Without him it would have been easy. I should have had them. But there he was . . . determined to have his way, determined to show me that the Church comes before the State. Who would have believed it of him?'

'Some of us would,' I reminded him.

He might have turned on me in rage but he did not. All his anger was for Becket. I think he blamed himself. He had been warned. He had thought that an Archbishop who was also his

Chancellor would go step by step with him. He had not known Becket, it seemed. In any case, Becket had changed. He was a different man from the one who had hawked and hunted with Henry. He was an archbishop now, not an elegant dilettante. He was a man of the Church and had taken up his new profession with a zeal which astonished all. Henry was beginning to see that, in thinking to make his way easy, he had created a great obstacle to his plans.

He had himself to blame—but instead he blamed Becket.

'I'll show him,' he cried, 'He will see what it means to bait me.'

He could never have been judicious where Becket was concerned. He must have either great love or great hatred for the man. Now it was hate and it burned fiercely.

What harm could he do Becket? Becket loved his possessions. He loved comfort, ease, grand living; his pallium could not make up for that. Very well, he would begin by robbing him of some of the manors in which he had taken great pride. He would begin with Berkhampsted and follow with Eye. They were two manors very dear to Thomas's acquisitive heart.

Perhaps Becket was hurt even more than he was by the loss of Berkhampsted and Eye when Henry took our son out of his care.

Young Henry came to me bewildered and sad. I greeted him warmly and told him how I had missed him.

He said he missed me too. 'But why do I have to leave Thomas?' he asked. 'Is it just for a while or for always?'

'It will depend. At the moment your father is not very well pleased with the Archbishop.'

'I hope I may go back.'

'You were happy there, were you not?'

Henry nodded and I saw the faraway look in his eyes.

'He was not in the least like an archbishop,' he said.

'I can believe that.'

'He was so merry. There was always fun. He was so kind. He always explained everything . . . he made it interesting. Has he offended my father?'

'I think you could say that.'

'But Thomas would never offend anyone. He is so kind and so good.'

I could see that young Henry loved the man as his father once had.

Henry questioned young Henry about the time he had spent in the Archbishop's household, but he was rather impatient with the boy when he saw that he had put Becket on a pedestal.

'He has his good points,' said Henry, 'but he is obstinate and he wants to put the Church above the State.'

Young Henry said: 'He is a churchman. That is why.'

'He is first of all one of my subjects . . . as you all are.'

'But . . .'

'Don't argue with me,' snapped Henry.

I saw the look in my son's eyes, and it was by no means one of affection. It occurred to me that he was comparing his father with Thomas, and it was the King who suffered from the comparison.

Becket obsessed Henry. Before we left Northampton he decided that he would meet the Archbishop alone. There should be just the two of them. They could meet in a meadow, and perhaps without any lookers-on they could settle their differences.

During this time Henry and I had grown a little closer to each other. I think he felt the need of my support. I was rather pleased at this and felt gratified because I had always viewed his friendship with Becket with suspicion. It was as though I was being proved right. He did not mention this, but the fact that he confided in me showed me his feelings, especially as he was growing affectionate again. He could share his thoughts with me, so I knew very well how much Becket was affecting him; and he did tell me in detail about that meeting in the meadow.

'I thought,' he said, 'if we got right away from our retinues, if he could forget for a while that he was the Archbishop of Canterbury and I the King, we might get on terms we enjoyed during our old friendship. I told him to dismount and I would do the same. We would walk together . . . nothing about us but the grass and the sky. We could both feel free to talk as we willed without an audience.

'He obeyed me and I took his arm. I noticed how thin he had grown. He takes his religion seriously. He really does see himself as God's servant. He used to see himself as mine. I said that he opposed me at every turn—we used to be such good friends—and he replied that he did no such thing. It just happened that my wishes clashed with his duty.

'Then I said that he was ungrateful. He seemed to forget how I had raised him up. Who was he? Thomas à Becket! Was his father not some merchant . . . his mother a Saracen? I told him to consider what he had now. I had lifted him from nothing to be my Chancellor. He said, "That is what I should have remained." "And now," I went on, "you are my Archbishop." "I did not want the post," he replied. "You insisted that I take it. I knew it would mean strife between us, for the Church and the State cannot always march together." '

'It is what your mother implied. Do you remember?'

He nodded grimly. 'I grew angry with him. "Why not?" I demanded. "It is for this reason that I made you my Archbishop. We worked together when you were Chancellor. Why the change of heart when you are Archbishop?" '

'And what did he say to that?'

'He said, "Am I not the head of the Church in England?" '

'And you reminded him that you were the head of all your subjects?'

'I did. He said he was indeed my subject—but God's first. You can imagine how this talk of God angered me.'

'I can indeed.'

'I called him ungrateful. He replied that he was not ungrateful for favours received from me through God. You see, he has to bring God into everything—and that did not soothe my temper, I can tell you. He went on, "I would never resist you if it were the will of God. You are my lord, but God is your Lord and mine also, and it would be wrong for both of us if I should forsake His will to follow yours." I told him that since he had become a churchman he seemed to be on very intimate terms with God. He knew of course what was God's will, and that rather conveniently seemed to coincide with Thomas's own. He smiled at me sadly and said the day would come when we should both stand before the Judgement Seat. I was angered by his sanctimonious tone. How different he used to be I shouted at him. "And to you God will say, 'Well done, thou good and faithful servant,' and to me, 'Get thee down to Hell. You have disobeyed the will of my good Thomas and as you should know he and I are always together in the right.' " I was getting more and more angry.'

I smiled. 'And you had gone there with the desire to make things right between you. It must have been very frustrating.'

'Oh, it was indeed. He is a very obstinate man. I said to him, "You think the King should be tutored by a rustic . . . a peasant such as you are." He replied, "It is true I am not royal but St Peter was not royal either and God made him head of His Church and gave him the keys of Heaven." "Ah," I said, "and he died for his Lord." "I will die for my Lord when the time comes," he replied piously. "Becket," I told him, "you have stretched too far and grown above yourself. You believe that because I have lifted you up I have made you more important than I am. You think you can defy me with impunity. Have a care, Becket. My patience, as you know, is not great." "I shall trust in the Lord," he answered. "I would not put my trust in any man."

'He enraged me and yet at the same time I had some respect for his fervour. I would be lenient with him. I said, "There is not really much about which we disagree. There are just one or two points. Just swear that you will serve me. Forget about your order. Come. Give your complete allegiance to the King. Then all shall be as it once was between us." I meant it. I would forgive him all the troubles he has caused me. I wanted to be on good terms with the man.'

'I know you have always had a great affection for him. None but Thomas à Becket would have dared provoke you so.'

'Still, he would not give me what I wanted. He kept saying, "In all things save when it would be in conflict with my order." I gave him one last chance. I said to him, "I have tried to reason with you, because of the friendship we once had. I have stripped myself of my royalty and come to you as a friend . . . as a commoner. I will put aside all the trouble you have caused me; you shall not suffer for it. You shall have Berkhampsted back . . . Eye, too. Young Henry shall return to you. Come, Thomas, what say you? Remember how we enjoyed life together . . . what friends we were? All you have to do is give me your word. You will obey the King . . . in all things." And what do you think he said to that?'

'I can guess.'

'He said, "I cannot deny my order, which is to deny God." I shouted at him then. I had waived my dignity . . . everything for friendship and all he could do was mutter about his order. He would not budge one iota. I told him I would put him back where he was before I set him up. Everything he had he owed to me. He had better be careful, I said. I had had enough of his disobedience. He thought because of the great friendship I had shown him he could treat me scurvily. "You will see," I told him, "what it is to tangle with kings." He did not flinch. He just bowed his head; and I left him. That meeting should never have taken place.'

'No,' I agreed. 'You have gone a long way to placate Becket.'

'No more,' he shouted. 'No more. Now there is a war between us and that augurs ill for Becket.'

'We shall spend Christmas at Berkhampsted,' said Henry. 'Becket will hear that we are there. It will remind him of the proud possession which is no longer his.'

He continued to be obsessed by Becket. Now he was turning over in his mind how he could do him some harm. He wanted revenge; but in his heart I knew he longed for the old friendship.

I was annoyed. He had cared for Becket more than he ever had for me. It was humiliating; but because of his obsessive love, his hatred was the greater, and what he wanted now, since there could not be reconciliation, was revenge.

Henry decided to appeal to the Pope. He believed he might very well be successful in this, for Alexander III was not in a very happy position at this time, and when their state is weak, Popes are often ready to placate powerful monarchs. Henry knew that Alexander could not afford to offend him. When the English Pope, Nicholas Breakspear, who called himself Hadrian IV, had died, there were differences in the Church and two rivals came on the scene. Henry promised his support to Alexander, who was now living in France, and it was to Alexander that the appeal against Becket was addressed.

Henry stressed that he was a good churchman. He was a ruler who wanted nothing but obedience from his subjects, and Alexander would understand that no king could effectively rule without that. He could not allow anyone—even though he held a high position in the Church—publicly to declare his disobedience. All he wanted was a word from his Archbishop that he would obey the King—and that he must have. He said that he wished the Church to be strong in England, for all knew that the Christian faith kept men righteous. Thieves, murderers and rapists were irreligious men and he wanted to rid his realm of them; but to do this he must have power to enforce his laws and he could not allow any man—even if he be a priest—to escape justice.

Henry was known as a man of purpose, and Alexander would understand that he could not be ignored. He might have supported the Archbishop if he had been in a position to do so. It always amuses me to see how these religious men are influenced by their personal needs.

The result was that Alexander wrote to Becket telling him that there must be no quarrel between the Church and the King and that if it was a matter of saying a few words it would be wise for Becket to say them.

I should have enjoyed seeing Becket's face when he read that. How did he feel about his master the Pope, who was not prepared to take a small risk when he, Becket, was staking his whole career and perhaps his life? But he was trapped. He had orders from the Pope and he must give way because of the uncertainty of Alexander's position, for Alexander, who needed all the support he could get, was not going to offend a monarch as powerful as Henry.

Becket sought a meeting.

I was with Henry when he was brought in. He looked very disturbed. He must have been feeling that he had been betrayed by the Pope.

I was mildly irritated to see that Henry's mood had softened at the sight of Becket. It was amazing that, after all that had happened, he could still feel affection for him. I believed he was telling himself that when this little matter had been settled and Becket realized it would be wise to stand firmly beside the King, they could return to their old relationship.

'Well,' said Henry expansively, 'what has His Holiness to say on our little matter?'

'He is of the opinion that I must swear to serve you without reservations.'

'Wise man. So our little difference is over, eh?'

'The Pope commanded it.'

Henry's genial mood began to fade. 'And you must obey *him*, eh?'

'I must, my lord King.'

'You must, of course . . . while you disregard me.'

'He is the Head of the Church.'

'And you still think that you were right and His Holiness is wrong?'

'I thought I was right in what I did.'

'And because he is not prepared to agree with you, you will do your duty and swear allegiance to your King?'

'I am assured from His Holiness that I must make this concession because you, as the King of this realm, cannot have your wishes openly disregarded and that you have given your word that you will not go against the laws of the Church.'

'You swear to obey me, Thomas?'

'I do, my lord.'

Henry's face was tinged with purple. I could see the love fighting with the hatred. He so desperately wanted this man to tell him that he would serve him, forsaking all other; he wanted not so much complete obedience from Thomas as love; he wanted Thomas to break down that cold reserve, that dedication to his Church, to be as he had been in the old days when they had roamed the streets of London together, sharing interesting conversation, private jokes, enjoying the fun which two people, close in spirit, can find in each other. But between them stood the Church. Thomas was a strange man. Perhaps therein lay his fascination.

Remembering the past was angering Henry. Why had it changed? And all because he had bestowed on this man high office in the Church. He had been a fool to do it. He had been warned . . . outspokenly by his mother, obliquely by me . . . and by Thomas himself. Henry hated to think himself a fool and it was typical of him that when the blame rested on himself he sought to shift it onto others.

His face hardened. 'I am glad of your allegiance, Thomas,' he said, 'grudgingly given though it is and on the orders of one whom you serve before you serve me.'

'My lord, then I trust all is well between us,' said Thomas.

'You opposed me in public,' said Henry, his lips tightening, so I knew he was controlling his rage. 'It is not fitting that you should give me your apology in private. I shall need you to make your oath of allegiance to me before the Great Council.'

Becket looked stunned and Henry laughed harshly.

'It will soon be Christmas,' said Henry, 'and, knowing your pleasure as well as your pride in the place, I, with the Queen and the Court, am spending it at Berkhampsted.'

* * *

That was not a very happy Christmas. I could not find much pleasure in spending it among what was some of Becket's splendour. I was glad when it was over.

The Great Council was to assemble on 25 January, and it was to be held in the hunting lodge at Clarendon, not far from Salisbury. We arrived on the 13th. The children were with us.

Young Henry was very thoughtful and I noticed that he avoided his father. The King could never understand children; he underrated their intelligence and treated them as little children, not realizing how quickly they become adults; and I think there is nothing children resent so much as this attitude.

Young Henry was aware of a great deal more than his father gave him credit for.

I said: 'Your father has had a difference of opinion with the Archbishop because the Archbishop stands for the Church and your father for the State.'

'But the Church is part of the State, is it not?' asked Henry.

'Yes, but the Church is under the rule of the Pope and the State under that of the King and sometimes it makes for differences.'

I explained about the King's desire that all criminals should be judged by the State and that there should not be special privileges for members of the Church.

'And Thomas wants those privileges?'

'Well, he would, you see, being the head of the Church in England.'

Henry pondered this. He was on Thomas's side not because he believed that Thomas was right but because he loved Thomas, and the plain truth was that he did not love his father. My feelings were mingled. I thought Henry was right in this matter. I could not see why murderers should go free just because they were clergy. I believed many of them were rogues and would be prepared to swear their innocence for the sake of escaping punishment for their misdeeds. But I had to admit to a great pleasure when I saw my children turn to me rather than to their father. Henry had disappointed me in many ways. I found it hard to forgive his blatant infidelity, especially in the days just after our marriage; and my nature was such that I enjoyed scoring over him.

Richard particularly clung to me. I think he actually disliked his father. My main pleasure now was in my children. I would defend them against their father always and I think they knew it.

A great deal of preparation was going on for this meeting in the hunting lodge. The leading churchmen, with all the most influential noblemen in the country, were arriving.

Henry said to me: 'This is going to be a most impressive occasion. It will do young Henry good to sit beside me and watch the proceedings. It will teach him a little perhaps.'

I wondered if that were wise. The conference would stress the clash between Becket and the King, and in view of the fact that our son had spent a long time in the Archbishop's household and obviously idealized him, and that his antagonist was the King, it seemed to me as if it might have an undesirable effect on the boy. I did not mention this to Henry, knowing in advance that he would not understand.

It was a tense moment. I was beside the King: on the other side was young Henry. I watched my son when Becket came into the court.

There were a few preliminaries, then Henry rose and said: 'My lords, you know what has gone before. There has been a little misunderstanding between myself and the Archbishop. I am happy that is now at an end. Thomas à Becket, Archbishop of Canterbury, has come to swear before you all that he will unconditionally serve the King.'

He turned to Thomas. The Archbishop's face was very pale, his eyes were brilliant. He was an impressive figure; his emaciated looks proclaimed his religious fervour. I thought of the hairshirt under the magnificent robes . . . verminous, most likely. I thought of Louis on his knees at our bedside. And I wondered afresh about these men who seem pointlessly to pursue their painful devotions to a god of their own conception, for this must be so. What god would wish those he loved to submit themselves to senseless torture for his sake? There was no logic in it. I despised them for their folly. Yet it was difficult to despise Thomas. There was indeed an air of saintliness about him. I should not have been surprised to see a halo spring up round his head. I glanced at my son, who was staring at Thomas, his eyes shining. I could see that he would be ready to worship the man.

Thomas stood up. He was going to bow to Henry's will. He

would never have the courage to do otherwise . . . not even Thomas. There were armed men in the hall and outside. Thomas would know that if necessary they would do what the King commanded. His enemies were waiting to pounce, chief among them Roger de Pont l'Evêque, Archbishop of York, who had always hated him and must have gnashed his teeth in envy over his rise to fortune. Roger was that very ambitious priest who had been in Theobald's household when Thomas was there and who had contrived to bring about the latter's dismissal. How he must have resented seeing Thomas Archbishop of Canterbury when he, for all his brilliance and scheming, had only York. Roger could be depended upon to do Thomas all the harm he could; and no doubt Roger was not the only one. A man who rose high could be sure that he would incur hatred, for no other reason than that he had risen, and the more spectacular the rise, the more people wished to pull him down.

I had to admit that Thomas was a brave man. There was a certain recklessness about him. He was as though he were courting martyrdom.

His voice was unfaltering; it rang out clearly in the hall.

'My lords, I swear to serve the King when that service does not conflict with my duty to the Church.'

I saw young Henry's face turn pale. He realized what was happening. The man he loved was defying his all-powerful father.

I waited. Would there be a rage here in the council chamber? Would he roll on the floor; would he kick and shout and gnash his teeth?'

Henry began to shout. He pointed at Thomas, his eyes bulging, foam on his lips. I prayed that he would not completely lose control. He was fighting to retain it, I knew. 'If this man does not observe the laws and customs of my kingdom, I will resort to the sword.'

Thomas stood calm as though waiting for the blow.

Henry was clenching and unclenching his hands. What would the assembled nobles think, all those dignified churchmen . . . to see their King rolling on the floor like an animal?

But Henry controlled himself sufficiently to stride from the room.

There was a long silence. I felt for my son's hand and held it reassuringly.

The meeting was broken up for that day.

* * *

Henry went into the court next day with documents setting out the laws which had been in existence in his grandfather's day. All had agreed, had they not, that his grandfather had administered the law to the utmost satisfaction of all. Had he not been known throughout the country as 'The Lion of Justice'? All he wanted was a return to those laws and a peaceful country in which it was safe for men to travel unmolested. The laws had lapsed since his grandfather's time. All he wanted was to return to them.

'And to prevent trouble rising in the future,' he said, 'I wish the Archbishop of Canterbury to put his seal to them.'

There stood that strange man, stirring us all—even myself— with a sense of awe. There was something quite spiritual about him. I wondered what it was. Perhaps the contrast to all we knew of his earlier life, his love of comfort, which showed even now in the fine material of his robes. I reminded myself again of the hairshirt. He was a mass of contradictions, that man.

Now he spoke in ringing tones. 'By Almighty God, never as long as I live will I put my seal to them.'

Then he took an unprecedented action: he strode from the hall.

We were all aghast. Roger of York could not hide his satisfaction. Henry was too shocked for rage. That would come later. My son looked shocked and bewildered. For a moment I thought he was going to burst into tears.

There could be no turning back now. My rival for Henry's affections was completely destroyed. This must be the end of Becket. But in my heart I knew that, whatever happened, Becket would always be there in Henry's thoughts. He would never escape from him.

Henry had recovered a little from the shock Becket had given him by his abrupt departure from the hall. He was debating what his next action would be.

I wondered whether he would have Becket arrested as a traitor. That was possible. Becket had refused allegiance to the crown . . . had openly done so. There was tension. Everyone was waiting for Becket's arrest. I thought he might welcome it. It would all be part of what I called his 'hairshirt mentality'.

There was a little trouble between the two Henrys. The King asked his son what he thought of the proceedings.

Young Henry said he thought the Archbishop very noble.

'Noble!' screamed his father. 'To defy me?'

'He did it for the Church . . . because he thought it was right.'

'Well, my son, he must be a fool then if he thinks it is right to go against his King.'

'The Archbishop is not a fool.'

'What then? I could have his head for this.'

'He does not care for his head. He cares for what is right.'

'Right!' cried the King. 'Right to defy *me*! Fine words from the heir to the throne.'

'The Archbishop always said we must tell the truth . . . no matter how hard it is. The great Christians did . . . even though it cost them their lives.'

'What has he been stuffing your head with?' demanded Henry.

'With truth,' said the boy, defiant in his loyalty to Becket.

I could see that Henry was still smarting from insults from Becket and was in no mood to listen to his defence from his own son.

I went to the boy and ruffled his hair.

I said to Henry: 'He is a boy, you know. It is right that he should respect truth. He is not yet ready for politics.'

The King was scowling. I had to pull Henry away. He would have stood there and faced his father; but I wanted no trouble for the boy and I knew how fierce the King could be.

He was staring at us as we left. I knew because I turned my head and saw. I gave him a placating smile, implying: He is only a child. Leave the children to me.

When we were alone I said to my son: 'You are not old enough to take up arguments with your father.'

'The Archbishop is right,' he said stubbornly.

'The King is the head of the country,' I reminded him. 'Kings make rules. All you father wants is to try those who commit crimes, whoever they are.'

'But it is against the law of the Church, and the Archbishop has sworn allegiance to the Church.'

'That is a quarrel which has gone on through the ages. Church against State. It is something with which you will have to deal when you are King.'

'I hope that when I am I shall have men like Thomas about me.'

'They can be very uncomfortable at times, as you have seen.'

'But he is right . . . right.'

'Do not let your father hear you say that again. Remember that we have to support the crown. Your father is the King. You will be the King. If it is to be a battle between Church and State, it must be the State for you.'

'I do not see why they cannot work together. All this swearing about small matters is not necessary.'

'You will understand one day. A king must be strong. Your father is that.'

He was silent but his eyes narrowed and his mouth was hard. I kissed him. 'Come. Forget the matter.'

He would not. Later I remembered that occasion, and it occurred to me that it was a beginning.

Everyone was waiting now for what would happen next. There was one thing which was certain. The matter would not be allowed to rest. The King and the Archbishop were at war with each other, and the King could not afford to have an enemy in a high place. It rankled all the more because he had put him there.

When it came to Henry's ears that Louis had written encouraging letters to the Archbishop congratulating him on the firm stand he was taking on behalf of the Church and in the name of God, he was furious; he raged and shouted abuse of Louis, that lily-livered half-man. Louis hinted that, should life in England become intolerable for Thomas, there would be a welcome for him across the water.

To make matters worse, a tragedy struck the family, and this again Henry laid at Thomas's door.

There was news from Matilda. Her letter betrayed her violent grief. Her young son William was dead.

Henry could not believe it. When last he had heard of William, his brother had been perfectly well—sad, of course, because he had been in love with the Countess and on account of consanguinity he had been denied—by that meddling priest Thomas of Canterbury—permission to marry her.

Matilda wrote: 'Dear William, he was always so gentle, so different from you and Geoffrey. He only wanted to live in peace and amity with the whole world. He never sought anything for himself. He only wanted love and he could have had it—but your Archbishop prevented the marriage. He never recovered from that disappointment. He was listless. When he came to me I was shocked by the sight of him. I nursed him myself but it was no good. He did not care to live. He caught a cold. There are so many draughts in the castle. I think he could have recovered, but he just did not want to live without the Countess. You should never have appointed that man as Archbishop. Now he has killed William.'

The letter dropped from Henry's hand. I picked it up and read it.

Henry's face was crumpled in sorrow. He had really loved William. Then suddenly his grief turned to rage.

'It is Thomas à Becket . . . always Thomas. He plagues me. He brings trouble into my life.'

'It would seem so,' I agreed.

Henry sank onto a stool and covered his face with his hands. Then he lifted his eyes to my face, and I saw the burning hatred there.

'This,' he said, 'I will never forgive.'

Tension was increasing all through that summer. I knew that sooner or later it would have to come to a head. Henry's mind was completely obsessed by Becket. I knew he would not rest while Thomas was in the country. He wanted to dismiss him, but he could not dismiss the Archbishop of Canterbury. All he could do was hope to humiliate him into resigning.

I did not think Thomas would do that. He would consider he had failed the Church if he did. He would want to stand firm and fight the good fight for the sake of the Church.

He did, however, make two attempts to escape during that summer, I heard afterwards. On one occasion he disguised himself as a monk and with only a few of his loyal servants rode to Romney, where a boat was to have been waiting to take him across the water to enjoy that hospitality which Louis had promised him. However, the elements were against him, and the boatmen would not risk their lives trying to cross on such seas. I wondered what he thought of God's being so careless as not to arrange better weather for His chosen one. He would always have an answer, such as, 'God has other plans for me.'

He could not stay in Romney and had to return to his palace. When he arrived late at night, his servants thought he was a ghost and some terrible fate had befallen him. They were terrified but at last he was able to persuade them that he was no ghost and they let him in; he was their own Archbishop and was still with them because it was God's will that this should be so.

Then came an opportunity to summon him to the court.

One of Henry's officers, John the Marshal, brought an action against the Archbishop's court. There had been a dispute over a piece of land in Pagham in Sussex, which John claimed as his; but it happened to be on Church land and the Church disputed John's claim to it. Then a court, set up by the Church, heard the case and set aside John's claim. Under the new law John could contest the case and have it tried in the Kings's court.

Henry was delighted, for here was a chance to come once more into conflict with the Archbishop.

The court was to be held in Westminster, and Henry, with great glee, summoned Becket to appear.

On the day set for the hearing, Becket did not arrive in court. He sent a message to say he was unwell.

Henry did not intend to spare him, though Becket had sent four knights and a sheriff with the letter in which he stated he was too unwell to attend court, and the case ought not to be brought, as John the Marshal had taken his oath on a hymn book instead of the Bible.

Henry then declared that he did not believe in Becket's illness. He said Becket need not think he was going to escape. The suit should be held on 6 October, which was a few weeks later, and it should take place at Northampton, where we should be at that time.

Henry had worked himself up into a passion, certain that Becket had been well enough to attend on the previous occasion, and when he was in court and Becket put forward his case, Henry refused to listen and accused him of contempt of court. He demanded that sentence be passed against him.

Henry was so fierce in his accusations that those who were to judge took fright and, realizing that he wanted Becket found guilty, condemned him to be 'at the King's mercy'. This generally meant that he would be required to give up all his goods to the King, but in most cases it was a figure of speech and merely meant the imposition of a fine.

But Henry wanted more than that. He wanted the sentence carried out to the letter. He sent his demands, which were enormous, referring back to the time when Becket had been Chancellor and money had passed into his hands. Everything must be accounted for. It was clear that the King's intention was to ruin Becket.

Sick and emaciated from insufficient nourishment, Becket was ill again and could not appear in court to face more charges. When he did not arrive, Henry humiliated him by sending several men to his chambers to be assured that the Archbishop was not malingering.

I think at that time Becket wanted to be a martyr. His feelings for the King must have been as strong as Henry's for him, and in my opinion he wanted to goad Henry into doing something which would cause him lifelong regret. He came into the court, bare-footed and carrying his own cross, implying that it was his only protection against a tyrant. I heard that his advisers clustered round him—one urging him to use his power to frighten the King with a threat of excommunication, another to remember the saints and meekly accept what was coming to him.

Henry was not present on this occasion. His feelings fluctuated; he swayed between love and pity for his old friend and hatred and the desire for revenge. He could not face him, so he sent the Earl of Leicester to sentence him. What the sentence would have been it was never discovered because it was never given. Becket told the Earl so sternly and with such conviction that he was committing a sin by attempting to sentence his spiritual father that Leicester refrained from doing so. And Becket left the hall, carrying his own cross.

The next day news was brought to Henry that the Archbishop had disappeared.

Henry fell into a rage. He shouted that the traitor had escaped him. He would go to France, where they would make a saint of him. It would be easy for him to work against the King there and he must be stopped.

He commanded that all ports be watched.

It was some time afterwards that we heard what actually happened. Being aware that the King's men would be waiting for him at the port of Dover, Thomas, disguised as a monk, had turned northwards and gone to Grantham and from there to Lincoln. There were many who regarded him as a saint and were ready to shelter him. So he was travelling in England for some days, and from Lincoln he sailed down to Boston, and then turned back to Kent. With him was Roger de Brai, who would serve him with his life, and two lay brothers, Robert de Cave and Scailman. It was a hazardous journey and they knew that one false step could lead them to disaster. Becket would be called a traitor now, and the fate of traitors was death.

They took their lives in their hands every time they rested for a night, but in due course they came to the little village of Eastry, close to Sandwich, and they stayed there for a while in the house of a priest until a boat could be found and the weather was clement enough to give them a safe crossing.

In due course they set sail and were fortunate enough to pass safely over the sea and to land on the sands of Oie, not far from Gravelines.

I wondered what Thomas à Becket's thoughts were when he went ashore from his little boat. Did he think of that other time when he had come to this spot with splendour and pomp, come on a mission from the King to ask for the hand of Louis's daughter for Prince Henry? Then he had been the King's beloved friend; now he was his bitter enemy.

The Fair Rosamund

Henry's reaction was what I should have expected. When he finally realized that Becket had escaped him and landed in Flanders and was doubtless on his way to take advantage of Louis's offer of protection, he was overcome with rage.

This time he did not attempt to suppress it. He raved and ranted, tore at his hair, screamed abuse, lay on the floor, kicked the furniture and, seizing handfuls of rushes, gnawed them.

I stood watching him dispassionately. Everyone else made haste to get out of the way when these moods took him.

He was aware of my analytical gaze. It angered him. He would have liked me to be terrified. I just thought he was behaving like a spoilt child.

At length he grew calmer. He stood up and, after kicking viciously at the legs of the table sat down heavily and stared into space.

'He'll go to Louis,' I said. He nodded.

'And Louis,' I went on, 'will make much of him.'

'Oh yes, indeed he will. He'll do anything to make trouble for me. He will be laughing at this. These two good men of the Church will put their pious heads together. I can see that. I must write to Louis without delay. I must tell him my side of the story. I shall demand that Becket be sent back to me. What right has Louis to keep a subject of mine?'

I shrugged my shoulders. 'If he is there and Louis allows him to stay, he will,' I said.

'Oh yes, yes, he'll be there . . . with his tales of the wickedness of the King of England.'

'I daresay he will tell what actually happened.'

Henry sent for writing materials. I saw what he wrote.

'Thomas, who was my Archbishop of Canterbury, has been judged in a court of a company of lords, a traitor against me. I beg you not to allow this guilty man to remain in your kingdom. Let not this enemy of mine have help from you, as I would never give to any of your enemies . . .'

Becket had gone but could not be dismissed. Henry would sit glaring before him and I knew he was wondering: Where is Becket now? What is he doing?

We left Northampton and travelled by degrees to Marlborough where we were to spend Christmas. I guessed that it would not be a very merry one, haunted, as I was sure it would be, by the ghost of Becket. We were already at Marlborough when messengers returned from France. They brought no reply from Louis but did report on the manner in which he had received Henry's information.

Louis had read the letter with some amazement and all he had said was: 'The King of England states that Thomas à Becket *was* his Archbishop. Has he been deposed then?' The messenger had not known how to reply to that, for in truth Becket had not been deposed. 'It must be by the King of England,' Louis replied. 'I can think of no other. I am also a king but I do not have the power to depose the humblest cleric in my country.'

The messengers reported that Louis had then said to the papal representative, who happened to be present: 'Pray tell my lord Pope Alexander that I hope he will receive the Archbishop of Canterbury in friendship. I fear that unjust accusations have been made against him which must be ignored.'

It was obvious whose side he had been on. It was no surprise. For all their show of friendship in the past, and the fact that Louis's daughter was married to Henry's son, they were enemies and, I feared, always would be.

The return of the messengers brought on another of Henry's rages, which were becoming more and more frequent—and it was all due to Becket. That man was the most important person in his life and always would be until the death of one of them.

He turned to me. There was a certain bewilderment about him, as though he were asking me where he had gone wrong. I felt pity for him and a slight return of the affection I had once had for him. Over that Christmas we were together again—not as we had been in the beginning, but Henry was a very sensual man and he did gain comfort from physical contact.

Our children made a bond between us. Henry's eyes would grow acquisitive as he discussed them. Through them he intended to govern the whole of France. Young Henry would be King of France one day. He had plans for Richard—another daughter of the King of France, young Alais—just to be on the safe side. Geoffrey? Well, there might be a marriage into Brittany for him. The whole of France would fall into Plantagenet hands. He was also thinking of our daughter, Matilda. She was eight years old now. Quite young, but it was not too soon to look round for her.

Then to my great dismay I found that I was once more pregnant. I had thought to be done with childbearing. I was nearly forty-three years old, and that was surely an age when I could expect to have a rest from the wearisome business. True, I was well preserved. I had always taken the utmost care of my appearance, and when a woman looks younger than her years she usually is. But there was no denying the facts: I was too old to want this now and in any case we had a good family—three boys and two girls; and I had had two by Louis before I began to breed Plantagenets.

However, what was, must be and I had to endure it, so I gave myself up to the contemplation of my daughter Matilda.

She was very dear to me—as all my children were, but Matilda had been my constant companion since her birth, and although we were very different in character—she was of a gentle nature, quiet and retiring—we were very close.

Henry, ever aware of the advancement of his family, had been putting out feelers for some time and he was delighted with the response he had had from Henry, Duke of Saxony and Bavaria, known through Europe as 'Henry the Lion', because he had proved bold and fearless.

I said: 'He is a little old for Matilda, is he not?'

'What does age matter?' demanded Henry. 'You are eleven years older than I. People shook their heads over that, did they not? And look at our fine brood.'

'Matilda is not yet nine years old. He is thirty-six. It is rather a lot.'

'I want this alliance,' said Henry. 'A mature man will be best for Matilda. She is quiet and gentle. He will understand her better than a young man could.'

I thought there might be some truth in that, and I found out all I could about the proposed suitor.

His father, another Henry, was known as 'the Proud' and was descended from the Guelphs from the noble house of Este, and his mother had been Gertrude, the only daughter of the Emperor Lothair, Duke of Saxony. This meant that Henry was the heir to two dukedoms; but as his father died when he was ten years old, he had had to struggle for his inheritance. He had distinguished himself and earned the sobriquet of 'Henry the Lion' at an early age, and in time he dealt with his enemies and proclaimed himself Duke of Saxony and Bavaria.

Some twenty years before, he had been married to Clementia, the daughter of the Duke of Thuringia. From this marriage there had been only one daughter. As usual this was a cause for complaint, and after seventeen years the marriage ended in divorce—on the usual grounds of consanguinity, of course.

Now here he was seeking the hand of our Matilda.

There was trouble, as usual, in France. My own Aquitaine was a source of anxiety. My people had never settled under Henry's rule. It was not what they had been accustomed to. They did not like the discipline he tried to impose upon them; they wanted their old style of government, when handsome and romantic men rode out to settle their differences with panache, and filled the Courts with laughter and song. Consequently there was trouble, and Henry could not stay in one place for long.

The conflict with Becket had kept him in England for two years. It was time he crossed the sea to govern his other possessions.

I was to remain in England.

Before Henry left, we received the embassy from Henry the Lion. It was necessary that they be treated with the utmost respect. It was a most splendid company that arrived and we had to meet their grandeur with everything as fine ourselves. Royal unions were always costly, for each side had to outdo the other if that were possible and it ended in everyone's being more extravagant than was wise.

There was inevitably trouble.

'It is a mercy that Becket is not here,' I said, 'or this little matter would be blown up into a great one.'

This time it was about the controversy which was going on in papal circles. Henry had supported Pope Alexander while the Germans gave their allegiance to his rival, Paschal III. This meant that the clergy were not present to welcome the German embassy. It was indeed fortunate that Becket was not in England or there would certainly have been trouble. However, the priests, no doubt remembering Becket's fate and not wishing to share a similar one, were determined not to offend the King, so they were particularly mild in their disapproval.

The necessary pledges were given, the contracts signed. I pleaded the wedding be postponed for say two years, when Matilda would be of a more suitable age. I had promised her I would insist on this and I was determined to fight Henry for the concession if need be.

He gave way. The relationship we had been enjoying since Christmas had softened him in that respect; he did see that his daughter was young to leave home—though, Heaven knew, many princesses had left at a much earlier age—and he did have some affection for his children. It was merely that he did not know how to show it.

However, I won the day and Matilda was to remain with me a little longer so that we could plan her trousseau at leisure and decide all she would want to take with her.

The child clung to me and told me she never wanted to leave me. That was gratifying, but it made me anxious about her. I soothed her and reminded her that it was the fate of all princesses to go away from their homes. 'But that does not mean we shall not see each other,' I went on. 'I shall come to see you. I am a great traveller, as you know. I am always on the move. I shall come to see how my Duchess of Saxony and Bavaria is faring.'

Henry left for Normandy in March. I now had to face the fact that several months of discomfort lay ahead of me. I was certainly not a stranger to childbearing, but I was getting rather old for it.

In the meantime I devoted myself to my children. Young Henry was getting a little proud of himself. He and Marguerite had their own establishment now, and he was convinced he was going to be King of France. Too much adulation came his way, and the King was now openly talking of having him crowned. That would be difficult, because the Kings of England were supposed to be crowned by the Archbishop of Canterbury. And where was the Archbishop of Canterbury? Everything seemed to come back to Becket.

For two months I enjoyed the domestic life with my children. My favourite would always be Richard. He was so tall, so fair and golden, quite the most handsome of them all in my eyes, though some would say that Henry was more so. Poor little Geoffrey had missed those good looks and lacked the height of the other two. One should not allow looks to influence one, but how could one help it? Moreover, Richard was so like me in character. He loved poetry and had a beautiful singing voice. I felt he would have been at home in my grandfather's Courts of Love.

I heard from the King. There was a great deal of trouble everywhere. He believed Becket was stirring it up. Not that he did anything very much. He was just there, playing the martyr and making Henry the tyrant. Of course, he was getting help from Louis. A plague on the man!

Henry wanted me. He needed me in Anjou and Maine. I must leave at once. Leicester and de Luci could take care of England, as they had so well in the past.

So in May I left England with Richard and Matilda. We stayed briefly in Normandy, paying a visit to the Empress Matilda in her palace near Notre Dame des Prés. She was delighted to see the children and me but I was saddened to see that her health was deteriorating. She had changed a great deal since her fiery youth and was giving herself over to good works. But she cared deeply for her family and was distressed by Henry's quarrel with Becket.

'It should never have happened,' she said. 'He should never have given him Canterbury.'

How right she was! On the other hand, she was delighted by her namesake's coming marriage. She said she had never really felt well since her illness five years before. But she did not altogether regret it, for being less active gave one time for reflection.

When we left her, we made our way to Angers, where I was to stay and act as Regent.

I was quite happy to be in Angers. It recalled the days when

I was the Queen of Love, and poets and musicians sang their songs to me.

I reviewed my life. I had had two husbands, and neither of them had given me the satisfaction I needed. Louis was incapable of it but he was a good and gentle man. I had hoped for much from Henry but he had failed me and the disappointment was bitter. Chiefly I resented his infidelity; his driving ambition I could understand; the childish rages could be excused; but his attitude to women, his picking them up and casting them aside, his ability to take equal satisfaction from a night with a prostitute and a wife who loved him . . . that was something I could not tolerate.

No, he had killed my love for him.

I had loved my uncle Raymond in Antioch. Looking back, it seemed that that was the most satisfactory love affair of my life. And I was old now and could no longer expect the raptures of youth.

Henry was back in England now, in conflict with the Welsh. He had failed there once, and failure rankled with Henry.

Meanwhile here was I in Angers, not greatly caring that we were separated. I knew I could rule my own people better than he could because I understood them. I had my little daughter Matilda to prepare for her wedding; and there was my beloved Richard, always a joy to be with. And in addition I was growing unwieldy.

August had come. In two months my child would be born. This was a wearisome time, when I was feeling exhausted by the least exertion. This was different from my first pregnancies, when I had eagerly looked forward to the birth. I had already proved my fruitfulness to the world and had enough sons to govern our empire and two daughters to make alliances beneficial to us. I had done my duty and had had enough.

I shall never forget that day. A messenger came to the castle, and as soon as I saw him I knew he had important news.

'A son!' he panted. 'A son for the King of France. The Queen has given birth to a son. There is rejoicing through France.'

I could not believe it. Louis the father of a son! After all these years of endeavour! It was not true.

'I do not believe it!' I cried.

'It is true, my lady. They are singing in the streets of Paris.

They are calling the child "the God-Given". They say he is going to save France . . . from the English.'

I felt dismayed and at the same time a kind of mischievous amusement. I was imagining the news reaching England. How would Henry take it? Would he lie on the floor and gnaw the rushes? It was almost certain that he would. And he would have good reason for anger on this occasion. His most glorious plans quietly dispersed by the birth of one small boy to the King and Queen of France! Our Henry could not be King because this little boy would wear the crown. Equally he would imagine Louis's joy, the hours of kneeling in thanksgiving. In the churches there would be paeans of praise to God who had granted this longed-for wish.

I was soon hearing accounts of that rejoicing. There was talk of nothing but the heir to the throne of France. Paris went wild with delight. Bells rang through the nights; the people danced in the towns, and bonfires were lighted at every street corner.

France at last had an heir. He was called Philip Augustus. He was the hope of France. Merely by being born he had scored the greatest possible victory over the English.

And Henry—in Woodstock, of course, where he seemed to spend a great deal of time nowadays—would be gnashing his teeth in rage.

It was a sobering thought that all his devious plans could be destroyed by one stroke.

In October our daughter was born. She was called Joanna.

I had expected Henry to come to Angers. Christmas was approaching, and it was a custom to spend it together with the family. I wondered what was keeping him in England. I had heard of no reason, and he was usually so restless. It was rare for him to spend so much time in one place. He was at Oxford or Woodstock most of the time.

Of course, he must have been deeply shocked by the birth of Louis's son, but I should have thought that event would hardly produce listlessness, rather would it have goaded him into action. I began to wonder whether he was ill. He must have fallen into violent rages when he heard the news from France. It had often occurred to me that he might do himself an injury when he was in such a state.

Christmas came. It was pleasant to have the children around

me, and the new baby brought joy to me. There was unrest in the provinces over which I had jurisdiction and, of course, the fact of Philip Augustus's arrival had weaned Henry of a certain power, and those who had hesitated to rise against him before might be bolder now. On the other hand the people had a certain affection for me, and I felt I could keep the revolt simmering without its actually boiling over. With his sweeping reforms, his disciplines and his uncouth appearance and manners, Henry had alienated my people.

We heard he was coming over in early March, but that was cancelled and he remained a week longer in Woodstock. It was not until April that he arrived in Maine, and then he travelled through Alençon and Roche-Mabille to Angers.

He was delighted with the new baby. Matilda was indifferent to his presence. She was getting apprehensive about her marriage, poor child. As for Richard, there was a suppressed hostility in his relationship with his father; for some reason they did not like each other very much. I wondered why: Richard was by far the most outstanding of our sons. *I* thought he was more handsome even than young Henry; he was more cultured, more balanced, less vain; moreover, he shared my love of music and poetry. Perhaps it was that which Henry did not care for. But Richard excelled in all manly sports in fact, more so than any of the others. Perhaps he objected to Richard's affection for me, for the boy showed it in every look and gesture.

However, our meeting passed amicably.

Henry expressed his fury over the arrival of Philip Augustus. I saw the red in his eyes and the purple in his face when he referred to the matter and he could easily have indulged in one of his rages on the spot. He said it was a disaster. We might have found another bride for young Henry if we could have seen into the future.

'Who would have believed that Louis would be able to do it?' he cried.

I said: 'It's no use harking back. We have to go on from here. Louis has his son. He'll probably have another now. The French throne will never come your way, Henry.'

'By God's eyes, who would have thought I could be cheated so?'

'Louis would not call it cheating. He will think it is God's reward for all the praying he has done.'

'It's true. We have to look elsewhere. There is this marriage of Matilda's. That will be a good thing. And I want Brittany for Geoffrey. Then there is a match for Eleanor and the new child.'

'Pray let us get her out of her cradle first.'

'Becket's causing trouble, of course.'

'Simply by doing nothing.'

'Posing as the passive martyr. Alexander has received him. Louis has arranged that. This alliance with Henry the Lion has come at a good moment. Alexander will be worried . . . and rightly so. My friendship with Saxony could mean I'm wavering towards Paschal. I could withdraw the obedience of all my Angevin dominions from Alexander. Oh yes, he'll have some anxious moments about this alliance, and that is good.

'But there is much to be done. I want this matter of Brittany settled with the union of our Geoffrey and the heiress, Constance; and Henry must be recognized as the heir of Normandy and Anjou; and Richard as the heir of Aquitaine. I am thinking of the King of Castile for Eleanor, and Sicily for Joanna. Unfortunately we should have to get Louis's approval.'

'You have been busy making plans. Is that what you were doing at Woodstock?'

'That and other matters,' he said.

He was showing his age. In fact, in spite of those eleven years between us, he looked older than I. I understood what a terrible blow the birth of Louis's son must have been to him. I still had a twinge of affection for him and found him physically attractive—in a minor way, it was true, but it did surprise me that it still existed.

I comforted him in the usual way.

He did not stay long with us. He was deeply disturbed by the rumblings of rebellion in all the provinces, and to my intense dismay, soon after he had left, I was once more pregnant.

I could not believe it. It was too much to be borne. I did not want another child. I had just emerged from the tiresome pregnancy with Joanna—and now it was going to start all over again.

I returned to England in the autumn.

Henry had said that he wanted young Henry to accompany him on a trip through the Angevin provinces as they must become accustomed to their future ruler. I felt that if there was going to be trouble, particularly in Aquitaine, it was better for me to accompany them. The people would be more likely to think kindly of me. But he was anxious for Henry to go, and now that I was going to have another child I did not want to do a lot of travelling.

It was October when I came back to England. I was at this time seven months pregnant, and although it seemed to be more or less an habitual state with me I felt tired and realized I was right to stay where I was and await the birth of my child in comparative peace.

Young Henry had changed. Perhaps this was since he had had his own apartments and was aware that he was soon to be crowned King. He was already giving himself the airs of a king, and Marguerite behaved as though she were Queen. I did not think this a very satisfactory state of affairs, and I was amazed that the elder Henry could not have seen how unwise it was to endow the boy with such ideas of his own importance. He was too young; moreover, he was surrounded by people ready to do him great honour at every turn, thinking no doubt of the power which would one day be his.

I was sure the King did not intend this. He was the King and would remain so until the day he died. He merely wanted to safeguard the throne for his son so that when he himself died there would be a king waiting to mount the throne. The memory of Stephen and Matilda lingered on.

Young Henry did not see it in this way. He was already the little King.

When I told him that his father wished him to go to France, he was dismayed.

'But I do not want to go,' he said.

Certainly he did not and I could understand why. Here he was, the idol . . . almost a king . . . deferred to in every way. Why should he want to go and endure discomforts, riding out to possible war with his father whom he would have to obey?

'Why should I go?' he demanded.

'Because it is your father's wish,' I told him.

'I do not want to go. I like it here.'

'Of course you do. Here you are treated like a king; there is entertainment in your apartments; you ride out with your subjects round you; everyone defers to you. Kingship is not like that all the time, my son. There are provinces to be kept in order. You have to learn that side of kingship as well as the pleasant side.'

'Why should *I* have to go now?'

'I tell you, because your father commands it.'

'But I . . .'

'You are his subject, Henry.'

'But I am going to be King.'

'Not yet. And when you are, it will be in name only. There is only one king of this realm, and that is your father. You must remember that.'

'I do not want to be with him.' He came to me and put his arms round me. 'I want to stay with you.'

I confess to a thrill of pleasure which I could not help feeling when my children showed their preference for me—which they did fairly frequently. I stroked his beautiful fair hair.

'We cannot always have what we want.'

'He does.'

'He is dedicated to his country. He suffers discomfort for what he feels must be done.'

'He is dedicated to his own pleasure! All last winter he was here with that woman. He stayed at Woodstock and Oxford . . . and there she was . . . like the Queen. He does what he wants. Why shouldn't I?'

'What woman was this?' He was silent for a while. 'Tell me,' I said sternly.

He replied: 'It was Rosamund . . . Rosamund Clifford.'

'And he was here . . . with her . . . through the winter?' He was silent again.

'Listen to me, Henry,' I said. 'I want to know.'

'Everyone in the Court knows. She was here . . . just as though she were the Queen . . . in your place . . . Why should he do what he wants when I . . .'

I was staring over his head. So this was the reason for that period of inactivity. He was here with Rosamund Clifford. Anger swelled up within me. I had known of his infidelities. I had grown used to them, telling myself that they were of no account . . . passing fancies which never lasted more than a day or so. Women . . . just women . . . And he, the restless one, with Becket making trouble for him on the Continent, with his provinces ready to revolt, with justice to maintain in England . . . had dallied at Woodstock and Oxford to be with Rosamund Clifford! Not for just a night . . . but all those months.

This was different from anything that had ever happened before.

I was certain of one thing. I was going to discover the exact relationship between the King and Rosamund Clifford.

Nobody wanted to talk at first. But they all knew. It was a feature in cases like this that everyone knows the intimate details while the one chiefly concerned remains in ignorance.

Gradually I learned the story. The alarming part was that the liaison was a lasting one. It had been going on for quite a few years.

She was the daughter of Walter de Clifford, I discovered, and Henry must have met her during one of his campaigns in Wales. She was certainly not like the prostitutes and serving-girls with whom he usually contented himself. Rosamund was a lady, and of outstanding beauty, by no means the sort of woman who would indulge in a fleeting affair with anyone—not even the King.

He was actually in love with her. That was what was so galling to me. He cared about her. She was not just a woman of the moment. He had brought her to the palace of Woodstock, and while I was in France taking care of the dominions there, Rosamund was living in my apartments as Queen!

This was too much to be borne.

At this time every vestige of affection I had had for him departed. I could think only of revenge. He had insulted me. He had married me for my possessions. Apart from those I was no more to him than any woman for whom he briefly lusted. I hated him.

And when I thought that it was this woman who had kept him in Woodstock all that time when he should have been on the Continent dealing with the troubles there, I was incensed. I had never known anyone able to charm him sufficiently to take him away from his commitments before.

I had to see this woman for myself. All those about me were too terrified to tell me anything. They feared what I would do—and what the King would do when he learned that they had told.

I said to myself: I will not harm this woman, but I will see for myself what she is like.

I had always thought Woodstock one of our most charming palaces. 'Woodstock' had originally been 'Vudestoc' which meant 'a woody place', and the woods were indeed beautiful. Henry's grandfather, the first Henry, had built an enclosure for wild beasts in which the lion, leopard and lynx had roamed. The first porcupine ever seen in this country had been brought there. Stephen had used the place as a garrison for his troops during his skirmishes with Matilda. Henry had always been fond of it, and so had I . . . until now.

So Rosamund had been installed here. But where was she now? She must be at Woodstock. He would keep her here so that he could summon her at any time. The only reason she was not in the palace now was because I was there. When I was absent on the Continent, he kept her there as his Queen.

I must see her. I must discover what sort of woman could keep Henry interested to the extent that he went to the great trouble of keeping her with him, and who had evidently been his mistress for several years.

I knew that I would get no information as to her whereabouts from those around me, for there was no one who would be bold enough to tell me where she was.

There was a maze built close to the palace. It consisted of a number of vaults, underground passages and arches walled in brick and stone. It was supposed to provide a diversion . . . a game for the courtiers to find their way out. Few people went there. I referred to it quite casually once, and there was a constrained silence which aroused my suspicions.

I determined to explore the maze. I did so, making sure that I should be able to retrace my steps. I made one or two fruitless excursions, and then one day I found a piece of silk thread in one of the passages. It was a fine silk as used in embroidery and looked as though someone had caught it up in a boot or shoe. I stooped and picked it up. It was a long, unbroken thread. I started to roll it into a ball, and I saw that it went on through the passage. I was surprised, for it led me into a part of the maze which I had never seen before. Then suddenly I saw a shaft of sunlight and came out into the open.

My eyes were dazzled after the dimness of the maze. Before me was a miniature palace. It looked mysterious in the November mist, and instinctively I knew I had found what I had sought. I approached cautiously, crossing the lawn to the iron-studded door.

I rapped sharply on it. I heard a shutter being drawn and I was looking into a pair of intensely blue eyes.

Rosamund Clifford! I thought.

'I wish to come in,' I said.

'But who . . .' she began.

'I am the Queen.'

A bolt was drawn. She stood back. Oh yes, she was indeed beautiful. Her rippling fair hair, falling about her shoulders, was in some disorder; her lashes were dark, as were her well-formed brows; they accentuated the blueness of her eyes and the corn-like colour of her hair; her cheeks had flushed to a rosy shade at the sight of me. She looked very frightened.

I stepped inside.

The hall was beautifully furnished. He would have given her all this. I could see at once the sort of woman she was. Meek, docile, ready to await his pleasure; with all that beauty no wonder he came back and back again to her.

'You are Rosamund Clifford,' I said. She bowed her head. 'I would speak with you.'

She curtsied uneasily and led the way. We were in a richly furnished chamber, and the first things I noticed were two little boys. They were playing some game and stopped short as I entered to stare at me.

'Your sons?' I asked.

'Yes, my lady.' She went on: 'William . . . Geoffrey . . .'

They ran to her. I could see him in them . . . the tawny curls, the leonine head . . . the Plantagenet arrogance, and I felt a surge of rage, not against this woman but against him.

She took the boys by the hand and led them to the door. The elder one . . . William, I think . . . could not resist looking over his shoulder at me. A woman had appeared; she took the boys, and Rosamund Clifford came back into the room.

She stood before me, her eyes downcast.

'How long have you been the King's mistress?' I asked. She was trembling and it seemed she could not find her voice. I went on: 'I know it is for several years. Those boys, are they his?' She nodded. 'And he has been coming often to Woodstock to see you, and you are always here in this place when he is not here, and if I am absent you take my place in the palace, do you not?'

'It was . . . his will.'

'And what of my will?'

'I . . . I told the King that it should not be.'

Suddenly I was sorry for her. I could see how it had been. She was no wanton. Perhaps she would not have attracted him so intensely if she had been.

'When did you meet him?' I asked.

'It was in Wales . . . where the King was. My father served him.'

'Your father is Sir Walter de Clifford, is that so? And you have brothers and sisters.'

'Yes, my lady. I have two brothers and two sisters.'

'You see, I know something of you, Rosamund Clifford. Do not think that your conduct with the King is a surprise to me. Anyone, whether noblemen's daughters or serving girls . . . they are all one to him. So it does not surprise me. But you are much talked of. And all because you flaunted yourself and your sinful behaviour at the palace . . . my palace . . . for I am the Queen and, as you know, the King's lawful wife. So the King first saw you in Wales.'

'I was at my father's castle of Llannymddyvri. The King was campaigning . . .'

'I know. And your father was pleased that you should behave thus with the King?'

'He is the King, my lady.'

'Yes,' I said slowly, 'he is the King.'

I knew I should not blame her. I could see it all so clearly. The campaign in Wales, all the women there would have been . . . and this one. She was different; her father was an honourable knight, and his daughter could not be treated like a serving-girl. I could imagine her attraction. She was outstandingly beautiful; her type would appeal to him; she was completely feminine. An English beauty and mild with it. A pure virgin when he first saw her. He would soon change that. She would be a little reluctant, yet overawed. That would add to his passion. He would soothe her. 'Have no fear. I am your King. I swear no harm shall come to you.' And so she succumbed and she was in love with him. Women fall in love with power, and kingship is supreme power . . . or almost. Master of us all . . . the lover. I could see it all so clearly.

But it had lasted. That was what rankled. He would not be faithful to her any more than he had been to me. Fidelity did not exist for Henry. But he did come back to her. She had his sons. How many women in England had Henry's sons? Too many to be remembered. There must be little Plantagenets in every village in the country.

I said: 'It must end.'

'The King . . .' she began.

'*I* say it must end. How dare you come to my palace! How dare you take my place!'

'It was the King's orders . . . I . . .'

I should not be hard on her, poor silly simpering little thing. She was like an insect, causing a moment's irritation. She had no power to resist him. I was terrifying her. Well, let her be terrified. Let her fear what I would do to her.

I would have looked formidable. I was clearly pregnant with her lover's child. What a situation!

I felt my face contort with hatred. She thought it was for her but it was for him.

'You are a harlot,' I said. 'Are you not afraid?' She nodded. 'Not of me, you little fool,' I said. 'Of God.'

I had struck the right note. This was one who would suffer a great deal from her conscience. She had obviously been brought up as a virtuous girl. And she had lost that virtue. But as it was to the King I daresay her family would find that acceptable. It was not her fault. But I was not going to let her escape lightly. I was angry and bitter, and my marriage was completely ruined, for it could not be revived after this, and she had done it with her simpering manners, her pink and white beauty and her virtue which could be assailed by the King.

'You are a whore,' I told her. She blushed painfully, and I went on: 'If you had not been, you could have married some good and worthy man. Then you would have been able to hold up your head and not bow it with shame as you must now. It were better that you had never been born. You should break this liaison with an adulterer.'

She was trying to speak but the words would not come.

'Yes,' I went on. 'Better if you had not been born. Are you not afraid to face me, the King's lawful wife and your Queen, to whom you as a subject owe allegiance? I could bring you a dagger and say, "Plunge that into your heart, or do you prefer a poison cup?" I could take your life. After all, did you not take my husband?'

'If you were to harm me,' she said with a shade of defiance, 'the King . . .'

'The King would say, 'Poor Rosamund, I knew her well. She was a very willing partner in my bed. But there are plenty of others ready to take her place. England abounds in whores. Why should I fret for one?'

'It was not so . . .'

'Oh no, with you and him it was romance, was it not? The adulterer and the wanton. There is one thing for you to do, Rosamund Clifford . . . if you truly repent your sins, and that is go into a nunnery. I recommend Godstow, which is not far from here. There perhaps, by the time your span runs out, you will have earned remission of your sins.'

I saw the sudden hope in her eyes. I laughed inwardly. I had sown a seed.

What would Henry say if he returned to Woodstock and found his mistress installed in a convent! That would be rather amusing.

'Think about it,' I said; and I left her.

I made my way back to the palace. I had given Rosamund Clifford something to think about. I wished Henry were here. I should have loved to tell him I had discovered his love-nest.

I was soon to have his child. That made the situation more ironic. I hated him. I began to dislike the child I carried because it was his.

Every vestige of gentle feeling for Henry had gone. Rosamund Clifford had killed it. This really was the end. I would never have another child by him, should never again share a bed with him. Our relationship was over.

I thought about divorce. He would lose Aquitaine, and for that I rejoiced.

I thanked God that I was still the Duchess. If I returned to Aquitaine, I was sure the unrest would end. I would rule as my grandfather and father had. I belonged there. Henry could go and gnash his teeth in rage—not because he had lost me but because he had lost Aquitaine. And France would be lost to him because of the birth of Philip Augustus. He would feel his possessions slipping away from him.

I would not live with him again. He would have to learn that

I was no Rosamund Clifford to accept his lecherous ways and be calmly waiting for him whenever he deigned to visit me.

This was a turning-point in my life. I was now making a great decision. I would leave this land of cool days and cloudy skies. I would return to my native country, where I was the ruler. And perhaps I would take my children with me. I was the one whom they loved, the one to whom they gave their allegiance . . . and not only Richard: the others too.

Henry would learn that, although he might have his will with Rosamund Clifford, it would not be so with Eleanor of Aquitaine.

My time was near. Another Christmas was approaching. I decided to spend it at the Beaumont Palace in Oxford, and there my child should be born.

Henry did not come to us for Christmas. It was a disappointment because I wanted to tell him what I had discovered and that I loathed him and had made up my mind to leave him.

It was frustrating that he absented himself.

My son was born on Christmas Eve.

He was unlike the other children. He lacked their golden looks and was smaller than they, a dark-haired creature. I could feel little love for him. It was a pity. The boy could not be blamed for his father's sins. It was just that he gave me no joy. In the past, though I had deplored my pregnancies while they were in progress, I was always thrilled when the child arrived. But this was not the case with John. I handed him over to his nursemaids.

My thoughts were occupied with my plans for a new life . . . without Henry.

The Turbulent Priest

I was in no hurry to leave England. I was feeling in limbo after the birth of John. I could not completely repress the revulsion the child aroused in me. Poor mite, it was unfortunate that he should have come at a time when I felt such an aversion to his father, and I was filled with a sense of shame every time I looked at him to remember how at one time I had enjoyed my relationship with Henry.

Moreover, it would soon be time for my daughter Matilda to leave England for her marriage. She clung to me. She was apprehensive of the future, as well she might be. But I was of the opinion that Henry the Lion would be indulgent as some men can be when they are so much older than their wives. I prayed this would be so.

I tried to make her excited about our preparations. We discussed her trousseau and the jewels she would have. And while I planned what Matilda would need, I was thinking of my own freedom, which could not be far away.

I wanted desperately to see Henry so that I could pour scorn on him. I wanted to tell him that I had discovered Rosamund's bower and how I wished him well of her, for he should never be a husband to me again. But that could wait. I had many plans to make and I did not want to be rash.

I would not lose my children. They were mine more than Henry's. I was the one to whom they gave their love. It always had been so. Henry would discover that in time.

So while I waited I planned, and the months passed.

Henry was occupied in Normandy and the Vexin. He had no plans as yet to return home. Trouble there must be rife. It could even keep him away from the fair Rosamund.

I saw little of the new baby and left him to his nurses. I tried to overcome my dislike of him, but in vain. My anger against Henry was so great that I was angry with myself, I supposed, for allowing him to get this child on me.

Henry was bent on using our children to extend his domain, and after leaving the Vexin he was in Brittany.

He had supported Count Conan, whom he intended to use to further his designs, for he wanted Conan's daughter, Constance, for Geoffrey. This would need a cautious approach as, although Conan might agree, the people of Brittany, like those of Aquitaine, were not eager to accept Henry as their overlord. In due course Henry was successful. Conan gave his promise and Geoffrey, aged nine, was betrothed to Constance, aged five. Henry was doing well: Saxony and Bavaria through Matilda, Castile for Eleanor, and even baby Joanna was given her part, with Sicily. And now Brittany. He was stretching out all over France. I wondered what Louis was thinking; still giving thanks to God, I presumed, for the God-Given, Philip Augustus.

Sad news came from Rouen. I knew that the Empress Matilda had been ailing for some time. Ever since she had caught a virulent fever some seven years ago there had been occasional recurrences of it. Early in the morning of 10 September she died.

Matilda's character had changed a great deal as she aged. In youth she had been fiery, ambitious, imperious and very reckless, antagonizing so many people with whom she came in contact. How she had mellowed! She had become very wise; she had always been clever but, losing her recklessness, she had given quiet thought to her problems and those of her family and had acquired a shrewd wisdom. If only Henry had listened to her over Becket . . . But one could not go on saying 'If only . . .'

On her deathbed, so pious had she become that she took the veil as a nun of the Abbey of Fontevrault.

I should have liked to be with her at the end. She and I had a great deal in common. We had admired each other, and that is always a reason for mutual regard. She had made a very careful will and had given a great deal to the poor. She had founded many religious houses and supported many more. She had set aside a large sum for the completion of the bridge over the Seine at Rouen—an object which she had started some years before her death. So she died full of good works.

I mourned her and I knew Henry would.

Now my great task was to see that young Matilda left the country for her future home in a fitting manner, and to do my best to make her believe that she could be happy in her new life.

We were to go to Dover and there embark for Normandy. Robert, Sheriff of Kent, was in charge of our passage and three vessels from Shoreham had been engaged to carry our small party and all Matilda's belongings. We were going to Argentan, where the King would be waiting for us. There we were to celebrate Christmas, after which Matilda would begin her journey to Saxony.

I was looking forward to my meeting with Henry. I had been thinking of it for a year, and many times had I rehearsed what I would say to him. I wanted to see his face when he knew he had lost Aquitaine.

And so we came to Argentan. It was to be a family Christmas. Henry greeted me warmly. He was always attentive after long separations. I received his embrace coolly in the presence of others.

He had the effrontery to come to my bedchamber, smiling confidently, certain that we were going to resume marital relations. I looked at him coldly. I said: 'Henry, there is something I have to tell you. I have decided I am going to leave you.' He stared at me uncomprehendingly.

I went on: 'I shall return to Aquitaine. It will be as though I never married you . . . except for the children, of course. They are mine and I do not forget it.'

'By God's eyes,' he said, 'you strike a dramatic pose. Does aught ail you?'

'I am well, thanks be to God. I have made a few discoveries. I went through your maze at Woodstock one day. I think a piece of embroidering silk must have become attached to your spur. It led me to her pretty little home. I must say it is very charming. Did you design it, or did she? You seem as though you have not understood. I am talking of Rosamund Clifford.'

His eyes narrowed and I saw the smile curve his lips.

'You were at one time extremely fond of her,' I went on.

'Don't tell me you were guilty of that weakness of some women
. . . and men even now and then. Were you in *love*?'

'With Rosamund,' he said. 'Yes. She is a delightful woman.'

'The mother of your two sons?'

'I admit the charge.'

'And you took her to live in the palace . . . in my place?'

'Ah, that is what rankles, is it? That is what you could not
bear. Yes, she did live in the palace. She was a more gracious
queen than you ever were.'

'*She* had to please her master. Has it occurred to you that I
do not have to please you?'

'Enough of this nonsense.'

'It is no nonsense. This did not happen yesterday. It was a
whole year ago when I found my way through the maze to that
charming abode of love. I have had ample time to think and I
have made up my mind . . .'

'Made up to what, may I ask?'

'You may indeed. Made up my mind that I have finished with
you.'

He threw back his head and laughed. He came to me and took
me by the shoulders. He was ready, I knew, for a little love play.
He was going to placate me, tell me that no other woman—not
even Rosamund—was of importance to him. I was the Queen,
was I not?

I threw him off.

'You could not tear yourself away from her. All those months
at Woodstock . . . and all that was happening to the dominions
overseas . . . it mattered not. You could not leave your mistress.
Very well, you are free now to set her up in the palace, to live
openly with her, for I shall not be there. Never . . . never . . .
Our marriage is over.'

'I did not think you would be so jealous.'

'Jealous? I? Do you think I envy your whores? No, I pity
them. That poor creature at Woodstock . . . awaiting your summons . . . You want to own the world . . . but most of all,
womankind, I do believe.'

'It is a dazzling prospect.'

'Laugh if you will. My mind is made up. I am not sure about
divorce. I don't think it is necessary. There are children enough.
I shall go back to my home. I shall go to Poitou. And I hope I
never have to see your face again.'

'Are you not being a little rash . . . just because you have discovered I have had a beautiful mistress? What are you envious of . . . her beauty? Her youth? You are eleven years older than I, you know.'

'Eleven years older in wisdom, I hope. But I have been foolish. I should have done this before. I have no need of you, Henry. I can go home to my own estates.'

'You will forget all this . . .'

'I have been thinking of it for over a year and I have made my plans.'

'What a fuss to make!'

'I have had enough. As soon as I saw your mistress and knew that you had set her up in the palace while I was absent, I knew that that was the end. Oh, she is pretty enough and the boys are fine ones. What a man you are for getting sons on harlots. We have your bastard Geoffrey in the nursery as proof of that.'

'A very pleasant boy he is.'

'He has been brought up in my nurseries, that is why.'

'You accepted him.'

'It was different. His mother was a camp-follower. I wonder you did not set her up as a queen. Your conduct is a constant scandal.'

'And your past is not free from it. You should not be surprised. Were you not brought up in a Court where it was the order of the day? I am tired of this nonsense. I will not be called to book for my misdeeds. I will do as I will.'

'With your low-born loose-living women, perhaps, but not with the Duchess of Aquitaine and Queen of England.'

'Even those two august ladies shall not dictate to me.'

'Nor shall any dictate to them. You speak of having your will. But at least you tried to hide your mistress from me in her cosy little place beyond the maze.'

'I thought to spare your feelings. Do you blame me for that?'

'I want no such kindness from you. Do you think I care how many mistresses you have? I know they are legion. It would be a superhuman task to try to count them.'

'You may be right.'

'And this one was different, was she not? You had a special fondness for her.'

He smiled reminiscently. 'I have,' he said.

'She has been as a wife to you and no doubt you wish she were.'

He looked at me, his hatred matching mine. 'I do,' he said.

'Very well then. Go to her. Go.'

'Don't be a fool.'

'It is you who are a fool . . . over this woman.'

'You are not planning to harm her . . . If aught happened to her through you I would kill you.'

'Oh, you feel as strongly as that, do you? And what do you think would happen to you if you harmed me? The people of Aquitaine hate you as it is. They would rise against you. In addition to all your troubles, you would have war with Aquitaine . . . and this time they would defeat you.'

'I would soon subdue them. Stop this folly. You are the Queen, no matter what other women there may be.'

'I will not have it. I shall never share your bed again.'

'So be it,' he said. 'You are past childbearing now . . . or soon must be. I am surprised you went on so long. You are no longer a young woman.'

'So you have already pointed out. And there are others who please you more.'

'I won't deny it.'

'I hate you,' I said. He smiled at me cheerfully.

'I shall go to Aquitaine,' I went on.

'It is not a bad idea. Perhaps you will be able to bring a little sense to the natives.'

'They are my people,' I said. 'I am going to rule them, and when I do, you will see there is no more trouble in Aquitaine.'

He was looking at me shrewdly. I knew that he was thinking that that could be true and that it would be an excellent idea for me to go back to Aquitaine and remain there for a while.

I hated him. He was not thinking of me but of his dominions. Then I felt exultant. Aquitaine was one he was not going to keep.

That was a strange Christmas. Neither Henry nor I wanted to publicize our differences. When he had seen that I was adamant and determined to leave him and settle in Aquitaine, he suggested that when the festivities were over he and his army escort me there. That would give the impression that, as there was a state of unrest in the country, I was going to stay there for a while and see if I could bring about a more peaceful atmosphere.

I could see that this was a concession I must make, for if it were generally known that there was a permanent rift between us, it could throw our affairs into confusion. So we left together as though we were on good terms.

As we came near to Aquitaine a shock awaited us. The country was in revolt under the leadership of the Count of Angoulême.

This was one of those occasions when Henry's genius for governing came into play. In a short time he had repressed the revolt, punished the offenders and restored peace—although an uneasy one—to Aquitaine. I had to be grateful that he had returned with me.

When he left, it was more or less calm, although there was an attempt to kidnap me when I was riding not far from Poitiers.

It was a band of rebels who had the idea of capturing me and holding me to ransom until their demands were met. I was alert for trouble and before they were able to catch me I had galloped back to safety, but the commander of the military force which had been left by Henry to guard the castle was killed in the affray. So it was clear how dangerous the situation still was.

But it was amazing how my presence there affected the people. Perhaps they guessed that all was not well between Henry and me, that I had left him and come back . . . alone. That was what they cared about. They wanted no foreigners governing them. I was a branch of the old tree. They had resented Louis, but Henry even more so.

I could sense the mood of the people. After all, they were my own people. When I rode out, they would cheer me. They let me know that they wanted me to stay here, to be their sole ruler. It was heartening.

Musicians and poets began to fill the Court. I restored castles to those from whom Henry had taken them when suppressing the rebellion. I wanted them to know that in my opinion they had rebelled against Henry . . . not against me.

I was in my own country. I was Duchess of Aquitaine, a title which pleased me more than that of Queen of England.

Bernard de Ventadour was one who returned. It was a great joy to bring back those evenings of music. They still wrote songs proclaiming my beauty—pleasant to hear but hard to believe,

though of course I took great pains to preserve my looks, and
although I was getting old, marching up high in the forties, for
my age I was still a handsome woman.

I had my children with me. Richard was my constant companion. We rode together, talked together, and he loved those
evenings when the musicians entertained us for he could perform with considerable skill himself. Young Henry was with us
now and then. He loved to be with me and was resentful when
he had to join his father. This made me gleeful. Eleanor and
Joanna had never seen a great deal of their father; they were
entirely mine. Little Constance of Brittany was with us, for she
had to be brought up with her future husband's family in accordance with custom. So I was happy. I was in charge of my own
domain and I had my family with me.

John was a problem. I often look back on those days and feel
a twinge of conscience about John. Perhaps he turned out as he
did because of his childhood. He was after all my child. But I
could not like him. All the time he reminded me of Henry's
deceit and that when he was being conceived Henry had been
thinking of Rosamund Clifford; and I despised myself for having
remained with him so long. John should never have been born;
he was conceived in deceit and reminded me too much of what
I wished to forget.

During that Christmas when I had made my intentions clear
to Henry, after we had recovered a little from our initial bitterness, and he had realized that I was determined to break up the
marriage, we had discussed one or two things calmly . . . for
instance, my return to Aquitaine and how I should be conducted
there, and we also talked of John.

I said: 'There ought to be one member of the family who
should go into the Church. You have distributed your dominions
among your sons, but what of John? What is there for him?'

'Poor John. He will be "John Lackland", I fear.'

'That is why he should be the one to go into the Church.'

'Archbishop of Canterbury . . . or perhaps a cardinal. Head
of the Church in this country . . . or maybe Pope. Either would
be useful to the crown.'

I could not help laughing. He turned everything to the advantage of the crown. However, he agreed that it was to be John for
the Church.

So I suggested that he go into Fontevrault, that abbey which had been founded by Robert d'Arbrissel and supported by my grandmother, one in which I had taken great interest. There John could be brought up. It seemed an ideal solution.

Peace settled on Aquitaine. I was there to stay, they believed. It was a return to the old days. We had pageants and ceremonies such as the people loved; we paraded in our splendid robes. I never lost an opportunity of staging these pageants. I did them well, as my forebears had. Aquitaine was content with the new rule, which was, after all, a return to the old.

I was content in my little world, but that did not mean I was not concerned with what was happening outside it. I followed Henry's actions with the utmost interest, rejoicing in his difficulties, though I must admit to feeling often an admiration—rather grudging—for his adept way of extricating himself from trouble and generally managing to get the better of his opponent.

He was in constant conflict with Louis. My first husband appeared to have changed since the birth of his son. The event had given him new vigour. He was more aggressive. Perhaps he was looking ahead to the days when the God-Given would take the reins. I was sure Louis would want to hand them over as soon as he could. Perhaps he would retire to a monastery then and relish a longed-for dream. However, I think Henry found it more difficult to hoodwink him than in the past.

There was a great deal of conflict between them over the Vexin. Their affairs moved to a stage when they were both seeking peace, and a conference was arranged to take place between them.

Louis, of course, did not like to see so much of France under Henry's domination and might have thought it would be better to proclaim Henry's sons rulers of the various provinces. I wondered afterwards if Louis had an inkling of the feelings of Henry's children towards their father. Henry was a strong man but he was not one to inspire affection in the young. It must have been apparent that our children turned to me rather than to him; and Louis, who did know a little of me, might have guessed at the state of affairs between Henry and me. One could not give Louis credit for shrewd planning; however, this scheme of his was, looking back, not without a certain wisdom. At the conference he suggested that the various Princes be given their lands and swear allegiance to their suzerain; and Henry, looking ahead to the future and always having in mind the possibility of his own demise, thought it advisable to have his sons accepted by Louis as official rulers of the provinces.

It had always been known that Aquitaine was for Richard; young Henry was to have Anjou and Maine, and Geoffrey Brittany. Henry, who had long been playing with the idea of getting young Henry crowned King, agreed with this, and at the beginning of the year 1169 the ceremony was to take place.

My sons left Aquitaine to join their father at Montmirail. I wished I could have seen the ceremony. It must have been most impressive—particularly my three sons. Henry and Richard were exceptionally handsome—both tall and dazzlingly fair with blue eyes and a nobility of countenance; Geoffrey lacked their handsome looks but was not an ill-looking boy by any means.

Louis would surely be thinking of his one and only *Dieu-Donné* and all the efforts he had made to get him.

Alas, I was not present, so it was left to my imagination. I could picture Henry's joy in his sons—particularly young Henry, who had always been his favourite, because I knew Richard's adherence to me irritated him a little, and Geoffrey lacked the charm of his brothers. But three such sons must make Henry very proud. So young Henry did homage to Louis for Anjou and Maine, Richard for Aquitaine, and Geoffrey for Brittany.

To stress his new friendship for Henry, Louis offered the hand of his daughter Alais for Richard. We did not know it then but this was to prove a matter of some consequence to Henry. There was an understanding between Louis and Henry that Louis did not wish to have his daughter put into my care, as he had shown when Marguerite was betrothed to Henry. But now, of course, Henry and I were living apart, so Alais was to go to the English Court to be brought up in the English manner, so that by the time Richard married her she should be a suitable bride for him. She was nine years old at the time, an exceptionally pretty girl, I believed; in fact, her beauty was the reason why she was to fall into such a scandalous situation.

There was one very important incident which occurred at Montmirail. Among the company was Thomas à Becket.

Thomas had been making a great nuisance of himself ever since his departure from England. He had gone to live in the Cistercian Abbey of Pontigny and was continually thundering forth threats of what would happen to Henry. At first Pope Alexander had been wary of giving him leave to denounce Henry too strongly, for his own position continued precarious, but later, when it improved, he allowed Becket more freedom to say and do what he liked against his old enemy. Henry threatened to expel all Cistercians from England if they continued to shelter Becket. Becket retorted by threatening Henry with excommunication.

It was a very unsatisfactory quarrel. I think, in their hearts, they most wanted to be together again. For one thing, Henry wanted young Henry crowned, and only the Archbishop of Canterbury should do that.

Just before the ceremony at Montmirail Becket had written to Henry asking that he be reinstated and that he and his followers might have back their rights and property. Henry said he would be prepared to accept Becket back, but the Pope insisted on a public agreement. It was for this reason that Becket had come to Montmirail.

There they met in a field. I wondered what Henry's emotions were when he beheld his greatest friend and worst enemy. Of one thing I could be certain: it must have been an emotional meeting. Thomas, I heard, fell on his knees before the King, weeping affectively. Henry took his hand and begged him rise.

Becket began well by asking Henry's forgiveness for himself and the Church. That Henry, of course, was very ready to grant. Becket then declared that, regarding their disagreements, he threw himself on the King's mercy and pleasure. That was enough. But being Becket he could not leave it at that. He was ready to obey the King in all things, he said, saving the honour of God.

I can imagine Henry's wrath. They had progressed no way. This had been Becket's cry right from the first. He would obey . . . save where his order was concerned. Now it was God.

Henry then addressed the spectators and told them that Becket had deserted the Church, creeping out in the night. *He* did not drive him away. He had always been ready to allow the Church to follow its rules, but whenever what the King desired was not what Becket did, he brought in 'his order' . . . or God. If Becket would act as those before him always had—and some of them saintly men—he would be satisfied.

The people cheered. The King had capitulated. He would receive Becket, providing Becket was ready to obey him.

But Becket stood out. He was not ready to return yet.

* * *

Exasperated beyond endurance by the man, Henry decided to go ahead with the coronation of his eldest son. Why should it be necessary that he be crowned by the Archbishop of Canterbury? The Archbishop of York would do very well. Moreover, he was no friend of Becket.

Becket was still not in England, and on 24 May young Henry, who was then fifteen, was crowned King of England in Westminster Abbey. Henry, generally so careless of his appearance and impatient of ceremony, did know when it was necessary to put on an elaborate show, and he spared neither effort nor money. The crown was made by the leading goldsmith William Cade at a cost of £38.6.0.—a very large sum of money.

Henry could be capable of acts of great folly, and this coronation was one, perhaps the greatest he ever made. It was obvious to me, and surely to others, that young Henry was becoming more and more aware of his position and taking advantage of it. When the cub is made head of the pride—even though it is intended to be in name only—the chief lion should watch carefully. Young Henry had revealed his character more and more as honours were heaped on him. He had never been the meekest of boys, and if he had been, the step would have been unwise.

It amazed me that Henry, so shrewd in most things, so quickly aware of his advantage, should make this tremendous mistake. He should have known the way things would go. There was an indication of this even at the banquet which followed the crowning, when the King waited on his son at table.

The Archbishop of York remarked to young Henry that it was a most auspicious occasion when a prince was waited on by a king. Henry arrogantly replied that it was not in the least unfitting for the son of a king to be waited on by the son of a count.

I wondered if Henry had a qualm then. Surely any man must have asked himself what troubles lay ahead when a son could at such time make such a reply.

Looking back, I marvel at Henry's blindness in this one matter. He had brought about a state in his dominions whereby all jurisdiction was subject to the direct authority of the Crown. The King was supreme. This made for great efficiency in the hands of such a man, but naturally there had been discords— and not only with the Church. I could not understand how he could nave been so short-sighted as to name another king—even though it was his own son.

It was foolish in more ways than one, for he incurred the wrath of Louis by not crowning Marguerite with her husband. Louis declared his daughter had been humiliated. The Pope, with Thomas à Becket, was incensed at the insult to Canterbury, for all kings should be crowned by the Archbishop.

In September that year the Pope sent letters of suspension and censure to Roger of York and all concerned in the ceremony, declaring that this was another example of the King's defiance of the Church.

Henry, realizing that there would be trouble until Thomas returned to England, proposed that he and Thomas should make the journey together and on English soil exchange the kiss of peace.

Thomas accepted the invitation, but when the time came for their departure, Henry sent word that he could not be there; he was delayed, he said, by matters of state and suggested that Thomas leave France under the escort of John of Oxford, a notorious enemy of Becket, who had once accused him of contending for Church privileges for the sake of personal gain.

Thomas, greatly fearing treachery, delayed a little longer, and it was not until the end of November that he set sail from Wissant, arriving on 1 December, at Sandwich, from where he made his way to Canterbury. The people, warned of his coming, crowded into the streets to greet him; hymns were sung; bells rang out. Canterbury wanted all to know how it rejoiced in the return of its Archbishop.

On the other hand, some of the King's officers were waiting for him. They demanded the immediate and unconditional absolution of those who had been suspended on account of the young King's coronation. Thomas replied that he would absolve all except the Archbishop of York, if they would swear to obey the Pope's orders.

Henry was spending Christmas at Bures, near Bayeux. I suppose everyone knows of that fatal Christmas and its aftermath. I was glad I was not there when this was happening. There I was, happy in my Court, with my troubadours about me, while Henry was stepping deep into a tragedy which would haunt him for the rest of his life.

Christmas at Bures. I could imagine it. Henry would be in

good spirits—just for the festive season, forgetting his worries. His eyes would be roaming round the room, looking for a suitable bedfellow. There would be jollity, music, games, Christmas fun.

Thomas was back in England. I guessed that was a relief to Henry. Thomas in exile had been mettlesome; in England it would be easier to keep an eye on him. He would not have the same freedom to consort with the King's enemies . . . with Louis and the Pope.

Yes, it should have been a good Christmas. He had achieved his longed-for wish in getting his son crowned; the others had all been acknowledge in their various domains. He must have been feeling pleased with himself.

Then there were visitors to the feast. I heard several versions of what happened and it was something like this:

Roger of York with the suspended bishops arrived. They had come to complain of Becket's latest ultimatum and insistence that they obey the Pope. Henry's first thoughts on seeing them would turn to Becket. He wanted to know that he had arrived in England and how he fared.

That gave Roger his chance. He replied that Becket was back and was the same as ever; he was roaming the countryside seeking to rally the King's enemies against them. Becket was very popular; he only had to appear and the people were shouting for him. He had made an effort to see the new King, taking presents with him and of course intending to turn him against his father.

I could picture Henry's brows drawn together and the colour beginning to rise in his face. Perhaps even then he was realizing the folly of his act.

But before Thomas had reached Winchester he had been stopped and ordered by young Henry to go back to Canterbury and perform his sacred ministry. He now declared that the young King was no king, for the ceremony of crowning could be performed only by the Archbishop of Canterbury—himself. He cursed all those who had taken part in the coronation. *All.* That meant Henry himself.

The rage would have been imminent, but Henry would hold it off. He needed to know more of Thomas's alleged perfidy.

Roger of York said: 'As long as this man lives, you will have no peace in your realm, my lord.'

Henry's rage would be getting the better of him. He shouted:

'So they tell me . . . a fellow who has eaten my bread now lifts his heel against me. When he first came to my Court, it was on a lame horse and he had a cloak for a saddle. And he would rule my realm. And you . . . you look on . . . you permit this to be. Will no one rid me of this turbulent priest?'

Four of Henry's knights listened to his words. They were Hugh de Morville, William de Tracy, Reginald Fitzurse and Richard le Breton. Their names will be long remembered.

What happened on the dismal Tuesday afternoon of 29 December of the year 1170 is known throughout the world. I often visualize the scene, constructing it from the many accounts I have heard:

Those four knights coming into Canterbury and making their way quietly and purposefully to the Archbishop 'on the King's business'.

It was about four o'clock. Thomas had already dined but the servants were at the table.

Thomas greeted the knights but they were terse in their response. Fitzurse was their spokesman. He said the King had sent them to order the Archbishop to absolve the bishops and restore those suspended from office. They accused him of attempting to deprive the young King of his crown and said he should stand judgement in Court.

Thomas's reply was to censure the bishops and in particular the Archbishop of York. He said he had not sought to deprive the young King of his crown. He had set out to visit him and was grieved not to have been allowed to do so.

Richard Fitzurse asked him from whom he held the archbishopric, to which Thomas replied that he held his spiritual authority from God and his temporal and material possession from the King.

'Do you not recognize that you hold everything from the King?' asked Fitzurse.

'I do not,' was the answer. 'We must render unto the King the things which are the King's and unto God the things that are God's.'

Members of the Archbishop's household, hearing the commotion, had come down to see what was afoot. Firzurse commanded them, in the King's name, to retire, but this they refused to do.

'Stop your threats and brawling,' said Thomas. 'I have not come back to flee again. I wish to go into the cathedral to pray.'

He left the palace and walked to the cathedral. I could picture him clearly, calm, serene, perhaps contented, for I often thought he was seeking a martyr's death. He entered the cathedral by the north transept and moved towards the altar as the four knights came in crying: 'Where is the traitor?'

'Here am I,' replied Thomas. 'No traitor but a priest of God. I do not fear your swords. I welcome death for the sake of our Lord and the freedom of the Church.'

'You cannot live a moment longer,' said Fitzurse.

'I submit to death,' replied Thomas, 'in the name of the Lord, and I commend my soul and the cause of the Church to God, St Mary and the patron saints of the Church. It is not my wish to fly from your swords.'

One of the men struck him between the shoulders. Another cried: 'You are our prisoner. Come with us.'

'I will not go hence,' said Thomas. 'Here shall you work your will and obey the orders of the one who sent you.'

De Tracy lifted his sword and hit the Archbishop on the head. As the blood streamed down his face he fell to the ground murmuring: 'Into Thy hands, oh Lord, I commend my spirit.'

There was another blow.

He received four wounds, all on his head, and there he lay . . . dead . . . the Archbishop of Canterbury, Henry's beloved and turbulent priest.

Revolt in the Family

When the news was brought to me, my first reaction was: What will this mean to Henry?

He was still in my thoughts a great deal, and I still smarted with humiliation when I thought of him; in my heart I longed for the day when I should see him brought low.

I found a great joy in having my children with me. Young Henry was in England at this time, playing the King, but Richard was here with Geoffrey, and there was Marguerite, Henry's young wife, who had been sent to me before Henry was crowned, presumably to get her out of the way. I could see no reason for Henry's refusing her the honour of crowning. It could only anger Louis.

By this time I had come to a new serenity. I loved this land; I was where I belonged; I loved the people and the easy way of life and appreciation of fine things, the gracious style of living. There was no unrest now. The people knew, I was sure, of my estrangement from Henry, and applauded it. I was their Duchess. They wanted no other.

When the day was drawing to an end, I liked to go up to the ramparts of the castle and look down on my city, touched as it was by the golden light of the setting sun. I had seen it thus so many times, and it had lived on in my childhood memories—Poitiers, *my* city, built on the slopes of a gentle hill with the Cain and the Boivre flowing past. There was the Cathedral of St Pierre. I remember the time it was built. How I loved it all

. . . the fine buildings, the flowers, the bright skies and the people.

And . . . I was far away from Henry.

Richard and I were as close as two people could be for there was deep understanding between us. I was fond of Marguerite too, and she of me. I loved Geoffrey. I tried to bind my children to me, for I loved them dearly and, of course, I took a special delight in their love for me for I felt that, in giving it to me in such measure, they deprived Henry of it.

And into this happy and peaceful atmosphere came the news of Becket's death. We were all stunned. Four knights had murdered him in the cathedral. The King's knights. That was significant.

'What will it mean?' asked Richard.

'For that we must wait and see,' I answered.

'Do you think the King ordered them to kill him?'

I was silent, wondering. I knew that whatever the case Henry was going to be branded the murderer of Thomas à Becket.

I could not sleep. I kept seeing Becket's cold, ascetic face, that expression of calm righteousness, the martyr's crown almost about his head even then. I saw Henry too, his face scarlet with rage, contorted with grief. He had loved the man. There was no doubt of that. The love had turned to hate, but it was never entirely hate . . . for love was always there.

How did Henry feel now?

We soon heard. People could talk of nothing but the murder in the cathedral. How dramatic that it should have been in such a place! It would add to Thomas's martyrdom. It would make him more holy than if he had been struck down in the street.

Henry had, of course, been stricken with horror. Thomas dead! No longer able to plague him, to arouse that hatred which was as strong as love had once been.

How had he received the news? He had taken off his royal robes and wrapped himself in sackcloth. He had wept openly and commanded to be left alone. He had returned to his chamber, and there he had stayed for three days, refusing food; nor would he see anyone. None could comfort him; there was no comfort for him. The days wore on and, although he emerged from his chamber, he would lapse into silence and then suddenly cry out: 'The pity of it! What a disaster! This is a terrible thing to have happened.'

It was indeed—for Becket . . . and for him.

The whole world was against him. They said he had murdered a saint, for even those who had been against Becket in his lifetime had now elevated him to sainthood.

I almost wished I could have been there. I should have liked to talk to Henry. I was sure he must be thinking of what effect this was going to have on the future.

Louis held up his hands in horror. I was sure he believed that God would strike his old enemy in some terrible manner. The Pope threatened all the Angevin dominions with interdiction and to excommunicate Henry unless he did penance for the murder.

Henry seemed to accept the charge, and the four knights were not taken to task in any way for what they had done. Henry believed in justice; he had asked why no one would rid him of the turbulent priest and those men had taken that as an order to kill the Archbishop. They had thought it their duty in the service of the King. He could not blame them. He accepted what had happened as his fault. He, who had loved Thomas as he had loved no one else, was his murderer.

The boys talked about it a great deal. Their attitude was changing rapidly towards their father. They had never loved him but they had been in awe of him. They had regarded him as the all-powerful monarch, and power earns respect, especially from the ambitious, and all my boys were that.

'The King of France is angry with him . . . so is the Pope,' said Richard. 'Will they rise against him?'

I said: 'We shall have to wait and see what happens.'

'If they defeated him,' went on Richard, 'I should still have Aquitaine and Geoffrey Brittany. Nobody could take Aquitaine from me.'

'Nor Brittany from me,' added Geoffrey.

'If our father were driven out of England, he might try to. I wouldn't let him.'

'No,' I put in, 'your father will not be driven out of England, and I should certainly hope you would defend your estates against all comers. You would not be worthy of them if you did not do that.'

I could see how strongly they were turning against their father, and I was not displeased.

The whole world was against him. I wondered what effect this would have on him. Would he be in despair? I did not think so. He was always at his most vigorous and inventive at times of crisis.

He ignored the threats and turned his attention to a project which had long fascinated him: the addition of Ireland to his dominions. Events were fortuitous. Just at this time Diarmait Mac Murchadha, the King of Leinster, had lost his crown, and he sent word to Henry begging him to help him regain it. If he did, he promised he would pay homage to Henry. Henry accepted the challenge. It must have kept his mind from Becket and the antagonism he had stirred up against himself. He raised an army—chiefly from the Welsh border, and sent it to Ireland, and very soon they had possession of the land from Waterford to Dublin.

Just as the papal legates were about to enter Normandy and carry out their threats, Henry decided he must go to Ireland, where his presence was needed. This he proceeded to do and by October had landed in Waterford.

He had sent strict orders to Normandy that no churchman should be allowed to enter the country during his absence; the same rule should apply to England. So no one could bring him messages from the Pope. He then gave all his thought and energy to the Irish problem and in six months he had made the people of that land realize that there was only one course open to them— submission to him. With his unbounded energy, he set about bringing trade to that country, and he succeeded in making it more prosperous than it had ever been before. The wise among the Irish welcomed this. He fortified the coastal towns and set up garrisons there. Dublin had been almost in ruins when he took it, but before the year was out it had become a trading centre. He spent Christmas in Dublin.

I could not help but admire him. It was typical of him to throw himself into this mighty project at the time when the whole world was against him and he himself must be tortured by the memories of a man who had dominated his life for so long.

He would probably have stayed in Ireland but for the fact that he heard rumours of what was happening in England. Did he then begin to realize what a great mistake he had made in setting up a second King? Young Henry was restive, eager to seize the crown; he was also very immature.

The older Henry had been groomed for kingship by his indomitable mother and had been made aware of all he had to learn and had set about learning it in a dedicated fashion. How different was his son! He was the sort of young man who would surround himself with sycophants; he was vain; he believed that governing a kingdom meant being idolized by those around him, being the centre of attention on every occasion. He should have remembered how his father worked, how he was constantly going into battle, how he never spared himself and suffered the hardships his soldiers did. Henry was young, of course. Yes, surely his father must now be realizing his great mistake.

So he went back to England where, I heard, he found young Henry truculent, demanding to know why he could not govern England or at least Normandy.

Henry told him not to be foolish. He had been crowned but there was only one King of England as long as he himself was alive. Young Henry would have to remember that he must obey his father—in all things.

The King's thoughts were now busy with marriage plans for our youngest, John. John was no longer at Fontevrault. He was now five years old and had been committed to the care of Ranulf de Granville, the Chief Justiciar of England. Always watchful for advantageous marriages for his offspring, Henry had decided on a marriage for his youngest with Alice, only daughter and therefore heiress of Humbert III, the Count of Maurienne. Henry had made a contract with Humbert that if he had no male heirs John should inherit all his lands. If on the other hand, he should have a son, there would be rich compensation for John.

This would give Henry command over the western passes of the Alps. Through his children he was going to have control of the whole of Europe.

In order to placate Louis, at the end of August Marguerite had been crowned with young Henry at Winchester by the Archbishop of Rouen. This had only increased my son's desire to rule. Resentment smouldered between father and son, and there were many who were ready to add fuel to this.

This was the state of affairs when Henry decided to spend Christmas at Chinon and summoned not only his sons Richard and Geoffrey to join him but me also.

I would have refused but my sons had to go, and I did not want them to go without me. I must admit that the prospect of seeing Henry again exhilarated me. I wanted to see how he had weathered the storm of Becket's murder which had still not abated. He was indeed a king. When he was threatened, he snapped his fingers and replied by adding Ireland to his dominions. It was impossible not to admire him.

Henry had aged. There was white in the tawny curls. But his vitality was as great as ever. He regarded me with a certain sardonic amusement.

There was great feasting, banquets with many courses and the finest wines that could be found in France, which meant the best in the world, I believed. But Henry was not interested in food and wine. I guessed it was a big strain for him to sit still while the rest of the company gorged themselves. He drank sparingly and showed clearly that he grudged the time spent on meals.

Richard and Geoffrey were in awe of him but their dislike was growing. The trouble he had had with young Henry had brought about a new sternness towards them all and he was determined to show them who was master.

I smiled inwardly. That was not the way to deal with them. It amazed me that such a brilliant tactician, such a born ruler, should be so ignorant of human nature. To have crowned his son in his lifetime was proof of that. And now followed his treatment of Richard and Geoffrey which could only alienate them.

I had shown him clearly that he could not expect me to bow to his wishes whatever they were. The partnership which had once existed between us was over. I had my dominions and, although he might think they were his, they were not. Aquitaine would have none of him and he knew it. Perhaps that was why he left me in peace to rule.

It was inevitable that that should be a stormy Christmas.

When we were alone, his conversation was all about our son Henry and how disappointed he was in him. The boy was pleasure-loving, thinking to spend his life staging tournaments; he thought kingship a round of gaiety with himself in the centre of the fun and everyone giving way to him.

'What did you think he would be like?' I demanded. 'A young boy having a crown thrust on him!'

'It should have made him more serious . . . more aware of his responsibilities.'

'You know nothing of people, Henry.' I told him.

'I know my own son.'

'You knew him so well that you put a crown on his head and then expected him to behave like a nobody in the nursery.' He glared at me but I laughed at him. 'You are a fool, Henry,' I said, 'if you think you can make a boy a king and then expect him to behave as he did before he had his crown.'

'*I* was always aware of what kingship meant. When I was a boy I always reminded myself that there was a kingdom waiting for me and how I should have to take care of it and guard it.'

'You had to win your kingdom. It is very different to have it graciously handed to you. I could have told you you were acting unwisely. You went to great pains to get that boy crowned, even alienating the Pope and not waiting for the Archbishop of Canterbury to officiate . . . leaving it all to Roger of York, who is now in trouble himself over it.'

'And you would not have crowned him!'

'Most certainly I would not. But the deed is done now and you will have to see what fruit it bears.'

'What do you mean? The boy will do as I say.'

I shrugged my shoulders and turned away. He strode towards me and gripped my arm.

'You are turning Richard and Geoffrey against me,' he accused.

I wrenched myself free. 'No, Henry,' I said, 'you are turning them against you.'

'What do you mean?'

'Look at yourself. Are you a good family man? Your wife will have none of you. You have indulged yourself with prostitutes. Your bastards are legion. You even set your mistress up in the palace in place of your Queen. My people of Aquitaine will not have you. You can take your laws and disciplines elsewhere as far as they are concerned. And now you complain that your sons do not fall down and worship you, and young Henry, whom you have made a king, is asking for more than a golden crown. Did you think to bind your children to you with lands and castles? I say, you do not know people.'

'You talk nonsense.'

'Nonsense to you, Henry, would be good sense to some. We shall wait and see.'

'You always brought trouble. I was a fool ever to take up with you.'

'Aquitaine you thought worth it.'

'And England for you.'

'I care nothing for England. I care only for my children.'

'So you have become the good mother, have you?'

'Ever since my children were born, I have been the good mother.'

'You were certainly the fruitful one.'

'An excellent thing in queens, is it not? I will tell you something: I know our son Henry. He is very young. He should never have been crowned in his father's lifetime. But you did not consult me. You did not consult me over the appointment of Becket to the archbishopric of Canterbury. Nor would you listen to your mother . . .'

His face was scarlet with rage. I thought: He is going to fall down and bite the hangings. I did not care if he did.

I went on: 'No. You knew best . . . so you thought. But let us not brood on past errors. Let us look ahead. You have made him a King. Now he must be treated as one. You cannot send him back to the schoolroom. Give him a little power. Keep the reins on him but do not treat him as a child.'

'Give him power! Let that young know-nothing ruin my kingdom!'

'He was at the head of affairs while you were in Ireland.'

Henry laughed. 'You know that not to be so. He had no power whatsoever. As if I would leave an untutored boy to govern England. Everything was left to the justiciars and de Luci. That is what he complains of. That is what angers him now that he has ideas beyond his capacities.'

'But don't you see? You gave him a grand coronation. He has been crowned with Marguerite. You cannot expect him to remain as he was.'

'He is worthless. He thinks of nothing but enjoying life. It is all sport and banquets . . . fine clothes . . . hunting and hawking. He learned that from you. I have told him that is not kingship. He has much to learn before he can take part in government. I had high hopes of him once. He seemed to be shaping well.' His eyes narrowed. 'Then he was with you. He was there in that Court with the troubadours of yours . . . those lily-livered poets who have no thought beyond turning a pretty verse. You have done this. You have ruined him . . . as you are ruining the others.'

'It is you who have ruined Henry with your crowning.'

'Nay, he would have been well enough . . . but he has ideas of a fancy Court with men parading themselves like peacocks, and the most important thing in life to make love to women through pretty verses.'

'Unlike his father, making love among the hay or in frowsty tavern wenches' beds.'

He laughed again. 'You give too much importance to these little things.'

'Not as much as you obviously gave, considering your numerous illegitimate children scattered all over the country.'

'Have done. You are of an age now to have finished with jealousy.'

'Jealous! Of you! I am glad to be rid of you. I would rather die than share a bed with you.'

'Never fear. You will not be forced to make that grand gesture. Your life is safe from me . . . as is your body.'

'I am glad of that.'

'And listen to me. I do not want my sons Richard and Geoffrey turned against me as you have tried to turn Henry.'

'My sons, Richard and Geoffrey, form their own opinions and if they have formed such of you which you do not like, do not blame me but look to yourself.'

'I can see that you and I will never agree.'

'Then at last you are seeing some truth.'

With that I left him.

Richard had been waiting for me. He was growing very suspicious of his father and knew how things stood between us. The scandal about Rosamund Clifford had reached his ears and he was ready to spring to my defence. He thought his father uncouth in dress and manners, and I was very touched because he was ready to go into battle on my account.

'You are angry,' he said. 'The King has been worrying you.' He looked so bellicose that I laughed.

'I will kill him if he hurts you,' he said.

I laid my hand on his arm. I said: 'Do not let him hear you say such a thing. It could be called treason. And, my dearest, I can look after myself. I need no defence.'

'But you hate him. I hate him, too. So does Geoffrey, I think.'

'And your brother Henry is turning against him.'

'John will be the only one who does not hate him,' said Richard. 'And he is too young to know. I expect he will, too, when he gets older.'

I said: 'We shall have to wait and see. I shall be glad when this Christmas is over.'

'And we go back to Poitiers.'

'You love the place, don't you?' Richard nodded.

'One day it will be yours, entirely. Your brother Henry longs for the crown but it will never be his while his father lives. Perhaps he hopes that won't be long. I hope you do not harbour the same thoughts about me.'

Richard was horrified, and I knew his emotion was genuine.

'Please do not talk so, dearest Mother,' he said. 'Life would be empty for me without you.'

He meant it. That was how it was between us.

And as soon as possible I left with him and Geoffrey for Poitiers.

It seemed that no sooner had we returned than we received another summons from the King. This time it was to join him in Limoges. The reason for this was ratification of the contract between Humbert's daughter Alice and John.

It was a long time since Henry had set foot in my province, and I was going to make him aware that he came as my guest— although I had not invited him.

There was a big gathering. Young Henry and Marguerite were there and John, the prospective bridegroom, had been brought forth. There was also Alais, daughter of Louis, who was to marry Richard when she was old enough. Alais was a very attractive girl and I was glad for Richard.

Henry was never happier than when making marriage plans which would bring him gain.

He behaved to me as though we had not had our differences at Chinon.

'I very much want this marriage,' he said. 'I know Maurienne is small but it is of strategic importance. It lies south of Lake Geneva and extends almost to the Gulf of Genoa. There one could control Italy. Oh yes, I attach great importance to this.'

All was going well when Humbert seemed suddenly to change his mind. There were Henry's other sons: Henry, crowned King of England: Richard with Aquitaine: Geoffrey with Brittany; and what had John? His father had called him 'Lackland'. Humbert was beginning to wonder what sort of bargain he was making.

Henry was greatly disturbed. There must be no hitch. He immediately added three castles in Anjou to John's inheritance. Humbert was satisfied, but there was one who was not.

Our newly created King had inherited Anjou, and he was not going to stand by and see his castles given to a younger brother. He immediately rose and declared before the assembly that he would never give up his castles.

The King laughed and turning to Humbert said: 'Take no notice of my son. He is but a boy. The castles are John's. I say so, and my word is law.'

He managed to convince Humbert.

Young Henry was furious. He came to me.

'I am tired of it,' he said. 'He treats me like a child. He arranges everything . . . even my friends. I was crowned King and I do not have the rights of the humblest of those about me. I will not endure it. I will not. I am the King.' A crafty look came into his eyes. 'And there are those who would support me,' he added.

I could imagine that. Oh, what trouble lay ahead for my arrogant husband, who thought he knew everything and could do so much better than anyone else?

'I am tired of living with him,' said Henry. 'I shall come to Aquitaine . . . and one day . . . one day . . . I am going to claim my kingdom.'

Richard came in while he was talking and stood listening, his eyes shining. 'He has been cruel to our mother,' he said. 'I will stand with you.'

'Then I'll do it,' said Henry.

There were dreams in his eyes, wild dreams. He would dream rather than achieve, I thought. But I could not help but be pleased by their criticism of their father.

I was looking forward to returning to Poitiers. These meetings with Henry were always disturbing. Our quarrels stimulated me, but during them I would see a cold and calculating light in his eyes as though he had plans for me. I knew he would be capable of anything and that I had to be wary of him.

My son Henry really hated him now. He said: 'I will come

with you when you leave. I will not stay with my father to be treated like a child.'

He was often with Richard and they talked against the King frequently. It was their favourite topic. They were working up a hatred against him. Young Henry said that several influential people in England were tired of the King's rule. They talked of the days of Stephen when men were more free. 'Free to roam the countryside and be robbed,' I might have said, for wise men should know that Henry's laws had made the country a safer place to live in. But I could not bring myself to say a good word for my husband.

When the time came for us to depart, there was a scene.

Young Henry said he was coming with us.

'No,' replied the King. 'You are mistaken. You are coming with me.'

'I prefer to go with my mother.'

'And I prefer you to stay with me.'

'Why should I . . . ?'

'Because I say so.'

'I am the King.'

'*I* am the King. You are my son and, if you deserve the honour, in due course you shall wear the crown. But you will have to be tutored for such a position and that is what I am going to do. That is why you will not go to your mother's Court. You will not be playing in tournaments and pageants, singing and dancing and frittering away your time. You will be learning the art of kingship.'

'I refuse.'

The King laughed. 'And I could put you under restraint until you calmed down.'

'You would not dare.'

The King's eyes had grown steely. He went to Henry and held his arm in such a grip that the boy winced. 'There is nothing I will not do to purge you of your folly. You will be under restraint most certainly if you do not take care.'

He could be very formidable, and the boy, though sullen, was afraid of his father.

Richard, Geoffrey and I left for Poitiers without him.

I heard news from time to time.

Young Henry was being recalcitrant, and the King was behaving very sternly towards him. His intimate friends, whom the King did not trust, were dismissed. Henry was not allowed to go out without a guard; he could almost be said to be under arrest.

I could imagine the resentment smouldering. The final outrage was that Henry should sleep in his father's room.

One day a messenger came to us with news. Young Henry had escaped.

He and his father had reached Chinon. Perhaps the King was growing old and was more exhausted than he used to be by hours in the saddle. They had retired for the night, young Henry sleeping as usual in his father's room. In the early hours of the morning while the King was in a deep sleep, his son slipped out of the room. He must have had helpers in the castle for horses were waiting for him.

I could picture Henry's rage when he realized what had happened. He would immediately set about bringing the boy back. He could not have gone far and it seemed they must soon find him.

The chase went on for three days, but young Henry managed to elude his pursuers, and finally he crossed the border into France and made his way at once to Louis, his father-in-law, from whom he could accept help.

When the King reached the French border and realized where his son had gone, he immediately sent messengers to the French Court. Louis would understand that there had been a little family misunderstanding. He wanted the boy to be told that if he returned they would discuss together how to settle their differences.

Louis's reply amused me as it must have others. He asked from whom the message came.

'From the King of England,' was the reply.

'That cannot be so,' said Louis in mock bewilderment. 'The King of England is here at my Court. You must mean the former King of England, for everyone knows that he is no longer King because he resigned his kingdom to his son.'

That should teach Henry a lesson. Oh, how he must be gnashing his teeth to contemplate his folly!

I waited for what would happen next, and to my surprise young Henry arrived in Aquitaine.

He was full of plans. His father was too old to rule. It was his turn. He wanted his brothers to join him. He would make his father see that he would have no more of this treatment. He could get people to stand with him.

My son was young and reckless, but there were others watching the growing tension with eager eyes. Louis was one. He had been casting anxious eyes on Henry Plantagenet for a long time. In Aquitaine, Brittany and even England, men were stirring themselves. The taxes were crippling. It was true Henry spent little on himself and that the money went in services to the country, but Henry's perpetual wars were costly and people in England were simply not interested in them. They wanted a king who would rule them and not one who must continually protect far-flung dominions which always seemed to be on the verge of revolt.

In fact, his sons were not the only ones who were ready to rise against Henry.

He was always at his most resourceful when he scented danger. I believed he did not take this desertion of his son seriously and had confidence in his ability to get the better of the petulant youth. He sent an order to the Archbishop of Rouen which showed me that he at last understood that I had great influence over my sons. If I would return to him, bringing our children, we could resume our old relationship, which he was eager to do.

I laughed. The arrogance of the man had to be admired. He really believed he only had to promise me a return of his affection—at least, I supposed that was what he was hinting at—and I would come running to him. I suppose he would have dismissed poor Rosamund Clifford, with whom he had been living more or less openly when he was in England.

I ignored him but Henry was not the man to relinquish his desires lightly. He must have been growing really anxious, for the Archbishop came to me and said it was my bounden duty to return to my husband with my family. He had promised me his love. There was a threat in this. If I did not return I should be open to censure from the Church. This moved me not at all. I was exultant. I was enjoying my revenge.

Now the rising against Henry was in full swing, and at the heart of it were his own sons. Louis was helping, but he was an unreliable ally. He still had no stomach for war, and although he entered into it, it was possible that he might not stay the course. Alas, my son Henry was far from wise. He made rash promises to any who would support him in his efforts to take the crown from his father. I wished I could advise him, but Henry was not the sort to take advice. He thought he was so wise—as only the ignorant do—and is there anything more calculated to bring failure?

He promised the county of Kent to the Count of Flanders for his services, and to the Count of Boulogne he offered the county of Mortain and more land besides; to Thibault of Blois, Amboise and rents from Anjou; and he even offered King William of Scotland Westmoreland and Carlisle if he would attack Henry on the Border. I could have wept for his ignorance and folly.

Although taxation had aroused certain resentment in England, the powerful lords had long realized Henry's great gifts and the benefits which had come to England through his reign. The Earls of Surrey, Arundel, Essex, Salisbury and Cornwall were behind him; the barons were with him; so was the ruler of Wales. Richard de Luci could always be relied on and when he realized how far the revolt had gone, with his usual energy Henry engaged mercenaries to augment his army. Then he went into action.

William of Scotland attempted an invasion, but Henry's illegitimate son Geoffrey, the one whom he had brought into my nurseries and who idolized him, quickly crushed that.

How foolish they had been to under-rate Henry. Whatever else he was, he was the great leader, the great soldier. Louis, deciding that he had had enough, withdrew; and one by one the territories taken by rebels were won back.

Henry was in charge once more, indomitable.

But he had no wish to make war on his sons. He called a meeting with Louis. Henry was lenient. He did not want to be hard on his own flesh and blood. He loved his sons—at least he loved Henry. He had always been proud of him.

Perhaps at this time he could see his faults very clearly, and if so they must have made him anxious, but he was not one to despair. He still thought he could make a king of Henry. He understood his ambition. He offered him castles and lands.

But my sons did not see themselves as conquered. They haughtily refused them and the meeting broke up. The fighting was at an end for the time being but the boys did not go to their father; they rode back to Paris in the company of Louis.

I was well aware that Henry's wrath would be turned against me. England was safe, and now he was left to deal with his Continental possessions. My sons were under the protection of Louis. He could not touch them. But I was not. Those about me warned me that I was in acute danger.

He was coming closer; he was passing through France, seizing the castles of those who had worked against him; and now all his immense energy was concentrated on the defeat of his enemies. He would be merciless to them, particularly as his sons were involved. That would have enraged him and I must not forget that he blamed me.

He was coming nearer and nearer to Poitiers. And why was he heading in this direction? Because he wanted to find me. He had designated me the leader of the revolt against him. I must not be here when he came, as he assuredly would.

I knew my advisers were right but I could not bring myself to go. This was my home. This was where I had my Court and my friends. I did not want to leave it.

How foolish I was! Each night I would go to bed wondering what the next day would bring forth; each morning I would say to myself: Should I go today? And I would still be in my castle when night fell.

It could not go on. There came a day when he was not many miles from the castle. His advance had been spectacular. Who would have thought he could have come so soon?

'His men will be everywhere,' I was told. 'You would be recognized at once.'

They were right. I should have left long ago and I must delay no longer. I dressed myself as a man . . . a knight. I piled my hair on top of my head and put on a hat which covered it. A few of my faithful friends came with me and we set off. I rose astride and tried to assume the manners of a man. I think I succeeded rather well. My little band was becoming quite merry. I was still young enough to enjoy adventure.

We realized how wise we were to have left. Henry's army was very close to the city. We should have to go very carefully—perhaps travel by night and rest by day.

We had not gone very far when we ran into a party of riders. I was not disturbed because they were my own people. They stopped and talked with us for a while and told us that Henry's forces were but a few miles away.

While we were talking, some strands of hair escaped from my hat, and in my attempt to push them out of sight my hat fell off and my hair was tumbling about my shoulders. The men stared at me. I saw the calculating look in their eyes. One of them said: 'It is the Duchess.' Their attitude changed. I saw the stupidity in their faces but it was hard to believe that I could be betrayed by my own people.

I understood their reasons. Their loyalty to me was forgotten in the contemplation of the reward they would surely receive from Henry for my capture.

Their numbers were greater than ours and they were armed. And so I was led away into captivity.

Once more I came face to face with Henry. I was his prisoner now but if he expected me to humble myself before him he was mistaken.

He regarded me sardonically.

'So,' he said, 'your attempt to escape has failed.'

'Because of traitors,' I said.

'Traitors to you, friends to me. I shall reward them well for their services, particularly as they are those whom you regard as your subjects.'

'Well,' I said, 'what do you propose?'

'To finish with the trouble you have been causing me ever since I set eyes on you.'

'What is it to be then?'

'You will see. I give the orders, you know.'

'When did you not? Though they have not always been obeyed.'

'Do not bandy words with me.'

'I do not give a thought to you.'

His eyes narrowed. 'You she-devil,' he said. 'You witch.'

'I thought you were the one who was descended from witches.'

'You would be wise not to provoke me.'

'I care not what you do to me.'

'You are a traitor. Do you know what happens to traitors?'

'You were false to me . . . always, even in the early days of our marriage. Are you still as lecherous as ever? Don't answer. I am not in the least interested.'

'You turned our sons against me.'

'I believe I have told you before that you turned them against yourself.'

'You incited them to take up arms against me.'

'They did not need to be incited. They hate you, Henry. Why do you think they do?'

'Because their mother turned them against me.'

'You insist on that old theme. What are you going to do with me? Kill me? Would you marry Rosamund? It would be scarcely fitting.'

'Be silent,' he said. 'Remember you are my prisoner.'

'I ask you, what are you going to do with me?'

'You will discover in time.'

'And now?'

I could see that he was working himself up into one of his rages. I wanted to goad him, to see him roll on the floor, biting the rushes. It would give me some comfort.

He might have sensed this, for there was no rage. He looked at me, his eyes narrowed, his lips curled: 'I am going to have you taken away.'

'Where?'

'I shall decide. It will be somewhere strong. You will be well guarded.'

'So you fear me?'

'It is you who should fear me.'

His voice was cold with hatred. I remembered how he had hated Becket, and yet there had been love in that hate. Were his feelings for me like that? I wondered if he ever thought of the passion there had once been between us.

He turned abruptly away and left me.

Later that day I was taken away. They did not tell me where I was going. I did not recognize the fortress when I reached it, and nobody would answer my questions.

And there I was incarcerated—the King's prisoner.

The Passing of Kings

It is hard to think now of that dreary time. I lived through it only because of Hope. I told myself it could not last. He could not keep me thus forever. At first I thought he planned to kill me, but later I guessed he did not want my death on his conscience as Becket's was. I was not ill treated, and after the first weeks I ceased to think of assassins who would come in the night and put an end to my life; I no longer wondered if every sip of liquid, every mouthful of food, would poison me.

He did not intend me to die. I had to live, deprived of everything I enjoyed. I have no doubt that he derived some joy from that.

Winter was with us. It was cold in my fortress but I had fur rugs to keep me warm. I was given food. But everything else I was deprived of. He just wanted to keep me alive, so that I suffered in my misery.

There was no news. My guards were silent. They had been ordered to tell me nothing, and they obeyed their orders.

How long? I used to ask myself. How long shall I be incarcerated here? It could be for years. What was he doing now? He had subdued his enemies, I was sure. What of my children? Where were they? I hoped they had not been misguided enough to take up arms against him afresh. They would never defeat him. He was undefeatable.

Winter passed—the longest and most dreary winter of my life. He could not have thought of anything that would have been more unacceptable for me.

Christmas came. How different from other Christmases! Where was Richard? What was he thinking now? And Henry and Geoffrey and the girls? They would surely think of their mother at Christmas time. And he . . . my enemy . . . he would gloat the more. He would be saying: 'Now she will see what happens to those who defy me.'

I hated him. I was sorry that he had not been utterly defeated and yet I was admiring him in a way because he would always win.

Spring had come. Each day was like another. I hoped for something to happen . . . anything rather than this dreary monotony. The days seemed long, and yet when I looked back I could hardly believe I had been here all that time.

Long summer days. I looked out at the green fields and felt more of a prisoner than I had during the dark days of winter. Could I have been here a year?

How long could I endure it? I should have to do something . . . find a way of escape.

It was a morning in July when I awoke to change. They were lowering the drawbridge, and there was activity everywhere. My door was opened. My sullen guards stood there. I was to prepare for a journey, they indicated.

My heart leaped with excitement. It was over then . . . this wearisome imprisonment. At last I was going to move. Where were we going? I wanted to know. They could not tell me. I should find out soon enough.

We were travelling north. Was he sending me to England? Perhaps, because he knew how much I loved my own country and he would want to take me away from it. Perhaps I should hear news of what was happening to my children. The hardest part of all was to be in ignorance of what was happening to them. I, who had been so much at the centre of events, to be shut away like this, a prisoner of a vindictive husband!

How I hated him! I would kill him if I had a chance. I hoped my sons would go on fighting him, let him know what an inhuman monster he was to me.

We were travelling north. We were almost certainly going to England. Barfleur. Right on the coast. This could mean only one thing.

Forty vessels lay in the Channel. I remembered the first time I had been here . . . an eager bride with a husband who, I had thought, loved me as I loved him. But even at that time he had been unfaithful.

How rough the sea was! The wind was lashing the waves fully. No one could put to sea in such weather . . . except Henry. He did not care for the weather. He could not bear inactivity.

I heard a little now of what was going on. There was more freedom. A woman called Amaria was given to me to look after my needs and act as maid. I liked her immediately, and she was to prove a great comfort to me. She was alert-minded, a gossipy woman with a talent for remembering and recording details. She was vitally interested in everything that was going on around her, and she had a capacity for disarming those with whom she came in contact so that she was able to extract confidences. She quickly grew fond of me and, understanding my craving for news, determined to supply all she could.

We travelled down to Salisbury, one of the most strongly fortified castles in the country. Henry was taking no chances on my escaping.

I settled into my new prison. It was an improvement on the old, particularly so because I had Amaria as my maid-companion and informant.

It was from her that I learned of Henry's penance. The whole country was talking of it, said Amaria. The King, dressed as a humble pilgrim, had walked barefoot over the cobbles, making his way to the cathedral.

'They say his feet were bleeding, my lady, and he did not complain. It was what he wanted . . . to suffer to make up for what had happened to the Archbishop. The Bishop of London was there to receive him.'

The Bishop of London! That would be Gilbert Foliot. That was interesting for Foliot had been no friend to Becket. He had always been jealous of him. I supposed he was penitent now.

'The King asked to be taken to the very place where the Archbishop had been struck down,' went on Amaria, 'and when they took him there, he lay on the stones and wept bitterly . . . so that his tears could fall where Thomas à Becket's blood had fallen. Then the Bishop went into the pulpit and told everyone why the King had come. He said that King Henry was praying for the salvation of his soul. He wanted it known that he did not order the death of the martyr but feared the murderers had mis- understood some words he had imprudently uttered and for that reason he sought chastisement and would bare his back to receive the discipline of the rod. That the King should act so! Nobody could believe their eyes, but it is true, my lady.'

'I understand him well. He knew this was the only way for him to escape from the burden which the death of this man had attached to him. He was guilt-ridden . . . and impatient of it. So he took this step . . . drastic as it is and unprecedented. What king has ever humbled himself so before? But it does not surprise me. He feels that the stigma of Becket's death is impeding his progress. Therefore he will take any step, however demeaning, to get this obstacle out of his way. And what was the King's reply to the Bishop?'

'That what the Bishop had said was what he had commanded him to, and he hoped his humble penance would be acceptable to God and the dead Archbishop. He said he had paid for lights to be set up at the tomb of the martyr and to be kept burning there. He had ordered that a hospital be built in honour of God and the blessed martyr. The Bishop then said that he would help with the building of the hospital and grant indulgences to all those who contributed to it. He himself should be joining in the King's penance, for he had said when the body of the martyr lay on the stones of the cathedral that it should be thrown into a dunghill or hung on a gibbet. Greatly he regretted that and repented of it.'

'The old hypocrite!' I cried. 'He certainly should have bared his back to the rod. What else did you glean, Amaria?'

'That the King went into the crypt, removed his top garments and knelt by the tomb, and each of the monks in the convent took a whip and struck the King three blows saying, ''As thy Redeemer was scourged for the sin of man, so be thou scourged for thy own sin.'' The King then prayed to Thomas à Becket and went round the cathedral stopping at the shrine to say prayers and ask forgiveness for his sins. He stayed there all day and the next night.'

'He would do it thoroughly,' I said.

'The next day he heard Mass and drank holy water which contained a drop of Thomas's blood which they had saved while he lay bleeding on the stones. Then the King left Canterbury.'

I could imagine him. The tiresome business had had to be enacted; he had had to humble himself; but he had not really done that. He would never humble himself. Any who thought he would must be mistaken. He had had to perform this unpleasant task, so with his usual energy he had performed it . . . thoroughly and efficiently. From now on the matter of Becket's murder was over for him.

Amaria, free to go where she liked, was often in town; she talked to the guards; she was a mine of information. Naturally curious and interested in people, she quickly understood that one of the hardest things I had to bear was being cut off from events. I believed she had an affection for me and was eager to please me, so she made this gleaning of information her greatest task and pleasure.

Soon after she had so graphically described Henry's penance, she came in with the news that the Scottish King, who had been making trouble, had been captured and made a prisoner at Alnwick. It had happened while Henry was doing his penance.

After his ordeal he had retired to bed. He spent a day there. He must have been feeling very weak to do that. I expected the monks had laid on rather hard with their whips. It must have been an opportunity too good to be missed. I wished I had been one of them. I would have given him a few sharp strokes.

The news of the Scottish King's capture was brought to him while he was in bed.

'They say, my lady, that he leaped out of bed,' was Amaria's version. 'He said it was a sign from Heaven . . . from Thomas à Becket up there. "We are friends once more," cried the King. "Now you will work for me. I shall go from victory to victory. We shall be friends as we were in the beginning." '

I laughed. Amaria amused me. But I think it must have happened something like that. Henry used everything to advantage. Did he really believe that the capture of the King of Scotland was due to Becket's help? One thing he would know was that the people would think so; and that would be important to Henry. What a combination—Thomas in Heaven, Henry on Earth. They would be invincible.

I knew he would be smiling to himself. The humiliation of walking barefoot, the sore back, the humble confession of guilt . . . it was all worth while. Now the people would believe that Henry was at peace with Heaven, and Thomas was on his side. Let his enemies beware.

* * *

I was moved from Salisbury to Winchester, where life was a little easier. I lived in comparative comfort. Of course I missed the fine clothes which I had always had in abundance; I missed my musicians and my Court of Poitiers.

My gaoler for a while was Ranulf de Glanville, which showed how important I was to the King, for he was one of his most trusted subjects. He was the Chief Justiciar of England and a man of many gifts. He was Sheriff of Lancashire and during the recent Scottish invasion had led the men of Lancashire into the attack which had resulted in the capture of the King of Scotland. It was Ranulf who had taken the news to the King. He had Henry's complete trust. I did not believe I would get any concessions from him.

Another of my gaolers was William FitzStephen, who was to write a biography of Becket, with whom he had been in close contact for ten years. During the time of his intimacy with Becket, Henry must have come to know FitzStephen very well. He had been a sub-deacon in Becket's chapel and entrusted with special duties.

I viewed Henry's choice of gaolers with mixed feelings. In the first place, I felt it a mark of respect for me that he would not give the post to any but those he trusted absolutely; but secondly it meant that my chances of escape were slight—or, more accurately, non-existent.

I had been in England over a year when I had a visitor, a Cardinal who had come to England and found himself drawn into a matter which Henry was considering.

He was very suave, friendly and compassionate.

'My lady,' he said, 'how different this life must be from that to which you have been accustomed in the past.' I could agree with him on that. 'I know you have always been interested in the Abbey of Fontevrault.'

'Yes,' I said, now very alert.

'How would you feel about going there and living a life of peace?'

'I have never thought I was suited to the cloistered existence. It is not in my nature to be.'

'But here you are . . . cloistered. You are a prisoner. There you would be free.'

'Has the King sent you here?'

He lowered his eyes. 'The King has suggested that I visit you.'

'With a purpose in mind, I see. To get rid of me by sending me to Fontevrault. I retire . . . and my retirement means that a divorce can be arranged for the King. Is that it? There is no need to mince words with me, Cardinal.'

'My lady, the King thinks of your welfare.'

'Not forgetting his own.'

'It seems this would be beneficial to you both. You are . . .' He hesitated. '. . . my lady, you are no longer young.'

'I am fifty-three years of age. Time, you suggest, for me to retire from the world?'

'You would find a life of meditation and prayer most satisfactory.'

'And if I took to it, so would Henry. A divorce would be easy, would it not? A wife who has retired from the world is as good as dead. And a divorce? Does he plan to marry again? Whom would he marry? His mistress, Rosamund Clifford? He lives with her openly now, does he not? Does he plan to have sons by her and replace my sons? I would never agree to that.'

'All the King wishes is to give you a life of peace where you can meditate on the past and earn remission of your sins.'

'He would do well to behave in like manner.'

'None of us is without sin, my lady.'

'And some are more overburdened by it than others. Let us be plain about this. I will not go to Fontevrault Abbey.'

'You would be Abbess of course . . . mistress of your world . . . the ruler of the abbey as you have been of the duchy.'

I laughed. 'You are trying to tempt me, Cardinal. The King has sent you and paid you well for it, I doubt not. You have come here to get my consent to go into a nunnery, giving him reasons for divorce, so making him free to take a new wife and get more sons . . . those whom he would mould to his way of thinking, unlike those who love their mother well and hate their father. Does he really think to marry Rosamund Clifford? It is impossible! But then he is a man who refuses to see anything as impossible. You will have to go back to the King and tell him no, no, no. I will not be forced into a convent . . . even Fontevrault. I will stay here, his prisoner, to plague him, a barrier between him and his fair Rosamund. Go back to him and tell him that he will have to think of another way of ridding himself of me.'

When he had gone, I found myself thinking of Fontevrault.

I might be fifty-three years old but I was not yet at that stage when I wished to think of the life to come. I believed I had a few more years ahead of me, and something told me that I should not be a prisoner for ever. I would not shut myself away from the world. I wanted to know what my boys were doing. Henry, too. He must think that I saw no release in sight and might as well shut myself away in Fontevrault where I should at least have the dignity of ruling my own little world. He did not realize that I should never give up and that my spirit was as indomitable as his.

Moreover, following his exploits, hating him fiercely, was a rather enjoyable occupation.

A year passed uneventfully for me. I heard that there had been a reconciliation between the King and young Henry. My son had been with the King of France; there he had raged against his father for imprisoning me and saying that he would like to do the same to him.

I was afraid that he swayed this way and that, wondering which way would be to his advantage. What he wanted more than anything, I was sure, was the crown of England; and Louis could not give him that. I often wondered how differently everything would have turned out if Henry had not made that vital mistake of crowning his son King while he lived.

Young Henry eventually decided that his father had more to offer than Louis and he went to him at Bures and fell on his knees before him—the prodigal son returned to the bosom of his family, having seen the error of his ways, and begging for forgiveness.

I was amazed at Henry's softness where young Henry was concerned. He loved that boy dearly. He could see only good in him. He had long assured himself that all that had gone wrong between them was due to my influence; he would not have been so gentle with Richard or Geoffrey. Delighted to have him back docile, playing the obedient son for a while, Henry promised him money and let him see how overjoyed he was to be friends with him.

I could have told him that the amity between them would not last.

People smiled at the softness of the King towards his son. They ate at the same table, slept in the same bedchamber. I guessed this was because Henry wished to keep an eye on the boy. I wondered how long it would last.

These little pieces of information came to me at intervals and I had to piece them together to get the picture, but knowing both my son and my husband so well, I was able to do this with ease.

I was amused when I heard that young Henry was planning to go on a pilgrimage during Lent of the next year to St James of Compostela. This idea was too much for the King to accept. He said very firmly that there would be no pilgrimage. I can imagine how young Henry sulked. The happy reunion was coming to an end; the King must surely understand by now that he could never make his son into another such as himself. What was strange was that he should have been so devoted to him. I should have thought Richard would have appealed to him more.

I was proud of my favourite son. He was already showing himself to possess unusual military skill. He was not quite nineteen years old but he was proving a resourceful ruler. At this time there was a great deal of trouble in Aquitaine. The people were disgruntled because they knew I was Henry's prisoner, and that made them very angry with him. They knew I had made Richard my heir. He was more like me than any other of my children. He loved music; he would fill his Court with troubadours. But there were always rebels to raise trouble, and Richard had not won the love which they gave to me.

Young Henry was becoming more and more dissatisfied, and finally the King gave him permission to go to Aquitaine to help Richard, who could do with some assistance.

The opportunity was apparently seized with eagerness. Anything to get away from his father's stern rule. What use would Henry be to Richard? I had no idea, but it did occur to me that he might dally on the way.

So young Henry set out. His father had insisted that a man in whom he had great faith—a certain Adam Churchdown—should travel with the entourage, and secretly I expect Adam had instructions to report on the young King's conduct to his father.

I was at Winchester when, to my great delight, Amaria came to me one day to tell me that my daughter Joanna was in the castle.

I was overcome with joy. Joanna, my youngest daughter, was very dear to me, as were all my daughters. I may not have mentioned them as frequently as my sons, but that is because, as girls in this man-governed world, they were not at the centre of events as my sons were.

Richard, of course, would always be first in my thoughts, and Henry and Geoffrey were a source of anxiety, but my daughters had been docile and loving, and my joy at knowing Joanna was under the same roof was intense.

Amaria, in whom I had confided to some extent, was well aware of my feelings, and with a little conspiring had arranged that my daughter's guardian should bring her just below my window so that I could look out and see her.

What joy it was to behold my daughter! She looked up at me, and I could sense her happiness at seeing me. Poor child, she was about to be sent away to a strange land and an unknown husband. It was the fate of princesses, but at such a time she should have had her mother with her.

Each day Joanna would be brought to that spot and we would gaze at each other. I was dreading the time when she would leave.

Then came a day which I remember now with an uplifting of my spirits. I was to be temporarily released from my prison. I was to join my daughter to help her prepare for her wedding to the King of Sicily. We should remain at Winchester and after my daughter had left the country, I should once again be confined.

I did not care. For the time being I was free and I was to be with my beloved daughter. With what joy we embraced!

'My child,' I said. 'I feared you had forgotten me.'

'I never would,' she declared fervently, and I was so happy.

She was afraid, she told me; she did not know what her husband would be like; she did not know what Sicily would be like. I soothed her. All would be well, I said. She was beautiful and talented and her husband must surely love her dearly.

She said: 'He has not yet decided that he will have me. He is sending his ambassadors to inspect me.'

'Assuredly they will tell their master that you are completely lovable.' I took her face in my hands. 'That is what you want, is it not?'

'I don't know,' she answered. 'I should not want him to turn from me. On the other hand if he did, I should stay here.'

We were able to smile together.

The ambassadors arrived. She was with me before she met them. I told her she had nothing to fear.

'Just be yourself,' I said. 'That is the best way to please them.'

I must have inspired her with confidence, for they thought her not only beautiful but dignified and delightful in every way.

She told me that when she had seen me at the window she remembered so much of the times we had together. She had missed me sadly and had implored the King to allow me to be with her. At first he had refused, but she had wept and told him how frightened she was, how lonely and sad, and how much she wanted to be with her mother. And at last he said yes. 'He said you would after all know what I should wear.'

'Well, we are together,' I said. 'And you will be happy, I promise you, for you are of a nature to be so. I have heard that your bridegroom is very handsome . . . and good, I am sure. I have seen a picture of him. He has long curling hair and a very fine complexion. He looked very impressive in his armour. It is said he is liberal to the poor, which shows a gentle and kindly nature. They are already calling him "William the Good".'

They were busy and happy days for me . . . like an oasis in a dreary desert. The Bishop of Winchester was appointed to entertain the Sicilian embassy, and I gave myself up to planning Joanna's wardrobe. Henry had arranged for his half-brother, an illegitimate son of Geoffrey le Bel, to be her principal escort. Henry always brought forward members of the family, even though they were illegitimate. Others who would join in the escort were the Archbishops of Canterbury, York, Rouen and Bordeaux.

Henry came to Winchester and I took my place in the Court celebration in honour of Joanna's departure. I could not help feeling a thrill of excitement at seeing him again. My feelings for him could never be negative . . . and I fancy he felt the same towards me. I noticed his eyes often on me. There was a certain triumph in them. He must have been thinking that I now understood that he was the master. It was true. He had the power to make me a prisoner. But if ever I escaped it would be a different matter.

He had aged considerably, I was gratified to notice. The disaffection of his sons, wars, state matters, penance . . . all this had taken a bigger toll of him than imprisonment had of me.

I wondered if he still found the fair Rosamund so delectable. She was still with him. It must have been something more than physical attraction there . . . as I suppose it had been with me. But that had not prevented his having mistresses all over the country. He still did that, from what gossip I heard, and I had no doubt that he would go on behaving so in the years to come. When he was tired of women, he would be tired of life.

Now we kept up the façade of convention for this important occasion.

Finally, we took leave of Joanna. She clung to me and I murmured words of comfort. We should meet again. She would come to England. I would be free some day and then, if that were possible, I should come to see her.

One fair August day she embarked and with a squadron of seven ships set sail for her new home.

I went back to my prison. But I felt refreshed. My daughter had begged that I should have a brief period of freedom. One day my sons would make sure that I was released altogether.

I heard gossip concerning the King and Rosamund Clifford. Everyone knew of her existence now. In spite of the fact that she was the King's mistress, she was meek and mild—so different from the Queen, they said, and so beautiful (they could not say that she was different from the Queen in that respect) that they accepted her. They said the Queen had been put away because she had plotted against the King, so it was natural that he should turn to Fair Rosamund for comfort. And to many others, they might have been told.

Amaria brought the news. 'Rosamund is very ill. She has gone into a convent. She wants to repent of her sins before she dies.'

'So she and the King are no longer together?'

'They say she is near death, and she does not want to die with all her sins upon her. She has gone into Godstow Nunnery, and there she practises the severest penances imaginable. They say she is very sad and afraid that she has come too late to repentance.'

'She should imitate the King. He very quickly achieved his reward. A flogging and Heaven makes the King of Scotland his captive.'

I believe Amaria thought that somewhat irreverent.

Soon after that I heard that Rosamund had died at Godstow and that she had so despaired of her sin in becoming the King's mistress that she had declared on her deathbed that only when a certain tree in the gardens turned to stone would they know that her soul had been received into Heaven.

Poor Rosamund! I had railed against her, but now I could feel sorry for her. It had not been her fault. The King had desired her and he expected his subjects to obey him. Rosamund had obeyed. I expected she had been fond of him. There *was* something lovable about him . . . though his children failed to see it. I had found it once, and if I were truthful I would admit that, hating him as I did, he still had some fascination for me.

However, he had lost Rosamund and she had been my greatest rival.

And still I remained his prisoner.

I often wondered how I was able to endure the restriction in which I was placed. Perhaps it was because I was getting old. I was at an age when most women would have considered their lives over; I was not like that. I was too vitally interested in what was going on. My hatred for my husband was a spur to my vitality. I wanted to live long enough to see what would happen in this battle between him and his family.

I had grown mellow with age—philosophical. That was why I was able to endure my prison and look on life with analytical cynicism. After all, I lived comfortably. I was not treated like a prisoner. Everyone about me remembered that I was Queen. Life was unpredictable. Those who were down one day would be up the next. I never let them forget for a moment who I was; nor did they.

I listened; I absorbed the news, fitting it together as I heard it, like pieces in a puzzle. I had time to consider it and perhaps because of that I was able to make a clearer picture than those who were in the thick of it.

There was always going to be trouble between Henry and his sons. They all had their grievances—young Henry chief among them because he felt the golden crown on his head and could not bear to see his father in possession of it. He did little in Aquitaine except find those who had rebelled against his father. Never far from his mind was the plan to oust his father and rule himself, alone. It was an ambitious plan, the elder Henry being the man he was; but if his son could get the strong battalions on his side, who knew?

I was very shocked to hear how he had treated Adam Church-down. The man was only doing his duty. Young Henry spent most of his time organizing tournaments—mock battles where his safety was assured and in which he was always the victor because those about him knew that was how he wanted it to be. This would not have been dangerous if the foolish young man had not gone about speaking against his father, plotting with his cronies as to how they could get an army together and take the crown from the old man and put it on the young head where it belonged.

Adam had, in duty bound, found it necessary to report to the King what was happening. Alas for Adam, his letters were intercepted and instead of going to the old King were taken to the young one.

My son should have had more respect for an honourable man. He knew that Adam was his father's servant. What he did was cruel and foolish. He wanted Adam to be humiliated and ordered that he be stripped naked, paraded through the streets— they were in Poitiers at the time—and whipped as he went.

I was horrified. Henry must have been too. He would never have done such a thing in his wildest rages. He must have despaired and realized that he could never make the king he wanted of his son. He might have been proud of Richard, but Richard had shown little affection for him. All his three elder sons were ready to turn against him.

There was only one, as yet untried because he was so young: John.

He could not say that John had come under my influence. Here was one son whom he might mould as he wished. He sent for John.

From then on, the young boy replaced Henry in his affections. John lacked Henry's good looks—he was smaller and darker— but he was young and therefore malleable.

The King made plans for his youngest son. The proposed marriage with Humbert's daughter had come to nothing; but William of Gloucester, one of the richest and most powerful men in England, agreed that his daughter, Hadwisa, should marry John, who would then become heir to all his lands in the west of England and Glamorgan, a considerable inheritance.

John was then declared King of Ireland—John 'Lackland' no longer.

Rumours were coming to my ears.

Amaria said: 'They say the Princess Alais is very attractive.'

'Yes. I am glad,' I said. 'I daresay it will not be long before she marries my son Richard. It is time he had a wife.'

'They say the King is very fond of her.'

'The King!' Something in Amaria's expression gave me a hint of what she might have heard. 'What do you know?' I asked.

She shrugged her shoulders. 'They say that now the Lady Rosamund is dead . . . that the King has taken up with the Princess Alais.'

'But she is to be his daughter-in-law.'

'I only know what I hear, my lady.'

I pondered this. Alais . . . and Henry. What would Louis have to say? How far had Henry gone in this? Surely he did not think he could seduce a daughter of the King of France as he might such as Rosamund Clifford?

But Henry would never consider such things. Moreover he despised Louis. She was very young. And Richard? What of Richard?

I could see a storm blowing up here.

Each day I hoped for news. It came sparsely. I could not believe how time was passing. Often I asked myself: Was I to spend the rest of my life a prisoner?

Was Henry hoping I would die? I had refused to go to Fontevrault, which would have given him his divorce. Did he want to marry again? Who this time? Alais? How would that affect her betrothal to his son Richard? What did he want to do? Raise a family? He was rather old for that. But I had no doubt that he saw himself as immortal. He would make up his mind that he would not depart this life until he saw his successor ready to take on the burden of kingship and not fritter away all the advantages he had brought to the country.

Our destiny was closely linked with that of France because our sway extended so far over that country. Philip Augustus was growing up. He must be fourteen or fifteen years old. The years of my captivity went by so fast that I lost count of them.

Louis had changed since the birth of the God-Given. He had become more statesmanlike and, after having waited so long and tried so hard, he was especially proud to have provided the heir of the Capetian dynasty.

At this time he decided Philip Augustus should be crowned. One might have thought he would have seen what had happened in Henry's case. Two kings in one kingdom made a dangerous situation. However, it did happen in France, and it might have been that Philip Augustus was a more docile son; in any case Louis had never valued his kingship as Henry had.

Having been so close to Louis at one time, I was always eager to hear news of him; moreover, what happened to him affected Henry closely. I heard that the coronation was going to take place at Rheims on 5 August of that year 1179.

How unpredicatable life is! We make our plans and then Fate decides to change them.

Louis had commanded all the nobles of the land to make their way to the cathedral of Rheims. Philip Augustus led his own party and, as always on such occasions when there was an opportunity to hunt, it was taken with alacrity. This was what happened on the way. Philip Augustus, rather like my son Henry, must have been gratified to think he would soon be crowned King. How could they be so foolish as to put crowns on the heads of young boys and expect to withhold the power that went with them? It might be that it would work in this case, but I had heard recently that Philip Augustus was a boy with a will of his own, and if he had any talent for ruling he would wish to work differently from the way his father had.

He showed his independence on this occasion. They were following the deer in the forest and Philip Augustus naturally decided that his should be the arrow which killed the hunted creature. He spurred on his horse and galloped ahead. His followers, I suppose, understood his desire and, not wanting to offend him, fell back, with the result that in due course they lost sight of him. There was consternation: the heir to the throne of France was lost in the forest.

Meanwhile Philip Augustus rode on. He realized he had lost the quarry, was himself lost and was out of earshot of the hunting party. All was silent in the forest. A mist arose; he was wet and cold. One can imagine his fear among the damp foliage and the tall trees; nature did not care whether he was a peasant or a king about to be crowned. After all the adulation he was accustomed to receive, the indifference of nature must have filled him with apprehension.

He began to feel dizzy and hot. He was not strong and they had had great trouble in raising him. When he was very young, his father had lived in terror that he would lose him.

He went deeper into the forest. He was lost and he was going to be ill. It was getting dark. It would be eerie in the forest and he had been accustomed to having people always around him. Now he was alone, alone in the forest which cared nothing for kings.

I have no doubt that he prayed. Who does not remember God when one's need is great? I suppose he thought God had answered his prayers when he came upon the charcoal-burners' hut. They took him into their hovel; they put him by the fire and forced some hot broth between his lips. He was fainting but he was conscious enough to tell them to go at once to the King.

Poor humble people, how bewildered they must have been! But the old man's son set off, and so well did he carry out his mission that by the next day men came to take Philip Augustus away.

I hope the charcoal-burners were amply rewarded. I am sure Louis would not forget to do that.

They took Philip Augustus to the nearest castle but by this time the fever had a hold of him and he was delirious. He had become very ill indeed and there was consternation throughout France. His life was despaired of, and it was feared that God was about to take back what He had given.

Louis's distress must have been great. The story was that he was so beside himself that he could neither eat nor sleep. Fearing that he would die as well as his son, the doctors gave him something to make him rest. He must keep up his strength so that he would be able to bear the blow which it seemed must inevitably come.

He dozed and it was then that he had a vision. He thought that Thomas à Becket came to him and told him that, if he repented of his sins and humbled himself at the shrine in Canterbury Cathedral, his son's life would be saved.

The consternation must have been great when Louis announced his intention of visiting Canterbury. Go into the heart of enemy territory? It must never be! But Louis was adamant. This was a message from God, and everyone must know that he was on special terms with the Almighty. Moreover, what would happen to France if his son died? He himself was a fast-ageing man.

He must go to Canterbury. God—through Thomas à Becket—would not have told him to go if it had not been for his own good. He had to save his son's life, no matter what happened to him.

They tried to put up obstacles. None of them believed in the vision. If Philip Augustus was going to die, nothing would save him. Could the King endure the hazardous journey? Everyone knew what the Channel could be like—and at his age . . . and in his health . . .

I wondered what Henry thought when he heard of Louis's proposed visit. If rumours were true and he had indeed seduced Louis's daughter, he must be feeling rather uneasy for Louis would surely expect to see the girl when he was in England.

I wondered how far Henry's relationship with Alais had gone, and if she were in love with him. Was it possible? He was hardly a romantic figure, apart from his power, but power I believe is one of the most effective aphrodisiacs. I could imagine his storming into the nursery . . . shouting orders . . . laughing . . . standing there, fascinating the beautiful little girl and inspiring her with awe. Would he be able to impress on her that she must betray nothing of their relationship to her father? And Louis? Would he have heard? If he had not, it would never occur to him to suspect. I was very eager to hear the outcome of the meeting.

Henry sent a letter of warm welcome to Louis. He would be honoured to receive him, and he would join his prayers to those of Louis for the recovery of Philip Augustus. He would make himself personally responsible for Louis's comfort and safety while he was in England.

I imagined their meeting. Poor Louis, how did he look now? Particularly old and ill, I guessed, after the sea crossing. Steeped in religious fervour, frantic with anxiety, without the slightest fear of what would happen to himself. Louis had never, at least, been a coward. His hatred of war had had nothing to do with fears for his own safety.

Henry took a brilliant assembly to Dover to await Louis's arrival. This would give him an advantage, for he would see Louis immediately he disembarked, racked with sorrow and probably ill after the crossing. Henry would be vital, glowing with health . . . a little patronizing to his rival. After all, he was opening his country to an old enemy; he was allowing him the benefit of praying at the Archbishop's shrine. Henry was always one to seize an advantage.

I could picture it so well, remembering Henry as I had last seen him. Although he was showing signs of age, he could still ride through the day without fatigue and his immense vitality had not abated, whereas Louis would look like an old man. Henry would gloat over the contrast. Louis was considerably older than Henry in any case—as I was. A fact of which he had enjoyed reminding me. How I wished I could have seen that meeting!

Together they went to Canterbury. Louis would be talking of his only son and envying Henry, who had several. Henry had suffered every bit as much as Louis but this was due to the perfidy of his sons. Did they talk of their children? Did Louis mention Alais? If so, I was sure Henry would skirt round the subject adroitly. He was such an adept at amorous intrigue. I would never forget how he had kept Rosamund Clifford's existence a secret for so long.

There was a great welcome for Louis in Canterbury. Henry had ordered that the bells of the city ring out as the French King entered it. The Kings rode side by side to the cathedral amid the crowds, silent, not because they did not welcome Louis but because this was a solemn occasion and all wanted to give the impression that they were praying silently that the life of the heir to the French throne might be saved.

In the crypt Louis knelt at the tomb of Thomas à Becket. He remained there all through the day and night, begging Thomas to plead with God to spare the life of his son. When he left the crypt, I heard that he looked like a corpse himself. Stricken with sorrow, fear and old age, it seemed that it was for the King of France people should be praying as well as for his son.

Henry's mind would be working fast. If Louis died, if Philip Augustus died, young Henry, married to Marguerite, could be King of France. Once that was what he had strived for, but did he pause to think now? His son would indeed be powerful; and he had already shown his father what he could do in his present state. Henry's mind must have been very busy with possibilities as he joined in Louis's prayers for his son.

Louis expressed his gratitude by promising the Convent of Canterbury free French wine every year and exemption from customs for goods exported for their use.

He was then ready to return to France, but Henry would not hear of it. The journey had exhausted Louis, as had the day-and-night vigil at the tomb. Henry would take him to Winchester and there entertain him in a manner fitting his rank.

Louis saw the wisdom of this. There was nothing else he could do. He was a man of faith. He believed that his son's life would now be spared.

In order to impress Louis with his friendship—and perhaps fearing that he might have heard rumours about Alais and himself—Henry took Louis to visit churches, where, I have no doubt, there was more praying; he also showed him the treasury vaults and begged him to take some precious object as a mark of the amity between them. How amused I should have been! If I had been Louis, I should have selected the most valuable object I could find, for I knew how Henry hated to lose anything of value. I believe he would have regretted the gesture as soon as he had made it. But there was little malice in Louis. He had never been interested in earthly possessions and took the smallest object he could find.

Louis declined further hospitality and declared he was sufficiently rested to make the journey back across the sea and return to his son for he was sure Thomas à Becket would not have failed him and that God would have answered his prayers by now.

And sure enough, when he returned to France, he found that Philip Augustus had completely recovered. Everyone was sure that his return to health had begun at that moment when Louis was on his knees at the tomb of the martyr.

It was a miracle.

It was of great importance now to go ahead with the coronation. My son Henry was at the French Court with Marguerite. He would be dismayed at the recovery of Philip Augustus, which had put the French crown out of his reach. I hoped he was not foolish enough to show it.

Before anything else there had to be a thanksgiving service at St Denis. The whole French nation must show its gratitude for the heir's return to health.

My son was to ride beside the King of France in the procession. Louis had been delighted by the show of friendship which had been given him in England and the fact that the King had prayed with him so earnestly for the recovery of Philip Augustus when the latter's death could have brought such power to his own son. Louis's faith in human nature was almost equal to his faith in God. It was naïve of him, but rather lovable in a way, and there was so little that was lovable about Louis that I wanted to remember it.

There was an incident during the journey to the abbey.

Louis had been looking ill apparently soon after his return. His wan looks had been commented on, and as they came near the abbey, one of the knights near to him saw him sway sidewards. He was just in time to catch him before he fell. He was carried back to the castle and the doctors were sent for. They diagnosed a seizure and thought he had not long to live.

Louis was paralysed in his arm and leg, but he did not die immediately.

Now the coronation of Philip Augustus was very necessary. Louis sent for the Count of Flanders and put the care of his son in his hands. The Count of Flanders had been one of those who had joined with young Henry against his father. I wondered what my husband thought to see him in such a position, guiding the new King of France, for with Louis incapacitated, that was what Philip Augustus would soon be. So poor sick Louis—unwise as ever—chose the Count of Flanders to guide his son through the coronation and after. My son with his wife Marguerite was present at this impressive occasion. What bitterness he must have been feeling! I knew my son well. He had come very close to winning the crown, and Thomas à Becket had intervened.

The old King had undoubtedly shortened his life by crossing the seas to get assistance.

So Philip Augustus went to Rheims while his father was in bed, and the boy's uncle, who was his mother's brother and Archbishop of Rheims, crowned him.

Louis would be praying, of course, for his son's welfare. In his mind he would see it all: his son-in-law Henry holding the crown which his brother-in-law would place on his son's head, and the Count of Flanders carrying the golden sword.

And there he lay in his bed, a broken man, worn out by a way of life which had been thrust upon him because of the antics of a wayward pig.

So he lingered on.

* * *

The situation in France was now more interesting to me than that in England. It was not so easy to hear gossip of another country, but messengers were always coming to and from the Courts and news slipped through. Amaria was an avid gleaner of such items. It may be that they were not entirely accurate, but with my knowledge of the two countries I was often able to sift the truth from the distortions, and that gave me a very good picture of what was going on.

What a mistake to crown young boys!

Louis, of course, had no alternative; Henry was the fool. Every turn in events seemed to point to the greatness of his mistake. So now there was a young King of England—although there was an old one still very much in possession of the throne, and an even younger one in France with a man, still the King, lying paralysed in his bed. The menace of youth was greater in France than it was in England.

From what I knew of the Count of Flanders, he was flamboyant and extravagant, although with the means to indulge his tastes. He was hungry for power, just the man to appeal to a boy as young as Philip Augustus, as he had to my son Henry.

Louis had been lucky in his wife Adela. She was a wise woman and anxious to protect her son. Seeing the effect the Count was having, she wanted to call in her brothers to help guide her son. These were Henry, Count of Champagne, and Thibault, Count of Blois, and each of them had married a daughter of mine—Marie and Alix. It was reasonable that Adela should call in members of her family, but it was not difficult to picture the fury of the Count of Flanders at such a suggestion.

The information came to me in such scraps that I could not see the whole picture until later . . . years later in fact, but I tell now the story as I have been able to piece it together long after it happened.

The Count of Flanders was, as was to be expected, a very ambitious man and he saw himself in a unique position. He knew exactly how to flatter the two young Kings and by carefully manipulating them he could become the ruler of the two countries. It was not easy in the case of England, where the elder Henry was very much in command, but the Count was building for the future. How different it was with the King of France! But first he must prevent the arrival at Court of the King's uncles.

How could he do this? Adela would have told Louis of her decision, and Louis was still King. Philip Augustus, like his young friend Henry, was King in name only while his father lived. But Louis was only half alive, Henry entirely so.

Young Philip Augustus was at odds with his mother, and when she told him she had asked his uncles to come and help him rule, the boy, egged on by the Count of Flanders, told her that he would not have them, at which she reminded him that he was not King while his father lived.

Adela told Philip Augustus that God was not pleased with those who did not respect His commandments, and one of those was 'Honour thy father and thy mother that thy days may be long in the land which the Lord thy God giveth thee.' Because of his exalted position, this applied particularly to Philip Augustus, who could not give orders without the stamp of the Great Seal which was in his father's possession.

The Count of Flanders must have been desperate. If those uncles arrived, it would be the end of his dreams. He would lose his influence over the young King. I believe that Philip Augustus, in spite of his youth, was not as easy to handle as my son had been. He was already showing an independent spirit.

The Count of Flanders, who had always been on good terms with my son, turned to him for help. Marguerite did not share her husband's admiration for the Count. He had, I heard, talked disparagingly of her father, from whom Marguerite had had nothing but kindness. This turned her more from the Count, who feared she might have some influence with her half-brother. He was a scheming man, this Count, and he sought to break Marguerite's position with her husband by arousing young Henry's jealousy, for Marguerite was an exceptionally beautiful young woman. What he did was diabolical.

One of the most honoured men in England was William Marshal, Earl of Pembroke and Striguil. He had a reputation for bravery and honour. Long ago, at the time when I had told Henry I wanted to leave him and it had been decided that I should remain in Aquitaine, he had come with me to quell the rebellion there. I had almost fallen foul of an ambush set for me by Geoffrey and Guy de Lusignan. In the skirmish my bodyguard, Earl Patrick, had been slain. Earl Patrick was William

Marshal's uncle, and William Marshal, who had been riding with him at the time, had been wounded and taken prisoner. I was very much impressed by both uncle and nephew and took an early opportunity of paying a ransom to Geoffrey and Guy de Lusignan for the release of William Marshal.

He was a young man who had delighted me. He fought with such courage and was so handsome and honourable—the kind of man I had always liked to have around me. I gave him arms and money and did all I could to further his career; and when he went to England, Henry, always quick to recognize a man's worth, put him in charge of young Henry. It was true that when the rebellion broke out Marshal was on the side of the young King, but in spite of this he did not lose Henry's favour, and he allowed him to remain in charge of his son.

William continued to distinguish himself. He was a success at the tournaments which young Henry so loved to organize, and this won him fame. He had great influence over Henry and Marguerite, and they were both very fond of him. He viewed with disfavour the influence the Count of Flanders had over young Henry. The Count knew this and decided to break Henry's friendship with Marshal. Insidiously he poured poison into Henry's ears. Wasn't Marguerite a beautiful lady? He had seen many admiring glances go her way. Even the virtuous William Marshal had rather a special way of looking at her, which was quite revealing . . .

It must have gone something like that.

Henry was very proud of Marguerite; she was much admired for her beauty and her charm. Marshal was a handsome fellow. One could imagine the words . . . sounding so innocent and being far from it. Women would admire Marshal. He had a certain maturity.

I wondered whether the Count of Flanders told Henry what he had done to *his* wife's lover. Not at that stage perhaps. That would come later when he was not discussing Marguerite, perhaps, but talking generally of the frailty of women. I had heard the story and despised the Count for it. He had the man flogged severely until he was almost dead and then hung him over a cesspool. The lover in question was Walter du Fontaines, who had won fame for his chivalry. He would doubtless point out that there were men who lost all sense of honour when it came to women.

I could imagine my son's jealousy being whipped up. He had the Angevin temper. He would have watched William Marshal jealously and misconstrued those glances which passed between him and Marguerite.

Eventually he could contain his jealousy no longer. He summoned William Marshal and accused him of being intimate with the Queen. I could picture William's amazement, his cold disdain of the blustering boy. I could imagine his pouring scorn on the sly insinuations of the scheming Count of Flanders with such dignity that Henry would quail before him. If he had any ideas of flogging William Marshal and hanging him over a cesspool, they must soon have been dispersed. William's calm conduct would put him at a loss. Henry was always inclined to bluster and remind people of his high office in case they forgot it.

All he could do now was stammer that William was dismissed.

William of course took his dismissal coolly and prepared to leave for England.

When Marguerite discovered that he had dismissed William and for what reason—for he could not keep it from her—she was angry. How could he have been so foolish? He ought to have known that the Count was lying. William Marshal had been a good friend to her and more so to Henry. This was nonsense, and the Count only wanted Marshal out of the way so that he could rule Henry as well as Philip Augustus.

Meanwhile the Count had induced Philip Augustus to steal the Great Seal from Louis's bedchamber and make an order forbidding the uncles to come to Court.

My son was ready to be swayed this way and that, and Marguerite had always had great influence over him. He must have felt rather foolish in dismissing Marshal because Marguerite could make him see how absurd the accusation was. I imagined that he hated to be compared to Philip Augustus, for they were in such similar positions: but he always remembered that Philip Augustus must very soon become the one and only King of France, and he would have to wait years before he was King of England.

I think it must have been Adela who asked for his help; that would please him. He liked to be thought powerful and then he could be magnanimous. Adela would have asked him to come to see her and told him how beset she was by her enemies, how she feared for her son. Her husband was no longer able to take care of his kingdom; her son was but a boy; there were warring factions all round the throne. Her brothers, whom she relied upon to help her, were forbidden to come to Court; she needed help and was asking Henry for it.

How he would swell with pride. He liked to see himself as a knight of chivalry; naturally he would help a lady in distress.

What Adela needed was help from Henry's father, and she wanted young Henry to go to him and tell him of her need. Perhaps he was a little piqued that it was his father whose help was wanted and his only indirectly. However, she was pleading and that was pleasant. Moreover, it was embarrassing being at the French Court where Philip Augustus was so much more important than he was; and there was all the unpleasantness over the Count of Flanders and the dismissal of William Marshal.

So young Henry quietly left the country and went to his father. They met at Reading. I heard that the King was delighted to see him, even after all the trouble he had caused. That faithfulness always amazed me. It must have been the only faithful feeling he ever had for anyone. He so wanted Henry to be a good and worthy son, preparing for his destiny, that I believe he continued to deceive himself that he would make Henry this in time.

He would have listened to what was happening at the French Court, and the thought of the Count of Flanders guiding the destiny of the King of France was something which needed his immediate attention.

With Flanders in control, Normandy would not be safe. Henry would have to leave England at once.

I did hear something of what happened at that interview, for there were people present during it and there followed the inevitable whispers.

Henry had expressed his fear for Normandy. He chided his son for sending Marshal away. A foolish act. He should be grateful to have such a man with him and not dismiss him for some frivolous reason. He would never be a great king if he could not recognize the value of men . . . those to keep with him, those to discard. It was a part of kingship to surround oneself with the faithful. The King of France was dying. His son was nothing but a boy. His Queen in despair had sent to him. Now young Henry would see the tables were turned.

'When my sons would make war on me, they went to Louis and he gave them support. Now that the Queen of France is in danger the King of England is ready to go to her aid.'

Henry said it was noble of him.

That brought a fresh homily. Kings were not noble where their countries were concerned. They served the needs of their countries. And if a country needed nobility, then would he give nobility and if a lack of nobility then he would give that?

'We have to curtail the ambitions of this Count of Flanders. We have to make Normandy safe. A king's first consideration is his own crown. Remember it.'

When he was with his sons, Henry had a habit of making every discourse an object lesson. He would make young Henry feel insignificant, humiliated. I doubt that encounter endeared the son to his father. It was rather pathetic, for what Henry wanted more than anything was the love of this son.

Henry set out for France. I was sure that news of his coming must have struck terror into the heart of the Count of Flanders. Louis on his deathbed; the King of France, a mere boy, and Henry of England, the greatest warrior of his day, on the march.

Henry, however, had no wish to do battle. He said he would first speak with Philip Augustus and the Count, and speak to them separately. The Count would naturally have liked to refuse to leave the young King and Henry alone, but he dared not.

I could well imagine that meeting. Philip Augustus a little sullen, trying hard to imply that Henry was Duke of Normandy and his vassal and Henry stressing that he came not as Duke of Normandy but as King of England. Henry could be impressive and Philip Augustus was but a boy, and it was no use trying to play the great King when he was in the presence of one.

Henry would be gentle. He would point out the delicate position Philip Augustus was in. His father could not recover; they had to face the fact that he would soon be gone. When a king died, dangers invariably sprang up in the country and they needed dexterous handling. The situation was always tricky. The King should not be alienated from his mother and his uncles. They wished to help him. The people would not be pleased if there was friction within the royal family.

Philip Augustus would try to bluster that he was King and he must do as he wished, and Henry would point out that kings ruled by the will of the people.

Philip Augustus could not stand out against the experience and power of such a man. He began to see that Henry was right, and because he was fundamentally sensible he began to come round to Henry's way of thinking.

Adela was delighted and grateful to Henry as gradually her son began to turn to her and away from the ambitious Count of Flanders.

Meanwhile Louis became weaker and weaker, and it was clear that the end was not far off.

Philip Augustus was overcome with grief. He was going to be a clever ruler, and a sign of that is to be able to recognize and admit one's faults. He saw that he had been led astray by flattery and that it would be better for him to listen to the advice of people who had his good and not their own interests at heart.

On a September night Louis passed away. I was glad to hear that Philip Augustus was at his bedside to the last and Queen Adela with him. Louis deserved to go in peace. Philip Augustus kissed his hand as Louis murmured a blessing on his son and wished him a long and happy reign.

I was touched and a little sad when I heard. I had despised him at times; I had wanted to get away from him; but we had lived intimately together and I had many memories of him.

I had always thought of him as 'Poor Louis'. He had tried so hard to perform the duties which had been thrust upon him. He was a good man but life had been too much for him.

Now he was gone forever. But we must go on. A new reign had begun and we had to learn what this would mean to us.

There was trouble in Aquitaine. In fact, there had been since I had been captured and imprisoned. The people wanted me as their ruler—no one else would do, not even Richard. Richard was a Plantagenet. He was a Norseman descending from William the Conqueror and bearing some resemblance to his famous ancestor. Tall, reddish-haired, a great warrior, ruthless in battle, restless, never so happy as when the sword was in his hand. He was, I was beginning to realize, not a ruler my people would have chosen. True, he had a love of music and surrounded himself with troubadours, but that cold disciplinary rule would never be accepted by my people.

It was being said that there would never be peace in Aquitaine until I returned.

I heard these reports and, although I was gratified, they worried me a great deal. For all his strength and energy—and he was becoming known as one the greatest military leaders in Europe—Richard had one physical weakness. He had not inherited it, I was sure, but during his battles he had slept in damp and unhealthy places and it had left him with a kind of ague which made him tremble. He must have found that most distressing. Although he did not fly into the kind of rages in which his father indulged, when the trembling was on him he could become quite ruthless and find a reason for punishing with the utmost severity any who had witnessed his disability.

The people of Aquitaine were making it clear that they did not want Richard. They wanted their Duchess back.

Richard was wise enough to know this. He told me about it afterwards, how he had vowed that he would force his father to release me. He was in this frame of mind when he went to Navarre as a guest of King Sancho. There he discussed the advisability of bringing me out of prison so that I could return to Aquitaine. He wanted the friendship of Sancho, for he believed he might intercede with Henry and make him understand the need for peace in Aquitaine, whose state was a cause of anxiety to its southern neighbour Navarre.

There were tournaments and jousts in honour of his visit, and in those Richard naturally shone as the outstanding hero. He enjoyed the tournaments of course, but being Richard, he would rather be involved in a real war.

Two important matters emerged from this visit. The first was that Sancho agreed to impress on Henry that in his opinion it was unwise to keep his wife captive for so long, particularly when she could be of use in bringing peace to one of the family dominions. The other was Richard's meeting with Sancho's daughter, Berengaria.

Richard was not one, I was to learn later, to be drawn to women, but he did become attached to Sancho's little daughter. She was very pretty and played the lute most excellently; she was gentle and sweet and adored the handsome warrior, hero of all the tournaments, so different from the men she saw at her father's Court, he being so tall with dazzling blond looks and piercing blue eyes.

Richard told Sancho of his feelings for Berengaria. Sancho was pleased but pointed out that Richard was already betrothed to Princess Alais, daughter of the late King of France. Richard said that he had no intention of taking his father's mistress. Had Sancho not heard of the scandal concerning his father and the young Princess? It seemed common knowledge.

Sancho may have kept his promise to write to Henry. If so, nothing came of it. Henry would resent interference in his affairs; he knew well enough that I might bring peace to Aquitaine, but doubtless he thought I might stir up strife with his sons against him.

I was allowed a little more freedom, but I remained a prisoner.

The King of France was in difficulty.

With the death of his father, Philip Augustus seemed to have grown up suddenly. The petulant gullible boy was left behind and the statesman began to emerge. He had had such a clear example of the inexperience of youth which led to an acceptance of false friends, when the Count of Flanders, realizing that Philip Augustus would no longer be his tool, plotted against him.

The King of England had said in that little homily he had given him when they last met that he wished to be regarded as the young King's father. So at this time Philip Augustus turned to Henry in his need.

Henry was not displeased. In his shrewd way he saw that the Count of Flanders could be a menace to him also and he wanted to subdue him. Ostensibly he sent his sons to aid the French but in fact their duty was to guard their father's dominions.

Philip Augustus was delighted. He was already on good terms with young Henry; he was glad to welcome Geoffrey; but Richard was the one who delighted him. Richard had military genius, and men were beginning to fear and respect him, which was a great asset in a battle. Richard's tenor voice was a joy to hear in song, and he played the lute like the true musician he was. Richard had begun to mean a great deal to Philip Augustus.

He wanted Richard always with him. They sat side by side at table. It was the delight of Philip Augustus to share the same plate with his friend. They laughed and joked together, and soon they were sharing the same bed.

With Richard's troubadours had come a certain Bernard de

Borne. He was a great poet and musician and compared with Bernard de Ventadour; and just as Philip Augustus had no eyes for anyone but Richard, Bernard de Borne was taken with young Henry.

The appearance of my two sons was outstanding in the extreme, and Bernard de Borne wrote verses extolling Henry's good looks and charm and attributed to him in verse the daring exploits which I am sure Henry often imagined himself performing. He was delighted with the poet and they became great friends.

Henry was not a young man to form attachments with his own sex—unlike Richard in this respect. Henry, like his father, had a keen interest in women, but this was different. Bernard de Borne knew how to flatter, and flattery was something Henry had never been able to resist.

The poet was well aware that the people of Aquitaine did not want Richard. His military skills did not appeal to an essentially peace-loving people who wanted their comforts more than anything else. His methods would never please them, and it must have occurred to de Borne that Henry would be a more suitable ruler. As he was my son, and continually complaining that his father withheld all power from him, why should he not seize Aquitaine?

It would be a simple matter to insert that idea into Henry's mind. My poor foolish son was constantly hoping that glory which he was unable to win by his own efforts would fall into his hands.

If only young Henry had been content to walk in his father's shadow and to learn from him! If only Geoffrey had not been such a trouble-maker; if only Richard could have understood my people of Aquitaine; if only Henry and I could have lived in amity—between us all we could have ruled over peaceful dominions. But it seemed it was not to be so. The Angevins were a quarrelsome brood. Sometimes I thought that story of their having descended from the Devil was true.

Young Henry therefore saw himself as the ruler of Aquitaine. I was sure he thought he could show his father how the people appreciated him.

De Borne was able to do a great deal with his writing; he was also a persuasive talker. He persuaded the people of Limoges that under Henry there would be a return to the old rule; the elder brother would understand them; there would be tournaments, jousting, a return to the old way of life. As a result, when Henry rode into Limoges, the people cheered him; they acclaimed him as their new ruler.

Meanwhile the King, having sorted out his affairs with Philip Augustus, turned his attention to Aquitaine. He knew that Richard was having trouble. He sent for Geoffrey. Geoffrey was not so much a soldier as a diplomat. He had a plausible manner and a tactful way with words. He was the one to help Richard, Henry decided, and he sent him out to talk to the trouble-makers and counteract Richard's somewhat abrasive manner.

How mistaken Henry always was in his sons! He did not know Geoffrey, who loved nothing more than to stir up trouble. Arriving in Aquitaine, he was met by Henry and Bernard de Borne, who told him that the people were preparing to rise and oust Richard, taking Henry as their ruler. Geoffrey, who was as jealous of Richard's military glory as Henry was, decided to come down on Henry's side.

I cannot imagine what would have happened if the King had not decided to go to Aquitaine and sort things out for himself.

Face to face with his father, young Henry's courage fled. He dared not tell him that he had been proclaimed Duke in Limoges. They marched together to Poitiers, where they were met by Richard.

What the people of Aquitaine must have thought, I cannot imagine. All I knew was that with the coming of the King order was restored. I think young Henry must have been very worried indeed for sooner or later his father must discover what he had been doing. He was so weak. Sometimes I was fearful, thinking of what would happen to England when he was its King. It would be a return to the days of Stephen, and doubtless his brothers would be plotting to take the crown from him. The King must not die . . . not yet . . . until Henry had reached a state of maturity which, in my heart, I feared he never would.

He was saved from the discovery of his foolish perfidy by my daughter Matilda.

Matilda was in deep trouble and was leaving Saxony for the protection of her father. Her marriage to Henry the Lion had been a happy one domestically but there was always trouble in the German states.

Henry the Lion had been quarrelling for some time with his

first cousin, the powerful German Emperor Frederick, and a year or so before, after a great deal of conflict between them, Duke Henry had been condemned by diet at Würzburg to forfeit all his lands. Naturally he refused. Hence the Emperor laid siege to Brunswick, where Henry and Matilda were living.

Matilda already had three children: Richenza and two boys, Henry and Otto, and she was pregnant at the time of the siege. The Emperor, in a chivalrous gesture when he heard of her plight, sent her a tun of wine and raised the siege. Whether he did this for altruistic reasons or whether it was because Matilda was the daughter of the most formidable soldier in Europe, I am not sure. It might have been a little of each.

In due course Matilda gave birth to Lothair.

But this time Henry the Lion realized the hopelessness of his position. Fearing the power of the Emperor, his followers deserted him and he was left with no alternative but to accept the Emperor's terms. These were harsh. He was to be banished from Germany for seven years, and during that time he must have the Emperor's permission if he wished to visit his country; only a few possessions were left to him—Brunswick, Luneburg, Hanover, Zell and Wolfenbüttel which, though considerable, were a small part of what he had previously owned.

King Henry had been watching affairs in Germany closely and he came to the assistance of his son-in-law. The Emperor had no wish to quarrel with one as powerful as the King of England, and he agreed that the period be reduced to four years and that the King's daughter, Matilda, should be allowed to remain in Brunswick with her children. The choice was hers. She might live in freedom on the estates left to her family, or if she wished to go with her husband, stewards would be appointed to look after her property. Matilda chose to follow her husband.

Thus it was that at this time, when my son Henry was in a precarious position, wondering whether his father would discover his perfidy towards his brother, this diversion arose to turn the King's thoughts from Aquitaine.

Little Lothair was too young to undertake the journey, and he must be left for a while, but Henry the Lion, with Matilda and the three children, Richenza, Henry and Otto, set out for Normandy.

The King met them there. He was deeply touched to be reunited with his daughter. He had such plans for his sons but I think it was his daughters who brought him most joy.

Almost as soon as they arrived, Matilda's husband, overcome with humiliation because of what had happened to him, decided he must go on a pilgrimage to St James of Compostela, who was at this time the most popular of all the saints; pilgrims from all over Europe were going to visit his shrine. There were springing up inns all along the road to Compostela, and whether or not the saint answered the prayers of those who prayed at his shrine, he certainly provided prosperity for the innkeepers.

There were great preparations for his departure, and before he left Matilda was pregnant again.

I do believe that for a short time at Argentan the King forgot his troubles and gave himself up to his grandchildren, in whom he found great pleasure. Matilda told me about it afterwards. She herself was surprised. The grandchildren adored him. It was amazing, said Matilda, to see Richenza climbing all over him, and the boys shouting with glee as he played war games with them. When he told them about the battles in which he had fought, they listened in silent awe; he wanted to spend as much time with them as he possibly could, and for once he forgot his dominions.

I could never feel indifferent about Henry. I could hate him fiercely. Who would not hate a husband who had kept her incarcerated for years? But I understood him. He had to keep me incarcerated, for how did he know what I would do if I were free? I was sorry for him in a way as I was not for myself. My captivity had given me time for reflection. My mind had always been too active for it to become sluggish. Here I was removed from events, looking in from the outside and finding it all fascinating. I was not one to sit down and weep for my misfortunes. I could see many sides to every question and, because I was so interested in people, I could understand their motives and realize that from their point of view they were in the right.

My feelings for Henry were similar to those he had had for Becket. I had loved him; I had hated him; but always he had been of vital interest to me, and I could picture his snatching that brief period at Argentan when Matilda's children played with him, showed their pleasure in having him with them and gave him what he had missed in his own children.

Young Henry could not learn his lessons. As soon as his

father was no longer there to overawe him, his ambitions began to return; and there was Bernard de Borne to feed them.

Bernard de Borne probably suggested that he had been too meek with his father. Men like the King of England understood strength and respected it.

Aquitaine was now out of the question. Richard was securely installed. The King had shown that he stood firmly behind him on that matter, and Henry must needs accept that this was so, and although the people thought Henry might bring softer rule, they had no wish to go to war.

There was Normandy, of course. Why should he not have Normandy?

With the praise of Bernard de Borne ringing in his ears, he wrote to his father demanding that he be given control of Normandy.

The reply came back. The King had no intention of relinquishing any of his possessions while he lived. He expected his sons to serve him and reminded Henry of the oath he had taken to do just that.

More frustrated than ever, raging inwardly, listening to the flattering poems of Bernard de Borne, young Henry looked around for trouble.

It came when he discovered that Richard had built a castle near the frontiers of Poitiers but which was actually in Anjou. Anjou, of course, was territory which would become Henry's on his father's death, and in building the castle Richard had encroached on land not his. This was the opportunity. Henry wrote to his father demanding that the castle be handed over to him.

I could imagine the King's groans when he read of this. I wondered if he went into one of his rages. Perhaps not; there would be no point in doing so. This squabbling in the family was dangerous. Did these sons of his not see that their strength was in their union! He wrote to Richard telling him he must immediately hand over the castle to Henry as it had been built on land not his.

Richard's reply was a blank refusal. The castle was necessary for defence.

'Hand it over or I shall come and take it,' replied the King.

Richard was first and foremost a soldier; he and the King should have been close; it was a pity they disliked each other.

The King knew that Richard was a good soldier. How well they could have worked together for the aggrandisement of the Plantagenet empire! But Richard hated him because of his treatment of me; and there was another matter: Alais Capet, who had been destined for Richard and with whom the King had fallen in love. His feelings for Alais were, I believe, similar to those he had had for Rosamund Clifford. It went deeper than lust. Both women were beautiful and gentle. I had been beautiful but never gentle. They were the kind of women he needed—not to plague him but always to be there to soothe him, with no recriminations when he returned from those little respites which he allowed himself. I believed he really loved Alais. Every time the proposed marriage with Richard was brought up, he eluded it. Richard would always remind him of the wrong he had done his son; and people hate those whom they have wronged. Thus his feelings for Richard, who would have been a man after his own heart.

Richard was too wise to enter into conflict with his father. He wrote back that he would never give the castle to his brother who had been working against him with the object of taking Aquitaine. The castle was necessary to the defence of Poitiers. If the King would judge for himself the importance of the castle to Aquitaine, he would be prepared to accept his decision.

The King immediately realized that the castle was important for defence, otherwise Richard would not have built it in that particular spot, and as it was very necessary to defend Aquitaine, he was sure that Richard was right. He wrote back that he accepted Richard's decision; he himself would decide about the castle when he saw it.

He was deeply disturbed, I was sure, about this discord in the family and he sent for Henry, Richard and Geoffrey to come to Caen, ostensibly to celebrate Christmas, but in fact he wanted a full understanding that these quarrels between them must stop: he wanted to impress on them the importance of solidarity in the family. He must have hoped that the Christmas spirit would incline his sons to reason.

I wished I had been there at that Christmas. Matilda's presence would have helped perhaps, but young Henry, spurred on by the flattery of de Borne and the conviction that he had been cheated of his rights, was determined to make trouble.

Christmas fare had been provided in plenty: pies of all description, game, great joints of pig and lamb, and all the best wines obtainable. The King, of course, was impatient of such feasting, but it all had to be provided to give an air of Christmas festivity.

Yet there was little of the Christmas spirit that Christmas. Henry began by reminding his sons that they had taken an oath to serve him, and now they were warring together. He insisted that they swear an oath of fidelity towards each other.

I wondered what young Henry must have been feeling. Could he refuse to take the oath? He would not dare. And yet could he at this very time be conspiring to take Aquitaine from Richard?

The King's affection for his eldest son continued to amaze me. How much wiser he would have been to give it to Richard. Surely he must see by now how worthless Henry was. But always he placated him; always he hoped to reform him; always he tried to achieve the impossible.

He went on to say that Henry was the eldest. They must remember that. One day he would be King of England. He himself held the rights over all their possessions at this time, but in due course Henry, as King, would have them. Richard would remember that he held Aquitaine through the will and grace of his brother Henry, and Geoffrey so held Brittany. The King wished them all to swear fealty to the brother who would one day be King.

How different Richard was from Henry. He was completely outspoken and immediately declared that he would not swear fealty to his brother. He pointed out with vigour that he had received Aquitaine through his mother, and that I had always intended that he should rule it; it was apart from any of the King's dominions. He had paid homage to the King of France as his vassal; that was traditional; he would swear fealty to no other.

I think the King must have been shaken. He was so used to browbeating everyone but he could not do that with Richard. He was always logical and mostly shrewd. What Richard said was true. Aquitaine was mine, not his, and I had given it to Richard.

There was a duel of words between them; the King could not give way and yet he knew that Richard was right. How foolish he was not to have grappled Richard to his side and let the others go. But this was one of the occasions when Henry was ruled by his affections rather than his common sense. Dearly he loved his eldest son, and nothing could alter that.

I daresay he found it easy to whip up his anger against Richard because he had wronged him so much. I wondered if it were true that Alais had borne his child. There had been rumours.

'You will obey me,' he shouted.

Richard retorted that he would do no such thing.

'Aquitaine is mine,' he cried. 'Given by my mother whom *you* have treated so shamefully. How dare you imprison the Queen? How dare you rob her of her freedom! Because you are afraid of her? That could be the only reason. You shall not treat me as you have treated her. And I tell you this: one day I shall free her. We shall snap our fingers at you. I shall swear fealty to neither you nor to my brother.'

How thrilled I was when those words were reported to me! He meant them. He always meant what he said. He was not called 'Richard Yea and Nay' for nothing. He had not forgotten me, and that love which had always been between us remained.

I could imagine Henry's fury. I could picture him, standing there, bow legs apart, face scarlet with rage, eyes flashing. It would not be the moment for childish rage. His voice would be cold and precise when he said: 'By God's eyes, I will not be treated thus by my own son. We will teach Master Richard a lesson.'

What a Christmas that must have been at Caen. And I not there to see it!

The King must soon have realized his folly. Teach Richard a lesson! What could that mean but that young Henry had his father's consent to take Aquitaine, but when he heard that Henry and Geoffrey were riding to Aquitaine, gathering supporters as they went, he must have been overcome with dismay.

There were times when even his doting affection had to be seen for what it was. Henry with Aquitaine! How long would he hold it? And Geoffrey, the young fool, with him! What were those boys thinking of? They had no sense. They wanted to *take*, all the time; they never wanted to *give* anything. They thought ruling was all pleasure. They had no notion of what it meant to govern wisely.

Would Richard be able to hold out against them? He was

infinitely superior in the field, but in battle numbers often counted.

Young Henry was in Limoges, the town which had acclaimed him as their Duke. The King must go to Limoges with all speed.

He was soon approaching the town. There could be no doubt who he was, for his standard-bearer carried the pennon above his head, which announced to all that here was the King of England. Arrows were falling about him; one pierced his cloak. It must have been aimed directly at him. From whom could the order have come? From his son Henry? His men gathered round him and told him he must return to the camp at once. It was obvious that there was an intention to kill him.

He saw the wisdom of this and retired.

I could imagine his feelings. Did his son want the crown so much that he was prepared to murder his father to get it? Did he really believe that? He would have grappled with himself; sentiment trying hard to get the better of reason. How strange that such a man should have such weakness. It did show that he was capable of love, for he certainly felt it toward his son.

I was glad that young Henry went to his camp. How touched the King must have been when the young man fell on his knees before him. He wept bitterly and said that when he saw the arrow pierce his father's cloak he was overcome with sorrow. So he had seen it? Had he ordered it? The King would not allow himself to believe that. It must have been some over-zealous soldier who sought to win honour.

Something of that conversation was reported to me.

'Father, when I saw that arrow touch you . . . and realized what might have happened, I was overcome with shock and grief.'

'It was shot by one of your men.'

'I will never forgive him.'

'He meant to serve you.'

'Oh, Father, forgive me.'

'It was not you who shot the arrow?'

'No. But one of my servants . . .'

'There must be an end to this strife between us. Do not forget I am your father. Do not forget you are my son.' He went on to impress on young Henry how much he had to learn. He tried once more to make him understand the responsibilities of kingship.

Henry protested that his father was siding with Richard against him and Geoffrey, although Richard had stalked out at Caen and refused obedience.

'There must not be war in families,' reiterated the King. 'If we do not stand together, we are doomed.'

'The people of Aquitaine do not want Richard.'

'Richard is the rightful heir.'

'Father, if you came to Aquitaine, if you asked the people which of us they wanted, they would listen to you. Will you do this?'

'I will consider,' said the King.

Young Henry went back to the town, and the King stayed in the camp outside.

I was sure he would not easily forget the arrow which had pierced his cloak. I could imagine how he spent that night. He must have been full of misgivings; surely the truth must have begun to dawn on him then. He must have seen that his son's tears and grief had been a pretence, that he wished to gain time for the fortification of Limoges, that he was ready to go into battle against his father.

Geoffrey was with him—two traitor sons, and Richard defying him.

The next day he rode towards the town intending to speak once more with Henry. He took with him only his standard-bearer and two knights. There could be no question that he came in any attempt to take the town. Yet he was greeted by a shower of arrows, and this time one of them struck and killed his horse. The King was thrown to the ground.

His standard-bearer and the knights knelt beside him in consternation.

'I am unhurt,' he said. 'It is just my poor horse who is killed.'

While the King was getting to his feet, young Henry came riding full speed towards him. He was preparing to weep, to tell his father how distraught he was.

The King said coldly: 'You should train your archers better. You see, the second time they have failed.'

'My father . . .' began young Henry.

But even the King understood now. He leaped onto the horse which his standard-bearer had brought to him and turned his back on his son.

How bitter his thoughts must have been as he rode back. His

sons were against him. They had defied him; one had tried to kill him. He would not be duped any longer.

He thought then, I believe, of Geoffrey, the son of a prostitute; he had never had anything but devotion from that one. How ironic that his legitimate sons should have turned against him, and he had only loyalty from his bastard!

There was one who had not stood against him. He was too young to do so. That was John.

Henry would always care for his illegitimate son Geoffrey and keep him near him; but alas, when all was said and done, he was a bastard. It was a legitimate son he needed to stand beside him and give him that affection for which he craved.

And there was John.

From that time he transferred his affections from his eldest to his youngest son. John became the centre of his ambitions.

I was very involved with my children even though I did not see them, and young Henry was constantly in my thoughts. I had known of his weakness long before it had been revealed to his father. I had eagerly gleaned everything I could hear of him, and in spite of our separation I knew him well.

I fervently hoped his folly would not destroy him.

One night I had a strange dream. I thought I was in a crypt. The coldness seeped into my bones; there was a faint light which seemed to beckon to me, and I followed it. When it stopped, I was looking at a man who was lying on the stones of the crypt, and that man was my son Henry. Looking closely I saw that it was not in fact my son but an effigy as one sees on a tomb; there were two crowns above his head—one the crown of England, the other in the form of a halo, and there was a look of infinite peace on the carved face.

When I awoke, I said to myself: My son Henry is dead.

It was some weeks later before I heard what had happened.

There was only one course open to the King. He was at war with his sons, and he was going to lay siege to Limoges. He was now ranged on Richard's side.

Young Henry must have been really frightened. Twice he had tried to kill his father and failed. It was no use weeping and expecting forgiveness now: he had obviously betrayed himself;

the only surprise was that the King had taken so long to realize his son's true nature.

Young Henry did not want war; he only wanted the spoils of war. He soon discovered that real war was very different from the mock variety he enjoyed at jousts. War was hardship, exhaustion and possibly death.

Geoffrey escaped from Limoges on a pretext of raising men and money. Henry realized that his father's tactics would very soon end in victory. He could not endure the thought of being his father's captive and one night crept out of town and joined some supporters who had raised an army in a nearby town. He was immediately told that money was needed if they were to continue with the campaign. Soldiers had to be paid. Henry did not understand these matters. He was the King—if in name only—and men must do their duty without pay; but his captains informed him that they would desert if not paid. Many of them were mercenaries. The money had to be found.

'The men must wait . . . wait,' he cried petulantly.

They came to an abbey where the monks received them as they wished to visit the shrines, and according to custom they were given food.

After the meal, when they visited the shrines, Henry was struck by the beauty of the monastery's treasures. An idea occurred to him. The sale of some of the chalices alone would feed an army for a month. What use were they in an abbey when he was so desperate? I wonder how long it took him to persuade himself. I am sure his captains attempted to warn him of his folly.

But Henry was reckless; he had betrayed himself to his father, and he guessed the old man could live another ten years with the knowledge that his son had made two attempts on his life. He had crowned him; he was King; nothing could alter that; but his father was a sly man; he might even attempt to do to his son what that son had tried to do to the father. He made up his mind. His need was great. They were going to rob the shrines of their valuable ornaments, sell them and with the money raise an army to take Aquitaine.

The monks were shocked beyond belief. They could not understand how any professed Christian could desecrate the shrines. But Henry did, and with his army rode on.

Robbing monasteries and abbeys was easy. There was no— or little resistance. This was the way.

The countryside was in terror at the approach of Henry's army. Everywhere monks locked their doors against them. This proved useless. What were gates against an army? They battered their way in.

I wished I could have talked to my son. He was like a man possessed. He had offended against all the laws of God and man; he had attempted to murder his father, and now he was robbing holy shrines. He was frantic, running on blindly . . . shutting his mind to all thought of the consequences of his actions because he dared not face them.

He came at length to the monastery at Grandmont, which contained the shrine of Rocamadour.

He was wealthy now. He could raise a bigger and better army, but the lust for plunder stayed with him. He knew that he was damned but instead of repenting his sins he wanted to add to them. He wanted to defy God as he had defied his father.

Those about him would have held back; they wanted to finish with this way of life; they wanted to return to their homes and forget the conquest of Aquitaine and the crown of England.

Perhaps he kept up a spirit of bravado. I think that would be typical of him. And when his men showed a reluctance to enter the monastery he would have called them cowards.

They broke in; he took the treasures from the shrines of Rocamadour.

That night Henry was in the grip of a fever. Those about him believed that God had judged him and condemned him. Perhaps they were right. As he was so ill, they took him into the house of a smith called Stephen so that he could receive some comfort.

His bravado vanished; his fear of what was in store for him was uppermost. He was sure he was going to die and that this was God's just punishment. He was guilty of attempting to kill his father and desecrating holy shrines. He feared the future and wanted to right as many wrongs as he could in the time left to him.

There was one man whom he had wronged and whom the King valued. He desperately wanted to see that man.

William Marshal was in Aquitaine and could come to him quickly. After he had sent for him, Henry despatched a messenger to his father begging him to come to him.

After two attempts on his life, the King was wary. His attitude had changed. He was no longer deluding himself about his eldest son. Henry had exposed himself too obviously for further deceit to succeed. This time the King listened to his advisers, who were sure that this was another attempt to do that in which he had twice failed.

William Marshal did go to Henry's bedside, but by this time the fever had taken a firmer hold on him.

I did hear later what he said to William. William had been a friend of his childhood; they had been close until the Count of Flanders had sown suspicion in Henry's mind about Marshal and Marguerite. He told William that he knew his end was near. He had been possessed by devils and feared eternal damnation. He blamed his ancestress, the witch. 'We Plantagenets are the Devil's spawn,' he said. 'We came from the Devil and we shall go back to the Devil.' William begged him to repent of his sins.

He was happier when a messenger came back with a ring from his father. The King did not trust him sufficiently to come himself but he was still his father and he did want his son to know that in spite of everything he still cared for him. They told me how Henry's ring had comforted him.

William Marshal had arranged for the Bishop of Cahors to come to the house where Henry was staying. He begged William to remain with him. By his bed was a crusader's cross which he had stolen from one of the tombs. He swore that if he lived he would take the cross to Jerusalem and place it on the Holy Sepulchre. He had written to his father. He had lied to him so many times; he had cheated and betrayed him. He wanted as many wrongs put right as there possibly could be. Would the King restore what he had stolen as far as he could? Would he look after Marguerite? He sent a message to me, too. He thought of me often. He had longed to see me, and he had begged the King to be more tender towards me.

Henry implored William Marshal to take the cross and if ever he went to Jerusalem to place it on the shrine in the name of the young King Henry.

He ordered that a bed of ashes be prepared, with a stone for a pillow; he wanted to wear a hairshirt. Then he declared himself the most wicked of sinners. He lay on his bed of discomfort for several hours, and it seemed that there he found a certain peace.

His repentance was complete.

And thus he died.

I would think of him as I had seen him in my dream. My poor, foolish son. I hope he found more contentment in death than he had in life.

Last Days at Chinon

Henry mourned deeply. He had so loved his eldest son. I knew he would be thinking of that handsome boy; he would be remembering all the glorious plans he had made for him; all had come to nothing.

And on his deathbed, with his sins heavy upon him, he had thought of his mother.

I was sure Henry wondered why my children loved me so much more than they loved him. But he did remember young Henry's words. Richard had reviled him for his treatment of me; Henry on his deathbed had pleaded that I be treated with more kindness. Henry could not ignore one of his son's last requests, so I received a visit from the Archdeacon of Wells.

He respectfully told me that he had come on the King's behalf and that I was to prepare to leave Salisbury for Winchester. This I should be happy to do, I told him. I preferred Winchester.

'The King wishes me to say that much will depend on your behaviour at Winchester. The King thinks that it would be well for you to be with your daughter, the Duchess of Saxony, at the time of her confinement.'

My heart leaped with joy. To be with my dear daughter. I could hardly contain my delight. This was surely due to my son's deathbed request.

'The King thinks you may need garments, and he is arranging for some to be sent to you.'

I was exultant. The end of my imprisonment must be in sight. Should I be invited to Court? What excitement that would be!

What was Alais thinking? *I* should not mind being at a Court where my husband's mistress was. After all, I was the Queen. I should find it very amusing. I should be plunged once more into intrigue. What a pleasure not to have to rely on hearsay.

And to be with my dearest Matilda, to watch over her while she was waiting for her child!

A hamper of clothes came. Delicious red velvet. I handled the soft materials, loving the feel of them. How I had missed my beautiful clothes over all these years!

My women crowded round me. Amaria was so delighted for me, and the prettiest of them all who waited on me, Belle, whom we called Bellebelle, danced with joy. They would all love going to Court.

We were moving too fast, I told them. I was not yet released.

I stroked the white fur which lined the cloak and thought of facing Henry. How would he look after all these years? How would I look to him? I had taken care of myself and had not allowed my imprisonment to cause me undue anxiety. I had been shut away from the world, so he thought, but I had managed to keep myself aware of what was happening. The years had been kind to me as far as my appearance was concerned.

Should I see them all again? Most of all I wanted to see Richard, I wanted to talk to him about his father's intrigue with his intended bride. But of course Richard would not have her now. There would be no compromise with Richard. It was either Yea or Nay, and as far as Alais was concerned it was most definitely Nay. What a joy it would be to see him! A boy no longer. A great soldier. And there was something else. He was now heir to the throne of England. What did Henry think of that? How I should love to know.

Well, I should soon be seeing and hearing at first hand all those things for which for so long I had had to rely on others.

Matilda was at Winchester, eagerly awaiting my arrival. We stood for a moment looking at each other. This was my daughter who had been a child when I had last seen her, and now she was twenty-eight years old, a wife and a mother who had endured much suffering.

There was no ceremony between us. We ran together and were in each other's arms.

'My dearest child,' I cried.

'Oh . . . my mother . . .'

We held each other at arms' length and stared eagerly.

'You are beautiful still,' she said. 'I remembered always how beautiful you were. I expected to find . . .'

'An old woman? I am an old woman . . . but I try to forget it. That is the best way. I will not admit that. I am not an old woman to myself, and therefore I can pass for being younger than my years.'

I looked at her anxiously. She was heavily pregnant and looked tired. She told me that the journey from Normandy had been exhausting in her condition but her father had wanted the child to be born in England.

'Besides,' she added with the lovely smile I remembered so well, 'it means that we can be together.'

There was so much to talk about during those days.

She told me of her life in Saxony, of how she had at first been impressed by her husband's power. She described the ducal palace in front of which rose the column of Löwenstein at whose top was a great lion made of brass. It had been put there because her husband was known as Henry the Lion. He had received the title, a story ran, because when he was in the Holy Land he had watched a fight between a lion and a serpent; the lion was getting the worst of the combat, so Henry destroyed the serpent and the lion was grateful to him and became his companion, always at his side.

'Was it true?' I asked.

She shrugged her shoulders.

'Did you not discover from your husband?'

'He liked us all to believe it was true, but I could never say for sure.'

'Men like to preserve legends about themselves,' I commented.

'Henry wanted to make Brunswick the most beautiful city in the Empire,' she told me. 'He built a magnificent church. I helped him in this. We planned to be buried there side by side. Who knows now?'

'Burials are a dismal subject,' I said, 'and now we are together after all these years let us not be dismal.'

I learned a great deal about her life: the joy she had in her children and how she missed little Lothair, who had had to stay in Brunswick; she looked forward to the birth of another little one.

The quarrel with the Emperor Frederick had been their undoing. He wanted all the governors of the Saxon towns to accept him as their overlord. She had discovered his intentions while Henry was on a pilgrimage to the Holy Land, and she had sent a messenger to him to tell him of her fears. They were anxious days until Henry returned. Before he had left he had built Der Hagen, a hunting park, for her.

'I always remembered Woodstock,' she said. 'I wanted to make a Woodstock there. Der Hagen was not quite the same, but I used to go to the hunting lodge there and think of England while I was waiting for Henry to come back. I thought a great deal of England, and it seemed a kind of haven to me then. But you know of our trouble and our exile.'

'I am glad of one thing,' I said. 'It brought you here. Do not speak of it though. It makes you sad. Here you are and we are together. Let us be happy for a while.'

'And all this time, dear Mother, you have been a prisoner, my father your gaoler.'

I laughed. 'Don't pity me, dearest child, for I do not pity myself—though sometimes the cold stones of Salisbury seem to seep into my bones. But I kept myself warm and I had good friends about me. My dear Amaria has been a great comfort over the years; little Bellebelle amuses me, and there are the other women too. They bring me news. I have enjoyed piecing it all together. It has been like a great picture puzzle to me, and I think that being apart from events I have perhaps been able to see them more clearly. I know so well all the actors in the drama, it is as though I sit before a stage watching their performances.'

'And now Henry is dead.'

I nodded. 'Poor Henry. He always strove for the unattainable. Your father made the biggest mistake of his life when he crowned him.'

'He knows it, but it does not ease his pain. He thinks a great deal about Henry . . . and Richard and Geoffrey and John . . . all the boys. He knows Richard hates him, yet I think he admires him in a way.'

'No one could help admiring Richard.'

'Yet it seems it is John he loves now. He talks constantly of John.'

'He must be about seventeen now.'

'He is ambitious, Mother. He wants to be King.'

I laughed. 'The crown is for Richard. Richard will be King of England.'

'But what of Aquitaine?'

'Richard will be the King of England and Duke of Aquitaine.'

'I think my father wants Aquitaine for John. I even think he wants the crown of England for him, too.'

'That will never be.'

'If my father decided . . . who could stop him?'

'Richard would. And he will never give up Aquitaine.'

She nodded. 'Yes, Richard is a great warrior.'

'Have you seen John?'

'Yes.'

'Tell me, what sort of a man is he? I saw little of him in his childhood, you know. He was at Fontevrault and then under the care of Ranulf de Glanville.'

'I do not like Ranulf de Glanville, Mother.'

'No?'

'I think he has allowed John to go his own way. He . . .'

'Tell me.'

'He is dissolute. There are always women and . . . he is rather cruel. I think he finds pleasure in hurting people. He is like our father in one way. He falls into rages. He lies on the floor and kicks and gnaws the rushes.'

'That is certainly like his father,' I said.

'But our father is never unjust in rages. When they are over, he does not look round to vent his spite on anyone who happens to be nearby.'

'No, he did not do that. And John does?'

She nodded. 'I know it may seem strange but I am sorry for my father now that he is turning to John. I think he is going to be very disappointed.'

'He was always a fool where his family were concerned. He could never see those who would be loyal to him. So now John is taking the place of Henry?'

'It would seem so.'

'From what you tell me, I would say 'God help him' then. And Geoffrey? You say little of Geoffrey.'

'He would be rather like John . . . but kinder. I think he is happy with Constance, and they have their little Eleanor. If John had someone like that . . . a wife to steady him . . .'

'Then we have to be grateful to Constance.'

'Geoffrey seems to be safe in Brittany. They accept him. I suppose because Constance is there. She is the heiress, in fact, and he is her husband, and as they seem happy together that pleases the people.'

'Let us at least be glad of that.'

There was much to be glad about during those days. Matilda would sit embroidering little garments for the child, and I would sing to her, read and play the lute. I sang some of the ballads I used to hear in my grandfather's Court. How it brought it all back . . . those stories of gallantry, chivalry, of ladies rescued from tyrants, of unrequited love.

There were Matilda's children to amuse us. They talked of their grandfather with affection. At least he had managed to win their hearts. They loved me, too. Sometimes I thought it a pity we did not forget ambition and become a happy family.

We talked of songs, and Matilda told me how, when Bernard de Borne was at Court, he used to write them in praise of her beauty.

'In truth, they were for my brother Henry,' she said. 'De Borne was in love with him. It was those verses of his which led to Henry's death in a way. He flattered him and wrote of him as though he were a mighty warrior . . . invincible . . . and that was how Henry began to see himself. It was the reason why he thought he could get the better of our father.'

'Poor Henry,' I said. 'He died penitent.'

'I pray his sins will be forgiven.'

'He did not repent,' I said, 'until he saw that the game was lost. I suppose it is at such time that we all repent our sins.'

'I heard about the bed of ashes and the stone pillow.'

'Yes. A humble recompense. Let us hope God forgave him as his father did.'

So the days passed, and to be free and with my daughter was wonderful to me. I felt like a young woman—alive, vital, deeply interested in all that was going on around me.

It was a happy day when Matilda came safely through her confinement. She had given birth to a healthy boy and we called him William after his great ancestor the Conqueror.

We celebrated his birth with much merry-making, drinking a special spiced ale made with corn barley and honey, and I laughed maliciously when I saw that it cost the King £3.16.10, for I knew he would resent having to pay so much for a mere drink—which showed my attitude towards him had changed little.

Orders came for a move from Winchester to Westminster, and I was to accompany the party. So I was to be received back at Court! I had to thank my son Henry for this. His father could not refuse his dying wish.

A saddle ornamented with gold arrived for me. Clearly he did not want me to ride through the streets looking impoverished. He would not know what the people's reaction would be, but one thing was certain: they would all be in the streets to see the Queen who for so long had been her husband's prisoner.

I was going to enjoy this, particularly as I guessed Henry was thinking of it with some apprehension.

Clad in my red velvet gown with my fur-trimmed cloak, mounted on my horse with his gold-ornamented saddle, I rode to Westminster.

I had been right when I suspected that there would be crowds to see me. They watched in amazement. I knew I looked splendid. I had taken great care with my appearance, and I was practised in the art of applying those aids to nature which are so effective. I had made sure that my dark hair looked almost as it had in my youth. My skin was unwrinkled; it had not been exposed to rough winds for years. They had been expecting an old woman; and in spite of my years I certainly did not look that.

At the palace I came face to face with Henry. He had aged considerably and was an old man now. All the defects he had had were more pronounced: the legs were a little more bowed; he leaned on a stick. I learned later that he had had a fall from a horse. Was it when Henry's men had killed the horse under him? He had ingrowing toenails which caused him some pain. Poor old man! Was this the greatest soldier in Europe? He was still, I supposed. Age could not alter that completely. His hair was grey and there was much less of it than I remembered. He was still careless over his clothes; still the same short cape, the hands that were more reddened than ever.

Yet for all this, one only had to look at him to know he was a king.

I felt a sudden emotion. It was certainly not love. I would never forgive him for what he had done to me. Hatred? Yes, in a measure, but not entirely. A little pity because he was no longer active and must have hated leaning on a stick—and pity too, for the unrequited love he had given to his sons.

Then I thought with a glow of pleasure: You are an old man, Henry Plantagenet. You are older than I am in truth, although you are eleven years younger.

'You are beautiful still,' he said.

I bowed my head. I gave him one of those looks which implied that I could not return the compliment on his looks. He understood. We still knew each other very well, and even after all these years we could read each other's thoughts.

'It is long since we met,' he went on.

'It was your pleasure,' I reminded him.

'It is now my wish that there should be no rancour between us while we are here.'

'Then the King's wishes must be obeyed.'

His lips twitched; he was admiring me, I knew; and I felt my spirits rise. I knew that there would soon be conflict between us and I welcomed it.

I thanked him for the clothes and the saddle he had sent.

He smiled faintly. 'I dareswear you needed them.'

'I did. I understand it is because Henry asked it that you freed me from my prison.'

'For this visit,' he reminded me.

'Then I must be grateful to him,' I said. He was moved at the mention of our dead son.

I said: 'He was my son too. I knew the end was near. I saw him in a dream.'

He was too emotional to speak for a moment.

'He was a handsome boy,' I said.

'There was never one as handsome as he was.'

'The end was sad. All that conflict. I know you loved him dearly . . . more dearly than any of the others.'

'He turned against me. He was led astray.'

I wanted to say to him: No, it was not as simple as that. When you crowned him, you created a rival. You were to blame. He had no love for you . . . yet on his deathbed he remembered me. You made me a prisoner but you cannot take that away from me. In the love of our children I have something for which you would give a great deal.

But I said none of these things. I was sorry for him.

'We both loved him,' I said. 'He was our son. We must pray for him.'

'Together,' he said. 'None understands my grief.'

'I understand it,' I said. I looked at him and saw the pain in his eyes. 'Because,' I added, 'I share it.'

He took my hand and pressed it; then he lifted it to his lips.

For a moment our shared grief had taken us right back to the days when we had meant a great deal to each other.

Then the greatest joy I had known for years came to me. Richard arrived at Westminster.

I stood staring at him. He had changed. He was so tall. I had forgotten how handsome he was; it was those blond looks inherited from his Viking ancestors, those bluest of blue eyes which could look like ice and which glowed like flames at the sight of me.

'My mother!' he cried and I was in his arms. I could not help it but the tears were in my eyes.

'This is wonderful . . . wonderful,' I cried.

'At last,' he answered. 'I have dreamed of this moment.'

'I have gleaned every bit of information I could about you. I have followed all you have done as far as I could. I have chafed with impatience because I could not know more. And now you are here. Richard, my dearest son.'

He looked at me, smiling. 'There is no one like you,' he said. 'You look wonderful. At first I thought it could not be. You are so . . . young.'

'I have kept myself young and I take a great deal of care to do so. There is so much we must talk of.'

'In secret,' he said.

'Oh yes . . . yes . . .'

'We shall find a way.'

'I intend to be at your side whenever I can be.'

'That shall be my endeavour, too. I have thought of you constantly. You have never been out of my thoughts.'

'You are to be a king now, Richard.'

'Aye,' he replied. 'But he will do all he can to deprive me of my rights.'

'Hush,' I said. 'We will talk of it later. We are going to prevent that, Richard. We are going to see that everything that is yours shall come to you.'

I was dazzled and bewildered. This meeting was something I had dreamed of for so long. I had never doubted that it would take place some day, but now it was here it seemed too wonderful to be true.

Later we contrived to be alone and we talked of Aquitaine.

'He can't take it from you,' I said. 'Aquitaine is not his to give or take. It is mine and I made you my heir.'

'He wants to give it to John.'

'Nonsense. I will never allow it. And you are the heir to England now.'

'He will try to deprive me of everything.'

'He will not succeed.'

'I am determined that he shall not.'

'He does not really want war between you.'

'No, he wants to get his own way without it.'

'We will defeat him. Why has he brought me here? Why has he suddenly released me?'

'Sancho of Navarre advised him to, and Henry asked it on his deathbed.'

'I know. But it would be more than that. He will have a reason which we shall discover in due course.'

'There is something else. All this time he has kept Alais here. She is my betrothed and everyone knows how it is between them.'

'She has been his mistress for years. Do you know what surprised me more than the fact that he has taken his son's intended bride? His fidelity to her. I had never thought he could be capable of it, as he has been to her and was to Rosamund Clifford.'

'He does not always act as one expects him to. I will not take Alais now. And I shall tell him why.'

'It is amazing how he keeps up the pretence. How old is she? She must be about twenty-five by now.'

'I prefer Sancho's daughter Berengaria.'

'And it is Berengaria you shall have. Even your father would not expect you to take Alais now. What is wrong in Aquitaine, Richard?'

'I do not understand it. I have brought law and order to the land. It is quiet now but one is never sure when disruption will break out. They did not like my father and they do not like me.'

I said: 'When my grandfather ruled, Aquitaine was happy . . .

well, as happy as a state will ever be. There were always dissenters . . . but never on the scale that there have been since I went away. There was music and laughter in the Courts.'

'Bernard de Borne inflamed rebellion with his poetry.'

'That was because he flattered your brother and made him believe all he told him. Sometimes poetry can inspire men and women to greatness. Why will not the people accept my son?'

'They thought I was on my father's side against you.'

'They hated my first husband, Louis, but not as much as they hated Henry.'

'They will hate anyone but you, Mother. You are the only one they will accept. I know of only one way to keep order and that is by strict application of the law. And that is what they will never wholly accept.'

'If I went back . . .'

'The King is a fool to keep you a prisoner. There are too many people who love and respect you . . . and admire you, too. I tell you this: as soon as I am King of England, I shall have you beside me.'

'I am fortunate,' I said, 'to be so deeply loved.'

And so we talked, but we knew that Henry would have his reasons for bringing us all together and most of all for releasing me from my prison . . . if only temporarily.

Christmas was to be spent at Windsor. Preparations were in full swing to make this a very special occasion. For the first time for years the King and Queen would spend the festival together. Special wines were sent to Windsor with food of all description. Musicians, *jongleurs*, acrobats . . . nothing was spared to make this a memorable time. I guessed it would have been so without such trifles.

Alais was there. She was a beautiful girl, very gentle, a little uneasy at this time, particularly as Richard was one of the party. He treated her with a cool disdain almost as though he were unaware of her. I know of no one who could present such an icy front to the world as Richard. Geoffrey was rather amused by the situation, I believe. One had the impression that he was hoping for trouble and if he saw a chance would do his best to provoke it.

John was there. I could not like my son John. He was different from the others. Now he was placating his father at every turn, being the dutiful, affectionate son. Surely Henry was not deceived. Oddly enough he seemed to be. It was strange that he who was so shrewd on all other matters should be so blind where his sons were concerned—believing what he wanted to rather than what was blatant fact.

There were meetings. At some of them I was present.

Henry was trying to persuade Richard to give up Aquitaine, and Richard refused. Henry raged and ranted and Richard stood firm.

Henry wanted to distribute the power among his sons, and for that he had to have my agreement. That was why I was there. He did realize that I was of some significance on the continent. I believed that a certain amount of his troubles there were due to his imprisoning me.

When he asked me to agree to the distribution of his possessions, of which John was to get the larger part, I stubbornly refused my consent.

'Why do you always go against me?' he demanded in exasperation.

'I only go against you when you act foolishly.'

'You are speaking to the King.'

'I am well aware of that for he never lets me forget it. I remember that he has been my gaoler for a great many years.'

'And could be for a great many more to come.'

'If it suits his purpose, I have no doubt.'

'Why cannot you listen to reason?'

'Why do you not do the same?'

'I am the King—I make the rules.'

'As we have seen on occasions . . . disastrously. Thomas à Becket, Archbishop of Canterbury. Was there ever a greater mistake? Yes, one. The crowning of your son in your lifetime. Think about that, Henry Plantagenet, and then ask yourself whether you have always listened to reason.'

'Be silent.'

I bowed my head. The shafts had gone home.

'There is going to be trouble in Aquitaine. They don't like Richard.'

'Do you think they would like John?'

'They are stupid ridiculous people. They spend their time singing romantic songs. They think that if you were their ruler it would be paradise. Richard will not give up Aquitaine to John. Perhaps he would to you.'

I stared at him.

He did not look at me and went on: 'You could spend some time there. Go among them. Let them see you . . . how well you have fared in prison. Satisfy their love of romance. I have no doubt they will make up songs about you.'

To go back to Poitiers, to be in my Court again, surrounded by musicians and poets . . . long summer evenings out of doors . . . the scent of pines and glorious flowers . . . long winter evenings around a fire . . . laughing, carefree . . . beautiful clothes to wear . . . he was opening the gates of Paradise.

'Think about it,' he said.

'Yes,' I replied. 'I will go.'

And I thought: Aquitaine returned to me and held for Richard.

What could be better?

From Windsor the Court travelled to Winchester.

I had told Richard about the King's suggestion.

'If Aquitaine is mine, it is as good as yours,' I told him. 'He is suggesting that I go there to keep order.'

'Which shows how worried he is. It is quiet for a while but revolt is always there . . . ready to break out. He thinks you will have a sobering effect and this is his way of bringing it about.'

'But if it is handed back to me—and that will have to be without double-dealing . . . if it is all fair and legal . . . I shall go there. I shall be free, Richard. And I shall see that, when I am no more, Aquitaine shall be yours.'

'You are the only one I would give it to.'

'So let us think about it. Let us consider every little detail so that he has no opportunity of cheating us.'

Richard agreed that we must do that.

As for myself, I was in a state of bemused delight. I could hardly believe it was true. After years of resignation to quiet living in Salisbury or Winchester or some such place . . . I was to be free.

Henry was ready to go ahead with his suggestion. Aquitaine was to be returned to me just as I had given it to Richard. Geoffrey was to go back to his dominions, and John would go to Ireland where he was the King.

I think it was clear to Henry that I was going to insist on this before I agreed to anything. Richard was to be the next King of England. He was the eldest son now, and the people would never accept either of the others.

Richard would suit England better than he did Aquitaine; and in his heart Henry must know that. Henry loved England, although he spent so little time there, but that was only because the other dominions were where trouble was always breaking out.

While we were at Winchester we were disturbed by the visit of Heraclius, the Patriarch of Jerusalem. Henry would have wished that he was anywhere but in England, especially when he was aware of what had brought the Patriarch. Saladin was on the point of taking Jerusalem. King Baldwin was dying and Queen Sybil was pleading for help from the whole of Christendom. Her son was an infant. Prompt action must be taken.

Henry, who was always anxious to appear to his subjects as a deeply religious man, listened sympathetically and declared that he would raise money without delay.

But it was not money that Heraclius wanted. He wanted crusaders.

Henry said: Yes, he could see that, but he himself was in no position to go and fight in the Holy Land.

Heraclius was desperate and did not mince words. He reminded Henry that when he had done penance at the tomb of Thomas à Becket he had promised to undertake a crusade to the Holy Land.

Henry was always upset by references to Becket. It was astonishing how that man still haunted him. I was sure he thought of him often. There would be constant reminders . . . places they had visited together in the days when Becket was Chancellor, before his disastrous elevation to the archbishopric . . . the conversations they had had. There must have been thousands of memories.

'I said I would go when the time was ripe,' he declared. 'And when the time is ripe, I will. That time is not yet.'

'This is the time,' declared Heraclius. 'The heathen is at the very heart of the Holy Land.'

'I could not leave my dominions now,' said the King and added: 'This is too important a decision for me to make alone. I must leave it to my ministers.'

Heraclius was shocked that he could rely on others to decide for him. Had he not taken an oath?

Henry could have retorted that the decision would not depend on them; he would follow their advice, yes, because their advice would be what he had commanded them to give him.

In spite of Heraclius's disappointment Henry called together a council headed by the Archbishop of Canterbury, who obediently rose and announced: 'My lord King, your duty lies in your own dominions.'

Heraclius could be very disturbing. Perhaps he guessed Henry's men were merely obeying his orders. He said he would call on another Archbishop, one whose blood had stained the stone of his own cathedral. He would remember that the King had made an oath to go to Jerusalem.

'When it was in his power to do so,' the Archbishop reminded the vehement Patriarch. 'The King has his duties here, and God will agree that it is his duty to remain in his own dominions.'

Henry rose and then said that he believed his council spoke good sense, and although in his heart he would be in the Holy Land, he must perforce think first of his duty. He would give money to the cause and he would help any of his subjects who wished to join the Crusade.

How fiery and how venomous these good men can become when they are flouted and prevented from carrying out their good works.

'You and your family,' cried Heraclius, 'came from the Devil and to the Devil you will return. No good will come to you, Henry Plantagenet. You have turned from God.'

Henry was trembling with rage.

Heraclius mocked him. 'I do not fear you,' he said. 'I fear only God, and He is on my side. Murder me if you will, as you murdered that saint Thomas à Becket. I could esteem the infidel in his ignorance who knows not what he does . . . yes, I could esteem him more than I do you.'

Henry was very shaken. That talk of God and Becket and the Devil unnerved him now that he was getting older.

I was sorry for him.

I had a feeling that I might comfort him more than anyone else could just now. I could laugh at the fiery Patriarch who used God as his ally to get his own way.

By chance I came across him alone in one of the chambers.

The door was ajar, and when I looked in he was staring pensively at the wall. I believe he often went to that chamber, and it was said that he liked to remain there alone and study the murals.

'Henry,' I said quietly.

He looked up and I could see that Heraclius and of course Becket were not far from his thoughts.

'The Patriarch is a very fierce man,' I said.

'He cursed me.'

'I dareswear he distributes his curses widely. It is a method of getting his own way. Not a bad one really. It is amazing how those so-called holy men can strike fear into the bravest.'

'I did say I would go on a crusade.'

'When the time is ripe. It has never been ripe and never will be, I fancy. You have not broken your oath. It is only when the time is ripe that you have said you will do it.'

'It is so.'

He put his hand to his head. A rare gesture with him. It suggested weariness.

He was standing before one of the paintings on the wall. I had seen some of them before. They were allegorical studies of life . . . very cleverly done. This one was new to me. It was of an eagle and four eaglets.

'This is new,' I said.

'Yes. I recently ordered it to be painted.'

'It means something.'

'Yes, I am the eagle. The four eaglets are my sons. Look. They are preying on me. There are Henry, Richard and Geoffrey.'

'And the fourth is John.'

'Yes, that is John. He is waiting until the others have all but finished me, and then he will pluck out my eyes.'

'Oh Henry,' I cried. 'What a terrible picture.'

'I face the truth now and then in this room. They are my own sons. I have given them affection. I have planned for them. I wanted them all to be great men. Between them they were to own the whole of Europe . . . and there is not one of them who has given me any affection. They are all ready to wrest from me what I have been preserving for them.'

'I did not realize you knew all this.'

'*You* know it?'

I nodded. 'You were a fool to crown that boy, Henry.'

'I see it.'

'You were told . . . yet you did it. You would listen to nobody. You did it hastily so that you could show Becket that you did not need him. You have thought too much of Becket.'

'I loved that man.'

'That was clear enough. You loved the wrong people . . . apart from Rosamund and Alais. Oh yes, I know about Alais, your son's betrothed and your mistress. They were gentle, kind, unquestioning. They gave you comfort. You did not get that from me. But it was more exciting, was it not? You and I could have done much together, but I was no Rosamund . . . no Alais. If you had been a faithful husband we could have worked together.'

'You did not care for me.'

'I did . . . in the beginning. It was when you brought that boy Geoffrey into the nursery that it changed for me. Unfaithful immediately after our marriage! It was too much for me to endure. But it is all over. You have treated me shamefully. That was a mistake. It has hurt you more than it has hurt me. Look at me. Look at yourself. And ask who has suffered more from your ridiculous behaviour . . . imprisoning your own wife, the Duchess of Aquitaine at that! Do you imagine I am the sort of woman who sits down and weeps and tears her hair at misfortune?'

'Never that,' he said.

'Then at least you have learned something. But it is too late for your eaglets.'

'They are against me . . . all of them.'

'Richard might have worked with you.'

'He hates me more than any of them.'

'Because of what you have done to me.'

'I did nothing more than you deserved. You are the one to blame. You always were. You turned them against me.'

'I have told you before. *You* turned them against you.'

'Enough of this.'

'Yes. It is too uncomfortable for you.'

'I might have known that you would plague me.'

'You plague yourself. If you do not want to think of your sons, why liken them to eaglets and have an artist depict them so that they may always be before you?'

He turned away.

'You do not know,' he said, 'what I would have done for just one of them to have been a good son to me. Instead of that, I have to rely on bastards. I can trust that other Geoffrey as I can trust none of yours. It is because they are yours. You turned them against me in their cradles.'

'As you like to think that, you must go on doing so.'

He looked old and tired. In spite of everything he had gained during a lifetime, in spite of his power and might, he was a sad and lonely man.

He leaned on his stick for a few moments and then turned and went away; and as I listened to the tapping of the stick, I felt pity for him and a certain sadness. I should have liked to comfort him, if that had been possible.

Freedom is one of the greatest gifts life can bestow, and like all great gifts it is only appreciated when it is lost.

To ride out again through my beloved country, to feel the sweet balmy air of the south, to see the people greeting me, calling long life to me in their warm and friendly voices—it was a pleasure to be savoured and remembered.

They saw me as the deliverer. I was their true ruler. They had glorified my grandfather and my father, conveniently forgetting certain strife which had been evident during their reigns. They saw in them the great romantics. Aquitaine was never the same as when we had our own among us, they said.

And I was the direct descendant, but being a woman, I had married and brought strangers among them. Now I was back. There were rumours of what had happened to me. I had been cruelly imprisoned by my monster of a husband, but now I was free to come back among them and take my rightful place.

The troubadours came back to Court, which was filled with *jongleurs* seeking to return to the ways of the old days which, looking back, they were assured had been full of pleasure.

They wanted no strangers among them. They wanted to live their lives as their grandfathers had. And I . . . the true heiress . . . one of themselves, was back.

Calm settled on Aquitaine.

Henry was right. This was what was needed.

So passed the days and life began to return to the old carefree ways. The people were happy.

A great deal was happening far away. I could not forget Henry as he had looked when he stood before that picture of the eagle and the eaglets. No wonder he turned to Alais for comfort. I think she must have cared for him, for it was not to her advantage to remain the mistress of an old man when she might have been the bride of a young one with a kingdom in view.

I wondered if Henry realized how dangerous were his eaglets. He was still deceiving himself about John. And John was the least likely to bring him happiness if all I heard of him was true.

My youngest son was wild, sadistic, profligate, a hypocrite and a liar, according to reports. Geoffrey might be pleasure-loving, suave and self-seeking, but he was not as bad as John. Richard of course was cold and stern and in a way high-minded; he would call his rule just, but some called it cruel. But John, from what I heard, was depraved.

Henry had been foolish to send him to Ireland. He ought to have known that that would end in failure. I could imagine John, surrounded by young men imitating him to curry favour. John would not care for the good of the country, of making it a prosperous addition to his father's Empire. All he would think of was his own pleasure.

Messengers brought news to the Court of how John had roamed the countryside looking for mischief, ridiculing the local inhabitants, because of the way they dressed and wore beards, which he was reputed to have tweaked provocatively and insultingly. The Irish would not accept that. Of course his main pursuit was women, and as he was the King he thought that all were at his command. He was immediately in conflict with Hugh de Lacy, who had been sent over earlier and was governing the country.

I remembered Hugh de Lacy. He was a very dark man, by no means handsome, with small black eyes and a flattened nose; he was short of stature and far from elegant; but he had power, I remember. I could imagine his dismay at having John giving orders above him.

After a while, having run out of money, John returned to England, where Henry apparently received him warmly, still deceiving himself that this was the one son who loved him. I could imagine John's playing the affectionate son, laughing inwardly at the old fool, determined to get what he could out of him.

Soon after that Hugh de Lacy was murdered. He was in the process of building a castle at Durrow when a man from Teffia with an unpronounceable name—I think it was Gilla-gan-inathar O'Meyey—picked up an axe and severed his head from his body.

Henry was deeply shocked and perturbed for de Lacy had kept good order in Ireland. John's comment was that it was the old fool's just reward.

In the meantime Geoffrey was at the French Court. Henry was uneasy about his sons' friendship with the French King. I wondered if Philip Augustus knew that Henry's worst enemies were now his own sons; and of course Philip Augustus was Henry's perennial enemy—just as his father had been. There would always be strife between the kings of France and England while England owned so much of France; constantly there would be on one side the desire to retrieve and on the other to acquire more.

But between the King of France and Henry's sons there was a great attraction. Philip Augustus was a clever young man, quite different from his father. He might not be as powerful on the battlefield as Richard, so successful at the joust as Geoffrey, but he had a subtlety they lacked.

At the Court of France Philip Augustus was now treating Geoffrey as an honoured guest. It might have been that he was trying to sow further distrust between Henry and his sons. That would not be difficult. However, the entertainment he arranged for Geoffrey was lavish.

Geoffrey loved tournaments above everything else. He was brilliant in the lists, and it was only natural of course that with a prince from England there should be rivalry between the two countries, and as the jousts were conducted as a war, the two sides should vie with each other for victory.

They had agreed that this should be a mock battle. The two sides were to face each other, and if one member of the party could be separated from the rest and forced to dismount, that was considered a capture. Later they would count their 'prisoners'.

Constance, Geoffrey's wife, was with him. She was pregnant at the time. They had one daughter only, Eleanor, named after me, and this time they were hoping for a son.

He wore her colours, I was told, as he rode confidently out. None quite knew how it happened. Perhaps he was over confident. Perhaps he was taken by surprise. The joust had scarcely begun when a lance struck his horse, and the creature reared and fell, throwing Geoffrey. He was called upon to yield in the name of the King of France. I could imagine his chagrin. He, Geoffrey Plantagenet, to yield to a knight of Philip Augustus! He raised himself and as he did so a rider and horseman came thundering past. The horse's hoof caught him at the side of his head and he lost consciousness immediately.

He was taken into the castle. Constance ran to his side while Philip Augustus shouted for doctors.

But when they came it was too late. Geoffrey was dead.

We had lost another of our sons.

I was grief-stricken and knew that Henry would be, too. What was this ill fate which dogged him? Did he remember the curse of Heraclius? Did he go into that chamber and look at the eaglets? One would not now peck him to death.

Two remained—Richard and John—and he was at odds with Richard and putting his trust in John.

I imagined that he would be even more fond of John now. He would delude himself in his grief that he had one son who loved him.

I remembered so much—Geoffrey when he was a baby, sweet and dependent. That was often how I thought of them . . . before they grew up, before the faults began to show, when they were royal babies and the years before them seemed full of promise.

I was due to return home. Aquitaine was quiet now . . . at peace. It had worked out as Henry intended. The duchy was mine now, and that meant a return to the old way of life.

I said I would come back to them again. Oddly enough, much as I loved my native land, I wanted to know what was happening. I felt I had to watch over Richard's inheritance, for I was sure the King planned to cheat him of it.

I was met at Dover. The King had given orders that I was to be taken to my old quarters in Winchester.

I could not believe this.

I was once more a prisoner.

What a fool I had been to come back when I could have continued my freedom in my beloved Aquitaine. I had trusted Henry.

I should have known better. I had settled affairs in Aquitaine; the duchy was at peace; the people looked on me as their ruler. So now, for the time being, he had no further use for my services; and having done his work for him I could return to being his prisoner.

For some time I was so overcome by hatred for Henry that I was unable to think of anything else. Later my anger abated a little as I saw that it was really as well that I was back. I could keep an eye on what was happening here, and I had to be watchful of him. He was planning to disinherit Richard and make John his heir. That was something I had to prevent, and I could do that better even as a prisoner here than I could in Aquitaine.

Constance's child had been born. I heard that Henry was delighted with a grandson and had wanted him named after himself. It amused me that the people of Brittany refused to allow this, and the boy was named Arthur, after their national hero.

Being an inveterate matchmaker, Henry was immediately planning remarriage for Constance—a match which would be advantageous to him, of course.

Henry was far from well. I gleaned little bits of news about his indisposition. The ingrowing toenail was making walking painful, but of course he spent a great deal of time in the saddle. There was something else. He was suffering from a vague internal disease and could no longer ride for a whole day without becoming exhausted. He had indeed not worn as well as I had. No one would have believed I was the elder. The thought gave me considerable gratification when I remembered how he had taunted me that I was eleven years older than he.

With the coming of autumn there was disturbing news from Jerusalem. Heraclius had warned of impending disaster; now it had come. Saladin, the legendary Saracen hero, had taken Jerusalem, and the tomb of Christ was now in the hands of the Infidel.

Everyone was talking of the need to save the Holy Land for Christianity, and all over Europe people were taking the cross.

I was appalled to hear that Richard had fallen victim to the fervour. At Tours he had vowed to undertake a crusade. Henry was enraged when he heard. When he had taken the vow at the time of his penance, he had been wise enough to add 'when the time is ripe'. Richard had shown no such good sense and seemed determined to honour his vow. I was disturbed, for if Richard went off on a crusade, that would leave the way clear for John. How could he have done such a thing!

Of course Richard was a fighter and to fight in a holy cause was an incentive to all Christians. There was a glimmer of hope. Crusades could not be undertaken in a matter of weeks. They needed years to prepare, and much could happen in that time. My thoughts went back to those days when Louis and I went off on our crusade. I remembered the fervour and the preparations, how I had fitted out my ladies with fine clothes and how we had looked forward to an exciting adventure. Exciting it had been but not always pleasant. There were times when I wished I were going with Richard. Then I laughed at myself. It had been considered rather absurd for a young woman to undertake such a venture. What of an old one?

There was conflict with France: Philip Augustus was demanding the marriage of Alais and Richard or the return of her dowry; he was threatening Normandy.

I knew now that Henry had no stomach for war. The old lion was tired, and tired men long for peace. Richard, caught up in religious fervour, although he hated his father, remembered the biblical injunction to honour his parents. John was with him, too, and that other Geoffrey the bastard, with William Marshal. With his sons and such men beside him, Henry's spirits must have lifted a little. After all, he was at heart a fighter . . . one of the greatest of his day.

The two armies were drawn up facing each other. Richard told me about it later, so I had a clear picture of what happened. It was night in the camp when one of Richard's men came to him and told him that a knight was asking to see him and when he was brought into Richard's camp, he was amazed to see the Count of Flanders. He came from Philip Augustus, he said, to remind Richard that he could not fight against the King of France, his suzerain, to whom as Duke of Aquitaine he had sworn fealty. Richard replied that the King of France was at war with his father and that meant at war with him.

'It is of that matter which the King wishes to speak to you,' said the Count.

'Does the King of France want a truce?' asked Richard.

'He wants to speak with you.'

Richard was always fearless. He must have known what a risk

he took. He went with the Count of Flanders through the enemy lines.

I knew of the relationship between Richard and Philip Augustus. Richard never kept anything from me. They had loved each other and there was a strong bond between them.

He said that when he arrived the King of France came out of his tent to greet him with such infinite tenderness that it was difficult to remember that they were on opposing sides; and when Richard asked what Philip Augustus wanted him for, he answered: 'Friendship. Could I ever be anything but your friend?'

Richard went into the King's tent. Philip Augustus was alone and unarmed. 'Take off your armour, Richard,' he said.

Richard protested, saying that he was in the midst of his enemies.

'I would not allow any to harm you,' replied the King. 'We should be together . . . not against each other.'

'Do you expect me to fight against my own father?' asked Richard.

'Has he not fought against you? He is betraying you, Richard. He has taken my sister, who was to have been your wife, and made her his mistress . . . and she a Princess of France! If she married you, you and I would be brothers. We must be friends. War destroys us both . . . and war against each other is unthinkable. The King of England is more your enemy than he is mine. Do you know he plans to disown you and set up another in your place?'

'I do not trust him, it is true, but he cannot do that.'

'Stay here.'

'No. I must go back but I will think of what you have said.'

They talked a while. Then Richard left. Philip Augustus said that, if any harm came to him in the French camp, those responsible would have to answer to him.

The next day, as soon as dawn broke, Richard went to his father. He was shocked to see the King look so ill. He shrugged off Richard's enquiries about his health. 'I am well enough. It is always thus first thing in the morning. I grow better as the day wears on.'

'The King of France would be ready for a truce,' Richard told him.

'He would impose humiliating terms.'

'You would have to give up the Princess Alais.'

Henry blustered. 'She is to marry you when the time is ripe.'

Richard gave him a steely look. 'Methinks she may be over-ripe. Tell me. Why are you so reluctant to relinquish her?'

'I could have talked to Louis. He was more reasonable than his son.'

'Louis was continually asking for the marriage to take place when he was alive. The ripening process has taken a very long time.'

'Some time ago I made a promise to go to the Holy Land,' said Henry. 'Now the need is great. I would go on a crusade if Philip Augustus would agree to a two-year truce.'

'I have already taken the cross,' said Richard.

'I know that well. We will go together. The King of France shall be told, and if he will agree to this truce we will make our preparations.'

Richard knew, of course, that his father would never go to the Holy Land. He was too old and ill; moreover he would never leave his own dominions. What he wanted was to evade war with France, for which he had no heart.

He sent envoys to the French camp. Richard regarded him with scepticism.

'How could I go on a crusade?' demanded Henry. 'How could I leave my kingdom? How could I trust the King of France?'

'You are repenting your rash suggestion already,' said Richard.

'You were once friendly with the King of France. You could perhaps arrange a truce. That is what we need. We do not want to go to war. We could come to terms and these you could arrange.'

Richard said he would go to the King of France.

Philip Augustus received him with the utmost pleasure. I pictured it all clearly. Richard standing bare-headed before him, taking his sword and handing it to him, then kneeling before him. Philip Augustus perhaps reaching out a hand to caress his beautiful red-gold curls, for the King of France made no secret of his delight in the presence of his enemy's elder son.

'I come on behalf of my father,' Richard said. 'He wants a truce.'

'That he might go on a crusade?'

'He cannot go on a crusade. He is too old and sick and would never leave his dominions.'

'If we fought now, I should certainly win,' said the King.

'My father has never been defeated in battle.'

'He knows he will be this time. It is why he asks for a truce. For you, I will consider a truce, but only for you, because if you fight with your father you will be defeated, and I know that would humiliate you, my friend. I do it for you, but there will be terms.'

'What are these terms?'

'First, that the King of England leave his son with me while we discuss them.'

'Would you make me a hostage?'

'Nay, only an honoured guest. It is because I want you near me that I will agree to this truce. If you leave me now . . . which you will not be prevented from doing, I shall go into battle and defeat the old lion this time. I will beat him so soundly that he will not be able to fight again.'

Richard knew this was possible, so he agreed to remain with the French while the terms were discussed.

Philip Augustus was overjoyed to have Richard with him. There was never a question of his being treated like a hostage. He was the most honoured of guests. The King would have him sit beside him at table; he insisted that they eat from the same plate. He told Richard that the greatest honour a King could bestow on a guest was to ask him to share his bed. The friendship was as it had been before—one of passionate attachment.

They talked together; they would have long discussions in bed. Richard told the King of his vow to go on a crusade.

'We will go together,' declared Philip Augustus. 'I, too, will take the vow.'

They talked of preparations for this shared adventure, but Philip Augustus's main object was to warn Richard against his father, for he was sure Henry was planning to take Richard's inheritance from him. Richard did not see how he could do so. He was the eldest son now, the legitimate heir to the throne of England and the dukedom of Normandy.

'Perhaps one day you will discover,' said Philip Augustus.

Henry would of course hear rumours of the relationship be-

tween the two young men, and it must have given him cause for
alarm.

Richard was being royally entertained by the King of France,
who seemed in no hurry to proceed. He was quite content with
things as they were as long as Richard stayed with him.

Henry would not have been able to understand the relationship between Philip Augustus and Richard. It was alien to anything he himself could experience. He wrote to Philip Augustus
saying that he believed the main difference between them was
the Princess Alais. He had decided that the Princess should
marry John instead of Richard, and John should have all his land
except Normandy and England.

How Philip Augustus must have laughed. Here he had actual
proof of Henry's duplicity. He promptly showed the letter to
Richard. Now surely he could not doubt his father's treachery.
Give John Aquitaine—the land for which he had fought! It was
his mother's, in any case. How could he ever have been such a
fool to range himself against his dear friend, the King of France?

The confrontation of the two Kings took place at Gisors, under an elm tree. It was not the first time the Kings of France and
England had met at this spot. The English, who had arrived first
at the scene, took up the position in the shade, leaving the hot
sun to the French.

I could imagine Henry seizing the smallest advantage glee-
fully.

Philip asked that the Princess Alais should be given to Richard as his wife and that fealty, throughout the English Court,
should be sworn to Richard as the heir to Henry's dominions.

Henry must have been astonished. It was as though it were
Richard who was making the terms. He was in a quandary.

The King of France signed for Richard to come forward.

'Here is your son,' he said. 'You will swear to these conditions before him.'

Henry hesitated and Richard went on: 'Swear that I shall have
my bride. Swear that I shall have the inheritance due to the eldest
son.'

There was no way out for Henry. He was trapped. He glared
with hatred at his son and began to shout: 'No, no. I will not
do it.'

'So,' said Richard, 'I see that what I have heard of you is
true.'

He turned his back on his father and approaching the King of France, took off his sword and handed it to him.

In the presence of his father he was offering allegiance to Philip Augustus.

How joyfully the King of France accepted it. Henry could not believe it. How could his son go over so blatantly to the enemy? I could have answered that. 'Because, my dear Henry, you have shown so clearly that *you* are his enemy.'

Philip Augustus, eyes shining with love and gratitude, said he would agree to a truce; the two Kings should meet in a month's time. Meanwhile Henry could consider his terms.

'Come,' he said to Richard. He gave him back his sword. Richard mounted his horse, and the two of them rode off together.

So Henry had lost another son—if not to death this time, to the King of France.

He went to Saumur for Christmas. It must have been a gloomy one. He would hear reports of the great friendship which existed between Richard and the King of France. They were always in each other's company and now were planning the crusade they would take together.

The two Kings met again as planned. Philip Augustus implied that he wished for peace because he wanted to give his mind to the proposed crusade. The Holy Land was in danger while they played out their petty quarrels. All he wanted was that Richard should have his bride and be proclaimed heir to his rightful inheritance. The marriage had long been arranged and Richard was Henry's eldest living son. Philip Augustus was only asking for what was right. There was another point. It would be necessary for John to join the crusade. This was so that he could not be up to mischief while Richard was away.

Henry raged to William Marshal and Geoffrey the Bastard at the insolence of the King of France. They must have been very unhappy—those men who really cared for him.

Henry said he would not agree to the terms, and Alais was to marry John.

Once more the conference ended in failure.

John joined him. Henry was at Le Mans, one of his favourite cities because it contained the tomb of his father, and he had often rested there to visit it.

It was while he was at Le Mans that he heard that Philip Augustus was on his way to attack him. He had given him many chances and still he refused to see reason; so now the French were on the march and with them Henry's own son, Richard.

'What have I done,' demanded Henry of William Marshal, 'that my own son would march against me?'

William Marshal was one of those honest men who could not lie even if it meant saving their lives. 'You have tried to rob him of his inheritance,' he said.

Henry must have smiled wryly. One could trust William Marshal to put a finger on the truth. He *had* tried to rob Richard of his rights because he wanted John, whom he believed to be his only faithful son, to have everything.

How tired he would have felt, how despondent. I never knew why, hating Henry as I did, I could feel sorry for him. The great raging lion, the invincible warrior. How did it feel to be brought to the stage when one's ageing body did not match one's valiant spirit?

From a high point he would see the French camp and know that his own son Richard was there with his enemy.

There was a high wind blowing straight into the French encampment. He had an idea. Fearing he might not be a match for the French and his son Richard, he would attempt other methods to win the battle. If he had fires lighted, the wind would blow them straight at the French camp and might destroy it completely. At worst it would do much harm and impede their advance. All means are fair in war.

He gave the order and the fires were lighted.

It was like a miracle. It was as though God was working on the side of the French against him. For no sooner were the fires lighted than the wind changed, and instead of blowing them into the French camp, they blew back to the town of Le Mans.

He could not believe it. The flames were enveloping the city. He cried out in anguish; then his rage overtook him. He shook his fist at the heavens. Such a disaster could only come from one place. God was against him. God had determined to destroy him.

William Marshal said it was an unusual change in the wind. Such things happened.

'It was deliberate,' shouted Henry. 'It was done to plague me. It shows God is not on my side. I have prayed to Him . . .

worked for Him, and He has deserted me in my hour of need. By His eyes, I will pray no more. I will curse Him who curses me.'

His son Geoffrey was in fear of what would happen next. He implored his father not to blaspheme. They needed God's help as never before.

'He has deserted me. I will plead with Him no more,' shouted Henry.

Geoffrey was greatly distressed. I think that must have comforted him a little. He had been good to Geoffrey, and Geoffrey had always adored him and had had that attitude towards him for which he had looked in vain from his legitimate sons.

Then came news that the French were preparing to advance. William Marshal urged him to mount his horse for they must retreat at once.

Henry, the great warrior in retreat! The humiliation must have been intolerable to him. Old, tired, sick, the only son left to him, John, about whom he must know he was deluding himself; and the bastard Geoffrey, of course, was the only one on whom he could rely.

Richard told me about an incident which occurred at that time.

Intending to parley with his father, Richard set out with a few men. Unarmed for combat and isolated from his party, suddenly he was halted by a man on a horse who had a lance which he pointed at Richard's throat.

'It was too late for me to do anything,' said Richard. 'He could have killed me. I knew the man. It was William Marshal. I said, "You are going to kill me, William Marshal. But see, I am unarmed." He paused for a moment, then said: "No, I will not kill you. I will not be the one to send you to the Devil." And with that he slew my horse from under me and rode off. I could only find my men and lead them back to the French camp, thus allowing my father to escape.'

I should always be grateful to William Marshal. I knew he was a good man. He might have considered it his duty to kill the King's enemy, and Richard at that time was one.

Henry must have known that he was no match for the French. Le Mans was a burned-out town, burned out by his act which made it all the harder to bear. William Marshal and Geoffrey and the others discussed what they should do next. Marshal thought they should make for Normandy, where they would find men to rally to their banner. The King was too tired to make plans. He wanted to know where his son John was; he wanted to discuss with him what was the best thing for them to do.

John could not be found.

'He has gone off to find men to come to our aid,' said Henry. 'Soon he will be with us. And then we shall be ready for the enemy when they come.'

There were messengers from the King of France. He wished to parley with Henry once more.

As usual Henry prevaricated. He felt ill and he looked it. I guessed he was too proud to be seen in such a state. No doubt he thought a few days' rest would be beneficial.

He tried to delay, but Philip Augustus made it clear he would wait no longer. If Henry did not agree to a conference, it would be a matter of all-out war.

So he rode to the meeting. Richard told me about it afterwards.

'The King could scarcely sit his horse. William Marshal and Geoffrey rode close to him, one on either side. I think it was because they feared he would fall from his horse.'

Philip Augustus's terms were that Henry must pay homage to him for his lands in France. He, Philip Augustus, and Richard were going on a crusade and as soon as they returned the marriage of Richard and Alais must take place. Richard must be proclaimed heir of all his father's dominions, and Henry must pay for the cost of the war. If he did not adhere to these conditions, the knights and barons of England were to desert him and join Richard.

'My father was overcome with shame, but there was no alternative. It was either submit or become the prisoner of the King of France. Can you imagine my father a prisoner! He had to accept. The King of France was insistent. He gave me the kiss of peace before all assembled there. We embraced and as his face was close to mine I saw the hatred there. You know how he could not hide his feelings. His lips were close to my ear. He said, "I pray God I live long enough to take my revenge on you." I took no notice. I thought it better not. And then he went away.'

I heard the rest from William Marshal later.

Henry was overcome with exhaustion, depression and the

pain he was suffering. The castle of Chinon was not far away and there he could rest for a while and recuperate his strength.

William Marshal said it was pitiful to see him attempt to mount his horse. Geoffrey, who could speak to him more frankly than the others, insisted that he be carried in a litter. The King protested. He, who had been more at ease in the saddle than on his own two feet, to be carried in a litter like a woman! But Geoffrey was firm, and it was an indication of Henry's weakness that at length he agreed. And so, by litter, he was carried to Chinon.

What distressed him so much was that after the incident of the fire at Le Mans several of his knights had gone over to Richard, which meant going over to the French. He could not abide traitors. He wanted to know who they were.

He said to Marshal: 'I want a list of those knights who deserted me. I am sure the King of France would not deny me this. Nay, perhaps he would take a pleasure in giving it to me.'

Geoffrey said: 'Perhaps it would be better to forget them. They are not worthy of a moment's thought.'

'Don't be a fool,' retorted the King. 'I must know my enemies and I regard these as such.'

Geoffrey suggested that he should try to rest.

'Send my son John to me as soon as he comes,' said the King.

He did sleep after that. There was terrible consternation in the camp, for everyone knew how ill he was. The fact that he would not admit it could not disguise it.

When he awoke he saw Geoffrey and William Marshal whispering together. He heard Geoffrey say: 'Better not to show it to the King.'

Henry was then fully awake, demanding to know what was not to be shown to him. They were holding something back. What was it? They tried not to tell him but he saw through their ruse and demanded to know.

At length they admitted that it was the list which Philip Augustus had obligingly supplied.

Why were they hiding it? They should bring it at once or feel the weight of his wrath.

I could imagine his anguish when he saw that the name at the head of the list of those who had deserted him was that of his son John.

He could no longer deceive himself.

Did he think of that picture at which he had often looked so sadly? Did he see how true it was? The old eagle worn out . . . finished . . . and the young eaglets waiting to finish him off. They could not wait for him to reach his end gracefully. They were ready to snatch from him that which he had been so reluctant to give during his lifetime.

Gone were all his illusions. He had gained much territory; he had been the most powerful man in Europe—but he had failed to win the love of his sons, and that was something he had dearly wanted.

He did refer to the picture, they told me. He said; 'You see, it was right. My youngest was waiting for the moment when it seemed that all was lost to me, that he might peck out my eyes. I no longer wish to live . . . unless it is to take revenge on them. They are her children . . . all of them. That she-wolf . . . who laughs at me. I made her my prisoner, but still she laughs at me, and she defeats me through her sons . . .'

I think he must have been delirious then. He talked about the early days of our marriage and of Rosamund and Alais . . . the three women who were most important to him among the myriads he had known.

Geoffrey was beside him, for he was uneasy when his son was not there.

'Would to God you had been my legitimate son,' he said to him. 'Why did it have to be the bastard who was loyal to me?' He asked Geoffrey to call him 'Father'. He said: 'You are the best son I ever had. The sons of the Queen have been my enemies, and the son of a whore my friend.'

Geoffrey and Marshal consulted together. They thought the end was near and they should call a priest.

There was no priest. In fact, they were almost alone with the King. He was dying and all knew it. Most of the knights were concerned for their own safety. What would happen to them when he was dead? There was no point in remaining if the King were dying.

I hope he did not know they were deserting him. Geoffrey and William Marshal kept that fact from him. They remained by his bedside and watched life slowly ebb away.

Then he looked at them with anguish in his eyes. He grasped

Geoffrey's hand, and suddenly the young man felt the grip slacken.

He bent over his father. The King murmured: 'Oh, the shame that I suffer now . . . the shame of a vanquished King.'

And those were the last words of Henry Plantagenet.

Richard's Marriage

When I heard the news of Henry's death I was deeply shocked. My mind was a jumble of impressions from the past. I did not know whether I was glad or sorry. The idea of a world without that maddening, devious personality, who meant no good to me, was somehow empty.

I supposed that everyone who had lived close to him must have been deeply impressed by him. He was no ordinary man. He was unique. Whenever I had encountered him I felt a great excitement; to do battle with him had been as stimulating as making love had been.

It was strange to remember that he had gone for ever.

But why should I mourn? I had been his prisoner for sixteen years. He had dared treat me thus. Now I was free. My beloved son Richard was King of England. Everything would be different from now on.

Even before orders came that I was to be released, people behaved differently. There were no more guards, no more locked doors. With Richard King, his mother would be the most important woman in the land.

William Marshal arrived at Winchester almost immediately. To my surprise he came from Richard. I could not help but be amazed after what I had heard of their encounter when Marshal had been on the point of killing him. Marshal himself told me what had happened and how it was that Richard had chosen him to be his messenger.

After the King's death he and Geoffrey had carried him to

Fontevrault Abbey and sent word to Richard that his father was dead.

There Henry lay, stripped of his jewels and all possessions, which those who deserted him had taken before they went. There were very few besides Marshal and Geoffrey who had remained faithful to him.

That was perhaps one of the saddest aspects of all.

Richard had arrived at Fontevrault and stood beside the dead King. It was typical of William Marshal that he did not attempt to make his escape, although it must have occurred to him that after what had happened he would have little mercy from the new King.

Richard had moved away from the corpse and signed to Marshal to follow him.

He said: 'There is work for you to do, William Marshal. I cannot return to England immediately. Go to my mother and, with her, guard my kingdom until I return.'

William was so taken aback that he stared at the King in amazement.

Richard said: 'I trust those men who are faithful to their kings, and I believe you will be so to the new one as you were to the old.'

William took his hand and kissed it.

'I will, my lord King,' he said.

I was delighted. Richard was not always by nature magnanimous, but I considered this a gesture worthy of a shrewd king; William Marshal's acceptance of him made me feel that everything I had heard of him was true.

A king needs men such as William Marshal about him.

Thus it was that he arrived in England and came straight to me.

William brought letters from Richard in which he stated that I was to have full command of the kingdom until his return. My orders should be obeyed as though they came from the King himself. I was delighted and gratified by his trust. It was my duty now to prepare the people for him. I knew they would be feeling a little dubious.

He had never shown much interest in England; he had been out of it for most of his life. I had to make them realize that he was a strong man, a worthy successor to his father.

A further shock awaited me. Following almost immediately

on the news of Henry's death came that of Matilda. She had in fact died a few days before her father. I was glad he had been spared the grief of knowing this.

He had skilfully negotiated with the Emperor Frederick and had made it possible for them to return to their own dominions; but I believe the strain she had suffered greatly impaired Matilda's health. It was sad that her husband was not with her when she died. He had been with the Emperor in the Holy Land and had taken their eldest son, Henry, with him. Thus Matilda died with only Richenza, Lothair and William beside her. She was only thirty-three years old.

The messenger who brought me this terrible news tried to comfort me by telling me that she had been buried with great pomp and ceremony in the church of St Blasius. As if that could console me! I was grief-stricken for the loss of my daughter as I could not be for my husband.

I went over the details of her childhood and our last meeting . . . and my sorrow was great.

But there was no time for mourning. Richard was left to me, and my time must be dedicated to his needs.

I could not tarry in Winchester. I must go to London as soon as possible.

Before I left I summoned the Princess Alais to come to me. I think she was very frightened, fearing what would become of her now that the King was dead. She stood before me trembling.

She was a poor thing, really. She had so little spirit. That was what he had found comforting; she would always be ready to obey without question. I despised her, and I reminded myself that while I had been a prisoner she had been acting as Queen, taking my place.

The tables were turned now.

'Your position has changed considerably,' I said. 'You must be wondering what will become of you.'

She looked blankly at me. I could see that she had been weeping.

'I, who was a prisoner here, am so no longer,' I went on. 'The King treated me very badly, but that is over now. What are you going to do now that he is no longer here to protect you?' She looked at me piteously.

'You can't expect Richard to marry you.'

'No,' she said quietly.

'No indeed. You could not expect the King of England to marry his father's one-time mistress. Oh Alais, who would have believed that possible—and you the half-sister to the King of France!'

'Perhaps . . . I should go home.'

'Do you think you would be welcome at your brother's Court? You are no longer a marriageable princess. So many people know what you were doing with the late King. I . . . his prisoner . . . was aware of it. As you know, your lover kept me in captivity for sixteen years . . . apart from that short period when he cheated me into going to Aquitaine to put my duchy at peace.'

'I . . . I did know.'

'For what reason do you think?'

'Because you plotted with his sons against him.'

'That is what he told you, was it? His sons were against him because he tried to cheat them. He crowned Henry and then would give him nothing. They were all against him . . . and he deserved it. Now, Princess Alais, you will remain in Winchester until I decide what shall become of you. We shall have to see whether your brother wishes to have soiled goods back in his Court.'

She shrank from me and I waved her away.

I gave orders that she was not to be allowed to leave Winchester. Then I went to London and summoned leading representatives of the Church and the nobility in order that they might swear fealty to the new King.

I stayed in London only for a few days, showing myself to the people as often as I could, smiling graciously and benignly, willing them to love me.

Then I decided to make a tour of the countryside. I wanted the people to welcome Richard as their King. They had been aware of the virtues of his father, which would have naturally increased in their eyes since his death. Henry had brought law and order to the country where there had been none, but recently the taxes he had imposed had alienated them, and I always believed that what they had resented more than anything were the stringent forestry laws.

William the Conqueror had been a great hunter; it was his main recreation; he had created forests and had had game placed there so that there would always be plenty of hunting grounds. Whenever he travelled round the country, the journey was broken by hunting trips. Most of his successors had been the same;

hunting was their passion—and Henry had been no exception. He had added to the forest lands and made new ones. There had been strict laws. No one was allowed to deface trees; moreover, cutting them down was a major offence; no one must touch the game. In fact, the forest was sacrosanct.

Infringement of the laws brought dire penalties: a man could have his hands or feet cut off, his tongue cut out, his eyes gouged. The King's forest must not be touched. There were wardens in the forests looking for offenders; even trespassers were thrown into prison, and they never knew whether they were going to be robbed of some vital part of their bodies.

I always thought that such laws should never have been. There was nothing like such to stir up strife, to underline the subservience kings expected of their people, and to arouse those bitter feelings which, when the opportunity arose, would come bursting forth.

I knew that the prisons were full of people awaiting condemnation. So I ordered that they should all be freed.

'Life will be different under King Richard,' I told the people. 'He wishes all his subjects to be as happy serving him as he will be to serve them.'

This was a very worthwhile move. King Richard's health was being drunk all over the country. Life was going to be good. He was a benign King; he cared about his subjects. He was going to make England a merry place to live in.

I had only a few weeks to prepare them, but I flatter myself I did so thoroughly, and by the time Richard arrived at Portsmouth the people were ready to welcome him as their King. They anticipated great celebrations. Coronations always won popular approval. A new reign could herald a new era, and people were always ready to believe that what was to come was better than what had gone before.

Richard greeted me with great affection. Such demonstrations were particularly touching when they came from him because he made them so rarely and when he did they were heartfelt. He was not the man to dissimulate. I could never understand how Henry and I could have had such a son; he was so different from us both; he was entirely straightforward, which I fear neither of his parents was.

He looked more handsome than ever. The English must be proud of him. The people like a handsome king.

I told him what progress I had made and how I had prepared the way for his popularity.

He said: 'I knew you would do well. What a fool my father was not to appreciate you.'

'Oh, he had to have his Alais . . . his Rosamund. He needed docile women and he certainly got what he wanted in those two.'

'What of Alais?'

I shrugged my shoulders. 'I suppose she will go back to France in due course. You will not have her.'

'Most certainly not. My father's leavings! Never!'

'It would be most repulsive,' I agreed. 'But do not let us concern ourselves with her. She is quite insignificant now. We have to think of your coronation.'

'Yes, I suppose that is necessary.'

'Indeed it is. A king is not a king until he is anointed.'

'Then we will get it over as soon as we can.'

'We shall do it as it should be done. The people need to be wooed, Richard. You do not know them. You have seen so little of them. They need treating with care. With the people of Aquitaine one saw the way they were going. Their anger or their love was apparent the moment they felt it. These people are different. They show nothing though they are filled with rage. They must be watched. You have to woo them, Richard, and you must begin with a grand coronation.'

'As soon as it is over, I shall make my plans to go to the Holy Land.'

'Now that you have become King?'

'I have taken the cross. So has Philip Augustus. We are going together.'

But it is different now, surely. You have a kingdom to govern.'

'I am blessed with a mother who can do that better than I.'

I was gratified but disturbed. It was unwise to leave the country. Henry had made that mistake. No, that was not quite the truth. There had been little else he could have done, for he had had his dominions overseas to keep in order. I often thought how much easier it would have been for him if he had been merely King of England. But that was not the case with Richard. He would be leaving his country to go to the defence of another.

He said: 'I shall have to raise money.'

'How?' I asked.

'There is only one way. Taxation.'

'The people will not take kindly to that from their new King.'

'But this is a holy cause. Any who cannot undertake the crusade should be glad to help those who can.'

'They don't see it like that. The Holy Land is far away. They do not like paying taxes to keep Normandy safe. How do you think they will feel about far-away places?'

'It is our Christian duty.'

There was nothing I could say. He was determined and I had always known that once Richard had made up his mind there was no changing it.

The coronation was to take place on 3 September, which some people said was unlucky. But I wanted to get it over as quickly as possible. A king is not truly a king until he is crowned.

Just before the coronation John returned to England. He was married to Hadwisa of Gloucester on 29 August. In spite of the fact that their father had tried to set John up in that place which rightly belonged to his brother, Richard received him graciously when he came to England. He granted him the county of Mortain, gave him £4,000 a year from land in England and agreed to the marriage to the heiress of Gloucester, which would greatly enrich him. Richard was determined to be magnanimous, thinking, I suppose, that, if he bestowed his bounty on John, his brother would be loyal while he, Richard, went off on his crusade. He was most generous, giving him the castles and honours of Marlborough, Ludgershall, Lancaster, Bolsover, Nottingham and the Peak among others. John expressed his delight, but even so, it occurred to me that he would have to be watched.

There was a slight hitch for a time when it seemed that the wedding might not proceed, for Archbishop Baldwin brought up the point about the couple's being related in the third degree. This however was overcome and the ceremony continued. After all, it was well to have those close ties to fall back on if the time came when the couple wished to part, I thought cynically.

And when he was safely married, none could call my son 'John Lackland' anymore.

I had lavished great care on organizing the coronation. I wanted to make it a day everyone would remember. I knew the people loved such spectacles.

I was glad that it was a bright and sunny day; that would help dispel the gloomy prognostications of some Egyptian astrologer who had said that any important matter undertaken on this day would be disastrous. The ceremony went well from the moment the archbishops and bishops arrived in Richard's bedchamber to conduct him to the abbey.

The clergy chanted as they walked along. John came immediately behind them. I wondered what he was thinking, his head lowered, his eyes veiled. After all, he had at one time believed that the crown would be his. He must be seeing himself in the position which was now Richard's.

How magnificent Richard looked as he walked with the royal canopy poised on lances carried by four barons and held over his head. The people were awestruck; and then they cheered. Slowly he came through the nave to the high altar, where Archbishop Baldwin awaited him. Baldwin would still be smarting over the controversy over John's marriage and no doubt wondered whether this new reign would bring conflict between Church and State as the last one had.

Relics had been placed on the altar—bones of saints and phials of their blood. Richard must swear on these to honour God and the Holy Church. Then he was stripped down to his shirt and hose for the anointing after which he was dressed in the tunic and dalmatica. He took the sword of justice in his hand; the golden spurs were placed on his heels and the royal mantle was put about him.

None could have denied he was one of the handsomest kings England had known. Tall, impressive, with his Viking looks, the great warrior, he was the perfect monarch in appearance. How different from his stocky father, inclining to be fat towards the end, those bow legs, that careless mode of dress, those reddened hands. Oh, so different! Richard was like a god from a Norse legend. My heart swelled with love and pride as I watched the anointing and with emotion saw them place the crown on his head; and the sound of the Te Deum echoing in my ears was wonderfully inspiring.

Richard was in truth King of England.

Feasting followed. I thought the day had gone well. There had been no discordant note, although there had been one uneasy moment when Richard and Baldwin came face to face at the altar. But that had passed and all had gone smoothly.

This was not to continue.

There had always been trouble between the citizens of London and the Jews. The Jews were a hardworking race and in their business deals always seemed to get the better of a bargain. This was resented by their gentile rivals. It was a form of envy, which seems to be at the root of most trouble.

Richard had ordered that there were to be no Jews at the coronation, giving the reason that this was a Christian ceremony and the Jews were not Christian.

Whether the Jews decided to defy the command or whether they had not been aware of it, I was not sure. Perhaps they thought that, if they brought costly presents, their presence would be welcomed.

There was one very rich Jew called Benedict of York. He brought a valuable gift for the King, but as he was making his way to the palace, he was recognized and the crowd immediately set upon him.

He protested: he had a valuable gold ornament which he wanted to give to the King. All he was doing was delivering it at the palace. The people would not listen to him. 'No Jews,' they screamed, and dragged him to the ground.

The poor man realized that his life was in danger. He had a quick mind. It was the Jews they were attacking. Killing was against the law . . . providing it was not a Jew, of course; so he had the brilliant idea of changing his religion on the spot.

'I am about to become a Christian,' he cried. 'If you kill me, you are killing one of your own.'

Some did not believe him, but others did. They did not want to face trial for murder. They knew what happened to murderers. The late King had been fanatically set on bringing law and order to the country, and he had done so by severely punishing violent acts.

'If he is a Christian,' said one of them, 'let him be baptized.'

This was a new turn to the revelry. The mob forced Benedict to go into the nearest church and insisted on his immediate baptism.

Meanwhile there was rioting throughout London. The shops and houses of the Jews were full of valuables. They were Jewish goods and therefore they belonged to Christians.

So what began as a day of rejoicing turned into a nightmare of horror for many people.

Richard was angry. What a beginning to his reign! He wanted peace. It was imperative that he have peace for he must go off to the Holy Land with an easy conscience.

I was with him when he sent for Ranulf de Glanville, one of the most able of his ministers and the man who had very often been my gaoler during my imprisonment. Neither I nor Richard felt any rancour towards him; he was a far-seeing man; he had always been respectful to me, looking ahead to the day when Richard would be King and his mother would be beside him.

Richard commanded Ranulf to put an end to the rioting. The people must be told that it was his intention to have no such disturbances. People must live in peace side by side, though they had differences of opinion on certain things, including religion.

Ranulf was certainly efficient. Very soon he had quelled the rising in London, and then Richard sent him off to stop it elsewhere, for when the news of what had happened after the coronation spread through the country, people in provincial towns thought they could enjoy a few pickings from the wealthy Jews.

There was a sequel to the story of Benedict of York. A few days after the coronation he begged an audience with the King.

Richard permitted him to come. He knelt before him.

'So you are the new Christian,' said Richard. The man was silent.

Richard went on: 'Were you not baptized on the day of my coronation?'

'I was, my lord,' the man replied.

'Are you a true Christian?' asked Richard. 'And will you abjure your old faith and cling to your new?'

Benedict raised his head. 'My lord King,' he said, 'I lied. I was in fear of my life. I was baptized. But I am a Jew and as such can never be a true Christian. In a moment of terror I renounced my faith. Now that has passed, I wish to tell the truth. I am ready to die for my faith.'

'Why are you so ready to die today when you were not a few days ago?' asked Richard.

'I spoke in a moment of panic. Now I have had time to reflect. I see what this means and I would rather die honourably than live ignobly.'

Richard said: 'You are an honest man and an honourable one. I respect these virtues. Forget your baptism and return to the faith of your fathers.'

Benedict was overcome with gratitude; he fell on his knees and kissed Richard's feet.

When I heard of this, I was filled with emotion. I knew my son could be a great king . . . if he would.

Once the coronation was over, Richard was obsessed by one thing: the need to raise money for the crusade.

I was beginning to be alarmed: he was proposing to sell all his castles; if anyone wanted a special favour, they could have it for cash. William Longchamp paid him £3,000 for the office of Chancellor. Was that wise? I wanted to know. Could such an important post be a matter of money? And why Longchamp? Just because he had been prepared to pay! Henry had said that Longchamp was the *son* of a traitor. His father had been deep in debt and disgrace not so long ago, and his grandfather was nothing but a French serf who had taken the name of Longchamp from the Norman village where he was brought up. First he had been in my son Geoffrey's service and, seeing an advantage in transferring to Richard's, he had done this. He was rather uncouth, slightly deformed, lame and by no means handsome. Moreover, he did not speak English and showed no desire to learn. He was certainly not going to find much favour with the people.

There were many anomalies. Charters were available to cities for certain sums of money; privileges were taken from monasteries and retrieved on payment. The people were amused at first, then outraged. It seemed as though an auction sale was being conducted throughout the country; and not for its own good either, but so that the King might raise an army to fight far away from home. There would have been a great outcry, I was sure, but for the fact that the money was sought to fight a holy war, and people were afraid to protest too much for fear of heavenly reprisals.

I protested to Richard that these acts could undermine his future as King. He had begun so well by releasing the people from prisons. He reminded me that that was my act. I said I had done it for him and he had seen how it had enhanced his popularity. The people had been ready to welcome him when he came home; but there were murmurings now. If there was one thing calculated to alienate the people, it was excessive taxation.

His reply alarmed me. He said: 'I would sell London itself if I could find a buyer.'

It might be that the people were more disillusioned because

they had expected so much. They had believed they were getting a more benign sovereign than Henry; now they were beginning to see that what they had thought of as Henry's harsh rule was for the good of the country, whereas everything Richard wanted was for the good of his crusade.

Preparations went on with speed. Richard's methods were bringing in the money. There was talk of little else but what military equipment would be needed. The fleet was being assembled.

I could not help comparing this with the crusade in which I had joined. Whenever I was with Richard, he would insist that I talk to him of my adventures. He was determined that the Third Crusade should be the one to bring final victory. He did not want to return until Jerusalem was in Christian hands. I was anxious about him, for, in spite of his magnificent looks, he was not as strong as might be expected. He had suffered from that distressing ague for a long time. He had tried to hide it but it was not always possible to do so; and I remembered the hardships I had suffered during my adventures in that inhospitable land.

I had always loved him so entirely—from the moment he first lay in my arms, a beautiful child even on the day of his birth—that it was hard for me to see faults in him.

I did find myself constantly comparing him with Henry. I had to admit that Henry had had very special qualities. He had been bedevilled by his need for women. I had often noticed how preoccupation with sex can impair people's careers. Not that Henry allowed it to interfere disastrously with his; but if it had been less important to him and had allowed him to remain faithful to me, our partnership could have brought us both much good, I was sure.

Henry had made those two vital mistakes in his life, of course—the bestowing of an archbishopric on Becket and a crown on his son Henry. Even so, he would never have made the mistakes Richard was making now.

I saw them clearly and I wanted to stop him; but I knew Richard's obstinacy. He had one thought now and that was to go on a crusade. I must not try to impede him. Let him go; and when he returned he would be a good King. Meanwhile I must hold the kingdom for him.

I was very worried about John. Rumours were circulating,

and I guessed John was at the source of them. It was being said that Richard wanted to be King of Jerusalem . . . and in that event John would be King of England.

How I wished that Richard had never taken the cross, that he had been content to rule over his possessions at home!

He was ready to sail by spring. He left the country in the charge of Longchamp as Chancellor and Hugh Puiset, Bishop of Durham, both of whom had paid highly for their appointments. I, of course, was to be at the head of affairs.

But I did not intend to remain in England. I had been captive so long and I was finding freedom sweet. Uppermost in my mind was the need to see Richard married. I was anxious about the succession. I knew John had his greedy eyes on the crown; but there was one who came before him, and that was my grandson Arthur, Duke of Brittany, the son of Geoffrey who had been born after his death; as Geoffrey had been older than John, his son came before John.

I thought Henry's illegitimate son Geoffrey might have had pretensions too. Henry had made so much of him and on his deathbed, when this Geoffrey was the only son who remained faithful to him, he had said something about his being his only true son.

A country without an heir is in danger. Richard was now thirty-three years old, an age when a King should be married and have produced several heirs. Of course, the circumstances of Alais's connection with Henry had been the cause of the present position, but I believed it should be remedied without delay.

I tried to get Richard to pay some attention to this all important matter, but it was quite difficult to draw his attention from the crusade.

'Richard,' I said firmly, 'You must marry.'

He looked absent-minded. 'Oh, that can wait until I return.'

'It cannot wait,' I said. 'It is imperative that you produce an heir.'

He looked at me steadily for a few moments, then he said: 'Dear Mother, I have no desire for marriage.'

'You . . . a King . . . can say that?'

'It is true.'

I had heard rumours. There was the passionate friendship with the King of France. 'The King likes better to toy with his own sex than with women.' That had been said. I had refused to accept it then. He was so good-looking, so essentially masculine.

He read my thoughts. He said: 'It is so. You see, women have little attraction for me.'

I said: 'Your friendship with Philip Augustus . . . you *were* lovers?'

'You could say that.'

'I see,' I said slowly. 'But that does not prevent your marrying and having a child. There have been other cases . . .'

'I suppose it will have to be done.'

'Of course it will have to be done. There is a crown to think of. Imagine what would happen if you did not have an heir. Think of John on the throne of England!'

'Arthur is the heir to the throne.'

'A young boy. Do you think the people will want him! He is a foreigner. You know how the English hate foreigners.'

'They could call me that.'

'No. Not with your fair looks. They say you are the perfect Englishman.'

'Who has lived so little in England.'

'You must remedy that, Richard. When this crusade is over . . . Oh, I wish to God it had not been necessary to do it so soon.'

'It was when the call came.'

'But your marriage. What of this Berengaria of Navarre? You mentioned her once. I thought you had taken a fancy to her.'

'I did. I do not want marriage . . . but if it were necessary . . .'

'It *is* necessary. We must approach Sancho for Berengaria.'

'What of Alais?'

'She shall go back to France. Philip Augustus must understand that in view of what has happened you can not make her your Queen.'

'He will expect it.'

'Then he must needs do so. I must arrange this marriage with Berengaria.'

Richard did not answer. I guessed his thoughts were elsewhere. But I began to plan vigorously.

I was a little taken aback by what he had admitted. True, it was not exactly a surprise to me. It was something which had been in my mind for some time, and because I had not wanted to admit it, I had allowed it to remain a vague suspicion.

Men had such leanings but they did not prevent their begetting a family, which they must do if they were kings. I could see that Richard was going to be very lackadaisical about marriage, and it was my duty to see that it took place as soon as possible. I was certainly not going to wait until his return from the crusade.

There was only one course open to me. I must go to Navarre. I must bring Berengaria out with me, and we must meet up with Richard somewhere and get them married.

For a women of my age this was an undertaking which might prove a little daunting. But I was no stranger to the hardship of crusading, and though at the time when I suffered from this I had said I never wanted to do it again, this was my duty. Richard must be married with as little delay as possible. And as Berengaria was the only marriageable woman for whom I had heard him express a liking, Berengaria it must be.

What I planned to do was to leave England in the hands of Longchamp and Hugh Puiset and go to Navarre. There was bound to be delay on the continent. Both Philip Augustus and Richard had many preparations to make. I must catch up with them somewhere and insist on the marriage. The difficult part would be to see that it was consummated.

I must lose no time in bringing this about.

I left England, taking the Princess Alais with me. I was going to return her to France. We had no further use for her. She was very sad and, I believe, genuinely mourned Henry. He had been, I am sure, very different with her than with me. I supposed she was never provocative. It would have been, 'Yes, my lord. No, my lord' all the way. I was a little sorry for her, although her meekness irritated me. Moreover I guessed there would be trouble over her, for Philip Augustus would not want her to be returned to him unmarried. He appeared to be insisting that Richard marry her. He would consider, of course, that, whatever Richard's inclinations—and his must be the same, marriage was outside that. It was the duty of a king to marry and produce children. That need not interfere with his mode of life.

I crossed the Channel in February. It was not a pleasant experience. But when was it ever? I had known it worse in the summer than it was that February. We went to Rouen, where I decided Alais should stay until we knew what to do with her.

She was in the kind of captivity which I had endured for so long. I often thought: The tables are turned now, Henry. And I wondered if he could know what was happening now.

I left Rouen and made my way south to Navarre. There I was greeted warmly, for they knew the purpose of my visit, and naturally a little country like Navarre would be delighted for its daughter to marry the King of England.

Berengaria was presented to me. She was not very young. Her father had resisted offers for her hand because when Richard had visited his Court he had hinted that he might marry her, and Sancho had lived in hopes since then; now that it seemed those hopes were about to be fulfilled, he was overjoyed.

I told him that my son had begged me to come and bring Berengaria to him. This was not exactly true, but I could hardly mention his reluctance. Sancho believed me, though he must have wondered why nothing had been done about the matter before.

It was pleasant to be in Navarre. It was not so very far from Aquitaine, and Sancho's Court was similar to those I had known in my youth. There were the troubadours and the songs that I loved so well. Berengaria played and sang. She was a pleasant creature, but her beauty was not of that wild, tempestuous kind which might have been able to divert Richard from his tendencies. She was simply a charming, fresh-faced girl, and although she was still young enough to bear children, it seemed to me imperative that she and Richard set about the task without delay.

Sancho the Wise was Berengaria's father, and Sancho the Strong her brother. The minstrels sang of them and of the Princess who was going to marry a great King.

It was all very pleasant and very reminiscent. It was as though the years slipped away as I sat and listened.

Berengaria remembered every detail of her first meeting with Richard.

'I thought he was the most handsome man in the world,' she told me.

'I think he still is,' I replied.

She wanted to talk about him all the time. I told her of his prowess with the sword and how people were already talking of him as the great hero of battle. He was wise too. I told her the story of Benedict of York and of William Marshal who had killed his horse from under him and yet at their next meeting Richard had given him an important post in his realm.

'And he is going now in the name of God to fight the Saracen and restore Jerusalem to Christianity.'

She clasped her hands, smiling ecstatically.

I murmured a little prayer that all would be well for her.

She told me that she had never since seen anyone like him and that she had loved him from the first moment she met him.

'There is no one like him,' I said emotionally.

'You love him, too,' she answered.

'I have loved him more than I ever loved anyone else,' I said truthfully.

'When he was here and I was only a child, he rode for me in the tournament. He wore my glove in his helmet . . . as knights wear something belonging to the lady they love to show they are riding for her.'

'So he loved you then.'

'Is it not wonderful that our love has lasted all these years?'

Poor child, I feared she was going to be sadly disillusioned.

She told me of her fears that he would marry the Princess Alais.

'He swore he never would,' I told her.

'Poor Alais. I feel sorry for her.'

'You should not. She did what she wanted. She took the lover of her choice. She did not think of shame . . . then. It is only now when he is gone and she is left to bear the result of that affair, that she doubtless repents her folly.'

'Yes. And I am happy, for all my dreams are coming true.'

'Very soon you will be Richard's bride. Much as I like your father's Court, I do not wish to tarry here. I know Richard is going to Sicily. My daughter Joanna is Queen of Sicily and she will welcome us. She is, alas, a widow now, and I do not know what plans she will make. But Richard will be there and so shall we. The wedding will take place at once and you, my dear Berengaria, will be Queen of England.'

'It is good of you to come so far for me.'

'At my age, you mean? I have travelled much in my life and, although I now look for comfort, travel troubles me less than it would most folk. Now, my child, as I said, I wish to leave very soon. You must be ready.'

'I am ready when you wish to go, my lady.'

She would be a delightful, docile daughter-in-law. I hoped Richard was not going to disappoint her too much.

Time was all-important. Richard was to spend the winter of 1190–91 in Sicily with the King of France, so I could not go to him with Berengaria while he was officially affianced to Alais. I had no doubt that Philip Augustus was making himself quite unpleasant on that account.

I decided we would wait in Italy for the appropriate moment. Richard could be informed of where we were and send for us when it would be in order for us all to meet.

By this time winter was coming on, but I dared not delay. If I missed the army in Sicily, I should have to travel all the way to the Holy Land, which could mean hardship. I was quite prepared to do it if necessary, for I must get Richard married. I could not rest until there was a child on the way.

It was an arduous journey but I was determined. For me it was full of memories, for had I not come this way all those years ago? Memories came flooding back; and what was most vivid was that day when I had learned of Raymond's death. Then I thought I had touched the very depth of misery. But one recovers. Grief fades and life offers other joys to console one.

Berengaria was a pleasant companion—so fresh and innocent, a quality which I found most endearing. All the time I was hoping she would not suffer too much when the realities of life were forced upon her.

My relief was great when at last we reached Naples. The ships which were to take us to Sicily could be seen in the harbour. But there was disquieting news. Trouble had broken out in Sicily and we were to await Richard's instructions before we set sail.

Chafing against the loss of time as I was, I found this hard to endure. I was even more disturbed when news of the state of affairs in Sicily filtered through.

I was so looking forward to seeing my daughter Joanna, whom I had not seen since she had been not quite eleven years old; she would be twenty-four now. I had wanted to be with her when her little son, Bohemond, had died; poor child, he had scarcely lived, and heirs were so important to kings and queens. Joanna had written to me; she had been heartbroken. And now her husband King William was dead and Tancred, the illegitimate son of William's brother Roger, had taken the throne.

I thanked God that Richard was on the spot. He would surely rescue his sister from the dire plight in which she clearly found herself.

I continued to be worried about the passing of time. I must get Richard married. He knew I was determined to and he knew I was right; but at the same time he wanted to avoid it; and moreover there was his friendship with Philip Augustus. I had no idea what the relationship between them was now and whether they continued to be lovers; but Philip Augustus, from what I could gather, was a king who regarded his personal life as being quite apart from his kingship.

So there I was in Naples, each day hoping for news, wondering what was happening between Richard and Philip Augustus and how they were spending the time. Richard had already distinguished himself. There was no doubt about that. People spoke of him with awe, the great Coeur de Lion—the Lionheart. I heard the very sight of him inspired people and his bravery was a by-word.

All the same, there were rumours. One which distressed me particularly was that he had gone to the door of a church wearing nothing but his breeches and there he publicly confessed to his homosexuality.

'How could you, Richard?' I said aloud. 'Why proclaim it? What if Berengaria hears of this . . . or worse still, Sancho of Navarre? What do you think they would do? Berengaria would perhaps be ignorant of what it meant but there would surely be those to enlighten her.'

And here was I, at my age, bearing all the stresses of travel, giving up my comforts in my determination to get him married!

There had long been rumours of his way of life. They had started when he and Philip Augustus had so blatantly shown their affection for each other.

Richard had been chosen to lead the crusade; his military reputation made it clear that he was just the man; but there were some who did not approve of the choice.

The preacher Fulke of Neuilly, while exhorting men to join the crusade, expressed a doubt that Richard was the man to lead it. Fulke stressed the fact that this was a holy war and, great soldier that Richard was, his private life was not such as to make him fit to lead an expedition in the name of Christianity.

'Thou hast three dangerous daughters,' thundered Fulke,

when he was preaching and Richard was in the congregation, 'and they are leading you to disaster.'

Richard stood up and said: 'I have no daughters.'

'But you have,' countered Fulke. 'They are Pride, Avarice and Lechery.'

Richard knew how to deal with such a man and I was proud of him when I heard what happened next.

He cried out so that all could hear. 'So . . . this men tells me I have three daughters. I will be generous and give my daughters away. I will give Pride to the Templars and Hospitallers, Avarice to the Cistercian monks, and my Lechery to the prelates of the Church.'

There was a murmur of approval throughout the assembly, for all knew of the pride of the Templars, the Cistercians had a reputation for greed, and there was immorality in plenty among the clergy.

I wondered how Fulke felt. Perhaps he would learn in future that it was better not to do battle with Richard either with the sword or with words.

But I was uneasy because Richard's leanings were becoming so well known.

It was March before I had a message that I should prepare to sail for Sicily.

What joy it was to be united with two of my children: my beloved Richard and Joanna.

There was much to tell. Joanna embraced me with fervour. I had always had a rapport with my children—apart from John, who did not seem like one of mine somehow—and although there were long periods when we did not see each other, the affection was there, instantaneous when we met, and it was as though we had never been parted.

Poor girl, Joanna had gone through a terrible ordeal. She told me how Tancred had seized power and imprisoned her in the palace where, when her husband was alive, she had lived in regal splendour. Joanna was the one of my daughters who was most like me. Matilda and Eleanor were of milder dispositions; Joanna was one who would fight for her rights, and for that reason Tancred had seen fit to shut her away.

I, who had been a prisoner myself, could well sympathize with her, and I listened with great tenderness to the talk of her sufferings.

'Always,' she said, 'I thought of getting a message to Richard. I used to tell myself that had my father been alive he would have come to my rescue but I need not fear for I had a brother who was now King and who would do the same. It was wonderful when he arrived with his fleet. There were the English ships lying off the coast—a hundred galleys and fourteen large ships carrying arms and provisions. It was a marvellous sight. I knew my deliverance was at hand. The people rushed to the shore to greet them. The galleys rode in, all the banners and pennons floating on top of the spears. The fronts of the ships were painted with the knights' devices.

'And there was Richard. Oh, my lady Mother, he is so magnificent. More like a god than a man. He is so much taller than the others; he stands well above them. The trumpets rang out. Do you know what the people said of him?' ''Such a one is worthy to rule an empire. He is rightly made King over people and kingdoms. He is greater even than we have heard of him.'' How different it was when the French fleet came in.' She laughed. 'They had suffered storms and stress, and the French King was very ill. I believe he is losing his enthusiasm for the crusade.'

She went on to tell me what a difference Richard's arrival had made. He had immediately demanded that Tancred free his sister, and so afraid was Tancred that he arranged for her to join her brother, and all that he had stolen from her was restored.

'I was taken to the hospital of St John's which Tancred had arranged should be made ready, so that I might reside there in comfort. Richard came to me there. What a wonderful reunion! And with him, my lady, was the King of France. He was most gracious and complimentary to me. People were saying that he would want to marry me, but I do not think that was so.'

She was very friendly with Berengaria. Indeed, it would have been difficult to be anything else, for the girl was so eager to please. Richard had received her with a cool courtesy which sent flickers of alarm through me.

I heard, too, what had happened to him.

When he had crossed to Calais at the beginning of the journey, he met Philip Augustus at Gué St-Rémi. They had been together a while, then they parted to meet again at Dreux. They were in complete amity—lovers, I presumed. However, they swore to defend each other's kingdom as they would their own.

Richard's great desire was not only to win back Jerusalem in the name of Christendom but to make the way there safe for pilgrims.

In Gascony he was seeking Walter de Chisi who had been robbing pilgrims on their way to Compostela, and when he found him he threw him into prison and confiscated his wealth.

Richard was certainly eager to fill his treasury. He knew that crusades were often more costly than had first been realized, and he wanted to make sure that he was not impeded by lack of money. Whenever he saw a chance of adding to his resources, he took it with both hands; and when he came to Sicily and found his sister in distress, he felt that it was his duty not only to rescue her but to fill his coffers at the same time. Such a purpose was worth a little delay, a little divergence from the main project.

He knew that for years King William had been collecting money because he himself planned to go on a crusade. Where was that money? It was said that, when he knew he was dying, William had left the money to his father-in-law, Henry of England, for Henry at that time had vowed to go on a crusade. Richard now claimed the money. It had been saved for a crusade. He was the leader of this one, and the money was rightly his, as he was his father's heir.

Finally something was settled with Tancred about the money, and Richard promised that Tancred's daughter should marry Arthur of Brittany, the posthumous son of his brother Geoffrey, whom he had named as his heir in the event of his having no children of his own. So there was no fighting between Richard and Tancred. Tancred was too wise to enter into that kind of conflict with the mighty Richard; and in any case Richard had what he wanted without it.

Tancred, a mischievous man, had done his best to drive a wedge between the French and English Kings. He had tried to get Philip Augustus to side with him against Richard. Philip Augustus, however, declined to betray his friend.

All this time there was between the Kings of France and England this tiresome matter of Alais. Philip Augustus thought that Richard ought to marry her. He wanted to see his sister Queen of England. It was no use Richard's protesting that he had no desire to marry at all, certainly not one who had been his father's mistress and very likely borne his child. There was something indecent about it. He would not have it.

Philip Augustus said this was nonsense. Alais was a Princess of France. She had been kept more or less in captivity by Richard's father. It was Richard's duty to right the wrong his father had done her and marry her.

Richard said he would not. Philip Augustus said he must.

Unable to snare Philip Augustus into treacherous intrigue against Richard, Tancred tried to incriminate the French King in Richard's eyes.

Richard said to me: 'I did not in my heart believe Tancred. But he showed me letters which he said Philip Augustus had written to him. In these letters it was suggested that he and Tancred had plotted against me. I guessed the letters were forgeries.'

'Tancred is a dangerous man.'

'We are all dangerous men, Mother.'

'But you did not believe that Philip Augustus would work against you!'

'It is what was suggested. But it was clumsily done. I did not believe that of Philip Augustus. But I made him think I did. He was so angry that I should have doubted him. To tell the truth, I was heartily tired of the subject of Alais. He would not leave it alone. He was always bringing it up. I quarrelled with him. I told him our friendship was at an end. He had betrayed me, I said, and therefore I was freed from the bond which bound me to his sister. I said: "My mother will arrange for me to marry Berengaria of Navarre, and that is what I shall do." '

'So you are no longer friends?'

'Nothing will ever be the same between us.'

'That is good,' I said. 'It was not a healthy friendship. And now, Richard, you will have a wife. You must devote your time to her. I have come so far. I want the marriage to take place now.'

I saw the evasive look in his eyes.

'But it is Lent,' he said. 'A king's marriage could not take place in Lent.'

'She is here, Richard. It will have to be soon.'

'When Lent is over, we shall see about it.'

'It must be then,' I said firmly.

* * *

I was very worried about what might be happening in England and the rest of the dominions. I tried to arouse Richard's anxieties but he was so immersed in the crusade that he could not spare more than a fleeting thought for his subjects at home.

I said: 'Richard, you have only just been crowned King. It is dangerous to have left your country so soon. What will the people think?'

'They should be proud that I am fighting God's war,' he replied.

'That is a superficial emotion. They are already groaning under the taxes which they paid to finance it. Primarily people are interested in that which is happening to *them*. And what of John?'

'Well, what of John?'

'Do you realize that he wants the crown?'

'He has no chance. Arthur is the undisputed heir.'

'That is the trouble. John thinks he is the heir, as his father's son. He is trying to persuade others that this is so.'

'If they believe him, they will be traitors.'

'That may be. But John is there, and many will not want a foreign boy to be heir to the throne. The situation is full of danger. If you were there, all would be well. Your father would never have gone away and left his kingdom unless he had to.'

'And look what he came to.'

'For the main part he ruled wisely and well. It was only because he was old and ill and heartbroken and because his sons were against him that he died as he did.'

'I do not intend to go his way. I shall be able to fight for my kingdom if necessary.'

'But it must not be necessary. Richard, I must go back. For your sake I must watch over England and Normandy and the rest of the provinces.'

'If you were there, I should know all was well.'

I sighed. 'I had wished to see you married.'

'After Lent, dear Mother.'

'Will you promise me that you will marry Berengaria as soon as Lent is over? We cannot have her here like this . . . unmarried. Sancho will take offence.'

'I promise.'

I was relieved. I knew he would keep his promise.

'You will be leaving ere long,' I said. 'Joanna can act as

companion to Berengaria. It will be better that the two of them are together.'

'It shall be.'

'John and Longchamp are bickering together. Longchamp was not a good choice, Richard.'

'Perhaps not. But . . .'

'I know. He paid a good price for the post.' I shook my head. 'This crusade is an obsession with you, Richard. I hope it does not destroy you.'

'Destroy me! My dear Mother, I am going to free Jerusalem for the glory of God.'

'It may be necessary to curb Longchamp. Have I your authority to deal as I think fit with them all?'

'You have.'

'And Geoffrey the Bastard? He is a good man. I believe John is trying to win him to his side. He should have the See of York. Your father always meant him to. I want to do all I can to get him installed in the post.'

'Do as you think fit. I know that will be the wisest and best for me. You have my complete trust.'

'And I have your word that the marriage will take place as soon as Lent is over?'

'You have.'

'Then I must return.'

I said a fond farewell to Richard.

'My heart goes with you,' I said. 'And I long for the day when I shall see you again.'

He replied that he would think of me and he placed the care of his kingdom in my hands because I was the one whom he loved and esteemed beyond all others.

I was gratified, honoured and touched, but I wished he had shown a little more enthusiasm for his marriage with Berengaria.

It was a sad parting with Joanna. 'Such a brief meeting,' I said, 'after all these years. Sometimes I wish I had been born in humble circumstances so that I could have my family about me.' I kissed her tenderly. I went on: 'Take care of Berengaria. She needs your care. She will soon be your sister in truth, for the marriage with Richard is going to take place as soon as Lent is over.'

Joanna was wise and worldly. She understood that Richard was not eager for marriage and she was quite fond of Berengaria in a protective kind of way. I was glad of that.

Berengaria clung to me. She adored Richard and was happy at the prospect of marrying him, but she was a little afraid of him. He was not exactly an ardent lover, although always courteous to her in a detached way. She was proud of him because everywhere he went people deferred to him; there could never have been a doubt that he was the leader of them all. But I daresay she wished he would have shown a little tenderness towards her.

However, I must leave them. But for the urgent need to get Richard married I should not be here now. I was deeply worried about John and the incompetence of Longchamp; and in such a mood I set out on the long journey back.

When I arrived in Rome, I was received by Pope Celestine III, who was gracious and helpful over the See of York. He agreed with me that, as it had been the wish of the late King that his son Geoffrey should have it, illegitimate though he was, this should be done. I did explain that Geoffrey had always been treated as a member of the family and brought up in the royal nursery; he had been a good and faithful son and was with his father at his death.

'Then he is your Archbishop of York,' said the Pope.

I was very tired and feeling my age. But I had achieved a great deal. I had taken Berengaria to Richard and he had given his word that he would marry her. I did not believe he would break that word; and I had settled this matter of the See of York.

Now I must rest awhile in Rouen, where I could be watchful of what was happening in Normandy and across the Channel.

It was a good task done, but my work was by no means completed.

It soon emerged that there could be plenty to disturb me.

John, of course, was bent on worming his way into power. He was spreading rumours that Richard had no intention of returning from the Holy Land and would doubtless become King of Jerusalem.

He was quarrelling with Longchamp.

Geoffrey, who had been in Normandy, attempted to return to

England to take up his new post and was arrested on Longchamp's orders and put into prison in Dover.

John, who looked upon Longchamp as his enemy, seized the opportunity this offered; he had the bishops and barons on his side and they, with the justiciars, summoned Longchamp to appear before them and defend his conduct. Longchamp made use of the time-honoured excuse of illness and did not appear. He was forthwith excommunicated by the bishops. Meanwhile Longchamp tried to ingratiate himself with John and agreed to stand trial, but when he realized that his enemies were determined to be rid of him, he decided it would be wise to leave the country.

His escape turned out to be quite a comic interlude. Fearing that he might be prevented from leaving the country, he disguised himself as a woman. He wore a rather showy gown and was mistaken for a harlot. One of the sailors made advances to him; there was a scuffle, and during it the sailor became aware of his sex. He shouted to his companions that this was no woman but a man. They gathered round, pulling at his clothes and taking off his wig.

He was held a prisoner until he gave up the keys of the Tower and Windsor which he held as Chancellor; and then he was allowed to depart.

In France Longchamp made his way to Paris, where he sought out a cardinal friend, explained his plight and begged the cardinal to help him to an audience with me so that he could tell me of the troubles which were being stirred up by my son John.

As I was well aware of the troubles John was stirring up, I saw a good way of ridding the country of the arrogant and incompetent Chancellor, and I turned a deaf ear to his pleading.

What I needed more than anything was to hear that Richard was married. News was so difficult to come by. But at last messengers arrived and then I felt more contented than I had for a long time. Richard and Berengaria had been married in Limassol, on the island of Cyprus. We were over the first hurdle; now I wanted to hear more than ever that a son had been born to them.

I was horrified when I heard of their adventures. None knew better than I the dangers they would be facing. But at least I was comforted by the knowledge that they were safe so far. I thanked

God that my practical, indomitable Joanna was there to look after Berengaria.

They had sailed from Sicily in their fleet of ships—Richard taking up the rear, a lantern at the poop of his favourite vessel, the *Trenc-the-Mere*, in which he was travelling. Berengaria was not in his ship as he had said that they were not yet married and it would be improper for her to be with him. She was travelling with Joanna.

Good Friday dawned. The wind had risen and was blowing angry clouds across the sky and Richard, speaking through the large trumpet he kept for the purpose, warned his fleet to be prepared for storms. When they came, it was difficult for the ships to keep together; the sails were useless, and Richard's voice was lost in the roar of the wind. The storm continued for some hours and when it was over Richard decided that they must call in at Crete to assess the damage to some of his ships. Then to his horror he noticed that some ships were missing, among them his treasure ship and the one in which Joanna and Berengaria were sailing.

I suffered with them when I heard how they had thought their last moment had come. Richard should have had them in his ship. Who cared for propriety at such times? But perhaps it was not propriety in Richard's case. I could well imagine he wanted a little respite from the adoring Berengaria.

However, when the storm abated, the ship in which Joanna and Berengaria were sailing was still afloat and before them was the island of Cyprus. While they lay at anchor, they were made aware of the precariousness of their position, for a party of English sailors rowed out to them with a story which set them tingling with alarm. They had been in one of the other ships which the storm had cast up on this coast. The Cypriots had helped them salvage what they could from the vessel, but when the goods were safely ashore, the islanders had taken possession of them and put the sailors into prison. When they heard that an English ship was lying off the coast, they had escaped from their prison, found a boat and rowed out to warn their compatriots what would happen to them if they came ashore.

Berengaria and Joanna were frightened. Here they were, off the coast of Cyprus and no sign of Richard. While they were wondering what would happen to them, they saw a small boat rowing out towards the ship. In it was a very splendidly attired naval man, who told them that the Emperor Isaac Comnenus knew who they were and would like to offer them hospitality. Would they therefore allow him to take them ashore?

I was glad that Joanna was there. Having heard the tale the English sailors had to tell, she was wary. She knew that, if she and Berengaria were captive in the hands of Isaac Comnenus, a big ransom could be demanded for them. The last thing Richard would want to do was spend money on them!

She said: 'Please bring the Emperor to us.'

'He is so eager to honour you,' she was told, 'that he wants to entertain you in his palace.'

Joanna said that they needed time to consider the invitation. They needed time to recover from their ordeal at sea.

'The Emperor will have luxurious apartments prepared for you,' they were told.

Joanna was adamant. They needed time to make ready. They knew that the Emperor would understand, and they thanked him most warmly for his consideration.

Clever Joanna! I tremble to think what would have happened had Berengaria been alone. I was sure she would have trusted the wily Emperor.

The captain of the vessel was greatly relieved that the ladies had avoided accepting the invitation. Later that day some of the shipwrecked sailors who had been imprisoned were fighting their way to the shore; several of them escaped and came out in little boats. They all had the same story to tell: they had salvaged the goods on their ships and these had been seized and they themselves taken away to prison and left to starve. They had been desperate and when they heard that an English ship was close by, they had broken free and made their way to it.

The weather did not improve. Each day they looked eagerly for Richard; each day they wondered how long they would be allowed to remain in peace. Fortunately the bad weather was a help to them. The Emperor was hurt that his invitation had not been accepted, said more messengers; they hinted that continued rejection might anger him.

Their fear increased. They had been three days there when they saw troops massing on the shore, and they thought the Emperor was preparing to attack the ship.

Then one morning they awoke to great joy. Richard, with his fleet, was coming to them. When they heard the trumpet from the *Trenc-the-Mere*, their relief and excitement were overwhelming.

It was Isaac Comnenus's turn to be afraid. The situation would be quite different now.

Richard was furious when he heard that the salvaged goods had been confiscated and his sailors imprisoned. His men were weary; many had been sea-sick; but he was going into battle. He rallied them; their comrades had been ill-treated by Isaac Comnenus, who was no friend to crusaders. They came ashore. They had no horses. A peasant was riding by. Richard seized him, took his horse and mounted it. Richard on horseback brandishing his sword was a sight to strike terror into those who opposed him. This was the fabulous Coeur de Lion. Few could stand against him. Certainly not Isaac Comnenus. Soon Richard had put his enemies to flight.

He went to the fort and spoke to the people, telling them he came in peace not war. He did not want to quarrel with them, only with their Emperor who had stolen his goods and ill-treated his men, and he would be punished for this. But Richard was not at war with them. The only war he wanted to fight was a holy war.

The people were submissive; the Emperor's rule was harsh and they had little love for him; and they were overawed, as all must be, by the sight of Richard.

It was in Limassol that Richard married Berengaria.

I knew I could trust him to keep his promise to me. Joanna wrote and told me about it. I was glad she did for she told me in more detail than the others would have.

The people were pleased to have a royal wedding in their town. The romantic situation appealed to them. Moreover, Richard was such an impressive figure. I doubt any of them had ever seen a man so handsome; Berengaria was a charming bride, and the fact that she had travelled from Navarre and had made the hazardous journey to her future husband was intriguing.

Of course, the Archbishop of Canterbury should perform the ceremony, but on this occasion it was quite out of the question, and Richard's chaplain Nicholas would have to serve instead. I daresay it occurred to Richard that there might be a possibility of postponing the wedding until he returned to England that the Archbishop of Canterbury might officiate, but he must have remembered his promise to me.

This was something more than a wedding for, having driven Isaac Comnenus several miles inland, Richard had decided to crown himself King of Cyprus. Thus he would make Cyprus safe for pilgrims. He had always said that making the way safe was as important as getting to Jerusalem itself. Many pilgrims had set out and many had been lost on the way, through the treachery of those through whose land they had had to pass. Now he was making Cyprus safe, there should be both a wedding and a coronation.

Joanna said that Berengaria looked very charming with her long hair parted in the centre; she wore a transparent veil held in place by a jewel. She was so happy that she looked quite beautiful in her long white gown. Richard looked godlike. Joanna rhapsodized over his appearance. She had never seen any man so splendid. His great height, his Nordic looks, his imperious manner were such as to make people worship him. They were ready to believe in his divinity; and since he had told them that he wished them no ill, they accepted him gladly, for Isaac Comnenus was far from a benevolent ruler.

Richard walked to the church, one of his splendidly apparelled knights going before him, leading his horse, whose saddle glittered with jewels. The people crowded into the feast and, when they saw this godlike being playing the lute so sweetly and singing to accompany it, they thought it was indeed a visitation from Heaven.

So at last they were married. Joanna knew my thoughts, and she added that after the feasting the bride and groom were conducted to their tent. In Joanna's opinion all ended satisfactorily.

I pray Berengaria be fruitful soon, I said to myself.

The wedding celebrations had been brief. I supposed Richard was more interested in the conquest of Cyprus; and Isaac Comnenus was not a straightforward person to deal with. Richard had announced that Isaac was his vassal and that he would rule Cyprus under him; but as he was committed to leave for the Holy Land, he proposed to put a deputy in charge of the island and take with him Isaac who must now muster up a company of his best soldiers.

On the morning when they were due to depart, Isaac had disappeared. He clearly had no intention of going to the Holy Land. He did not consider Richard ruler of his island; he had merely appeared to capitulate in order to gain time.

But Isaac was no match for Richard, even though, during the fighting, Richard was taken ill with the return of the ague which plagued him from time to time. That he should be enfeebled angered him, but when the fever was on him there was nothing he could do but rest.

Urgent messages were coming from the King of France. Where was Richard? Why was he not with him? Was he or was he not supposed to be leading the crusade?

The King of France would have to learn that one of the greatest tasks facing the crusaders was to make the way safe for pilgrims, and that was what Richard was doing. In his messages Philip referred to him as Duke of Normandy, implying that he was ordering Richard to obey him. That always infuriated Richard as it had Henry. He sent a message back to say that the King of England would come in his own good time and took orders from no one.

But he was eager to go. He was afraid that Philip Augustus would take Acre without him.

He set two men whom he could trust to administer the island. Isaac was in silver chains, and his daughter was in the care of Joanna and Berengaria. So Richard set sail.

The Cyprus adventure had delayed him considerably; but he had made the way safer for pilgrims, and his fame had increased.

Now he was ready to join forces with Philip Augustus and to throw himself into the all-important battle for Acre.

The Road to Châlus

The months were passing. Christmas was upon us. News came that the key town of Acre had fallen to the Christians. I was delighted. This would mean that they were ready to march on Jerusalem. I prayed that their crusade would soon have achieved its purpose and Richard would be back with us.

I spent Christmas at Bonneville-sur-Touques. It was very quiet but I was in no mood for merriment. I was very anxious about Richard. I was sure the climate he was enduring would bring little good to his health, and I was uneasy about England and the French provinces.

Then I had disquietening news. A *jongleur* came to the castle. He had been in Paris and could tell us that Philip Augustus had returned home from the crusade.

'He is very ill, my lady,' I was told. 'His hair has fallen out and his nails are dropping off.'

'Was it some pestilential fever?'

'No one knows. He said he was forced to return home because of the treachery of the King of England.'

'This is nonsense,' I said. 'He is more likely to be treacherous than my son.'

'It is what he is saying, my lady. He says that the Franks captured Acre and that Richard Plantagenet would take all the credit for it.'

'A likely story. How dare he!'

'The people of Paris are giving him a hero's welcome.'

I was very uneasy. They must have quarrelled, and this, like most lovers' quarrels, would be violent. I knew Philip Augustus was jealous of Richard. How could he help it? Philip Augustus was a wily King; he could be more devious than Richard; but he lacked Richard's charisma; he was no Coeur de Lion. I had heard it said that, as soon as they saw Richard, men clustered about him and were ready to go wherever he led. That must have been galling to Philip Augustus. It was true he had loved Richard but that was one part of himself; the rest was all king, and kings of France would always regard kings of England as their natural enemies.

Philip Augustus was saying that his illness was a result of poison and, in view of his relationship with Richard, had half suggested that Richard was behind the attempt to poison him.

I thought the quarrel must have gone very deep.

Philip Augustus was determined to show his anger. He went into Normandy and at Gisors demanded that his sister Alais be returned to him. The Seneschal refused to give her up. I supported him in this. Alais must remain where she was for a time. I did not want more stories spread about her seduction by Henry and her desertion by Richard.

It looked to me as though we might be at war with France and, with Richard far away, that was the last thing I wanted.

However, I was mistaken. Having just returned from what was evidently an exhausting experience and being truly very sick, Philip Augustus had no stomach for war at such a time.

I should have looked elsewhere for trouble.

Messengers came from England with disturbing information. My son John was spreading the fabrication that his brother Richard had no intention of coming home, and as the people could not continue without a king, he, the late King's son, was ready to be crowned. For this purpose he would need allies. He must have heard of the quarrel between Philip Augustus and Richard, and the French King was just the ally for him. With Richard away and with the French King's help, it should be an easy matter to take the crown. What revenge for Philip Augustus! What glory for John!

Now I was really worried. I could no longer stay in France. I must go to England with all speed.

It was February—just about the worst time of year to cross the treacherous Channel, but no matter, I must go.

I suffered the journey and made my way to Windsor, where I summoned all the barons and the clergy to come to me.

When they were assembled, I said: 'I have information that my son John is gathering together a fleet and an army of mercenaries. His object is to go to France and solicit the help of the French King in gaining the crown. He is ready to give up certain overseas possessions in return for this help; and Philip Augustus is ready to give it. I have heard that he is offering John his daughter Adela in marriage and proposing to give her all Richard's Continental lands.'

The Council was grave. They did not approve of the King's absenting himself from his country. He was asking for trouble in doing so. But by now they knew something of John's character, and the last thing they wanted was for him to usurp the throne. They agreed with me that it must be stopped. The best way to do this was to threaten to seize all John's English lands the moment he attempted to cross the sea.

Sullen and angry, John knew he dared not leave the country. He went down to his castle of Wallingford to brood over the wrongs he had suffered.

But I knew this would not be the end of his endeavours. I had to be watchful all the time.

I did immediately despatch a messenger to Richard telling him he must come home. His throne was in danger. We had foiled John once, but we might not be able to do it again. John was obstinate and he longed to get possession of the crown. He was unstable and cruel. It is sad to have to admit this of one's son but it was true. I was glad that the barons were aware of it.

But we had a mighty enemy in the King of France. His love for Richard had turned sour, and there is never greater hatred than that which has grown out of an old love.

News came in now and then from the Holy Land. Richard was going from success to success. His name was continually mentioned. He was the hero of the Third Crusade. I was sure that it was he and his men, not Philip Augustus and the French, who had taken Acre.

There was talk of a mighty Saracen warrior who it was said was a match for Coeur de Lion. His name was Saladin. There were stories of a meeting between the leaders. Saladin was as outstanding among the Saracens as Richard among the Christians. It was certain that two such men would have the utmost respect for each other.

Richard's illness persisted. There were bouts of ague and fever. I think they were his real enemies.

Richard and Saladin had come to a point when they must make terms, and Saladin's brother wanted to marry Joanna. I was outraged at the thought; so, it seemed, was Joanna. But Richard apparently was so impressed by Saladin that it did not occur to him that the proposition was not acceptable. Why should not Christian and Saracen love each other rather than make war? Joanna might convert Malek Adel to Christianity. But what, I asked, if Malek Adel made a Moslem of Joanna?

Inevitably it came to nothing. I could imagine Joanna's rage at the suggestion.

There had been a truce. Saladin would not surrender Jerusalem, but he allowed the Christians to make pilgrimages to the holy shrines when they wished, and he gave them a strip of the coast between Jaffa and Tyre so that they could travel unmolested.

Many of the crusaders went to Jerusalem and worshipped at the shrines. Richard did not go.

He was reputed to have begged the Lord not to let him set eyes on Jerusalem: he had set out to deliver the Holy City from the enemies of Christianity, and in this he had failed, so he should be denied a sight of it. He had made the way easier for pilgrims, but that was all his campaigning and tremendous expense had been able to achieve. His greatest enemy had been the ague and the fever, from which he suffered still; they had plagued him just when he should have been going into battle.

He respected Saladin, and Saladin respected him, but he had failed in his mission, and he could see there was no use in continuing. It was time to go home.

My relief was intense. So now he would come back and I could hand over the reins of government to him. I need not lie awake wondering what mischief was brewing in John's mind.

I was an old woman. It was time I had a little rest.

I was planning that Richard should be home for Christmas. I was happy and excited. There should be minstrels and the music he loved. How I longed to see him again.

Berengaria would be with him. Was she pregnant? What joy there would be if she were!

I was very happy.

But Richard did not come home for Christmas.

The weeks passed and still he did not come. I began to realize that something was wrong.

Each day I waited for news. Tension was rising. I knew that John was biding his time. Where was Richard? Why did he not come back home? We had known that he was on his way, but why did he not come?

Something terrible had happened. It was frustrating to live in ignorance. He had just disappeared without trace.

I think that was the most agonizing period of my life. I had seen many tragedies, but this, wrapped in mystery as it was, seemed the hardest to bear.

I needed him. The country needed him. He must return soon or all England, all Normandy and his possessions in France would be thrown into confusion. The people were becoming restive. What sort of king was this to desert his country and go off to fight in other lands? And now the fighting was over, why did he not come home?

Joanna and Berengaria had arrived safely in Rome. They had sailed on the same day as Richard but not in his ship. I could glean nothing from them. They had not seen Richard since they left the Holy Land.

It was the same story whichever way I turned.

Richard had simply disappeared.

Then one day Richard's chaplain, Anselm, arrived at Court. He had a tale to tell which threw a faint glimmer of light on the mystery. This was the story he told me.

When Richard had arrived in Acre after leaving Cyprus, the French King, who had been eagerly awaiting his arrival, was overjoyed to see him. He made a significant gesture by wading out to the galley in which Berengaria had been sailing, lifting her in his arms and carrying her ashore so that she need not get her feet wet. That implied that all animosity over Alais was at an end.

The two Kings embraced affectionately. Now the conquest of Acre seemed certain. It had been inspiring to see the effect Richard had on the men. He looked magnificent, of course. They cheered him, the sick rose from their beds, and they cried:

'Coeur de Lion is here. Now we shall be victorious.' There were men from Germany, Italy and Spain as well as from France.

Now the Kings of France and England conferred together and planned to march on Jerusalem once Acre had fallen. Philip Augustus warned Richard of the mighty Saladin. Moreover, the Saracens had a deadly weapon which they called Greek Fire. Richard knew of this: he had encountered it before. It was sulphur, wine and pitch mixed together with Persian gum and oil, which produced an almost inextinguishable fire. A mixture of vinegar and sand was the only substance that appeared to be of any use against it—and that not very successfully. Greek Fire had impeded progress considerably.

Richard had a new contrivance with him called Mate Griffon. It was a tower on wheels which could be run up against a castle wall, so that men on top could step onto the castle and take it. It was easier than battering the way in.

They planned the assault on Acre. Richard wanted to perfect his weapons before they began. There was a mangonel, a machine which threw stones high in the air so that they fell into a city, causing great damage. This was jocularly called 'the Bad Neighbour'. The Saracens invented a machine to throw the stones back which they called the 'Bad Kinsman'.

In the midst of these preparations Richard was attacked by the ague and fever. Anselm had no need to tell me of his frustration. He was really ill. Berengaria and Joanna nursed him. Berengaria was delighted to look after him, for when he was well she scarcely saw him and she was deeply enamoured of him.

The King would have liked them to wait until he was well before they began the assault, but that was not possible. He could not, however, be prevailed upon to stay in his tent while the battle was going on. He ordered that a litter be brought and he was taken out on it; he shouted his orders to his men; but to see Richard the Lionheart in such a state robbed them of their spirit.

The battle ceased temporarily and the siege was still unbroken. The strangest thing happened then. Richard had heard a great deal about Saladin. His followers saw him and immediately believed in victory. It was the same as with Richard. But Richard was sick, and it was said that he was near to death.

The two men were very much aware of each other. Richard

was eager to meet Saladin. He knew that he had a formidable enemy and that in his state he could not hope to compete with him. Richard's view of Philip Augustus as a soldier was not great. He might score in diplomacy but the battlefield was another matter. Richard knew that Acre could not be taken with Philip Augustus in command.

He must meet Saladin and see if some terms could be arranged. Saladin was not only a great fighter but a man of honour. He was too fine a man to show meanness or pettiness, and he and Richard respected each other as one great leader did another. They instinctively knew certain things about each other because they were so much alike. Richard sent a messenger to Saladin's camp asking if he would meet him.

Saladin's reply was that he could not talk with the King of England except over food and drink, and if they ate together as friends, how could they fight each other?

The messengers were allowed to return to their camps unharmed.

Then this strange thing happened. Richard was in his bed, prostrate with fever, when one of the guards came to tell him that a messenger was without and wished to speak with him.

'Bring him in,' said Richard.

The guard did so and remained, suspecting treachery. Richard commanded him to leave.

The messenger leaned over Richard and touched his brow.

'You know who I am,' he said.

There was such accord between them that Richard had no hesitation in answering: 'You are Saladin.'

'I am Saleh-ed-Din,' he said.

'Why do you come to me on my bed of sickness?'

'Because I have a talisman which can cure you.'

'We are fighting against each other.'

'You are my enemy on the battlefield. In the sick-room you are my friend.'

'Is it possible to be both?'

'We will prove it to be.'

He held a stone object in his hand. The King was helpless before his enemy but he had no fear. It might have been an assassin's dagger which was held over him, but, helpless as he was, Richard believed that this man had come in friendship.

When the stone was laid on Richard's brow, he was aware of a coolness sweeping over him. He felt a little better.

'You need chicken and fruit. You do not have them in your camp. They shall be sent to you.'

'This is beyond belief.'

'There is much that is beyond belief.'

'But why . . . why?'

'You are a great warrior.'

'Better for your cause that I should die here miserably like this.'

'No. You may die in battle. So may I. That is what is intended for us. I want to face you out there. It is decreed that we shall be enemies. We might have been friends . . . and for this night we are. You serve your God and I serve mine. Perhaps it was your God who sent me here tonight and my God who bade me come.'

He laid a cool hand on Richard's brow.

'You speak strange words,' said Richard, 'but I feel the fever going out of me.'

'So should it be.'

'You are a brave man to come through our camp.'

'Allah protected me.'

'I shall add my protection to his. You shall not be harmed when you go back. Shall we meet again?'

'It is in the hands of Allah and perhaps your God. And now I shall go. I believe you will find the fever is past.'

Richard called his guard and told him that the messenger was to be escorted from the camp, and if any harm came to him, whoever caused it would be answerable to him.

All were surprised when that very night Richard slept peacefully, and next morning the fever was gone.

He might have thought he had had a dream, but gifts began to arrive that day. There were grapes, dates and young chickens with the compliments of the Sultan Saleh-ed-Din.

When I heard that story, I was amazed. It seemed to me so strange. I could have believed that Richard had suffered an hallucination. But then Saladin was an unusual man, as Richard was. There was some bond between them. Richard had always been an admirer of his own sex. Perhaps there was some invisible rapport between such men. They were two of the great heroes of the day. One worshipped Allah, the other the Christian

God. Perhaps the two were not so very far apart. If that were so, why this war? Why could we not sit down and come to terms about the differences? If the Saracens owned Jerusalem, why should not the Christians be able to visit the shrines in peace? And if the Christians owned it, why should they shut it to the Saracens?

However, that almost mythical meeting between the two leaders made me ponder. I must confess I doubted its authenticity, but the fact remained that from that time Richard began to recover.

Anselm's story continued. The King of France also became ill. He had been less affected than Richard but made far more of his illness. In Anselm's view he was getting very tired of the campaign. It was always thus with the crusades. People set out with such fervour, dreaming of the glorious deeds they would perform and the recognition they would get in Heaven; but when the reality was thrust upon them, it must occur to them that there were easier ways of earning eternal salvation.

As soon as Richard was well, the storming of Acre began; there were great losses on both sides, but the town, in due course, surrendered and Saladin was in retreat.

I wondered what his thoughts were at that time, and if he regretted saving Richard's life, as he appeared to have done. It was inexplicable. It was obvious that Richard was the leading spirit in the battle, and victory would not have been certain without him.

There was still the battle for Jerusalem to be fought.

An unpleasant incident occurred. When he was inspecting the walls of the city, Richard noticed the flag of Austria flying there. He demanded that the Duke of Austria be brought to him and before his eyes tore down the flag and ground his heel on it. The Duke of Austria was naturally furious at the insult, but Richard said: 'We come as Christians; we are one army; we cannot have every leader who has brought a handful of men claiming victory for his country.'

The Duke of Austria went away muttering that he would remember the insult. Richard had made a bitter enemy.

It was Philip Augustus who claimed his attention. The French King had been very ill and wanted to go home. He came to Richard and told him that he was worried about his country. A king could not remain away for so long and expect all to be well. That was true enough. I wished Richard had felt the same. Philip Augustus was longing for home. He hated being in this inhospitable land. The flies pestered him; the mosquitoes were dangerous; many had suffered from them; then there were the accursed tarantulas. Philip Augustus said that if they remained here one of them would die, and he did not intend it to be himself. He went on to say that he loved his country and his duty lay there. He was beginning to see that the task they had taken on was hopeless.

'Hopeless!' cried Richard. 'When we have just taken Acre!'

'These Mohammedans are great fighters,' argued Philip Augustus. 'Sometimes I think they are invincible.'

'We have a cause,' Richard reminded him.

'Have they not? Their Allah seems often to work better for them than God does for us.'

'That could be called blasphemy.'

'Then blasphemy is truth. I believe this man, Saladin, is a very wise one.'

'I would agree with that.'

'He is a noble enemy.'

'But the Saracens are in possession of Jerusalem. If you go now, you will break your oath.'

Philip Augustus called attention to the weight he had lost, to his thinning hair and his broken nails. 'All this I have suffered. It is God's way of telling me to go home.'

'I have been in a worse state than you have.'

'You have *always* suffered from the ague.'

'Philip Augustus, tell me, have you made up your mind to go home?'

'I will leave you some of my knights to command when I go.'

'I thought you were my friend who would want to be with me.'

'I would be no good to you dead. And what of this Saladin? Why did he send food to you when you were ill?'

'I do not know,' said Richard.

Philip Augustus looked at him suspiciously. 'They say he is a very noble-looking creature.' Richard was silent.

'And you met him?' asked Philip Augustus.

Richard told him of his experience.

'He came to your tent by night . . . uninvited?' said Philip Augustus suspiciously.

And after that there was a great coolness between them. Richard said that he could see that Philip Augustus was going to break his oath.

The French King said that his country was more important to him than anything else. 'To stay would be to condemn myself to death. I will leave you to make friends with our enemy. What of Tancred? You became friendly with him, too.'

'You have a jealous nature.'

Their friendship was considerably strained when they parted.

It became clear that Richard missed the French King. He tried to console himself with music and became greatly pleased by a young boy named Blondel de Nesle who was an excellent musician; he and Richard composed songs which they sang in harmony.

While Richard was repairing the walls of Acre, Saladin attempted to bring about a truce and sent his brother Malek Adel to Richard's camp to discuss terms. It was while he was there that Malek Adel had seen Joanna and been so impressed by her charms that he wanted to marry her. That Richard should find such a suggestion feasible told me a good deal about his respect for the Saracens. Joanna, naturally, had been indignant and the project came to nothing. There was no truce, and the battle for Jerusalem persisted.

There was a great deal of trouble among the crusaders. I suppose that was inevitable when there were so many nations involved, each trying to claim credit for his own country's achievements. Richard, as leader, managed to engender a certain amount of enmity and venom, and the task of delivering Jerusalem—daunting as it would have been without any of these disturbances—became almost impossible.

Meanwhile Richard was receiving urgent messages from me which must have given him anxiety. He had to fortify the towns he captured and garrison them to make them safe for pilgrims. It was a great task he had undertaken, and plagued as he was by bouts of recurring fever, life was not easy.

He was depressed. He was discovering more and more how formidable were his foes; and in Saladin they had a leader equal to himself. Moreover, the climate could be more easily borne by the Saracens. It was another enemy. The heat brought the perpetual flies, the poisonous insects, and with the passing of the summer came the torrential rains and the mud.

However, Richard continued to conquer towns and make them safe for pilgrims; and all the time he was plagued by my entreaties to return home.

I, who understood him so well, suffered with him. I could picture his frustration. He had thought to capture Jerusalem long before this, but Saladin was there, with a skill and valour which matched Richard's own.

There came a time when Richard intercepted a caravan full of food and ammunition on its way to Saladin's camp. That was a great achievement and must have cost the Saracens much anguish. Soon after this a great battle took place at Hebron Hills. The crusaders won the day and captured five thousand camels and mules laden with gold and silver as well as provisions.

After winning such prizes it seemed that the way was open to Jerusalem, and Richard believed he was on the point of taking the city and bringing the crusade to a glorious end. But Saladin was too clever to allow this happy conclusion to come about. He spread rumours throughout the Christian camp that, fearing their advance, he had poisoned all the drinking wells outside the Holy City.

It turned out to be not so, but Richard could not ignore such a rumour. He returned to Jaffa and by doing so lost his great chance.

Such are the fortunes of war. A successful general must win at the crucial moment, and Saladin's rumour of poisoned wells had cost Richard Jerusalem.

Richard knew there would be no easy victory. Saladin had had time to fortify the town, and the bad news from home, Richard knew, meant that if he did not return he was in danger of losing his kingdom.

There was nothing to be done but make a truce with Saladin. It was a heartbreaking finale to what was to have been a great enterprise. The peace terms were just. Richard had made it possible for pilgrims to visit Jerusalem. He himself did not visit the Holy City. He could not bear to. He cried out in his anguish: 'Sweet Lord, I entreat You, do not suffer me to see the Holy City since I am unable to deliver it from the hands of Thine enemies.'

Poor Richard! He must have felt defeated and for such a man

defeat was the worst thing that could happen. He had to admit that, after all the lives that had been lost, all the gold with which his people had supplied him, he had failed.

He was going back to his country with his mission unfulfilled.

Joanna and Berengaria went off before he did. Berengaria was often in my thoughts, and I wondered what she thought of her husband's aloofness. As far as I could gather, they had rarely been together. What hope was there of an heir? Very little, I feared.

Richard eventually sailed away. Anselm said he leaned over the rail watching until the land had disappeared and murmured: 'Oh Holy Land, I commend thee to God. May He of His mercy grant me such space of life that I may one day bring thee aid. And it is my hope and determination, by God's will, to return.'

In due course Joanna and Berengaria arrived in Rome. As for Richard, he sailed off . . . into mystery.

Richard may have failed in his mission, but his fame was known throughout the world. Everywhere people talked and sang of Richard the Lionheart. He was reckoned the greatest soldier of his age, although he had been unable to conquer another who was said to be as great as himself, Saleh-ed-Din, known throughout the Christian world as Saladin.

Anselm, who had sailed with him, had been able to tell me much up to this point.

In glowing terms he told me of the encounter with pirate ships and how Richard's courage impressed the pirates who allowed him to board their ships. Richard had decided to go home overland; he knew that he had many enemies and wished to travel incognito. He therefore sent his ships back to England while he, in the garb of a merchant, proposed to make his way across Europe. The pirates agreed, for a sum of money, to take him where he wanted to go.

Richard left Anselm on the ship, and that was the last the priest had seen of him.

I was desperately anxious. Where was he? How much better it would have been if he had stayed with the ships. How could he have thought he would be safer travelling overland dressed up as a merchant! Richard was the sort of man who could never be anything but a king and whatever garb he was in would not disguise that.

I was glad to have heard Anselm's story but frustrated that it stopped short of the vital part.

And so we waited, but news of Richard did not come.

I could not believe he was dead. I wondered how long it would be before John claimed the throne. If Richard's absence continued, the way would be clear for him. And what of Arthur? His mother, Constance, was ambitious for him. Would he attempt to claim the throne? And what would the choice of the people be? Arthur, the young foreigner of whom they knew little, or John of whom they knew too much.

And so I waited, fearful of the future.

Then one day there was news. I had very good people working for me in those Courts where I thought there might be information useful to me—and none was more important than France. Philip Augustus's love for Richard had now turned to hate, so I could expect treachery from that quarter, and I respected Philip Augustus as one of the wiliest kings in Europe. How different from his father! And for that reason I greatly feared him.

News came from the French Court that Philip Augustus had had a letter from the Holy Roman Emperor, a very good friend of his at the time, and it explained the reason for Richard's continued absence. A copy of this letter had been smuggled out of France and brought to me.

It ran as follows:

Richard the King was crossing the sea for the purpose of returning to his dominions and it so happened that the winds brought him, his ship being wrecked, to the region of Istria at a place which lies between Aquileia and Venice where, by the sanction of God, the King, having suffered shipwreck, escaped, together with a few others. A faithful subject of ours, Court Maynard of Görtz, and the people of the district, hearing that he was in our territory and calling to mind the treason and accumulated mischief he was guilty of in the Land of Promise, pursued him with the intention of making him prisoner. However, the King taking flight, they captured eight knights of his retinue. Shortly after, the King proceeded to a borough in the archbishopric of Salzburg, which is called Frisi, where Frederic de Botestowe took six of his knights. The King hastened on by night, with only three attendants, in the direction of Austria. The roads, however, being watched and guards being set on every side, our dearly beloved cousin Leopold, Duke of Austria, captured the King in a humble house in a village in the vicinity of Vienna. In as much as he is now in our power and has always done his most for your annoyance and disturbance, what we have above stated we have thought proper to notify to your nobleness . . .

Given at Creutz on the fifth day before the calends of January.

When I read this, I felt an immense relief. So he was alive! That was great cause for rejoicing. Next came the serious consideration of what we must do. We had to start to work at once for his release.

I remembered what Anselm had told me about his quarrel with Leopold of Austria, and it was very unfortunate that he had been the one to capture Richard.

What was happening to my dear son? Whatever it was, I told myself, he would be able to withstand his enemies, and they would not for long triumph over him.

But what were we to do?

It seemed that we must first find out where he was.

The news travelled fast. Soon everyone was talking about the capture of Coeur de Lion. What sort of prisoner would he be? A caged lion. I could imagine him prowling about his dungeon, his frustration, his attempts to escape; and I prayed for his safe return to me.

Why had he ever undertaken this crusade? What good had it done? Made it possible for Christians to go to Jerusalem. For how long? Saladin might honour the pact, but what of other Saracen leaders? What mistakes people make! First Henry, now Richard.

A wonderful thing happened soon after that. It was like an incident from one of the romantic ballads which used to be sung at my grandfather's Court.

Blondel de Nesle, the charming young mistrel of whom Richard had been so fond, had adored his master. When he heard that Richard was a prisoner in Austria, he went in search of him. That would seem almost laughable—a young man with nothing but an exquisite voice and a musical talent to set himself such a task. His method of search was original. He would rely on his talents. He went to Austria, knowing only two things: his beloved King was a prisoner and he was in a castle in that country. With the confidence of youth and the spur of devotion, Blondel set forth on what most people would have said was an impossible task.

He travelled through Austria and sang outside every castle he could find. I could imagine his strong voice carrying over the air. He sang a song which he loved beyond all others because he and the King had composed it together. No one had sung it but those two. It was in the form of a duet.

Blondel sang this song beneath the walls of castles and one day when he sang he heard a voice taking up the duet. They sang in unison; then each took his part.

There was no doubt that Blondel had found the King.

He came home with speed. One could hardly credit the story, yet it was true. No one knew that song but Blondel and Richard; and Blondel would know the King's voice anywhere.

Richard was a captive in the tower of Dürrenstein Castle. He was in the hands of a bitter enemy but at least we knew he was still alive.

John was furious that Richard had been found. He had been fervently hoping that his brother was dead. He had already gone to Normandy, declaring himself King of England and Duke of Normandy. I was glad the Norman barons rejected him. Then he had gone to Paris and become a close ally of Philip Augustus.

I had to bring Richard home somehow.

Now that the news that he was incarcerated in Dürrenstein was broken, he had been taken out of Leopold's hands and delivered into those of Henry Hohenstaufen, the Holy Roman Emperor.

I knew what would happen next. A ransom would be demanded. How delighted Richard's enemies must be! It was not so much the King himself whom they hated but the power of the Plantagenets. The Emperor, Philip Augustus, Leopold of Austria and the rest had seen that empire extending over Europe. It had been the realization of Henry's dream. They wanted to smash it, and they thought to do so by demanding a ransom that would cripple not only England but the French provinces as well.

Richard was taken to Haguenau—no longer the prisoner of the petty Duke of Austria but of the Holy Roman Emperor—

and the ransom asked was 100,000 silver marks. Two hundred hostages would have to be submitted until the money was paid, and those hostages must be from the noblest families in England and Normandy.

I could hardly believe it when I heard it. How could we raise such an amount? But we should have to do so. The people were already complaining of the taxation necessary to finance the crusade. How much better it would have been if that money had been used for England's needs, and Richard had remained at home.

But at least we could now communicate with him. He wrote to me, his beloved mother. What joy it gave me to read his letters! He had seen a draft of that letter which the Emperor had written to the King of France, and he was indignant. There were other matters, too, which annoyed him. He wanted to know why he should be held in captivity like a common thief. He had not taken Jerusalem, and that was held against him. He would have taken it but for the treachery at home in England which had made it necessary for him to return. Philip Augustus had slandered him. This was due to pure jealousy because the King of France had broken his oath and, being unable to endure the hardships of the crusade, had shirked them. He was angry because he, Richard, had been more successful in battle.

This was true, of course, but I thought it wiser to hold back recrimination until after his release.

It was a busy time that followed. I had to think of every means of raising money. And what a difficult task it was! It was not so long since we were making demands for the crusade. Richard was proving an expensive monarch. But it had to be; England was unsafe while Richard was a prisoner. John was not to be trusted, and now that Philip Augustus had become Richard's vicious enemy we were in danger. I gathered together a council of barons and clergy and we decided on new taxes. We had to ask for a quarter of their income from all men; a fee of 20 shillings from every knight; and we must have gold and silver from every abbey and church in the country; the Cistercians, who had no gold and silver but whose wealth was in sheep, must contribute a year's wool. No one could escape.

All through those anxious weeks, the waggons came into London with their goods, and they were all placed in coffers and stored in St Paul's Cathedral.

While I was calculating the accumulation of the ransom, I had to be watchful of John. He was with Philip Augustus and was offering him parts of Normandy and Touraine if he would make him ruler of all Plantagenet territory in France. I was relieved that the people of Normandy had rejected him, and I succeeded in getting the barons' agreement to confiscate his English territory so that he could not offer that as bribes to the King of France; while Normandy remained loyal, John was a pest rather than a menace.

That had been a year I would never forget, and I hoped never to pass through another like it. It was December before the ransom was ready. It was loaded onto one of the ships. I must go to deliver it. I would not let such a task be left to anyone else.

I took with me a company of all the highest in the land and arrived at Speyer in January. There I learned that there had to be a delay. I could not imagine why. We had the ransom for which they had asked. What more did they want from us?

To my horror it transpired that Philip Augustus and my son John had offered an equal sum to the Emperor if he would keep Richard prisoner. I was appalled by such venom from Richard's one-time great friend and his own brother, and I was amazed that the Emperor could contemplate acting so dishonourably, after having settled terms with which we had complied.

Fortunately the Emperor's advisers were also shocked by the idea of accepting money to keep Richard prisoner, and they prevailed upon him not to tarnish his reputation by such an act. He therefore declared that he would release Richard if he would be a vassal of the Holy Roman Empire.

I was able to see Richard. He took me in his arms and we embraced warmly.

'It is so wonderful to see you,' I cried. 'I would never let myself believe you were dead . . . but it was hard sometimes, Richard.'

'One of the hardest things to bear in my captivity was the thought of the anxiety I was causing you,' he replied.

'Let me look at you. You don't appear to have suffered much.'

"It is true. This climate has suited me better than that of Acre, and Dürrenstein was more comfortable than the Holy Land.'

'It was wonderful the way young Blondel found you.'

Richard laughed. 'I thought I was dreaming. To hear that pure young voice out there. Then I knew who it was . . . and I answered in song. Thank God I have a good strong voice.'

'I have rewarded Blondel.'

'I am glad of that.'

'Oh, it is good that we have found you. John . . .'

'I know of John. He is a young fool . . . urged on by Philip Augustus.'

'He hates you now, Richard.'

'I know. It is the way of the man.'

'And now the Emperor wants to make you a vassal.'

'I will never agree.'

'But the alternative . . . to stay here. It is what he demands, and remember he is in a position to demand.'

'I will never do it.'

'I have had consultations with the justiciar. The act would be quite meaningless. It would be considered illegal.'

'Then why does he ask it?'

'He is a proud man. He wants to see Coeur de Lion kneel before him.'

'I cannot do it, Mother.'

'Do you want to remain a prisoner? Do you want to let John take over your kingdom? John as King . . . can you imagine that? The Emperor is on good terms with Philip Augustus. Think of what they might concoct between them.'

'Do you mean kneel to him? Make myself a vassal?'

'It is meaningless and will bring about your release.'

'It is hard to do it.'

'Never mind if it brings your freedom. Better to pretend to humiliate yourself for a few moments than lose everything you have.'

He did at last see the point of this but before paying homage to the Emperor he defended himself before those who had accused him of treachery and accumulated mischief, and with such skill and grace did he do this that the Emperor was moved to tears. He went to Richard and embraced him.

Thus, after being a prisoner for a year and six weeks, Richard was free.

On a March day we landed at Sandwich and on our way to London passed Canterbury to give thanks at the shrine of St Thomas à Becket.

London gave a great welcome to the returning King. There

were banners everywhere and singing and dancing and general rejoicing. For this day the citizens had forgotten what it had cost to bring him out of captivity. He was the returning hero; he might not have captured Jerusalem but he had been acclaimed wherever he went . . . Coeur de Lion, the greatest warrior the world knew. Richard was made for pageantry. He stood out against all others with his magnificent height and dazzling fair looks; his godlike appearance made of him a natural hero.

So the return of the King was celebrated.

But there was one who was not there to welcome him: his brother John. I guessed he was in Paris, gnashing his teeth with Philip Augustus, asking himself what his best move would be.

It was wonderful to be with my beloved son. Now that he was home, I told him, he must not go away again; and I think he agreed with me. Prison had had its effect on him. But, of course, he was an adventurer by nature.

'You must now show yourself to your subjects,' I told him. 'You have been too little in England. The English want to see their King. We shall make a tour of the countryside. It is the perfect time of the year to do this. Spring is the best time in England.'

He was very grateful to me for all I had done. He knew that I, and I alone, had kept his kingdom intact during his absence, and he was fully aware of what a difficult task it had been. He was ready to take my advice.

There followed a happy time for me. We were together, as close as ever. We talked freely and frankly. He told me how he had travelled across Europe disguised as a merchant.

'I called myself Hugo of Damascus. It was interesting to stay in inns and to hear the talk of how King Richard was travelling in disguise across the country. One innkeeper told us that he would have to report our presence to the governor because we were strangers and they were told they must be watchful everywhere for the King in disguise.'

'That should have been a warning to you.'

'It was. Then there was Roger.' His eyes were soft, he was smiling. 'I wish you could have met Roger. He was such a charming fellow. I knew him for a Norman as soon as I saw him; he had the fair looks and long limbs of a Viking.'

'One of your own kind,' I said.

'We met on the road. He asked us where our destination was

and we told him England. He then said that we could spend a
night or two at his castle. I liked the man on sight. Do you know,
dear Mother, I trusted him. The others did not. They were very
suspicious. But then they were suspicious of everyone.'

'And rightly so.'

'Yes, indeed, rightly so. But there was a feeling between
myself and Roger. I knew he would not betray us.'

'Because of his handsome looks?'

'Oh far more than that. There was a rapport between us. He
gave us a great welcome at his castle. I can see it now . . . the
smell of roasting venison, the sweet sound of music, the warmth
of the great hall. He had a good voice and we sang together; we
played a game of chess. I checkmated him. I think he may have
allowed me to.

'He said to me after the game, "You are no ordinary merchant. I think you are a great nobleman." I had a feeling that
he knew who I was, and I asked him if this were so. I said to
him bluntly: "Do you know who I am?" And he answered, "I
think I do. You are the great Coeur de Lion. There could not be
another who looks as noble as you, and I have heard that the
King of England is the most noble-looking man on Earth." Such
was the understanding between us that I did not deny it.

'He looked worried. He said, "You are in danger. There are
those here who would make you prisoner. There is an order
throughout the land that any who suspect a travelling merchant
may be the King must immediately get a message to Frederick
of Betsau." He was more afraid for me than I was for myself,
and I found that touching.'

He paused, looking straight ahead, smiling tenderly.

Then he went on: 'He said, "You must leave here at once.
You are unsafe. In a few hours they will be here to take you."
"You have not told them I am here?" I asked. He fell on his
knees and, taking my hand, kissed it. He said, "I was to set the
trap. I was to bring you here. I was to have you here in bed
when they arrived to take you. There is little time to lose. Go
from here. But do not travel with your companions. You must
have just one to accompany you." "You have deceived your
master," I said. He nodded. "Why so?" I asked. He said,
"Because, my lord, I love you." I knew he spoke the truth.

'I went back to my friends. I told them what had happened.
They said they knew that Roger was laying a trap for us, but I

replied that he had opened the trapdoor and we should all be the better for having walked into it. So we rode away and I travelled with only one page to look after me.'

'When I think of the dangers through which you have passed, I tremble,' I said.

'Life is all danger. Compared with what we suffered in the Holy Land, this seems like a small adventure.'

'And it was when you were with your page that you were taken?'

'Yes. Perhaps we were careless. He used to go into the town to buy food. I would be outside in the country. I gave him jewels to sell. We had to have food somehow. It was inevitable, I suppose, that sooner or later someone would ask what a young page was doing with such gems. What we think of as of little value seems very grand to some people. My page was taken and threatened with torture. Poor lad, he was a good boy, but he did not want to lose his eyes or have his tongue cut out, so he told them where I was. We were staying the night at the cottage of a workman and his wife. They were glad to have us for a little recompense. When I heard the horsemen approaching, I went into the kitchen and tried to look like a yokel watching the meat on the spit.'

I laughed at the thought. 'You could storm the walls of Acre with more success than you could pretend to be a yokel watching meat on a spit.'

'There were two guards and a captain. They burst into the kitchen. The captain said, "You are the King of England and I have come to arrest you." "On whose orders?" I asked. He replied, "On those of my master, Duke Leopold of Austria." I knew I could expect little mercy then. Leopold of Austria, my great enemy!'

'Oh Richard,' I said, 'we should never make enemies. They have a habit of turning up at the most awkward moments.'

' "I demand you give me your sword," said the captain. I replied, "I will not give my sword to you, Captain. Your master will have to come to take it." He was nonplussed. I doubt he had ever arrested a king before. He set one of his men to guard me while he went off, and after a while he returned with Leopold, who was smiling smugly. He said, "This is a little different from the walls of Acre, eh?" I replied that there was naturally a difference, but he was arrogant then and I saw no change in him now. "But the positions are reversed," he said. "You are my prisoner. There are men all over Europe who will sing my praises and rejoice when I have you under lock and key." "Those who are afraid of me, you mean," I said. "Weak men who yearn for the glory they have not the courage to win."

'You were in his power. Was it wise to speak to him thus?'

'I said what I meant, and you may rest assured he was discomfited.'

'But you were his prisoner . . . and all that time. You must never put yourself in danger again.'

'I am home now. There is much to do here. It is my great pleasure to be with you and to know that you are well.'

'Now that you are back,' I said, 'what of Berengaria?'

'She is happy enough where she is.'

'She would be happier with you. Richard, she must come to England. She cannot stay so far away. She must be brought here, and when she comes you must live together as man and wife. There must be a child. Think of John and Arthur. His mother, Constance, is a very ambitious woman. It would be disastrous if there was war.'

'I intend to live a long time yet.'

'Long enough to get an heir and see him climb to manhood. But Richard, Berengaria *must* return.'

'Yes,' he said, 'you are right.'

But I knew he would shelve the matter. He did not want a wife.

Our tour was successful. The people clearly rejoiced in such a handsome King. What a difference appearances made! And with his reputation they were proud of him.

I thought: We must keep it so.

After leaving Canterbury we came to St Albans, and from there we went to Winchester where Richard was crowned again. That was a splendid ceremony.

There were certain castles which had been passed over to John because people believed that Richard was never coming back. These had to be retrieved. Those who had rallied to John were now required to come forth and beg forgiveness of Richard. He forgave them freely. Richard had never been really vindictive; he had been away for a long time, and they had thought him dead, he reasoned—well, they had given their allegiance to his brother because of this. If they gave it back to him, they would be forgiven for having strayed. It was understandable.

Then to Nottingham to receive more penitents.

Having travelled through England, he must now visit Normandy, where there had been a great deal of unrest. John was in France, and it would be as well to see him and let him know that, now his brother was back, there must be no more dallying with treason.

I was to be with him. I wanted to see the meeting between him and John. I greatly feared strife in the family.

I travelled down to Portsmouth with him, but although it was April the weather was too rough for a ship to sail, and we had to wait nearly three weeks before setting out.

Then to Caen first, where we planned our journey.

It was amazing and gratifying to see how those who had been ready to defect to John were only too happy to come back to Richard now they saw him. It might have been that John was getting such a terrible reputation that they had all been afraid to defy him. He was already showing himself to be cruel and sadistic, and naturally if he were about to be King they did not want to upset him.

John must now know that he was beaten. He came secretly to my apartments, for he wanted to see me alone, he said.

As soon as we came face to face, he fell on his knees and buried his face in my skirts.

I said to him coolly: 'You thought it wise to come to me.'

'I have been a fool, dear Mother. Please understand. I meant no ill. But the country needed a king. I have been a wicked brother to Richard. You cannot blame me more than I blame myself.'

I said: 'Get up. At least you admit your fault. Your brother Richard is the noblest of men. You should be proud to be his brother.'

'I am. I am.'

'And serve him with your life.'

'I will. I will.'

I was not so foolish as to believe him. He was repentant now because he was afraid of Richard, of course; and when the next opportunity to betray his brother came, he would seize it with both hands.

'I do not know what I must do to show my repentance,' he went on. 'Perhaps I should run my sword through my heart.'

I fancied he was looking covertly at me to see what effect this statement had. I was scornful but I was thinking: There must be a reconciliation . . . a public one. But we shall have to watch Master John. He is bound to be up to mischief sooner or later.

I said: 'Get up off your knees and talk sense. As for taking your life, that is the coward's way. I will not have any son of mine a coward.'

'But I have sinned. I should be punished. Richard hates me. You must hate me.'

'I think Richard does not respect you enough to hate you,' I said. 'He looks upon you as his feckless young brother.'

John smirked. I think that was the impression he was trying to give.

'Mother,' he said. 'Dearest Mother, please tell me what I must do.'

'Go now. I will speak to your brother. It may be that he will find it in his heart to forgive you. If he does, you will be fortunate. It would be something for you to remember if ever you felt inclined to play the traitor again.'

'I swear to God . . .'

'I should not if I were you. Those who break their vows to men are treacherous, those who break them to God much worse.'

He went away and I thought a great deal about him. I had never liked him. I remembered always that it was at the time of his birth that I discovered I no longer loved Henry, and I had resented the fact that I was pregnant with his child. Perhaps I had been at fault. I had sent him to Fontevrault. I had given all my love to the other children—particularly Richard—and there had been none to spare for John.

Now I saw him clearly—ambitious, avaricious, self-seeking, sensual as his father was; but there was something sadistic about John which had never been there in Henry. We should have to be careful of John. Naturally I did not believe in his repentance but I should have to pretend to. We had to break John's friendship with the King of France. We could not have brother against brother.

I told Richard my feelings in the matter.

'He is coming to ask your forgiveness. You must give it to him, Richard.'

'Willingly.'

'No, not too willingly, but for the sake of expediency. Never forget that, if the opportunity arose, he would betray you. But let it be thought publicly that you are good friends.'

I was present at the reconciliation scene. John went to his brother and threw himself at his feet. He would have given quite a good performance but he was always inclined to over-act.

He seized Richard's legs and gazed up at his brother.

'I deserve to be punished,' he said. 'Punish me, Richard. Devils possessed me. How could I behave so to a brother I hold in such great honour . . . as does the whole world. I am so proud of you, Richard. I would I could be more like you.'

'It was evil counsellors, not devils,' said Richard. 'You are young, and the young fall easily into the scheming hands of unscrupulous men. Come. Do not grovel there. Stand up.'

John did, and Richard kissed him.

There was peace between the brothers.

There was still no mention of Berengaria.

I brought up the matter again. 'You are thirty-six years old, Richard. It is time you had a son.'

'I have many years left to me.'

'That is what I pray for. But you should have children by now. If you do not live with your wife how can you get legitimate sons?'

'She shall come here.'

'When?'

'When I have settled Normandy. There is much to do here, Mother.'

Later he said he thought we should send for Arthur.

'Why?' I asked.

'So that he learns to speak English and becomes accustomed to our ways.'

'You mean . . . because he may be the future King?'

'It is a possibility.'

'Can you imagine the conflict? Do you think John would allow that to happen without a fuss?'

'John is young and headstrong.'

'All the more reason why we should be careful.'

'That is why I believe it would be a good idea to send for

Arthur. People should get to know him. He is a handsome boy, I believe.'

I knew in my heart that one of my hardest tasks would be to get Berengaria and Richard together.

I was an old woman, and the agony of Richard's captivity had taken its toll of me. Now that Richard was home and was taking over the reins of government, I needed a rest—if only a temporary one.

I had always been interested in Fontevrault. It seemed to hold the very essence of peace within its walls. I told Richard that I intended to go there and stay for a while. He thought it an excellent idea and encouraged me in this. I would be close at hand if needed.

I felt as near contentment as I could be there. Richard, my beloved son, was safe and well, and the only regret he gave me was the avoidance of his wife. I understood that the state of marriage did not appeal to him. It was difficult to understand why he—who appeared to be the very essence of manliness— should have what was almost an aversion to women . . . not as women, of course, but as a sexual attraction. No two could have been closer than he was to me. But nature is strange—and so it was. If only he had been the father of sons, so that my mind could have been at rest and I could visualize a safe Plantagenet empire, I could have been a very contented woman.

The weeks began to pass quickly. They were very peaceful, with each day very like another. I surprised myself that I could be happy in such a life, but I supposed it was because I was so tired.

Then I was constantly receiving visitors, and Richard and others wrote to me frequently, so that I was well aware of what was happening in the world outside.

My daughter Joanna had married Raymond of Toulouse. She had met him when she was with Richard on the crusade and had fallen in love with him. That seemed incongruous in view of the conflict which had always existed between our two houses. I wondered whether he was a good choice. Joanna was headstrong and would have her own way; she was more like me than my other two daughters; and Raymond had been married three times before. I was a little concerned, for his record in marriage was not one to inspire much trust.

His first wife, Ermensinda, had died; his second, Beatrice, had been living when he was in the Holy Land. Richard had taken the daughter of the Emperor of Cyprus as a hostage and she had lived for some time with Berengaria and Joanna. Raymond had become so enamoured of her that he tried to persuade Beatrice to go into a convent. She was a spirited woman, and her retort had amused me. Yes, she said, certainly she would go into a convent providing Raymond became a monk. However, he was said to have made her life so miserable that she preferred the life of the cloister, and in time gave in; so he married the Cypriot princess.

I am afraid Raymond was not meant to be a faithful husband: he soon tired of his third wife and on some pretext divorced her. That left him free for Joanna. He must have been a very fascinating man to have captivated my daughter, particularly as she would have witnessed his romance with her predecessor. The fact remained that she married him and in a short time gave birth to a son, another Raymond.

I hoped she would be happy. Perhaps, being strong-minded and forceful, she would keep the wayward Count in order.

Alais, now restored to her brother, was married to William of Ponthieu, a vassal of Philip Augustus. Not a very brilliant marriage for a Princess of France, but I supposed it was the best Alais could hope for after her shady past. I thought she might find contentment. Alais was the kind of woman who would make a man happy. She must be if she had been able to keep Henry's devotion all those years; gentle, docile, ready to submit to her lord in all things. Well, that was what most of them wanted.

Arthur had not come to England. His mother, Constance, would not allow him to do so. She must have been afraid of treachery. I thought she was rather foolish. She was ambitious for her son, and she should understand that, if in time he was to become King of England, he must learn its ways and speak its language. But no, she was adamant.

Then a strange thing happened which brought about that which I had for so long been trying to achieve.

When Richard was hunting in Normandy and riding a little ahead of his party, he was confronted by a man who stood before him and lifted his arms above his head, causing Richard to pull up sharply.

"What are you doing here?" demanded the King.

'I would speak with you,' replied the man.

'Do you know who I am?'

'I do.'

'Who then?'

'King of England, Duke of Normandy and sinner.'

Richard was amused. 'You are a bold man,' he said.

'You will need to be bolder when you face One who is greater than an earthly king.'

A religious fanatic, thought Richard. The country abounded with them.

'Repent,' said the man. 'Repent while there is time.'

'You are an insolent fellow. Do you know I could have your tongue cut out?'

'Do so, sinner. And remember Sodom and Gomorrah. You will be destroyed if you do not repent . . . destroyed as were the Cities of the Plain.'

The King was angry and drew his sword, but he did not strike the man, who walked quietly away.

The rest of the party had joined him and were prepared to catch the man, but Richard shook his head.

'Leave him,' he said. 'He suffers from a madness, poor fellow, which is no fault of his own.'

That was typical of Richard. It was only rarely that he wanted revenge.

Oddly enough, very soon after that encounter he had an attack of fever and was very ill indeed. In fact, his life was despaired of. He may have remembered the old man in the woods and wondered whether he was indeed a messenger from God.

Hugh, Bishop of Lincoln, went to visit him. He was a man who had often been in conflict with Richard but whom Richard admired for his courage. Like the fanatic in the woods, the Bishop was not afraid of speaking his mind. He told Richard that he had an immediate need of repentance.

'Does not every man?' asked Richard.

'You, my lord, are the King. Your responsibilities are heavy. You do not live with your wife, though it is your duty to give the country an heir. Instead you pursue a way of life which is against nature. Mend your ways. Life is short. If you die now, you will have failed in your duty. Give up your way of life. Recall your wife. Admit your sins.'

'You dare to talk to me like this!' said Richard.

'My lord King, I dare,' was the answer.

'I could order that your tongue be cut out. How would you like that?'

'I should not wish to burden your soul with further sin.'

Conflict always made Richard feel better. He was amazed at the boldness of Bishop Hugh.

He said: 'I respect your courage. You are right. I have sinned. There is the future to think of. Pray for me. If I have another chance, I will recall my wife. I will try to do my duty.'

Bishop Hugh fell on his knees in prayer. He stayed at the King's bedside and when he finally arose Richard's fever had left him.

Richard travelled to Poitou where Berengaria was living. Poor girl, she must have been very lonely now that Joanna had gone. I wondered what she thought when she sat with her embroidery, or plucked half-heartedly at her lute or rode in the forest.

What indeed were her thoughts when Richard came riding into the courtyard?

I knew that in the beginning she had idolized him, but what had the years of neglect done to her love? She must have known why he left her. She knew of the handsome men and charming boys with whom he surrounded himself.

And now he was here . . . come for her . . . implying that he intended to play the faithful husband.

I know Berengaria's type of woman. Meek, docile, not unlike Alais. I rejoiced. All would be well now.

Such a man as Richard should have many children . . . sons to follow him . . . to save the throne from conflict with John and Arthur . . . to continue to build up that great Plantagenet Empire which had been Henry's dream.

Philip Augustus and Richard were now deadly enemies. That was not surprising when one considered the position of their domains. What was to be marvelled at was that they had ever been friends.

Philip Augustus was no Louis. He might not have been a great general but he was an astute monarch; he was constantly seizing every advantage and now was posing a threat to Normandy since the all-important Vexin had come into his possession.

Richard built a castle where it overlooked the little towns of

Andelys—Petit and Grand—right on the banks of the Seine. Set high on a hill it had commanding views of the countryside, and advancing armies could be seen from miles off from whichever direction they came. It stood there in defiance of Philip Augustus, and Richard named it Château Gaillard—the Saucy Castle.

When Philip Augustus heard of this, he said: 'I will take it, were it made of iron.'

These words were reported to Richard. His reply was: 'I will hold it, were it made of butter.'

Thus the rivalry continued and the once-dear friends were now the bitterest of enemies.

There was a rumour abroad.

A peasant, ploughing his master's fields, had discovered a wonderful golden treasure, said to be figures of gold and silver, worth a fortune. The land belonged to Acard, Lord of Châlus.

Richard was intrigued. Perhaps there was more treasure on the land—and treasure found in his dominions belonged to him. He needed money. The exchequer was always low and taxes were unpopular.

Then it was said that the value of the treasure had been exaggerated—it was nothing but a bag of golden coins; and Acard was a vassal of Adamar of Limoges, who himself claimed the treasure. This seemed like defiance to Richard, and that was something he would not tolerate. He would make immediate war on the insolent barons.

So he marched.

It was Lent—not the time to make war. These things were remembered afterwards.

All Richard wanted was the treasure. Let them give it to him and the war would be immediately over.

Richard arrived before the castle of Châlus. It would be an easy matter to take it. How could they possibly defend it against the great Coeur de Lion? No doubt they wished they had handed over the treasure since it was not so very great, but it was too late.

It was so tragic—so ridiculous that so trivial an incident could bring about such a momentous event.

It was revenge, I suppose.

The castle was not a great fortress but it did stand on an

elevation which gave it an advantage. Even so, it would be no great task to take it.

It was a March day—one I shall never forget. Richard was inspecting the fortifications when suddenly an arrow struck him on the shoulder. It had entered below the nape of his neck near his spine and was so deeply embedded that it could not be withdrawn. He mounted his horse and rode back to the camp. There his flesh had to be cut away to remove the arrowhead.

I think Richard must have known that death was close, for he sent to me asking me to come to him. I prepared to leave at once, first sending the Abbess Matilda to tell Berengaria and send the news to John. Then I left Fontevrault with the Abbot of Turpenay.

We did not stop all through the night.

When I reached him, I knew there was no hope. He lay there, my beautiful son, with the knowledge that he must go, his work unfinished. His great object now was to make his dominions safe. He wanted me there beside him . . . not only because the love we bore each other was greater than we had ever given to any other but also because he believed that I was the only one in whose hands he could safely leave his kingdom.

Arthur had not come to England; therefore it must be John who followed him. There could be trouble but it was too late to avert it now.

Berengaria arrived. She was at his bedside. He looked at her sadly, apologetically. I knew he was wishing he had been different.

They had found the man who had shot the fatal arrow. He was young, little more than a boy. His name was Bertrand de Gurdun.

When he heard that his murderer had been arrested, Richard wanted to see him. He was amazed that one so young could have been responsible.

He said: 'Why did you want to kill me, boy?'

'You killed my father and my two brothers,' was the answer. 'You would have killed me . . . for a pot of gold. I wished to avenge my family.'

The King nodded. 'Have you any idea what terrible punishment I could order for you?'

'I care not. I have done what I set out to do. I have laid you, tyrant, on your deathbed.'

'This is a brave boy,' said Richard. 'No harm shall come to him. Let him go free.'

That was typical of Richard. He understood the boy's motives. He would have done the same himself.

From the moment I arrived, I was at his bedside. I would not leave him.

'Richard,' I said, 'you must live. You cannot die like this . . . in such a place . . . for such a reason.'

'We die when our turn comes, dear Mother. What I regret most is leaving you. Do not weep. This is the end for me. I sought to take Jerusalem and I died fighting for a bag of coins.'

'Richard, you have been ill before. You have been plagued by the fever, but you have always recovered. You must do so now.'

'You must watch John,' he said. 'It has to be John. Arthur is not in England . . . and they would not have him. Pray, Mother. Pray for peace in the realm. Send for the Archbishops. They must hear me. They must understand that it has to be John.'

They came and stood by his bed. I was there with my poor Berengaria.

'Farewell, dearest Mother,' he said. 'There has been much love between us two.'

And then he died and I felt that my heart was broken. I could have borne anything but this.

I had lost my son, the one in the world who had meant more to me than any other being.

I was alone, desolate, the most unhappy woman in the world.

I found some consolation in writing. I wrote: 'My posterity has been snatched from me. My two sons, the young King and the Count of Brittany sleep in the dust, and now I have lost the staff of my age, the light of my eyes, and I am forced to live on.'

With Blanca in Castile

What did I want to do now? Return to Fontevrault? To nurse my wretchedness? To shut out all memory of his bright presence?

On Palm Sunday Richard was buried in the church of Fontevrault. The journey from the Limousin had been a slow one and from cottages and mansions people had come out to stand in awe as the cortège passed, knowing that there lay the corpse of the man whose name was known throughout the world; the greatest of warriors, Coeur de Lion.

There was no real peace for me. I had to turn my mind from grief and think of what might happen now. Richard had said that John should be King; but it would be a matter for the barons and the justiciars to decide. It was Arthur who was, in fact, the true heir. Geoffrey, his father, had come before John. I could see that it was a weighty problem: Arthur just twelve years old. An unsuitable age! And the only alternative: John.

William Marshal would be one of those who helped to decide, and he was a wise man who would put the needs of his country before everything else. Then there was Hubert Walter, Archbishop of Canterbury. Men I could trust, both of them.

John arrived at Fontevrault. He over-acted as usual. He expressed great sorrow at his brother's death and assumed an attitude of piety.

John was acclaimed as the next King, not because of the high opinion anyone had of him but as the lesser of two evils.

As soon as he was sure of this, his attitude changed and we had a glimpse of what he would be like when he assumed power.

It was during High Mass. Bishop Hugh of Lincoln, who was officiating, could not resist the opportunity of reminding John, during his sermon, of his duty, telling him frankly what sacrifices were expected of a king. I must admit I found it all a little tedious and wished the man would stop moralizing, but I resigned myself to the fact that the sermon must soon come to an end. John was less patient. He interrupted the Bishop.

'Cut it short,' he ordered. 'I have had enough.'

There was a brief silence before the Bishop went on as though there had been no interruption.

But John, proud of his newly acquired kingship, wanted to show his authority. He shouted: 'I said cut it short. I want my dinner.'

Once more the Bishop ignored him. John took some gold coins from his pocket which he threw up and caught, and then he jangled them in his hands.

The Bishop stopped his sermon and asked what John was doing.

'I am looking at these gold coins,' replied John, 'and thinking that a few days ago, if I had had them, I would have kept them for myself rather than give them to you.'

'Put them into the offering box,' said the Bishop, 'and go to your dinner.'

If this was an example of what we were to expect from John, I wondered if the bishops were already regretting their choice.

My mind was taken from apprehensive contemplation of the future by the arrival of Joanna at Fontevrault.

My daughter was in a very sad state. She was pregnant and had been on her way to Rouen to see Richard. Her husband needed help and she had known that she would not appeal to Richard in vain. He had always been a good brother to her and she would never forget how he had come to her aid when she had been Tancred's prisoner in Sicily.

When she heard that he was dead, she was prostrate with grief.

I was delighted to see her but horrified at her condition. But caring for her did something to assuage my grief. None could take the place of Richard in my heart but I was deeply fond of all my children, and for Joanna to be in need of my love and care at such a time brought me solace.

I often wondered as I sat by her bedside whether she realized that this marriage of hers had been a mistake. She had been sent to Sicily to marry the King when she was twelve years old, and there she had found a kindly and faithful husband; that had been a happy marriage. It seemed ironic that the man chosen for her had been a better husband than the one she had chosen for herself. Of course, she never said a word against Raymond but, in view of his past record with wives, I did not believe for a moment that he would turn into a faithful husband.

Now Raymond was in great difficulties and needed help. Richard was dead; John was unreliable; and she herself was suffering from illness and a difficult pregnancy.

I was very worried about her and grew more so. I insisted on nursing her myself. We talked together of the long-ago days when the children had all been in the nursery together . . . all dead and gone now, except Eleanor, who was married to the King of Castile. Matilda was dead . . . William, Henry, Geoffrey and now Richard . . . all my sons, dead . . . with the exception of John.

We wept together. How sad and ironic, I thought, that I, an old woman, should have outlived all those young and vital people.

And now it seemed that I was going to lose Joanna.

I felt so bowed down with grief that I was expecting the worst, so it was no surprise to me when she became very ill indeed. Perhaps, had it not been for her pregnancy, I might have nursed her through that illness. But she was sinking fast. She had one great desire and that was to be a nun of Fontevrault. It seemed a strange request to make, but I feared it would be the last one she ever would, so I wanted it granted.

The Archbishops were against it, declaring that it could not be done without the consent of her husband.

I said: 'Her husband is far away fighting for his lands. Can you not see that my daughter is dying? What do rules matter if she can have a little contentment in her last hours?'

She would never take up the life of a nun, for she would never leave her bed, and I was determined that her last request should be granted. And in the end I had my way.

Just before she died, my daughter Joanna was received into the Order of Fontevrault. The Archbishop of Canterbury was in Rouen at that time and I sent for him. It was he who gave her the veil. Then the Abbot of Tarpigny and the monks offered her to God and the Order of Fontevrault.

It must have been the first time a pregnant woman had been received into a convent.

It brought great comfort to Joanna; she changed and seemed to come to peace. She gave birth to her child and died; and in a short time the infant followed her.

I wondered what fresh blows Fate could bestow on me. Of all my children there were only two now living: John and Eleanor.

What followed was scarcely unexpected. Constance of Brittany might not have wanted her son to come to England but she was determined to fight for his inheritance.

There were many who said he was the true heir to the throne. The Bretons under Arthur and Constance were on the march. Angers had fallen into their hands; and Maine, Touraine and Anjou had accepted Arthur as their ruler.

John was worried. He must have wondered whether he had gained his kingdom only to lose it. Philip Augustus had decided to back Arthur. So the position looked dangerous.

John immediately went to Normandy, where he was to be proclaimed Duke at Rouen.

Here again he showed his complete unsuitability for the position which had come to him. In the church were a number of his ribald friends, and during the solemn religious service they were laughing at the ritual and ridiculing the ceremony in audible terms. John kept turning to look at his friends and at one most solemn moment was seen to wink at them; when the lance was handed to him, he was paying such attention to them that he let it slip to the floor. What a foolish young man he was! Did he not know that the people were always looking for omens?

I could see that the peace to which I had looked forward was not to be mine. I had to rouse myself. I had to forget my age. I could see the Plantagenet Empire slipping away. John would have to grow up quickly. He had so much to learn.

In the meantime I sent for Mercadier, the chief of the mercenaries, who was always eager to serve if the price was good.

I had remonstrated with him about his actions when Richard had died. He had seized Bertrand de Gurdun and had him flayed alive. So Richard's last benevolent act came to nothing. I hoped the boy knew that Richard had had nothing to do with his death and that if the King had lived he would not have suffered that terrible end.

But Mercadier, for all his cruelty, was one of the best soldiers of his day, and fighting was his business. He gathered together his army of mercenaries and I went with the army for I was determined that what had been lost must be won back without delay.

Arthur was only a boy and Constance a woman, but after Geoffrey's death she had married a Poitevin nobleman, Guy de Thouars, and together they were not to be thought of lightly, particularly as they had the help—though intermittently—of Philip Augustus.

Mercadier soon put them to flight.

John brought out an army and took Le Mans. Alas, he did not capture Arthur as he had hoped to, and the boy escaped and put himself under the protection of Philip Augustus.

I was so tired. I kept telling myself that a woman of my age should be at peace, not in the midst of conflict, but there was so much at stake, and who would act if I did not? There was one thing I could do. I had done it before and it had been successful. I must show myself to my people.

I returned to Fontevrault and gathered together a retinue of bishops and nobles; and then I began a tour of my estates.

I did not this time attempt to promote my son John as I had Richard. I just wanted to show myself as their own Duchess, the one whom they had always loved and only rejected because of husbands brought in to govern them.

I was no longer the beautiful young woman, but they seemed to respect my age. They cheered me and extolled me because I was so old; and though exhausting, it was well worth while. They were as loyal to the old woman as they had been to the young.

Brittany might be lost to us but at least I had saved my native country.

Having now established the fact that I was the ruler, I must perform the painful duty of doing homage for my land to my suzerain. It was unfortunate that he should be the King of France.

In Tours we came face to face. He received me with courtesy and spoke of Richard with emotion. He had loved him, I know, while he had worked to destroy him. I had seen such emotion once between Henry and Becket.

We looked at each other steadily and with respect. I knew that he would be a formidable enemy, and John would be no match for him. It was for this reason that I was undergoing this humiliating ceremony. My lands belonged to me, I was telling him, not to my son John . . . although, of course, he would be my heir. But old as I was, I was very much alive.

I believed there was something which was of the utmost importance. That was an alliance between our countries, and what could bring that about better than a marriage?

Philip Augustus had a son; my daughter Eleanor had a daughter. There should be a marriage between them, and to bring this about would be my next task.

There was no one else I could trust to do this. I must see my grand-daughter and assure myself that she was prepared for what lay ahead. I must bring her to her bridegroom.

To undertake the journey to Castile was a little daunting, but I knew it must be done, so, having assured myself that Philip Augustus saw the advantage of this alliance and was agreeable to it, I immediately set about making my preparations.

My pleasure at the prospect of seeing my daughter outweighed my apprehension at the thought of the rigours of the journey. People would say I was not of an age for such arduous travel but I saw through this match a means of making peace in Europe. My family would be allied with that of Philip Augustus, and I was very anxious that the bride I should bring to him would be acceptable.

I had not seen my daughter Eleanor since she was nine years old, and she was now thirty-eight and had borne Alfonso of Castile eleven children. I wanted to spend a few months at her Court grooming the grand-daughter I should choose to be the future Queen of France. So my journey was necessary, and discomforts must be forgotten once more. Perhaps, once I had brought this to the desired conclusion I could settle down to the peace of Fontevrault.

I left Poitiers and travelled down to Bordeaux. Unfortunately my way led through the land which belonged to the Lusignan brothers. I remembered passing this way once before, when Henry and I were about to part. It all came back to me so vividly . . .

how I had been riding with Earl Patrick when we had been waylaid by Guy and Geoffrey de Lusignan who had killed Patrick and tried to make me their captive. I had escaped but it had been one of those alarming incidents which one never forgets. And as I was thinking of this I noticed a party of horsemen riding towards us. They surrounded us, and to my horror I saw that what had happened before was about to be repeated.

I demanded to know in whose name they dared obstruct us. Then a man rode up to me. He was obviously the leader—a very handsome, elegant person. He bowed low and said that he was Hugh le Brun de Lusignan and he would offer me hospitality for the night.

I thanked him and said I had a long journey before me and I must ride on.

He smiled at me in a rather impish fashion and said: 'My lady, I am afraid you have no choice. I shall insist on giving you the comforts due to your royal person.'

With horror I realized that he intended to abduct me.

This would be for a different motive than in the past. They were not now attempting to force me into marriage. This would doubtless mean ransom. I looked round at my retinue. We were in no position to repulse them. We had been foolish to ride into Lusignan country without sufficient protection. I saw there was no help for it. To my fury I was forced to ride beside my abductor, Hugh le Brun, to his castle.

There I was housed in the finest apartments. He was determined to treat me with the utmost respect. At the table he insisted on serving me himself.

I said: 'You are a bold man, Hugh le Brun. Has it occurred to you that, though you have the advantage now, it will not always be so?'

'I wish your ladyship no harm.'

'Then why behave in this uncouth manner?'

'Because I wish myself much good.'

'You mean you will demand a ransom. Since King Richard was held by his jealous enemies there have been those who have developed a taste for this sort of thing. Do you intend to ask a ransom from my son the King?'

'No, my lady, from you.'

'Then you had better tell me.'

'What I want is the county of La Marche.'

I was astounded by his impudence. Henry had seized La Marche from the Lusignans some years earlier. Richard had fortified it. It was an important stretch of land.

'You are talking nonsense.'

Hugh le Brun lifted his shoulders and smiled. 'It seems that your ladyship likes my castle.'

'I find little to admire in its owner.'

'Perhaps time will change my lady's views.'

'I believe that would only strengthen my dislike.'

'Then it is a pity, for if you do not give me La Marche you will be here a very long time.'

I was dismayed. I lay awake at night thinking of the implication of this. How should I reach Castile? What would happen to the match I so desired? One must settle this matter quickly for when matrimonial arrangements are allowed to hang fire they have a way of evaporating.

I was frustrated and angry. For two days I fumed against Hugh while he remained charming and unmoved.

At length I saw that I could be here for a very long time unless I gave way to his demands. So, cursing the fate which had brought me into Lusignan country, deploring the wily tactics of my kidnappers, while admiring them, I began to see that the difficulties of freeing me in the long run would be more costly than giving up La Marche.

So at length I agreed.

Hugh le Brun took, as he said, a reluctant farewell of me when the transaction was made; and thinking regretfully of what the incident had cost me, I continued my journey.

Everything seemed worthwhile when I arrived in Castile. I was enchanted with my daughter Eleanor. She was beautiful still, even though she had borne eleven children. Hers had been a successful marriage. She was one of those women almost certain to enjoy a happy marriage providing her husband is not a monster. Her nature was gentle, kindly, while she herself was highly intelligent and accomplished. She was the perfect wife and mother.

When I had spent a few moments with her, I thought what a tragedy it was that we had lived so much of our lives apart.

The Court of Castile reminded me of that long-ago one over which my grandfather and father had reigned. Everything was

comfortable and elegant. It was wonderful to hear the troubadours again; to be with my daughter was such a pleasure that I
felt happy as I had not thought to be ever again after Richard's
death.

We talked of the old days when she with the others had been
in the nursery. She told me how the children had looked forward
to my visits. They had all sought to win my favour, she told me,
for they had loved me dearly even though they were a little afraid
of me. They had not loved their father and as soon as they
sensed—as children do—that there was trouble between us they
were all prepared to defend me, and hated him the more . . .
all except Geoffrey the Bastard, who thought his father was the
most wonderful being on Earth.

It brought it all back . . . incidents which I had forgotten. I
was back there in the nurseries when they were all about
me . . . my dear children . . . and towering above them all, my
golden boy, my Richard, whom I should never see again.

Then there were my grand-daughters—the purpose of my
visit. The eldest, Berengaria, was already spoken for. She was
affianced to the King of Leon. The next was Urraca and then
came Blanca.

It studied them intently—two beautiful and enchanting girls.

I said to my daughter: 'This is a great opportunity. There
could scarcely be a better match than the future King of France.'

My daughter replied: 'I have spoken to Urraca and told her
what a wonderful match this is and that she is the luckiest girl
in the world for one day she will be Queen of France.'

'You have a family to be proud of,' I told my daughter. 'What
great good children can bring us . . . and what sorrow.'

'Dearest Mother, life has been cruel to you.'

'When Richard went, I thought I had nothing to live for.'

'I know he was always your favourite. In the nursery we
thought it was natural that this should be so. There was something magnificent about Richard.'

I could scarcely bear to speak his name, and she knew it and
reproached herself for reminding me, but I told her she was not
the one who had reminded me, for he was always in my thoughts.

'I am so happy to be with you, my dear,' I said. 'I think of
all my children you have been the most fortunate.'

'I have a good husband. We live happily here in Castile. And
then there are the children, of course.'

'I want to get to know them well while I am here. It might be that I shall never see them again.'

'Dear Mother, you must visit us and next time stay . . . stay a long time.'

'The years are creeping up on me. Sometimes it is hard to remember how old I am.'

'Then forget it, for, dear Mother, *you* can never be old.'

'Ah, if only that were true.'

So the days passed and I spent hours with my grand-daughters.

Urraca was a charming girl, but it was Blanca in whom I was more interested.

Blanca was beautiful—not more so than her sister, but she glowed with an inner light. Was it intelligence or character? I was not sure. All I knew was that Blanca had some special quality. There was a determination in her nature, an alertness; she loved music, and she was quick to reply in discussion and very often right on the point. Perhaps I am a vain old woman but I thought I saw something of myself in Blanca; and as the days passed I began to realize that she was the one I must take with me as the future Queen of France.

It was difficult explaining to her parents. They had planned that it should be Urraca. They had prepared her for the part she must play. They had impressed on her what a great honour it was to be chosen. There could be few such grand titles as Queen of France in the whole world.

But in my heart I knew it had to be Blanca.

I broached the matter with my daughter.

'It will have to be Blanca, you know,' I said. Eleanor looked at me in astonishment.

'She has all the qualities,' I went on.

'For what, dear Mother?'

'For marriage with Louis of France.' My daughter was silent with shock.

'I know,' I went on, 'that we have thought of Urraca, but I am convinced it will have to be Blanca.'

'But we cannot change now.'

'Why not? I am to take back one of my grand-daughters, and I say that one must be Blanca.'

'What of Urraca? She is the elder.'

'You will find a good husband for her, particularly if her sister is to be the future Queen of France.'

'Dear Mother, for what reason?'

It was difficult to explain. I supposed she loved both her daughters dearly and perhaps could not see the bright jewel she had in Blanca.

I sought to explain. It was not that there was anything wrong with Urraca. It was just that Blanca was endowed with very special qualities . . . a strength which I recognized clearly, as I had it myself, courage, resourcefulness. I said: 'The French would never like a woman called Urraca.' My daughter looked at me disbelievingly.

I elaborated the theme. 'No. They would never get used to it. She would be a foreigner to them all her life.'

'You mean because of her name . . .'

'Whereas Blanca,' I said, ' . . . that will become Blanche. That is a very beautiful name. The French will love it. My dear, don't look so taken aback. One of your daughters will be Queen of France. What does it matter which one?'

'Blanca,' she murmured. 'I hadn't thought of Blanca. She is younger than Urraca.'

'That is no obstacle. She is twelve, is she not? Old enough to go to her future husband. I shall take Blanca.'

My daughter was silent. She remembered from the old days that people did not argue with me. When I said something should be so, it was.

The girls were amazed, of course. Urraca, who had been very apprehensive about going to France, was now dismayed because she was not going. Blanca was surprised, but she took the announcement as I knew she would. She hated to displace her sister but could not fail to be excited by the brilliant prospect which was opening before her.

We spent a good deal of time together. I talked a great deal about the Court of France as it had been when I had been its Queen.

'You will mould it to your ways,' I told her. 'I am going to call you Blanche from now on. That is the name by which you will be known in France. It is merely a version of your own name and this one is prettier, don't you think, Blanche? It suits you.'

So we were often together and played the lute and sang. I was delighted by her elegant manners, her quiet wit and her budding beauty. I was glad I had made the journey. Otherwise they would

have sent Urraca instead; and my instinct told me that Blanca—
Blanche as she now was—was the one destined to be Queen of
France.

After the initial surprise at the substitution, there was no resistance to my suggestion, and the time came to say goodbye to
the pleasant Court of Castile. I travelled in a litter for quite long
stages of the journey, for I grew very tired if I stayed too long
in the saddle.

My grand-daughter rode beside the litter. I always liked to
have her in sight. She was a great joy to me. I gloried in her
beauty and her intelligence and love grew quickly between us.
We stayed at castles and inns on our journey and I would always
have her sleeping in my room or even in my bed. I talked to her
a great deal. I wanted her to be prepared. The fact that I, too,
had travelled from my home to become a Queen of France had
made a great bond between us. I drew myself back into those
long-ago days and as I talked of them memories came flooding
back.

I told her of my grandfather's Court and the manner in which
he had abducted Dangerosa and carried her off to his castle. I
remembered the legends sung in ballads by the *jongleurs*. I would
often sing them to her. It was amazing how the memories of
them came flooding back and I could remember the words
of romanticized adventure as well as the music.

'How strange,' I said, 'that my husband was Louis VII of
France and yours will be Louis VIII. My Louis was a good,
religious man, but good men at times can be tiresome . . . and
so can the other kind. I had a taste of both, so I am well qualified
to judge.' And I would tell her about Henry, the great Plantagenet, her own grandfather who had been so different from Louis.
'We should have been good together,' I said wistfully. 'But he
could never be faithful. Women were his weakness.' I did not
add that I thought it odd that his son Richard should have been
so different.

I realized how much my grand-daughter had done for me.
There had been hours when I had forgotten to grieve for Richard.

We came to Bordeaux. It was comforting to be in my own
castle. Here our ways divided: there was one road to Paris, the
other to Fontevrault. I was feeling exhausted. Even the exhila-

ration I drew from my grand-daughter could not disguise it. Fontevrault offered complete peace; there I could rest my weary limbs for a short time and shut myself away from all the burdens which I knew were waiting to fall upon my shoulders.

I sent for the Archbishop of Bordeaux. I told him that I had brought my grand-daughter from the kingdom of Castile, and I wished him to take her to Paris and present her to the King, who was expecting her. I had just undertaken a long journey and I thought I could not go much farther. I would entrust him with the task of taking the future Queen of France to her prospective husband.

I was touched to see Blanche's dismay when she knew I was not going with her to Paris.

'All will be well,' I assured her. 'They will welcome you in Paris. The Archbishop will take good care of you.'

'Oh dearest Grandmother, I shall miss you so much.'

'We have been so happy together, have we not?' She nodded, her eyes brimmed with tears.

'Dear child, one of the saddest things in my life has been that I have not been able to stay long with those I loved.'

'I don't know how I could have done all this without you,' she said. 'I should have been terrified of going to the Court of France . . . but I am not now. You have explained so much. You have *done* so much for me.'

'And you will never know what you have done for me, my child. You have helped me over the first stile, and I have put a little of my grief behind me.'

I took a sad farewell of Blanche and she left Bordeaux in the retinue of the Archbishop. Soon she would be in Paris and my mission accomplished.

I intended to rest a few days in Bordeaux to strengthen myself for the last lap of my journey.

Mercadier had joined me. I was rather moved. He had in fact had his own mercenary army, but when the news of my abduction by Hugh de Lusignan had come to him, he asked to be attached to my entourage because he wanted to make sure I was protected from any more such villainous attempts. I was delighted to receive him into my service.

It was Easter time. There were processions in the streets. I would sit at a window looking down. It was so comforting to wake in the morning and to know that I had not to hurry down and start another day's long journey.

But soon I was ready to go on.

This time I should have the doughty Mercadier to look after me, which was as well, for we had to pass through the valley of the Charente where I might meet with dissatisfied vassals like the Lusignans.

A shock awaited me.

There had been a brawl in the streets. Two men had drawn their swords and fought and one of them had been killed. To my sorrow and dismay, I learned that one of them was Mercadier.

So I had lost my protector.

This further disaster made me realize afresh how I longed to be shut away from conflict.

I just wanted to be alone, to meditate, to rest my weary limbs, to write of the past, to relive it all again and to ask myself whether what had happened to me had been due largely to myself.

I wanted to go back to Fontevrault.

Fontevrault

I now look forward to passing the days which are left to me in the peace I find at Fontevrault.

My grand-daughter was married to Louis Capet; John was crowned King of England, and he must now be realizing his responsibilities. Philip Augustus continued to alarm me, and as long as I lived I would do my utmost to see that his dream of destroying the Plantagenet Empire was never realized.

The days were slipping away . . . reading, writing, living over the past, reflecting on what might have been if one had acted differently. It was an amusing game.

John divorced Hadwisa of Gloucester. The marriage had never been a success. Henry had arranged it because of the immense wealth Hadwisa brought into the family, but that, of course, was before it was thought that John would be King. Hadwisa was childless, so the divorce was not a matter for regret.

However, John seemed incapable of doing anything without causing a great deal of trouble. In the first place he became infatuated with Isabella, the daughter of the Count of Angoulême. She was very young and very beautiful and she aroused such passions in John that he determined to have her. He would probably have abducted her if she had not been the daughter of a powerful man, but being so she was worthy of marriage.

Although he was bent on a union with her, he allowed negotiations to go ahead for the daughter of the King of Portugal. He thought that amusing. Another matter which gave him cause for mirth—and I must say I joined him in this—was that Isabella was betrothed to Hugh le Brun de Lusignan, the man who had had the temerity to seize me and demand La Marche for my release.

Of course the King of England was a far better proposition than Hugh le Brun, and the Count of Angoulême had little compunction in breaking Isabella's engagement to Hugh le Brun and accepting John's proposal for his daughter.

But what enemies John had made over this matter of his marriage! The King of Portugal and Hugh le Brun would never forgive him and would seize every opportunity for revenge; although I could not help feeling pleased about Hugh le Brun's discomfiture, I did think that to alienate the King of Portugal was an act of sheer folly.

From my retreat I felt I could look out on events and that it would not be necessary for me to be caught up in them. But could I turn away? Sometimes I wondered to what end John's folly would bring him. The care of such a wide empire had strained Henry's resources to the full and he had been a great king. Richard had spent most of his reign out of England, and I had to admit that that had not been good; and now came John, with his reckless folly. Where would it end?

Constance had died. I hoped that meant that we should hear no more of Arthur's claim. He was too young to do very much alone; and although he had his adherents, he was very much a figurehead only.

I felt we need not worry quite so much about Arthur . . . for a year or so at any rate; and then most probably I should not be here. I could not expect to live many more years.

I had always had my eyes on the French King. I would never forget those years I had spent as Louis's Queen; France had been my home for so long that I felt I was part of it.

I had always been aware of the fact that Philip Augustus was a man to watch. I recognized a clever ruler when I saw one and, for all his faults, Philip Augustus was that. In spite of the fact that he had been in love with Richard, he had never dreamed of neglecting his country on that account. He had married Isabella of Hainault, and his son Louis was now the husband of my own sweet Blanche.

Isabella had died and a marriage had been arranged for Philip Augustus with Ingeborg, a Danish princess, but after the marriage service he took an instant dislike to her and wanted her sent home. She appealed to Pope Celestine who ignored her pleas. I wondered what had brought about such a violent revulsion, for Philip Augustus had a great sense of duty to his country, and the object of this marriage was to provide heirs. In such cases when the encumbrance came from a not very influential family it was generally easy to find some reason for annulment; but Ingeborg had a powerful friend in Pope Celestine.

Philip Augustus had for some time been in love with Agnes de Meran and was now determined, in spite of papal disapproval, to marry her. Eventually he did this, but Celestine had now been replaced by Innocent who was ready to exert his authority. He threatened Philip Augustus with excommunication if he did not go back to Ingeborg; and faced with this Philip Augustus was obliged to take her back; but he kept Agnes with him. What would have been the outcome I cannot imagine if Agnes had not conveniently died. Philip wanted the children he had had by her legitimized and was now in consultation with Rome on this matter.

I was rather pleased about this, for it kept Philip Augustus occupied with his own affairs; I trembled to think what might become of Plantagenet possessions in France if he was able to give his full attention to the task of wresting them from us.

I was becoming more and more enamoured of the life at Fontevrault. I was feeling better. The place refreshed me and I realized that I could be content to spend what was left of my life here. I liked the ways of the convent. It seemed a good idea to give myself up to good works. It was said to be a way of expiating past sins, and I daresay most would agree that during my long life I had committed many.

I seemed to have become a different woman; the fire of my youth had gone and had taken with it my love of adventure. I would never have believed that the day would come when I could be content with the quiet life and enjoy the peace of it.

But perhaps I had not changed so much.

That peace was shattered suddenly. Philip Augustus had come to terms with Rome. Agnes's son and daughter were to be recognized as legitimate. Now he could turn his attention to what had always been an ambition of his: the disintegration of the Plantagenet Empire which had for long been a source of irritation to France.

His father had been weak; he was not. Henry FitzEmpress

had been strong; the present King of England was weak. Philip Augustus was ready to go into action.

In snatching Isabella from Hugh le Brun, John had committed an act of aggression against a vassal of Philip Augustus, and as Duke of Normandy John was summoned to appear in Paris to answer charges against him. He naturally refused to comply with this order.

Philip Augustus then declared that John should be deprived of all the land he held under the King of France.

John snapped his fingers at such a decree. Philip Augustus responded by knighting Arthur and betrothing him to the daughter who had just been declared legitimate. This was tantamount to saying that Philip Augustus supported Arthur's claim to the throne of England and that he would help him to achieve it. Moreover, he gave him an army and sent him off with his blessing, to capture his rights.

John was at Le Mans when the news came to Fontevrault that Arthur was marching on to Poitou. My country! I was alert. Though my people had been loyal to me, they would not rally to John, who was a stranger to them. I had thought I had done with action, but I could see that my peace was at an end. I believed that if I appeared at the head of a small force my people would support me.

There was nothing to be done but leave the peace of Fontevrault. It seemed that I still had a part to play.

I made preparations at once. I gathered what little force I had. I believed it was my presence which would induce my people to rally to my side. They would not allow Poitou to be snatched from me. I was sure of their loyalty.

So . . . though I was close on eighty years old, I rode forth.

We had come to the château of Mirebeau on the borders of Anjou and Poitou. It proved a bad choice for it was not strongly fortified, and I had not been there very long when news came that Arthur and his army, with that of the Lusignans, had had word of my arrival and were marching on the castle.

I laughed and said: 'Whenever these Lusignans are about we can expect an attempted abduction. They seem to make a habit of it . . . with me as their intended victim.'

I sent a message to John at Le Mans telling him he must come to Mirebeau with all speed. We then set about fortifying the castle.

It was a horrifying experience to see the armies approaching, because I knew that we could not hold out for long. They would be triumphant, knowing that I was inside the castle and that it would be a simple matter to take me.

Night was almost upon us when the armies encamped outside the castle walls. From a top turret I could see them clearly. I saw Arthur for the first time. My own grandson! He was a handsome boy. I was moved, as I always was by members of the family. I might have been fond of that boy. What a sad thing it was that he was there now, plotting to take me prisoner.

For my own fate I felt little concern. Perhaps one does not care very much when one gets old. My life was finished. What did it matter to me if they killed me in the attempt to take me? It would be that I reached the end a few months . . . perhaps a few weeks . . . before I should at Fontevrault.

What good fortune that they decided to delay the attack until morning! So are great events decided. They had marched through the day and were weary. There was no hurry, they thought. The prey was in her trap and there could be no escape with the army surrounding the castle; and in the morning it would be an easy matter.

I found myself looking forward to an encounter with my grandson. From what I had seen of him, he was a little arrogant, a little imperious. Well, he was but a boy and when too much respect is shown to the young it is not good for their characters.

I slept not at all and that was a long night. I lay on my bed waiting for the morning.

What hope was there that John would come? When had anything John did been a success? I had tried for so long not to see his faults, but of course I had been aware of them. Here I was . . . surrounded by the enemy . . . about to be abducted. Held for ransom, I supposed. How much would John think his mother was worth? It was not the money which was important. The Lusignans did not want the people of Poitou to know that I was coming to them. They wanted them to think of me as an old woman dying at Fontevrault. Then they would say: Here is Arthur. Is he any better than John? Why bother to remain under the rule of foreigners?

It was a clever idea to prevent my reaching my people, and we should have found a stronger fortress than Mirebeau. But there was nothing to do but wait for morning.

Life is full of surprises. For once my son John acted as his father would have. When he received the message that I was at Mirebeau, he rode with his army all through the night and arrived at the castle at dawn. Arthur and the Lusignans were taking a leisurely breakfast before beginning what they would look upon as the easiest conquest of their military careers.

With John was that military genius William Marshal. The timing was perfect, with Arthur and the Lusignans feasting, prematurely celebrating their victory: they were unarmed and when John arrived they were surrounded.

There was no real battle. It was all over very quickly and Arthur and the Lusignans were John's prisoners.

John came into the castle, his eyes alight with triumph. He embraced me. I was so surprised and delighted that I reciprocated warmly.

'I heard you were in danger,' he cried. 'I rode through the night. And see! We arrived just in time. There was no battle. We caught them unprepared.'

I had been mistaken in him. I thought in that moment: He is Henry's son, a true Plantagenet.

I wish that could have been true. I think that is the only time I can recall when John acted with good sense, for it is no use winning if one does not know what to do with victory.

He forgot that those men he had captured were noblemen. They had been defeated in battle and it was the mark of a good general that he treat honourable enemies with respect. In war a good leader is fierce; in victory he is magnanimous.

How elated John was to survey his prisoners: Arthur who would take his throne; Hugh le Brun who would have taken his bride. His great desire was to humiliate them.

He acquired farm carts in which cattle were carried from place to place. He chained and fettered his prisoners and forced them to stand in the carts with their faces close to the beasts' tails as an added insult. John was sadistic by nature. I had long realized that. These prisoners, who were of the noblest families, including his own nephew, were to be paraded through the streets and taken to various places selected for them.

The two he must have had a special delight in humiliating were Arthur and Hugh le Brun. Hugh was tall and handsome;

John was far from that. And this was the manner in which he treated his rivals.

He was foolish. He did not see the disgust on the people's faces or, if he did, ignored it. He did not realize that these people were making up their minds that they would not willingly have such a man to rule over them if he could behave so to their noblemen—many of them members of their own families.

Hugh le Brun was sent to Caen; many others were sent to England and imprisoned in Corfe Castle. Arthur was taken to Falaise.

I had tried to reason with John. He smiled and nodded but I knew he was not listening. I could not warn him; others had tried to. I knew that William Marshal was completely shocked by this treatment of the prisoners and had tried to instil in him the folly of such conduct.

I think I knew at that moment of victory that all was lost.

I stayed in Poitiers. I must if I were to hold the country together. I knew that they were going to reject John. Philip Augustus would know it too. John might have Arthur but he was on the way to defeat, and he did not seem to be aware of his precarious position. He was so enamoured of Isabella that he stayed in bed with her until dinner time. This passionate relationship between them was the talk of the Court. At least, I thought, there will be children.

John neglected his duties—and Philip Augustus was one to take advantage of that. He felt his way cautiously. He made leisurely progress through the country, taking castles as he went. There was little opposition. Nobody wanted to be ruled by John. There was nothing I could do. While I remained in Poitiers, Aquitaine would be faithful to me as long as I lived, but that would not be forever.

And then . . . ?

I had to watch events and see John plunge farther and farther into disaster.

The Lusignans offered a heavy ransom for Hugh le Brun, and foolishly John accepted it, so freeing him and adding to his dangerous enemies.

There was Arthur. What became of Arthur is a mystery. There have been many rumours. There is one story that Hubert de Burgh, the castellan of the castle, was ordered by John to castrate him and put out his eyes and that Hubert found himself unable to perform this dastardly deed. He hid Arthur and told John that he had died while the foul deed was being done and that he had buried him in the precincts of the castle. John, it seemed, was satisfied.

The subject of Arthur would not die down. Where was he? people were asking, including Arthur's immediate family and the King of France. Suspicion turned on John. Rumour was rife, and John began to be worried. Arthur had disappeared. He was presumed dead, and John was the suspect.

John affected great sorrow, and Hubert de Burgh, not knowing how to deal with such a situation and wondering how he was going to keep Arthur concealed for ever, confessed to John that he had not carried out his orders and that Arthur still lived in a secret room in the castle. John assumed great delight, congratulating de Burgh, and Arthur appeared on the streets of Falaise.

Everyone was satisfied.

But, of course, John would not allow Arthur to remain at liberty. He was taken to the castle of Rouen and never seen again.

I think I can guess what happened: John murdered him there and threw his body into the Seine. That is the most likely solution, and I fear there must be truth in it.

I despaired of John.

One by one those places which Henry had been so proud of were falling into the hands of Philip Augustus: Le Mans, Bayeux, Lisieux . . . and others.

It had happened so quickly that I could scarcely believe it possible. All that Henry, with my help, had built up, to crumble so soon. It would not be long before all our French possessions passed out of our hands.

Rouen itself was in danger. Messages were sent to John in England. Reinforcements were needed. There must be no delay. But John was revelling with his worthless friends; he was spending his nights and half his days in bed with Isabella. That was more important to him than the Plantagenet Empire.

I was helpless. What can an old woman of eighty do? If I had been younger, I would have done everything possible to rid the country of my son John.

I think the final humiliation was the loss of Château Gaillard—Richard's castle, built to hold out against the enemy for centuries. 'I will hold it,' Richard had said, 'were it made of butter.'

When it fell to the French, I knew that was the end.

I went to Fontevrault. What was there to do now but wait for my departure to another life? So I shut myself away. I follow the quiet life of the nuns; and I am reliving my life by writing of it as I remember it from all those years ago.

I often think of Henry and his dream of possessing the whole of Europe. Women influenced his life more than men; there had been Rosamund, Alais and myself. But for his relationship with the three of us how different would his life had been? And with me it had been men: Louis, Raymond of Antioch, Henry and Richard. All the King's women and all the Queen's men—how much had they shaped the course of history?

Looking back, I see that what I had always wanted was love. I had been born into the Courts of Love and all my life I had been trying to return to them—not as they had been in my grandfather's day but of my own making. With Louis it had been impossible; with Raymond there had been that blissful interlude which was necessarily transient; with Henry I believed I should find what I sought, and how bitterly disappointed I had been; Richard I had loved selflessly, and perhaps that is the best way to love.

But it is all over now. That which Henry had so painstakingly built up is being lost, and soon there will be nothing left but England.

John has done this. John, who should never have been born. Nor would he have been if I had learned of Henry's perfidy earlier. John was not conceived in love, and all the time I was carrying him I was obsessed by my hatred of his father. It all comes back to me clearly now.

So he was born, this monster, this sadist who tortures and torments, who must know that an empire is disintegrating while he sports in bed with the woman he took from Hugh le Brun.

What more is there to say?

So I lay down my pen and wait to pass out of a life which I have, I think, lived to the full. I am glad to be going at this time for I know my son John will plunge further and further into disaster. What will become of him? What will become of England, which is all that is left to him now?

I shall never know.

Bibliography

Abbott, Edwin A., *St Thomas of Canterbury*

Appleby, John T., *Henry II, The Vanquished King*

Appleby, John T., *John, King of England*

Ashley, Maurice, *The Life and Times of King John*

Aubrey, William Hickman Smith, *The National and Domestic History of England*

d'Auvergne, Edmund B., *John, King of England*

Aytoun, William E., *The Life and Times of Richard the First*

Barber, Richard, *The Devil's Crown*

Bié, Madeleine, *The Châteaux of the Loire*

Bryant, Arthur, *The Medieval Foundation*

Bryant, Arthur, *The Story of England, Makers of the Realm*

Castries, Duc de, *The Lives of the Kings and Queens of France*

Costain, Thomas B., *The Pageant of England, 1135–1216; The Conquering Family*

Dark, Sydney, *St Thomas of Canterbury*

Davis, H. W. C., *England under the Normans and the Angevins*

Duggan, Alfred, *Thomas Becket of Canterbury*

FitzStephen, William, his clerk (translated by George Greenaway with contemporary sources), *The Life and Death of Thomas Becket*

Funck-Brentana, Fr (translated by Elizabeth O'Neill), *National History of France, the Middle Ages*

Green, J.R., *Henry II*

Green, Mary Anne Everett, *Lives of the Princesses of England*

Guizot, M. (translated by Robert Black), *History of France*

Hampden, John, editor, *Crusader King, the Adventures of Richard The Lionheart on Crusade, taken from a Chronicle of the Times*

Hill, Lieut-Colonel W. *Our Fighting King*

Holbach, Maude M. *In the Footsteps of Richard Coeur de Lion*

Hutton, the Rev. William Holden (arranged by), *Thomas of Canterbury. An Account of his Life and Fame from Contemporary Biographers and other Chronicles*

James, G.P.R., *History of the Life of Richard Coeur de Lion, King of England*

Johnston, R.C., *The Crusade and Death of Richard I*

Kelly, Amy, *Eleanor of Aquitaine and the Four Kings*

Lloyd, Alan, *King John*

Meade, Marion, *Eleanor of Aquitaine*

Norgate, Kate, *England under the Angevin Kings*; *John Lackland*

Pernoud, Régine (translated by Peter Wiles), *Eleanor of Aquitaine*; (translated by Henry Noel) *Blanche of Castile*

Pine, L.G., *Heirs of the Conqueror*

Pittinger, W. Norman, *Richard the Lionhearted, The Crusader King*

Poole, A.L., *From Domesday Book to Magna Carta*

Robertson, James Craigie, *Becket, Archbishop of Canterbury*

Rosenberg, Melrich V., *Eleanor of Aquitaine, Queen of the Troubadours and the Courts of Love*

Salzmann, L.F., *Henry II*

Seward, Desmond, *Eleanor of Aquitaine, the Mother Queen*

Stephens, Sir Leslie and Lee, Sir Sidney (editors), *The Dictionary of National Biography*

Strickland, Agnes, *The Lives of the Queens of England*

Thompson, Robert Anchor, *Thomas Becket*

Wade, John, *British History*

Warren, W.L., *King John*

Wilkinson, Clennell, *Coeur de Lion*

About the Author

Jean Plaidy is Victoria Holt. Under the Plaidy pseudonymn she has written over forty-five historical novels for Fawcett Books, including the Georgian Saga, the Plantagenet Saga and the Queens of England series. Ms. Plaidy resides in England.

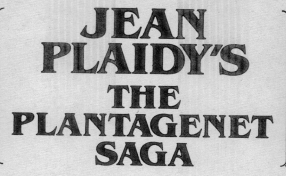